SOLAR
REBOOT

MATTHEW D. HUNT

SOLAR REBOOT
By
Matthew D. Hunt

DEDICATION

There are many people I'd like to dedicate this book to, but the two that stand out most are Tony Todd for inspiring and encouraging me in the first place; also to the late Richard Hatch for not only inspiring me but encouraging me, patiently answering questions when I had them, and making me think and reach beyond what I thought were my limits. Richard asked for nothing other than honesty and friendship, and gave that in return tenfold. I hope in my future endeavors that I can do the same for others.

AUTHOR'S NOTE

This book was originally a spec for a miniseries or TV show, which I am still considering. But overall, it is just supposed to be an enjoyable read. The science in it is not perfect, the locations in it are not perfect, the people in it are not perfect, but they're perfect enough for me, and for my story. I enjoyed writing in detail about all of my characters, trying to ensure they were not two-dimensional or uninteresting, and I hope you enjoy reading this as much as I enjoyed writing it. One other thing that I've added to this book, which I have not seen in many, is to give the reader and general public a small glimpse of what life is like living with Type 1 Diabetes. My son, now 10 years old, has had it for eight years, and if you'd like to find out more about it, please look up information at JDRF.org. Once again I thank you and I do hope you enjoy reading this book.

Sincerely,
Matthew D. Hunt

SOLAR
REBOOT

MATTHEW D. HUNT

CHAPTER 1

Scientists would have said it was still spring, that summer wouldn't come for almost another three weeks. Climatologists said there was no sharp dividing line, that the change of seasons was a gradual transition that humans gave name to for the sake of their own convenience.

But stuck in the back of a taxi cab in Manhattan, Alex Robinson thought the dividing line seemed much sharper, and that it had come last night. He and Piper had landed in JFK to a smattering of spring rain, the chilly, misty kind that didn't soak so much as it seeped through clothing. They'd made their way to the hotel with short tempers and all possible speed, and gone to bed expecting more of the same when they awoke. But morning had brought shining sun and a clear blue sky, and down on the streets it felt like the pavement had heated them from below just as much as the sun from above. Now the voices on the cab radio were blathering on about highs in the mid-eighties, and more of the same all week.

"How's your pump?" said Alex as the weatherman gave way to some story about a celebrity scandal.

"It's fine, Dad." Technically Piper had her seatbelt on, but from the way she lay sideways across the back seat, her feet in between them and her head wedged firmly between the window and the pages of an issue of *Seventeen*, Alex didn't think the restraint provided much protection. Fortunately, traffic was at a standstill.

"I told you you couldn't read that magazine for another five years."

"And Mom told *you* that I could read it if I want, and to stop bugging me."

"Your spares are in your backpack?"

"You think I carry extra issues of *Seventeen?*"

"Your spare meds."

She sighed, abandoning the magazine as a futile effort and dropping it on her chest. "The pump has enough to go for three days. I just changed it, you know that!"

"But you brought your spares."

"I don't need them."

"But you brought them."

"*Yes,* Dad. They're in my backpack, along with two extra magazines."

"I knew it."

She smirked and kicked him, shoving the magazine into her bag in favor of her phone.

"That's much better. Now I can pretend you're reading something educational."

"I'm checking Twitter."

"Don't ruin the dream."

"Nicki Minaj got the flu and had to cancel a concert."

"No father has ever been prouder."

She glared at him over the top of the screen. He held his hands up in surrender and let her browse, her eyes soon glazing over from the information dump. His attention went back out the window, squinting whenever the sun managed to poke its way out from between the skyscrapers. The sky was a strange shade of blue—too much red in it, closer to purple. Alex wanted to attribute it to city smog, but he'd been to New York plenty and had never seen that color. It bothered him. But then, according to Piper, most things did.

He knew he could never live in New York. Before a month was out he'd go insane from the people and the claustrophobic press of the architecture. But it certainly had its appeal as a place to visit, if for no other reason than it was the polar opposite of the forest.

Or maybe it was just a different kind of forest. Here the wild animals were the desperate poor who'd managed to get their hands on a weapon, and the rangers were men in blue who carried handcuffs and pistols. Just like back home, some of the rangers were more trouble than the animals, and just like back home, the animals weren't too dangerous if you knew what you were doing. But step into either environment without knowing the lay of the land, and you could end up dead real quick.

–scientists at NASA are now reporting that the solar flare is much larger than they had anticipated–

Alex's mind snapped back to the radio in an instant. He leaned forward, gripping the back of the seat in front of him. The cabbie looked over out of the corner of his eye, but Alex ignored him.

–and may in fact be the largest such event on record. Though telescopes first picked up the flare a few days ago, estimates of its size were, in NASA's own words, grossly in error.

"Excuse me, the radio—" said Alex.

"You want music?" said the cabbie. He leaned over and punched one of the numbered stations. The speakers blared the latest Top 40 single from some artist Alex didn't know.

"Ooh, I love this song. Could you please turn it up?" said Piper, sitting up in her seat.

Alex leaned back, looking out the window again. The sky was too red. Almost purple.

* * *

The whistle shrilled, blasting in the attendees' ears off the concrete walls of the gym, and the girls hit the water. Alex winced as the other parents around him erupted into screams.

5

No couch-borne football fan watching the Super Bowl ever cheered louder than a parent at a swim meet. He took a breath.

"Go Piper! Come on!"

He had to join in, not because he thought it did any good—the girls were underwater, they couldn't even hear their parental groupies—but because if he didn't, everyone saw him as the only jerk in the bleachers who wasn't cheering for his little girl. But as the swimmers neared the end of the first length and made their turns, the crowd settled down. Alex sank into his chair to think.

Something was bothering him, an errant thought tugging at the coattails of his mind, and it wouldn't go away no matter how much he tried to dismiss it. More than a decade in the woods had taught him that when a feeling like that stuck around, you listened. But often, as now, there wasn't much to listen to—just a sensation, like a sense of *something* standing just behind you, and you couldn't turn fast enough to get a good look at it.

"Which one is yours?"

Alex blinked, startled, and looked over. It was one of the moms. She was one seat over from Alex, but took his look as an invitation and scooted into the chair next to his.

"I'm Jackie. My daughter's Elizabeth, in lane three."

"Alex," he said. After a second, he realized he should offer his hand, and did. "I'm Piper's dad. Lane . . . uh . . . six."

Jackie flashed a dazzling smile with too-white teeth. "Ooh, she's winning!"

His heart sank as he realized she was right. He hadn't noticed. "Yeah, she's been training really hard."

"They all work so hard at it, but y'know, there can only be one winner."

She leaned back in her chair, resting an elbow on the armrest between them. Alex caught the whiff of something herbal in her hair, completing the picture painted by her upscale clothes and accent. Professional mom, probably from the mid-west, with a spouse rich enough to let her spend the money on the family however she liked. He hoped her smile wasn't hiding anything more. Too many parents saw these out-of-state swim meets as an opportunity to meet other unhappily married adults and use their hotel rooms for what they were really designed for. And since most of their husbands were white-collar business types, they tended to gravitate toward Alex as something refreshingly different and rugged.

"So what do you do?" said Jackie.

Alex shifted imperceptibly in his seat, sliding away from her. "I'm a forest ranger."

Her jaw dropped at what was clearly the most *fascinating* thing she'd ever heard. "No. Way. Like, full-on? Yogi bear style?"

He forced a polite smile. "Yogi wasn't the ranger, but you've got the idea." *Who uses 'full-on' and 'style' like that anymore?*

"That's got to be so interesting. How do you even get into that? I mean, it's not like they send recruiters around to colleges looking for rangers, do they? Or wait . . . do they? Where are you even from?" She said it with the air of someone who's just realized they never knew this vital detail about a lifelong friend.

"Seattle area. Oh, shoot, text from the wife. Give me a minute."

She smiled and leaned away. Hopefully that meant she got the hint. Alex pulled up his phone, hoping Jackie didn't notice the screen had no notifications on it, and tapped at the keys.

Rescue me. Soccer mom being too friendly. Bad touch. I need an adult.

No response for a long moment. From the corner of his eye, he spotted Jackie looking at him while trying not to look like she was doing it. So he angled the screen ever so slightly away from her, and then typed and deleted random words a few times so it would look like he was still texting. Finally, salvation came in a blue text box from Cameron.

I know a guy in New York. Real black-ops type. It's better if you don't know too much more.

No sniper rifles though, okay? I don't need the cover-up like last time, Alex typed back with a grin.

I get results. The rest is up to you.

He barely suppressed a guffaw, then gave Jackie an apologetic smile. It was a calculated move. Nothing like seeing a man giggle as he texted his wife to douse the romantic spark of a potential affair.

How's it going??

Did you just double-question-mark me? Alex teased.

Don't make this a thing.

Either it was a typo or an error, Cam. One question mark is acceptable. Three isn't orthodox, but colloquially established. Two is an abomination, Alex quipped.

You made it a thing. I am going back to work.

WAIT! I regret! Hey, did you hear about this solar flare? Alex asked.

Nothing came back for a very long minute. Alex immediately regretted sending it, but he'd been desperate to keep the conversation going. Jackie's hand had been edging back toward the armrest, almost as if it had a mind of its own.

I can safely say I did not. And I'm guessing you're worried.

Worried? Me? Never.

Alex. I can safely say we've never even used the words "solar flare" in all our years of marriage. Is something wrong, or is this one of your things?

To be fair, my things are often things that are also wrong.

I wouldn't say often.

Never mind. I shouldn't have brought it up. It's just one of my things, Alex texted back, trying not to worry her.

You promise?

I'll call you later. Race is almost over.

He mashed the power button and shoved the phone into his pocket. The swimmers were on the last lap. "Go Piper! Whoo!" he shouted, feeling like a pep rally cheerleader. The girls hit the edge of the pool, Piper in a close second place. The whistles blew, making him wince again, and he shuffled through the bleachers toward the stairs down. He'd completely forgotten Jackie, and didn't see her disgruntled huff as she went the other direction.

* * *

He called Cameron later, from the hotel room, while Piper was in the bathroom doing her level best to get the chlorine out of her hair. It was never a completely successful operation, but Piper was religious about it.

Ten rings in, Cameron still hadn't picked up. He waited. In the hospital, there could be a ton of reasons she couldn't get the call, one of which might well be that her hands were currently covered with another person's blood. It didn't help to be impatient.

Finally the line clicked. "Hey."

Her tone of voice was one Alex knew well. "Hey. What's wrong?"

"A bunch. Most recently, a dead guy on the table."

"Christ. I'm sorry, Cam."

"It happens. At least it wasn't anyone's fault here. So how's astrology treating you?"

"Astronomy. Astrology is horoscopes."

"Sweetie."

"Sorry. It's nothing. Probably. Did you hear about it?"

"I googled it after your text. News is saying it's no big deal."

"Scientists are saying something else."

"Well, if you can believe *them*."

"I'm really sorry, Cam."

"Please just . . . don't talk about it, okay? I should probably

9

get back. Turns out there's a ton of paperwork surrounding corpses."

The water shut off, and a second later Piper walked into the room. Alex cursed inwardly. "Actually, I was hoping you could do one thing for me tonight after work."

"I want to do precisely zero things after work tonight, unless those things are bottles of wine or taking out my frustration on your nubile body. One of those isn't an option."

"Please, Cam. Humor me. Or, don't humor me. Just, please."

"What?"

Alex eyed Piper, who was brushing her hair with the studious look of someone who was eavesdropping and trying not to be seen doing it. "Pick up some flats of water, and some canned food. And some extra meds for Piper."

"Canned food."

"The best stuff. Name-brand only. Go wild. Treat yourself."

"More canned food than we already have."

"And extra insulin for Piper."

"Once again, I feel the need to bring up wine as the only thing I was planning on tonight."

"Please, Cam. I know it's annoying, just . . . please." He tried to *will* his sense of urgency through the phone without letting it come out in his voice. Piper was smart—brilliant, actually. No way he could completely slip this under her radar, but there was no reason to freak her out. He hoped.

After a long and pregnant pause, he heard the resigned sigh he was looking for. "Okay."

"Thank you."

"When you get back, I'm going to wreck you."

"I'm looking forward to it. So much so that I stepped the flight up to tomorrow morning."

"What?"

"What?" said Piper, head snapping around to glare at him.

"Red-eye flight. We'll be there in the early afternoon. Don't worry about picking us up, we'll take a cab."

"Dad!" said Piper, anger turning to pleading in an instant.

"Alex, are you sure nothing's wrong?"

"Nothing's wrong," he said. An Oscar-worthy performance. "I just can't wait to see you. Okay, I have to explain myself to a pissed off pre-teen. Love you. Bye."

"Love you."

He hung up. Piper immediately turned to face him from her bed.

"Dad, we were going to go sight-seeing tomorrow."

"I know, sweetheart, but we're going to fly back early."

"Why?"

He paused. How to explain to her? What words could describe his growing itch, a sense that he didn't even totally understand himself?

"It's complicated."

"No it isn't! I wanted to see New York."

"We're going to come back plenty of times, Piper. I swear, next time we'll block out a whole week to go around and see stuff. The Empire State Statue. The Building of Liberty."

"Neither of those things are things."

He spread his hands. "See? That's the kind of stuff we'll learn on our sightseeing tour next time we come."

"Dad—"

"I'm sorry, Piper. The flight's already been changed, and we can't switch it again. Besides, Mom needs us. It's been a really rough few days for her at the hospital."

She glared. Her arms folded. Twice she opened her mouth, only to shut it again immediately. He could almost see the arguments flitting into her mind, being dissected, and tossed aside. Finally, she simply threw herself back on the bed.

"Fine."

Smart, he thought. *Oh, the monumental trouble we're in for in the next few years.*

11

"Sorry, sweetie. I'll make it up next time. I promise."

"Whatever."

He lay back on his own bed and fished for the remote. The TV clicked on with a high-pitched buzz—it was an old beast of a machine, not even a flatscreen—and he clicked over to the news, looking for an update on the flare.

"No. I don't want to watch news. Give me the remote," Piper insisted.

He almost resisted, but then he remembered that he'd just robbed her of a day in the city that she'd been looking forward to for weeks now. So he flipped the remote around and dropped it in her outstretched hand.

Soon she was watching some entertainment talk show, and Alex tuned out. He pulled up his phone and got on the Internet, looking around for any news. There was nothing new—or at least, nothing concrete, just wild speculation. And waiting for web pages was painfully slow; his connection had gone suddenly spotty, down to just one bar.

He clicked the phone off and dropped it on his chest with a sigh. Something in the back of his mind wanted out—not the next morning, but *now*. They should pack their things and taxi to the airport and pay for the first flight back to the west coast they could possibly find.

Deep breaths, he thought. Tomorrow morning, six a.m. He could wait fourteen hours. They could spend one night in a hotel. Nothing bad would happen.

Nothing.

He got up and went to the window. The sky outside was blue.

CHAPTER 2

Cameron threw her scrubs into the hamper a bit harder than she strictly needed to and went straight for her locker. Someone in the locker room called out a greeting, and Cameron waved without even looking to see who it was.

A bad day had gotten worse. The ER doctor had found himself "too busy" to speak to the family about the dead patient, so that had landed on Cameron. She could have foisted it off on someone else, she supposed. But she'd never been in the habit of passing the buck, and she sure wasn't going to start now.

It was the worst kind of family. She could understand the ones who just got sad and quiet, letting her slip off so they could be alone with their grief. She had a strange kind of respect for the ones who got mad. They didn't want to accept it. Anger was their solution, albeit a flawed one, and they turned it on whoever delivered the news so they didn't have to face the truth. Cameron knew all about that; she'd seen plenty of it in the service.

But the worst were the ones who thanked her. Thanked her for trying, for doing what she did. They always wanted to know what the last moments were like. They wanted her to go over every detail—did he open his eyes? Did he say anything? Did he know what was happening? Was it peaceful? Too often, the answers to those questions were worse than the simple fact of what had happened. And answering them meant that Cameron had to relive the incident over and over again.

Didn't they understand that this was just life? Dead was dead. A blink didn't make a difference. Then again, most people hadn't seen people die. Certainly not as many as Cameron had.

And now Alex wanted her to get survival supplies because he was afraid of . . . something.

She sighed as she looked out the locker room door into the hospital gym. Through the window, she could see the sun edging its way toward nightfall.

Screw it. She'd go paranoia-shopping later. It's not like the stores were going to close.

She threw on her tank top and shorts savagely, tugging her hair as she put it in a bun. And as she so often did, she wondered why she'd ever gone for a job like this. As though she hadn't watched enough bodies go still in Iraq and Afghanistan. As if she hadn't spent enough time with other people's blood spurting out to soak her hands, her clothes, sometimes her face. What kind of sick masochist went from active-duty Army medic to ER nurse?

It was an easy job to get, it pays well, and it has benefits. All things the family needs.

Cameron ignored the helpful prodding of the more analytical side of her mind. She wasn't interested in analytical just now.

The punching bag got the full brunt of her wrath. No treadmill or weights today. Cameron wanted to hit something, as hard as she could and as often. Soon the sweat was dripping down her face, sometimes running into her eyes until she swiped it away. Her knuckles began to burn, her shoulders to ache. It felt good, the way a lesser pain always feels like pleasure compared to something much, much worse.

"That's always been a good look for you."

Bam. One last pound, and she stopped. She turned

14

around, suddenly aware of how heavy she was breathing. Wade stood there, mouth cocked in a half-smirk like it often was, lean but well-muscled arms folded across his tank top. The front of his hair had always had those liberty spikes, but he'd bleached them recently, and they reminded her of a peacock's feathers.

Can't believe that was ever a thing.

But she always kept those thoughts to herself. Partly because acknowledging it ever *had* been a thing felt like inviting more of the same. And partly because she looked at his well-cut body and knew without question why they'd been together in high school.

"Hope you've had a better day than I have, grunt," she said, matching his smirk.

"From the black eye you're trying to give that bag, I don't doubt it, Army girl. Want to put some bruises on something that can hit back?" Wade shot back.

Cameron glanced at the ring in the corner. It wasn't uncommon for her and Wade to spar. She didn't have many partners she felt comfortable with; they usually folded in seconds. But Wade gave almost as good as he got. And there was that unspoken camaraderie there always is between two people who used to wear the kind of uniform that gets shot at. She wondered if that was why she'd ended up where she was, and he'd become an EMT. Both jobs with long hours and high adrenaline, where you stared down life and death every day. Rather than leaving the military, sometimes it just felt like a tour extension.

She shook her head. "Can't. Got some shopping to do. Just needed to work out some stuff."

"I'm real good for that," he promised. "We can do no gloves. Makes it twice as fun. Just don't hit me in the face; that's how I fill my weekend nights."

Cameron chuckled. "If I ever saw you outside of work, I'd spend it hitting your face, too."

He shook his head. But then he must have seen something in her eyes, because his tough-guy face grew a little more concerned. "Hey, you okay?"

"Yeah." She said.

"You sure? I heard about the guy—" Wade started to say.

"I don't want to talk about it." Cameron snapped.

"I get that. Wanna drink about it instead? I've got a bottle of Blue that's been waiting for a special occasion." Wade asked with a smile.

"The way I feel like going at it tonight, you shouldn't offer me anything pricier than motor oil. But I'm good. Like I said, shopping." She threw a towel over her shoulder and headed back for the locker room. He watched her go, and she tried to ignore it. But at the last second she turned, just before stepping out of sight.

"Let me see how this weekend goes. Maybe we can throw down some time, if Alex and Piper don't need me." Cameron offered.

"You call, I'm there." Wade replied.

She nodded and went to change.

* * *

Costco was terrible. No, Cameron reflected—it was a bona fide disaster. Seattle was entering the season of barbecues and backyard pool parties, and it seemed that every living soul in a hundred mile radius had decided to stock up at once. The store, normally so efficient at wrangling its customers, was woefully unprepared.

Five times while pushing her cart through the faux-warehouse aisles, Cameron swore to herself that she was walking out. Five times she ground her teeth and pressed on. She had told Alex she would do this.

After filling her cart to the brim with canned goods and flats of bottled water, then suffering the quiet strangulation of a cash register line that was overly long, she emerged into the evening air like someone breaking free from the grave. She'd taken particular care choosing her wine tonight, and then picked up a second bottle at the last second. And she'd already decided to pick up Chinese from her favorite take-out joint, a place too greasy to justify on most occasions.

Tomorrow she would have a husband and daughter in the house again. But tonight she deserved a reward.

She stopped to fill up the Jeep just a few blocks away from the restaurant, and less than a mile from the house. Alex hadn't asked her to do that, but she knew how his mind worked by now. This wasn't the first time he'd taken it into his head that they might need to bug out at a moment's notice. The things that made him nervous—possible riots, food shortages, mad cow disease—never seemed to amount to anything, and Cameron never failed to point that out to him. But he'd always shrug and smile at her and say, "Well, then there was no harm in preparing for them."

It was endearing to look back on, in its own way. But when it actually happened, it was nothing but annoying.

By the time she reached the house, the smell of Chinese had filled the car and Cameron's stomach was roaring its displeasure. She snatched the take-out bag, then leaned back and snagged the bottles of wine from one of the bags in the back seat. She'd unload the rest of the groceries later, or maybe the next morning. It's not like they were going to spoil. That was kind of the point.

She kicked open the door to find her neighbor Bettie standing just on the other side of the fence. It gave Cameron a little start. From the way she was leaning her arms on the fence, her eyes fixed on Cameron, it was like she'd been waiting. Cameron smiled to herself. Bettie was old, and her kids rarely came to visit her. Loneliness made her inquisitive and interested in everything the Robinsons were doing, but since she had an undeniable charm, it wasn't too much of a problem.

"That's a whole lot of food you got there," said Bettie, teeth shining bright against her chocolate skin as she grinned. "You having some kind of feast when Alex and Piper get home?"

"If I was putting on a banquet, I sure wouldn't feed them Campbell's," said Cameron. "It's just some stuff Alex asked me to pick up."

"That boy's so paranoid about everything." Bettie said with a smile.

"He'd say he was cautious, not paranoid. I wouldn't say anything either way, even if I agreed with you—which I do." Cameron said with an ironic grin.

Bettie laughed at that, and Cameron smiled. With most people she found herself acting reserved and aloof, even if that wasn't always how she felt. But Bettie was impossible not to like.

"What's giving him goosebumps now?" Bettie asked.

Cameron shrugged. "There's some kind of solar flare, or something. I don't know too much about them."

"I heard about that," said Bettie, her mood suddenly dampening. "The talking heads are acting like it's no big deal. But Mister Tyson ain't so sure." She was, Cameron suspected, Carl Tyson's biggest fan, and half her conversations with the Robinsons were about some new space phenomenon he'd been talking about on TV.

"Well, I guess he'd know better. What does he think's going to happen?"

"He said he don't know. That made me a little nervous, believe me. And then there's that sky." Bettie said pointing.

Cameron arched an eyebrow. Bettie simply pointed behind her, west toward the sunset.

The sun was edging out of sight now, and she was well used to seeing it glow red, or sometimes orange in the heart of summer. But today, something was different. There was a curious cast to the sky, something . . . *off.* It was almost purple. Not the lilac that came bouncing down from clouds in the upper atmosphere, but a deep and foreboding purple, turbulent, and almost black.

"That sure is an odd sunset," she said, feeling a twinge at the back of her mind.

Is this what Alex feels like? she wondered.

"Like I said. I see something like that, and then I hear that Mister Tyson don't even know what might happen? I don't much blame your husband for being nervous." Bettie said.

"Well, I'm sure it's fine. I mean, they say solar flares happen all the time, and we never even notice."

Bettie nodded slowly. "They do say that."

"Right. Okay. Well, I'd better be getting in. Unless you want to come in for a bit?" Cameron hoisted the bottles of wine, swinging them back and forth temptingly.

Bettie smiled again. "You sure are sweet, honey. But I'd better not. My son says he's coming by in the morning. Knowing him, that's probably a damn lie. But if it's true, I don't want to be walking around with an ice pack on my head. You enjoy yourself."

"I plan to," said Cameron. "You have a good one, Bettie."

She walked up the path and into the house, and not once did she let her eyes stray to the purple sky in the west, slowly darkening to black.

* * *

The take-out proved no match for her vicious assault. To avoid dishes, and because there was no one around to pretend to be civilized for, Cameron pigged out straight from the carton. She wasn't even halfway through before she cracked the first bottle of wine and poured herself a glass. It was a modestly priced vintage she'd tried and liked once, and never varied from, and it was especially sweet after the long day.

She was halfway through her second glass when the house-lights flickered.

Cameron looked up, eyeing the fixture suspiciously. It had nothing to say for itself.

The twinge at the back of her mind increased its intensity.

She forced herself to shake it off. The remote was right where she'd left it—something she could never say when Alex and Piper were home—so she flicked on the TV to keep her company while she finished her food. Idly, she flipped through the channels, looking for something interesting. But almost without realizing it, she left it on a news channel, and left it there as she kept eating. The anchorman blathered on about something controversial happening in Iran.

"As though that's supposed to be news," she said out loud.

The TV flickered. Not the white noise of traditional static, but a digital spike. The image went pixelated for a second, and then for a moment more the host's every movement was followed by a strange, almost-transparent shadow, like a ghost moving across him.

What the hell? she thought. They had satellite, not the rinky dink cable that was always so spotty in this area. Static wasn't supposed to even be a *thing*.

She tried changing the channel and then switching back. The digital glitch vanished, and the picture came through clear as day. Cameron leaned back with a sigh, surprised at how relieved she felt. She looked outside without thinking, toward the west. But the sunset was already gone, and she only saw houselights shining defiantly against the black of night.

. . . eastern seaboard has gone dark, prompting the governors of most east coast states to issue statements. They are asking their citizens—

Cameron's attention snapped back to the television. They'd moved off Iran, and now there was a big map of the U.S. on display. Most of the east coast was painted in orange. She grabbed the remote and turned the volume up. Facts trickled in with the words, slowly, a drip at a time, no one talking fast enough to give Cameron all the information she wanted to hear. But eventually she got the picture: the power was out for just about everyone, with no clue when they'd be able to restore it, or even what had knocked it out.

And it was "unclear" whether or not it had anything to do with the solar flare they'd reported on earlier.

Her throat went dry. Cameron knew a spin when she heard it. She'd been subjected to plenty of them when she was in the service. Everyone in the government clammed up at once, and the media filled the void with whatever they could.

That's when things got "unclear."

She looked out the window again, and at that second, the power went out. The lights through the window vanished, and the house turned pitch-black for a long moment while her eyes adjusted.

Cameron gripped the arm of the couch for a moment, until she heard the *click-click-click-BRRR* of their backup generator starting up. She breathed a sigh of relief.

Sometimes it was good to be married to a prepper.

The TV took another second to power back on, but when it did it only sank her hopes again. The satellite was gone. Not fuzzy, completely gone. She clicked through, hoping it was just the news, but it wasn't. Nothing came through except when she switched over to pick up broadcast channels, and those were so fuzzy she couldn't make out what anyone was saying.

Her mind wouldn't let her sit still any longer, so she jumped up and went to the kitchen. From a drawer she pulled a flashlight, then went out the front door and over to Bettie's house. She gave the front door three sharp raps and waited.

The second door opened at no time at all, and Bettie peered out at here, her wrinkles thrown into sharp relief by the light of a candle.

"Cameron? What's wrong?"

She let out a deep *whoosh* of breath. "Nothing. Just . . . I

21

just came to check on you. Make sure you were okay. Because of the power."

"It scared me half to death. I was on the pot. But I'm okay. You?"

"Yeah. We've got a generator, and it kicked right on."

"Sometimes Alex's ideas don't seem so bad, do they?"

"I was just thinking that. Do you want to come over?"

Bettie shook her head. "Thank you, but I'm fine. Now I just want to go to bed and wake up when I can turn my heater back on."

Cameron smiled. "Okay. Good night."

Back in the house, without the benefit of the TV to keep her distracted, everything seemed suddenly too quiet. She found herself going back and forth to the front windows, looking out at the rest of the neighborhood. But no matter how many times she checked, no one else's lights came back on. She was only grateful they didn't come poking around her place. Probably too late for most of them. Maybe half the people on their street went to bed early, and most likely wouldn't realize the power had even gone out until they missed their alarms the next morning.

Struck by a thought, she pulled out her phone and swiped up Alex's contact. But when she tried to text, she had no signal.

"Damn it," she muttered, shoving the phone back in her pocket.

Nothing to do and no one to talk to. What was she supposed to do, just stand there waiting like an idiot?

Alex and Piper would be home the next day. She could clean up. Yes, that would be something.

She went through the house, looking for things to put in order. The take-out was the first obvious choice, and then the few dishes in the kitchen sink. But she ran out fast. Cameron had never been especially messy, her discipline a holdover from military life. In the couple of days since Alex and Piper had left, the house had actually gotten a lot cleaner.

A book, she thought. She could read. That was something people did, right? Or at least they used to. She went to Alex's office and picked something off the shelf, not even glancing at the title, then curled up back in the living room with it. She even tossed a throw blanket over her legs, completing a look that was about as *not* her as you could get.

Five minutes later she realized she was still on the first page, because she kept glancing back and forth at her phone every few seconds.

She threw the book on the coffee table with an exasperated sigh.

This is fine. Totally fine. Alex and Piper wouldn't land until the afternoon, and she wasn't working tomorrow. She could sleep in basically as late as she wanted. That meant she could stay up until her phone worked again, and then text Alex just to set her mind at ease.

Once upon a time, she had had a perfect go-to solution for waiting around bored, and she already had just the right supplies for it. So she poured herself another glass of wine, filling it to the brim, and drank deep. As the alcohol crept in, she fiddled around with her phone so she could keep her eye on the signal bars. Apparently there were a few games she'd downloaded forever ago and then forgotten about—or, more likely, Piper had downloaded them to her phone when she wasn't looking.

One by one they gave her half an hour of entertainment at a time, until she struck on one that completely ensnared her. She tapped away at it over and over again, mesmerized by the bright colors and flashing lights, snatching another sip from her glass every few seconds.

"This thing is *fantastic*," she said, and paused. The words had been slurred. She looked over at the coffee table. When had she opened the other bottle?

Then she looked back at the phone and realized she had a signal bar.

She smashed down on the home button and opened the texting app as quick as she could, surprised by how badly she wanted to send it and cursing as her fingers fumbled over the keys. In seconds she was done, and she tapped *Send*. The progress bar slid across the screen for what seemed like an eternity.

It clicked, and the app said "Sent" just below the words.

She sighed and leaned back, mental adrenaline fading away. All of a sudden she felt too tired to even move herself to bed, so she curled up on the couch under the throw blanket.

Everything will be better tomorrow morning, she thought as she drifted off.

CHAPTER 3

N ear 5:00 in the morning, Alex was dragged painfully from sleep by the sound of sirens.

At first he had to lie there for a moment, listening through the grogginess of sleep as he tried to place the sound. As he placed it, nerves crept up his back. Sure, sirens were rare back home, but in Manhattan they were part of life's backdrop. He'd slept through them plenty, on this trip and on several before. Why, then, had they woken him?

Because there were too many, and too loud.

He sat up in his hotel bed. Piper still slept in her bed across the room, undisturbed. He slipped from his bed as quietly as he could and made his way to the window. The curtain was an ancient thing, and it squeaked harsh against its rust as he pulled it aside. Nothing on the streets below, no flashing lights, but he thought the sirens must be just around the next corner. And now that he focused, he could hear their variety; ambulances, cop cars and fire trucks, all joining together in a chorus like the warning bells that cities used to have in medieval times.

But something was wrong. Something else. For a long moment at that window, he couldn't place it. More time looking raised the hairs on the back of his neck higher, rather than soothing him.

Then it hit him. Manhattan was dark. No lights shone from the windows of the dozens of skyscrapers in view. The city that never slept was out cold.

His phone. He snatched it up and swiped it open, meaning to find a news site that might have word about the outage. But he stopped as he saw a notification: a text from Cameron. He swiped it open.

Power went out. Generator kicked in, but lights are still out in the neighborhood. Heard the same happened on the east coast. Update?

That wasn't too odd in itself, but then he saw the time the text had been sent. It was just a half hour ago, almost 1:30 am Cameron's time. That, more than the words, formed a deep pit of worry in his stomach.

He had no signal to reply, and he cursed the city's thick buildings that gave such spotty reception. That meant he couldn't search any sites for updates, either.

The TV, then. He searched in vain for the remote, then gave up and went to turn it on by hand. Immediately he smashed his finger down on the volume button, knocking it down to mute before the picture had time to come up on screen.

But there was no picture. No signal whatsoever. Just blank static. Frowning, Alex thumbed the channel buttons up and down. The result was the same. White snow, glaring at him in the darkness.

He tried to fight back the panic building in his chest. Think. There had to be some way to find out what was going on. If the Internet and cell wouldn't work, and the TV was down, then there was always . . .

Alex went to the room's alarm clock. The thing was a brick, an ancient relic that was nevertheless pointless to replace. Why get newer, better alarm clocks when every tenant had a cell phone to do the job? But the clock had one thing Alex's phone didn't: a radio setting. And better yet, its red digits shone in the darkness of the room. A backup battery for power, in case of power outages. No hotel wanted to deal with angry guests who missed their morning wakeup call.

First he unplugged it and took it into the bathroom so the noise wouldn't wake Piper. Then he turned it to AM radio and began spinning the tuning dial. What signals he could find were spotty and weak, but finally he found one strong enough to be heard through the static. He fingered the dial carefully, getting it in just the right spot, until a calm, smooth voice slithered out of the speakers.

—power remains down in the city, with only backup generators providing emergency power until state government figures out the problem. We've heard a few reports that the problem has spread to other grids across the country—or, I guess "spread" is the wrong word, isn't it? It's not like a virus, I guess, ha ha. Anyway, if you're out there listening in the dark, thanks for choosing to spend your time with us, and keep yourself safe. Maybe stay inside, play some board games with the family. I don't know about all of you, but I can't get a phone signal to save my life, and for the first time I'm having to talk to my family, ha ha. Reminds me of what life was like in the nineties. We'll give you more updates as we have them, but until then we've got a story from Frank "Stank" Savage, who went out to see one of my personal favorite bands—

Alex turned the radio off with a growl of impatience. What kind of idiot babbled about a concert when his whole state—heck, for all they knew, the country—was in a blackout?

Indecision turned to action in the span of a second, and he left the bathroom. He shook Piper's shoulder gently until finally she came awake, blinking at him in the near-pitch darkness.

"What? Stop shaking me."

"We've gotta go, sweetie. I need you to get up and start packing your things."

"Why?" said Piper, waking up fast. "What time is it?"

Alex clicked his phone. "A bit after 5."

"Oh my god. No. Let me go back to sleep." She turned over and dragged the covers above her head with a savage wrench.

Alex slowly pulled them back down, with Piper fighting all the way. "Come on, honey. We need to go."

27

"*Why?*" Her voice had taken on that plaintive whine that was perfectly calculated to drive Cameron and him crazy, although just now he could hardly blame her. "The sun's not even up yet."

"I know. And the power's out, too. I'm guessing all flights have been cancelled. So we're going on a small road trip. If you're tired, you can sleep in the car."

Piper still fought valiantly to keep her head under the covers, but she was fighting a losing battle. "A road trip where? Come on, it's not like we're going to drive all the way home. And when the airports are back up, we're just going to be further away from them."

Alex sighed, then put on his "stern father" tone. He hated it, but he needed her out of the bed. "Piper, we're leaving. Get up. Now."

The covers finally came down, and she glared at him through the darkness. "*Fine.* But I'm sleeping in the car, and you can't try to force me to stay awake to keep you company."

He barely kept from sighing in relief. "Okay. No problem."

"*And* we're getting breakfast before we leave."

Alex ground his teeth. Not only was the hotel restaurant stupidly expensive, but more importantly, it meant more time. But he'd have to pick his battles. "Fine. Get up. We're leaving in ten."

* * *

The restaurant, of course, was far worse than Alex had feared.

Despite his ultimatum, it was twenty minutes before Piper was ready to leave the hotel room at last. He tried to take the stairs, but she refused. The elevator was still working—hotels always had emergency power setups for what they considered vital necessities—and by god, Piper meant to use it. By the time they reached the lobby he was a ball of impatience, surprising himself by not bouncing from the elevator walls. He was half ready to veto the whole breakfast plan and carry her out the front door if he had to. But it would be good to get food in their bellies, especially if his creeping sense of unease turned out to be something more than just paranoia. But as soon as they reached the restaurant, he wished he'd tossed Piper over his shoulder and run.

"Elizabeth!" Piper beamed and ran to one of the tables, hugging a girl Alex didn't recognize. But her name was familiar, and a moment later he realized why—she was one of the girls from the swim meet, the daughter of the woman Jackie who'd been flirting with him in the bleachers. And there, at the same table, Jackie studied Alex over the heads of both their daughters. Under her cool stare, he briefly considered pretending he didn't know who Piper was, and walking right by the table.

"Come on, dad. Let's eat with them."

Well. So much for that plan.

Alex tried to smile and gave a mumbled greeting before brushing past and going to the hotel's buffet. Despite its incredible expense, it was probably worth it. There were heaping trays of eggs, bacon, sausage and oatmeal, with chefs waiting behind glass screens to prepare custom omelets for pickier guests. Alex passed them by, but Piper stopped and had them make a cheese and mushroom omelet.

After that painful ordeal, they made their way back to the table where Elizabeth and Jackie were waiting. Piper sat and fell immediately into an animated conversation with Elizabeth. Alex tried not to look at Jackie, remaining very focused on his food. Fortunately his silence was a little less conspicuous with the girls' chatter. First they talked about the meet, complaining about how sore their muscles were after yesterday, and then they quickly moved on to the power outage.

"It's crazy how dark the city is, right?"

"I know. I wonder why our hotel rooms didn't have light, but there's lights on here."

"They *always* have lights on in the lobby. I think it's like a law or something."

It isn't, thought Alex, but he kept his mouth shut.

"Why are you even up this early?"

"We always get up early. Our whole family does this morning routine thing . . . what's it called again, mom?"

Jackie stopped studying Alex to turn to her daughter. "The Miracle Morning."

"Yeah, that. We do it, plus my dad, even though sometimes he skips it when he does his poker night thing."

"Weird. You just wake up early?"

"Wake up early, exercise, yoga, that kind of thing. It's supposed to make the rest of your day better."

Piper turned to him. "Maybe we should try that, dad."

Alex tried not to laugh out loud. He'd heard of the routine, and the very idea of Piper getting up that early for *any* reason, much less exercise, was ludicrous. He barely managed to say, "Sure, sweetie," without spitting out the eggs in his mouth.

Piper missed his quiet snickering and returned to Elizabeth. "Are you guys flying home today?"

"We were," said Jackie, butting in. "But our flight's been cancelled. It looks like all the airports are down until they figure out how to get the power back up."

"Yeah, our flight got cancelled, too. We're going to drive at least part of the way home instead." Piper's frown turned into a look of sudden realization. "Hey! Where do you guys live again?"

"Pittsburgh," said Elizabeth.

Piper turned to Alex. "Dad, that's west of here! If we're going to drive until we can find a flight the rest of the way home, why don't we just take them with us? Then it wouldn't be just the two of us in the car."

Alex wanted to die. But fortunately, and unexpectedly, Jackie swooped in to save him. "That's very sweet, but we're going to stay in the city. We'll just wait for the airport to get back up and running, and until then we're going to have some fun in the city. It's not like we're in any rush to get home."

"That's what I want to do," Piper said, glaring at Alex.

He speared his last bite of eggs and gulped it down quickly. "Sorry, sweetie. But speaking of which, we should really get on the road. Traffic's going to get pretty clogged up on the way out of the city. Might as well try to get a jump on it."

"I'm not even halfway done with my breakfast," said Piper.

"Well then, less talking, more chow. Come on, chop chop."

Piper and Elizabeth rolled their eyes at each other. Alex thought he even saw Jackie looking toward the heavens for a second. Piper took a few more bites in quick succession, but soon started talking with Elizabeth again. He had to keep butting in, getting her to eat more and more until she finally said she was done. Then, with a haste that he knew had crossed the line way into rudeness, he ushered her up and away from the table.

"What is your *problem?*" said Piper. "We're going to be in the car with each other for hours, if not longer. Can't I even eat one meal with a friend of mine in peace beforehand?"

Alex tried to hide his concern behind a goofy smile as he tousled her hair. "Oh, come on. I'm a much better friend than Elizabeth."

"No."

"We're buddies."

"We're not. I don't even have 'buddies.'" She was pouting, but only because she was trying to hide a smile.

"Chums."

"No."

"Pals."

"Stop it."

"Oh hey, look, a bus." An express transit waited with a sign on the front that read *New Jersey*. Before she could even answer, Alex had Piper on board. They settled into seats, and in a few minutes the bus took off.

* * *

They'd taken the first empty seats they'd found, right near the front. Looking toward the back of the bus, Alex realized it was nearly empty. From one of his multitude of mirrors, the driver noticed Alex looking around.

"Lotta people aren't going to work today," said the driver. "When power goes out, you get that a lot. People figure their work can't call them to complain, so they play hooky. If their boss calls them on it tomorrow, they'll just say they couldn't make the commute. Subway's down, too. Plus, there's never many people going *to* Jersey in the morning. Most of the bodies are moving the other way."

It was a stunning amount of information, especially considering Alex hadn't even asked for it. "Crazy," was all he could think to say.

He pictured his own job, a frequently lonely station buried in the middle of the Washington woods. He could take days off if he wanted to, and most times people wouldn't even notice. But you didn't become a ranger without liking the job, or at least you didn't stay long.

Piper had tried to go online almost as soon as the bus started driving, but with no Internet she'd swiftly kicked on some music. Now she leaned her head against the window, watching the passing crowds and buildings, some overly-percussive pop beat blasting from the little white earbuds. It reminded Alex of his own phone, and he pulled it out to check the signal. Still nothing. He glared out at the skyscrapers, keeping a weather eye on the signal bars.

As the bus cleared the city, emerging from the Holland Tunnel into New Jersey, two bars finally sprang to life. Alex swiped his screen with fingers that were suddenly shaking, and tapped Cameron's contact. He heard only silence in the earpiece for a few seconds, but then finally the familiar *br-r-r* of a ringtone sounded in his ear.

"Hello?" Cameron spoke with a slow slur.

His heart skipped a beat, and Alex leaned back in his bus chair with a sigh. "Cam. Thank goodness. Are you okay?"

He heard a sharp rustling, probably of bedsheets. "Of course. Why? What happened?"

"Nothing," he said, heaving a deep sigh. What was wrong with him? There was no reason for this sense of anxiety hiding just at the corners of his mind. But he couldn't shake it. "Nothing. I just haven't been able to call since we woke up. The city's power is out. Apparently it's the same all across the country, and some others, too."

"Yeah, we're still on the backup generator here, too. No idea when they're going to get it sorted."

"If they do."

She was silent a moment. "What do you mean?"

"Nothing," he said quickly. "Hey, listen, flights have been cancelled all over the place, so we're going to get a rental and drive west."

"You're going to drive all the way home?"

"Maybe. If flights come back up, we can stop in Pittsburgh or Cleveland, catch a plane from there. But just in case . . ."

"Okay."

He blinked. He'd expected an *In case what?* "Really?"

"Sure. Piper must hate you right now."

Alex glanced at her across the bus. She caught him looking, and met his gaze with a glare. "Nah, she's fine. Hey, listen. If it gets any worse there—or, I don't know, even if it stays the same for too much longer—head to the cabin, okay?"

"You really think that's necessary?"

"I hope not. But if the power stays down for a week, or even a couple of days, a city isn't the place to be."

"We're hardly in Seattle, babe. No one's going to—"

The call cut off. Outside the bus, the sky . . . *rippled*. It was like a wave of hot air rushed across it, coming from the west, and where it came the sky turned reddish, edging toward purple. Alex watched it for a second, awestruck, then looked down at the phone. The signal bars were gone, and no amount of staring brought them back.

* * *

The bus pressed on, oblivious, and soon dropped them off at a Metro car rental place in Jersey City. The streets were empty, and a brisk wind had struck up. The sky was still purple. Alex tried to ignore it all, focusing on the door of the rental shop as he hustled Piper toward it.

"What did Mom say?"

"Nothing much. Power's down there, too, so it's probably a good thing we're not trying to fly."

"I am *not* going to get excited about this road trip, so you can stop trying."

"Ten-four."

In the front office, a single greasy twenty-something stood behind the counter. She looked bored out of her mind, and the presence of customers didn't seem to do anything to alleviate it. Alex tried to win her over with a smile as he stopped at the counter, but she didn't return it. Her bronze name badge read *Mindy*.

"Hey, I'd like to rent a sedan, one-way."

The girl sniffed and tapped a button on her keyboard. After staring blankly at her screen for a second, she looked back to Alex and shrugged. "Sorry, sir. Our computer system seems to be down."

Alex looked back over his shoulder. The front door still very clearly had an *Open* sign on it. "You're a car rental place. And you can't rent cars? Why are you even open, then?" As soon as the words left his mouth, he knew the answer: Mindy probably saw it as a total dream to come in to work and get paid for hours where she couldn't even do her job.

Sure enough, she shrugged. "Boss didn't call to tell me to take the day off. Plus, people can still return cars. Can't just leave them stranded, or whatever, I guess."

Alex took a deep breath and let it out in a *whoosh*. Piper tugged on his sleeve. "Come on, Dad. They're closed. It's not like there's anything we can do about it."

He gently pried her fingers from his arm. "If someone comes back with a car, what would you do? I mean, some of them have to pay, right? How do you process them?"

Mindy stared at him for a moment, then sighed and looked over his shoulder at the clock. It provided no help, so she met his eyes again. "They fill out a form with their payment info. We'll process it whenever the computers come back up."

"Okay. So can I please have one of those forms to take *out* a rental?"

"I'm sorry, sir, but we can't know if your credit card—"

"I'll pay cash," he said. "And you can photocopy my driver's license and insurance information. I've got it on me."

Another long-suffering sigh. But Mindy levered herself away from the counter and went to a file cabinet to retrieve a paper form. Piper leaned in close to Alex, whispering.

"Dad, don't be so mean. She just works here."

"I'm not trying to be mean, I'm just—"

He had to stop abruptly as Mindy returned with uncustomary speed. She probably wanted them out of the office as fast as possible so she could go back to doing nothing.

"Here you go, sir. Just fill this out. I'm afraid we only have a single car available for you."

Alex looked at the form. A Mercedes G-Class, for $169 a day plus a $500 deposit. He glanced up.

"This is the only car you have available?"

Mindy met his stare dead-on. "I'm afraid so, sir."

Touché, Mindy. Touché.

Alex forced himself to swallow several angry words and filled out the form. They could get something cheaper in whatever city they ended up at the next day. And at least the G-Class had a lot of carrying room. If power was still out the next day, he meant to pick up some supplies. As quickly as he could force Mindy to move, he paid for the rental, gave all his info, and took the keys. They drove away from the rental shop as fast as Alex thought he could without getting a ticket. It was twenty minutes since the sky had gone purple.

He felt a little better once they hit the 78, and better still when the freeway carried them out of the city proper and into the suburbs. Now they were surrounded by green forest on all sides, except for the occasional turnoffs into the little communities and small towns that surrounded New Jersey's city sprawl. Alex breathed a long sigh of relief at the familiar feel of nature all around him, at the freedom from claustrophobic humanity.

"Jeez, Dad. You're so hyper." Piper's nose was buried in her phone again. "But at least the car's nice."

"It had better be," Alex muttered. Louder, he said, "I just wanted to get moving. You know me—I hate waiting."

"We couldn't have even taken one day? I wanted to hang out with Elizabeth."

"I know, honey. But listen, about that. We can't just offer to pick people up on this trip, okay? I want to get home as fast as we can."

Something about his tone caught her attention. She clicked off her earbuds and pulled them from her ears. "Why? Is something wrong?"

He shrugged, trying to ignore the nagging feeling scraping at the back of his neck. Hard to do when it just kept getting stronger and stronger. But how could he explain it to Piper, when he himself didn't know why he was so nervous? He could hear, or imagined he could hear, a keen whine in the air, like the scream of a plane's engines. *Just nerves,* he told himself.

"I don't know. Maybe. You've seen how the sky is acting. And the weather looks like it's going to kick up soon. I just don't want to waste any time. The faster we get home, the happier I'll be."

Now Piper was looking out the windows, eyebrows furrowed anxiously. "So the sky's a weird color. So what? What does that mean?"

The whine grew louder. Not nerves after all, but a plane. Probably flying in to Newark. The sound agitated Alex's already-frayed nerves. "I don't know. And that's what's got me a little worried. That, and the power going down. If they don't get it back up soon, it's going to get worse. And listen, sweetie, I don't want to worry you. But if it does get worse, it could get a *lot* worse. That's why we need to look out for each other, and not pick people up like this is a regular road trip. Okay?"

Piper swallowed hard, and to his relief she nodded slowly. "But . . . Elizabeth, and her mom. They're going to be fine, right? I mean, it'll be safe in the city?"

Now it was Alex's turn to hesitate, for just a moment longer than he should have. "I'm sure they will be. People tend to band together when things get hard. It might be a little exciting in the city, but they'll be fine."

Suddenly the whine in the air became a roar. On instinct Alex slammed on the brakes. The Mercedes compensated for the sudden lurching speed change, and he guided it to the shoulder. Just as he pulled the car to a stop, the earth shook with a tremendous explosion. A colossal tower of fire bloomed to life in the field across the freeway, and the debris of a passenger jet flew from the crash like the rain of hell.

CHAPTER 4

Cameron woke to an explosion that rattled the house windows.

Instinct took over, a subconscious compulsion gained from years sleeping in deserts half a world away, and she leapt over the back of the couch to huddle behind it for cover. Panic made her heart thunder in her ears, and she stared around wild-eyed as she looked for the source of the explosion. After a minute she came back to herself. Blinking hard, she lifted her head up over the couch again.

Though the whole house had shook, it didn't look like any windows had broken. She went around to check them all, just to be sure. Then she realized she didn't have her phone, and went to retrieve it from the side table by the couch. There was no signal. The time read 6:15am. Forty minutes ago, her call with Alex had been cut off, just before she'd drifted back to sleep.

Now that she was sure the house was safe, her head was starting to throb. Too much wine. She stumbled into the kitchen and threw some coffee on, then went back to the living room. The TV was still out. But their sound system had a radio connection, so she flipped it to a news station.

. . . working to confirm reports that multiple flights have gone down all across the country for unknown reasons. Details are very hard to confirm at this time. We are working to get any solid information about which flights may have suffered failures, or why. So far as

we know, there is no indication that this is any kind of attack, and we ask for your patience—

Cameron turned it off. A plane crash. That would explain the explosion, she supposed. But why? It couldn't have anything to do with the power outage, could it? Planes certainly didn't rely on ground power to stay up in the air.

The murmur of voices outside distracted her, and she returned to the front window. On the street outside, several of the neighbors had converged. It seemed almost abnormal how many of them there were—did that many people really live in this neighborhood? Cameron was never a social butterfly on the best of occasions. Except for Bettie, she doubted she knew the names of most the people she saw outside.

As though summoned by the thought, Bettie appeared on the sidewalk, looking over the low white picket fence that rimmed Cameron's front yard. Before Cameron could duck back out of sight, Bettie saw her. She lifted a hand and waved energetically.

"Cameron! Come on out! Something's happened."

Time to be a social butterfly after all, it seemed. Cameron sighed. If she didn't go out, Bettie would no doubt come after her to see if anything was wrong. She gave a brief wave to tell Bettie she'd heard, then went to get some proper clothes on.

Outside, about two dozen people had gathered. Cameron stood off to the side of them, where she was quickly joined by Bettie. She caught brief snatches of the conversation. A few of them had heard the same news Cameron had about the planes, and they were filling in the others.

"Where'd the plane go down?" said one of them, a soccer mom Cameron barely recognized. She had her hands buried in the pockets of a flannel sweater, though it wasn't even below sixty outside.

"I think I saw it up north. Just caught the tail end of the explosion." Cameron was almost certain the guy's name was David. He was a real roughneck type, huge mutton chops hanging from his face and a veteran's cap on his head. She'd always thought those caps were self-aggrandizing, especially for newer vets. A ninety-year-old guy wanted to sport his World War II cap? Sure. But who went around boasting they were a backup convoy driver in Iraq in '98?

As the others babbled on, Cameron studied the crowd more closely. There were several more like David, thick men with beer bellies and red cheeks. More than one of them had a pistol on their belt. That raised her hackles. Sure, they probably had permits. But she'd lived in this neighborhood for more than a decade, and while she wasn't friendly with these people, she was sure she'd have noticed if they made a habit of carrying guns around with them. This wasn't normal procedure. They were packing because they were scared.

Her ears pricked up at the conversation again, focusing more closely now. "One thing's for sure," David was saying. "We've gotta set up some kind of neighborhood watch."

"There's already a neighborhood watch," Bettie pointed out.

"Oh yeah? Who's in it?" said David.

Hilariously, only the soccer mom from before raised her hand. Cameron fought the urge to snicker.

"That's my point. This is probably some kind of terrorist attack, and—"

Cameron was somewhat gratified to hear indignant shouts spring up from many in the crowd, matching the rise in her own pulse. Normal people didn't just go tossing around the T-word like that.

"The news is saying there's no evidence it's an attack of any kind, terrorist or otherwise," said a pencil-necked guy in spectacles and a bathrobe. Cameron hoped that wasn't his everyday attire.

"You believe everything you hear on the news?" said David. "They wouldn't tell us if it *was* a terrorist attack, unless the towel-heads were right on the street with their—"

More angry shouting. Some of the other armed men started edging toward David, forming a little group around him.

A decision crystalized in Cameron's mind: she was getting out. *Now.* With people tossing out slurs and flashing weaponry already, she didn't need Alex's paranoia to tell her things were going to get worse long before they got better.

Bettie's head was turned the other direction for a moment. Cameron took a slow step back, and then another. Quickly she whirled and walked back for her house, doing her best to ignore the argument that grew louder and louder behind her.

* * *

The Jeep was already loaded with most of the stuff she wanted to take with her. She opened the garage and pulled it in, opening the back to load in a few more things. First she grabbed two sleeping bags. The cabin had plenty of blankets, and places to use them, but it never hurt to be prepared.

Sounding a lot like Alex right now, Cam. She shook the thought away.

Next she grabbed every last supply they had for Piper—the spare pump, some backup meds, and the needles for emergency injections they'd never had to administer. She had plenty of canned food in the car already, but she loaded up with everything left in the house; meager compared to the backup stores at the cabin, but enough for about ten meals. Who knew how valuable those meals might turn out to be.

Finally, there were weapons. Cameron might not have felt the urge to walk around brandishing them, but she and Alex always had a couple on hand. But the only thing she could get to was a little Ruger 10-22. Practically no stopping power. It would only be useful against another person if they were ignorant enough about guns to think it was dangerous. There was also a pistol, a Smith & Wesson M&P Shield, but it was

41

in a safe under the bed that only opened to Alex's fingerprint. Cameron had never seen much need to program her own print into the lock, and now she cursed herself for it. But it would be fine. They had half a dozen guns at the cabin, and she wasn't expecting much trouble on the road there.

Ding-dong.

Well, crud.

Warily, Cameron went to the front door. She put an eye to the peephole only to discover David on the other side. He stood tall, one hand on the piece at his belt, eyes roving across the neighborhood over his shoulder.

No chance he was here for any good reason, Cameron supposed. She thought about pretending she wasn't home. She'd been quiet as she approached the door so he wouldn't hear her footsteps. But with a twinge of anger, she decided against it. Screw this guy, and screw his gun-nut buddies, if they thought she was going to hide in her house so they couldn't see her. She jerked the doorknob almost savagely and threw it open.

David turned to her, mouth set in a grim line, and gave a solemn nod. "Hey there. It's Cameron, right?" He offered a hand.

"David, isn't it?" She didn't answer him, or put out a hand to take his.

His mouth twisted a little, and he withdrew the hand. "Daniel, actually. Lotta people get it wrong, though, so don't worry about it."

"I wasn't worried."

The twist turned into a frown. "Well, I just wanted to let you know, the neighborhood agreed to set up a watch. There's gonna be a bunch of us around, so if you see something, you need to tell us about it."

"I need to, huh?" Cameron felt a familiar tightness in her chest, and her knuckles were white as they gripped the edge of the door.

"Yeah, you do." Evidently Daniel had decided manners weren't worth it. "No telling what kind of trouble could be coming down on us, and it's up to all of us to—"

He stopped, eyes moving past her to the kitchen just down the hall. Cameron cursed inwardly. The extra food was all splayed out on the kitchen table, and the sleeping bag was on one of the chairs. She refused to look at it, and kept her eyes on Daniel's face.

His eyes narrowed. "You going somewhere?"

"That is exactly none of your business."

"It's everybody's business now. We don't know what's going on, and it's safest for everyone to stay put. We don't know who might or might not be involved in these plane crashes."

She couldn't stop herself—she laughed out loud. His frown deepened. "You think I had something to do with the plane crash? Hilarious. Do you know what I do for a living? Do you know where I come from, my history?"

"I don't, and ain't that part of the problem? Now listen, where's your husband?"

"I'm gonna ask you to get the hell off my porch." She stepped back and began to swing the door shut.

"Now hold on—" His hand shot forward and grabbed the doorknob, while his other seized her forearm.

Cameron released the door to wrap her hands around his wrists, pulling his arms halfway through the doorway. Then she struck the door with the full weight of her body, slamming it on his elbows and making him cry out in pain. Kicking the door open again, she dragged his hand down and around, slamming his face into the jamb. She twisted his hand up just enough that she was *reasonably* sure it wasn't sprained, then spun him once more and struck him in the throat with the heel of her hand—though not too hard. He fell to the ground, choking and gasping. Cameron leaned down and grabbed the pistol from his belt. Then she took the extra magazine from the pouch just beside it.

"You really ought to button this in place," she said. "It's dangerous otherwise. Good luck on patrol out there."

She slammed the door as he was still struggling to get back to his knees.

She'd have to move quickly now. He might or might not get it into his head to come after her alone, but even if he left he'd definitely come back with friends. She stuck the gun in her waistband and the mag in her jacket pocket, then hauled the rest of the supplies to the Jeep as fast as she could. She wanted to do one more sweep through the house and make sure she wasn't missing anything, but she felt the time ticking by like gunshots. She jumped into the driver's seat and hit the button to open the garage door.

The street was clear, and she breathed a sigh of relief. But as she pulled out and turned right to head east toward the freeway, she slowed to a crawl. Out there on her front porch sat Bettie. The old woman's gaze wandered back and forth, aimless, like she was waiting for something but didn't know what it was. They focused on Cameron, though, as she pulled the Jeep to a stop and rolled down the passenger window.

"Hey. I'm heading for the mountains. You want to come along?"

For a long minute, Bettie thought about it. Then, "Let me grab my tooth brush." She got off her rocking chair and headed for the house. The chair swung back and forth, empty, gently creaking in the silence of the street. As soon as Bettie walked inside, though, Cameron began to worry about how long the wait would be, and whether those idiots would try to interfere again. But within five minutes Bettie was coming out of her door with a bag. As Bettie climbed into the passenger seat and Cameron hit the gas, Bettie shot her an amused look and quipped "I wanna be Thelma."

CHAPTER 5

Alex opened the car door and climbed out, but stayed next to it. One hand rested on the car door, the other on the roof. He could not tear his eyes away from the burning wreckage before him, nor could he force his muscles to put him back in the car and drive them away. An instinct told him to run forward, to see if anyone could be saved. Another part of his mind told him how stupid that was; there was only fire and twisted metal, and a terrible wound in the earth that stretched for a hundred yards. No one could have survived that.

Another crash, much closer, drew him suddenly back to the present. On the other, eastbound side of the freeway, two cars had collided. Most likely the drivers had been as transfixed by the plane crash as Alex was. It wasn't much, just a little sideswipe, and the vehicles coasted to a stop on the other side of the center divider. But rather than get out and exchange angry words, or insurance information, the drivers only sat and stared at the burning flames.

That drew his attention back to the here and now. Quickly he looked back into the Mercedes, at Piper who sat in the passenger seat. Her face and both hands were pressed to the window; her phone lay on the floor, forgotten.

"Piper." She didn't turn. "Piper!"

Slowly she looked to him. Her eyes were filled with tears, and more had already left their streaks across her face.

"Don't look at it, Piper. Just keep your eyes off it."

"What happened?" she said. "Why did it go down?"

"I don't know."

"But . . . were there people on it?"

"I hope not. I don't know." Was it really a lie? Yes.

"Are you going to go look?"

Alex lifted his head out of the car again, surveying the wreck one more time. Maybe he was wrong. People survived under incredible circumstances. Some people fell out of planes with no parachute and somehow walked away. Maybe someone . . .

He batted the thought away immediately. If anyone had been thrown clear of the crash, he could search for hours and never find them. And if anyone had still been alive in the plane when it went down, they weren't any more. He could feel the heat of the flames even where he stood.

"Hey! Hey, man! Can I get a ride?"

The shout drew Alex's attention, and he turned to see someone approaching from further down the freeway. A homeless man, draped in a thick parka despite the heat of the morning, his face covered in dirt and more than a few teeth missing. He waved a hand rapidly in Alex's direction.

"Hey, man, c'n I get a ride? I'm heading west for Philly, you going that way?"

Alex swallowed, then got in the car. He slammed the door, threw it into drive, and hit the gas. The bum flipped him off as he passed, and Alex heard his angry shouts despite the roar of the wreckage.

"What did he want?" said Piper.

"To come with us. Don't worry about it. We need to stop and pick up some supplies."

"What about the plane?"

"The cops will come soon to take care of it."

"Should we call them?"

"We can't, Piper!" The words came far, far too harsh,

and he regretted them immediately. In a softer voice he tried again. "I don't have signal. Do you?"

Through the tears that rose in her eyes at his voice, she looked down at her phone again. Slowly she shook her head.

He tried to give her a reassuring smile. "They'll get word, somehow. They found out about these things before cell phones existed, you know? They'll take care of it."

Piper didn't answer him. She just turned back and looked through the rear window, watching the orange glow that was even now fading over the tops of the trees.

* * *

They needed supplies, and they needed them quickly. Now Alex wished he'd picked them up after getting the car, but he'd been in too much of a hurry to get out of the city. They needed an army surplus store, outdoor survival stuff, just in case they had to camp on the road. The next sizable city on the road was . . . Bethlehem? Alex thought so, but he couldn't be sure. He reached for his phone to look it up, then cursed quietly as he realized they still didn't have Internet.

"Hey, keep an eye on your signal, okay? If you get the Internet back, I need you to look up a surplus store in the next town."

No answer. Alex glanced right to see Piper still staring out the window. Her face was hidden, but in the mirror he could see tears still making their slow, silent way down her cheeks.

"Hey. Hey, Piper." He gripped her shoulder, squeezing it gently. "Piper, look at me. Come on, look at me."

Reluctantly she turned, swiping one sleeve across her eyes, another across her nose as she sniffed hard. "What?"

"It's okay. You don't have to feel bad about crying."

"I don't . . . I mean, I'm not. I just keep seeing it. There *were* people. There had to be."

Alex sighed and shook his head—not a denial of her words,

but a simple expression of pain. "You're right. I'm sorry, but you're right. But it's done now. There's nothing we can do about it. So try to stop thinking about it."

"I *can't!*" she cried. "I *just* saw it, Dad!" Anger made her tears brim closer to the surface, and they came faster now, her voice breaking with each word and coming only with effort.

He looked out the window again, at the sky that was too purple. Beside him Piper kept sniffing, furiously trying to rein in her tears. Alex swallowed hard and spoke in a quiet voice. "I know it's hard to forget. I know what it's like to have those things flashing in your mind, over and over again, no matter."

Sniff. "You do?"

"Sure. Most people my age do. My grandpa died in a plane crash a few years before you were born, in . . ."

He let the words hang, and Piper looked at him expectantly. Then realization struck her like a thunderbolt, and she put a hand to her mouth. "Wait, what? I didn't know that."

Alex shrugged. "Yeah, well. You never knew him, of course. And it's not the sort of thing to bring up all the time. After it happened, I saw those images playing out over and over again in my mind. Didn't matter if I was watching them on TV for the thousandth time, or if I was outside trying to get some space. I couldn't forget it, and I kept picturing him in that crash, somewhere in those buildings."

Piper wrapped her arms around herself. "God. It must have been so much worse. But . . . how did you . . . I mean, how did it—?"

"What made me finally stop thinking about it?"

"Yeah."

Alex gave her a little smile. "Actually, your mom."

She blinked and leaned forward, like a cat listening to a can opener. "*That's* when you met Mom?"

"About six months after, but yeah. She was on leave from her second tour, and you could imagine what things were like for her back then. When I saw her, it was like I could see the same thing in her eyes that I could feel behind mine. Both of us had things we couldn't stop seeing, even though we wanted to. And we brought each other out of it. She was tough with me when she needed to be, and sweet when she needed to be. I tried to be the same. And it's the same thing now. I'm here."

Piper didn't answer right away, but just kept looking out the window. After a minute, she gave a long sigh. "Okay."

"Okay?"

"Yeah."

"Good. Now we need to figure some stuff out. Starting with food. I hope you're hungry."

A road sign told him Bethlehem was just ten minutes ahead, but right off the road he saw the blinking neon lights of a diner. He steered the Mercedes to the off-ramp and pulled into the parking lot.

* * *

Without a word, Piper went to sit at the counter. Alex lingered at the door, looking around the room. The diner was nearly empty. A few customers sat at tables in the corner, a few more at the counter near Piper. Most seemed to belong to the big rigs out in the parking lot. Everything was quiet. The silence jarred his nerves, and after a moment he realized why: diners always had the staple background noise of a radio in the background, or the low hum of a TV, and this place had neither. The two screens mounted near the ceiling were black. He rolled his shoulders and went to sit by Piper.

The woman behind the counter took their order quickly and dropped it off at the kitchen with hardly a word, then came to fill Alex's coffee cup. He sipped at it gratefully. Sleep had been fitful, and not long enough, and he suspected he'd be facing many more days of the same. Coffee would soon be almost as valuable as drinking water, and he decided to savor every sip of it.

A couple of seats over, a grizzled old trucker sat munching on some hash browns. He saw Alex looking at him and nodded. Alex nodded silently in return.

"Come from the city?" said the trucker.

Alex blinked in surprise. "Yeah. Just this morning."

"Can always tell city folk. Especially since I know the regulars here. If you ain't one of them, you're a passer-by from the city." The trucker nodded sagely at this, as though someone else had said it.

Alex smiled. "Guess you got us there."

The trucker seemed to take that for an invitation, because he scooted one stool over until he was next to Alex. For half a second Alex tensed, but he quickly pushed the nerves aside. *Just a friendly guy looking to talk,* he told himself.

"You came from the east, huh? Saw that plane crash by the freeway? Terrible."

Alex's throat went dry, and he was suddenly very conscious of Piper by his elbow. He could feel the tension radiating from her, and tried to stall the line of conversation. "We passed it by. Were you coming from the east as well? Where you headed?"

"Arizona. Or at least, that's where I was headed. Who the heck knows what's going on any more. I can't raise my company on my cell, and no one there's listening to the CB. If they're even in the office. Maybe they went home, like sensible folks would. And now we got planes falling out of the sky, and God only knows how many people dying in crashes like that. Terrible times, just terrible."

"Excuse me," Piper whispered, and Alex heard the sob in her voice. She got up and nearly ran for the restroom. Alex closed his eyes and sighed.

The trucker watched her go, his face melting into a look of regret. "Aw, crap. I'm sorry, buddy. I didn't even think of . . . I mean, I didn't mean to upset her."

"Don't worry about it," said Alex, though he was sure he'd

be dealing with the fallout of that comment for the rest of the day at least. "You said your company's not picking you up on the CB. How about other rigs?"

"Oh, they're on, all right. It's like our own network of carrier pigeons crossing the country. Name's Gary, by the way. Pleasure."

"Alex. What are they saying?"

Gary leaned back to look over Alex's shoulder toward the restroom. Once he was sure Piper was gone he leaned back in, lips twitching mightily from the depths of his massive beard. "It's dark stuff, son. Dark stuff. That plane ain't the first to come down, and likely ain't the last. Airports everywhere are shut down till they figure out what the hell's going on. Storms are coming in, too. Big ones. Hurricanes in Florida, earthquakes in L.A., you name it. I just came through the midwest, passed through two towns I know in Kansas. This morning an F5 wiped them both off the map. Ain't been able to talk to a soul there to see if they're all right."

Alex's throat grew drier with each word. He shook his head, drinking another long sip of coffee. *What the hell is going on?*

"Some of the boys are saying it's the end times, though I don't know if I believe in all that kind of stuff." Gary punctuated the declaration with another bite of hash browns.

"Well, I appreciate you letting me know. Though, when Piper comes back . . ."

"Lips are sealed, son. Piper, huh? Beautiful name."

Alex forced a smile. "Thanks. She hasn't decided she hates it yet."

Gary chuckled. "Just about to hit the teens, right? Don't worry. They're bad, but not as bad as people like to say. I got two of my own, though they're grown now. Gonna try to get them on a HAM as soon as I can find one."

Alex winced. Their cabin in the mountains had a HAM. He'd meant to tell Cameron to keep it on, but the moment he'd actually reached her on the phone, the thought had completely fled his mind. He'd have to keep an eye on the cell signal and try to text her if he could—or hope she'd think of the HAM on her own.

"How far west you heading?" said Gary.

"Seattle area. We've got a cabin out in the woods."

Gary gave a low whistle. "That's a long drive. Any place you can hole up a little closer, until this all blows over?"

"Who's to say it will? Besides, my wife's there. She'd kill me if I didn't try to bring Piper back ASAP."

"I hear that. But you keep yourself away from cities, hear? If I keep going to Arizona, I ain't going through any place with a population bigger than a thousand. People are gonna get crazy, if they haven't already, and more so the worse it gets."

"You're probably right. We've got supplies."

"Get more," said Gary. Then he straightened suddenly. Alex glanced to his right and saw Piper emerging from the bathroom, still swiping at her nose with a tissue.

"Hey, sweetie," he said, once she took her seat beside them again. "You okay?"

"I'm fine."

"You've got a heck of an old man here," said Gary, clapping Alex on the shoulder. Piper glanced up at him, then ducked her gaze again. "Sounds like the two of you are gonna have a lot of fun on the road. Make sure you take a second to see some sights, will you? He sounds like a bit of a worrywart. Can't let him suck all the fun out of the drive."

Piper chuckled and looked up once more, smile reaching all the way up to crinkle her eyes. Alex gave Gary a grateful nod. The trucker beamed, rummaging in his pocket.

"You're young, so I'll bet you haven't seen half the sights the ole U.S. of A. has to offer. They're something else, I'll tell you. Here's something to help you find them." His hand emerged from the pocket, holding a small furry object. "That's a jackelope foot. Helps guide you where you need to go, and it's dang good luck besides."

Piper took the thing with a look of confusion. "A jackelope? What's that?"

Gary's eyes went wide, his mouth hanging open in a perfect picture of shock. "Why . . . why, you never learned what a jackelope was? Heck, what do they teach you all in school these days? You don't seem like no slouch, son. You must have shown her a jackelope or two?"

Alex kept his face stone serious. "Of course I have. Piper, don't you remember? We saw some jackelopes when you were five."

"Oh, *five*," said Piper, rolling her eyes. "Like I'm going to remember back then. What do they look like?"

"Well, it's all in the name, see. They're like a mix of jackrabbits and antelopes. Little rabbit bodies, but huge old antlers springing out of their foreheads." Gary held his hands about two feet apart. "They can get about this big, though most are a touch smaller."

Piper gaped at him. "Rabbits with antlers? You're joking."

Gary raised his left hand. "Hand to God. Heck, ask your dad. He took you to see them, after all."

Alex fought as hard as he could, barely managing to keep the grin from his face. "He's right, sweetie. You've seen them, even if you don't remember."

Piper's brow furrowed, her eyes narrowing to slits. "You know . . . come to think of it . . . I think I *do* remember something like that."

Gary snapped his fingers. "See? Told ya. Keep an eye out for them this time around—you got that foot on you, you'll see them for sure."

She looked at the "jackelope" foot with fresh interest. "Really? Can they, like . . . sense it?"

"Well, scientific folk don't like to agree, but everyone knows they can," said Gary, tapping his nose confidentially.

Alex marveled at the man. He seemed like he would have been perfectly at home spinning this tale in front of a warm fire, while the stars danced above and wolves howled in the distance. "Anyways, I'd best be getting on my way—wherever that might be. Your lunch is on me."

"No, that's not necessary," said Alex, trying quickly to rise.

Gary put a firm hand on his shoulder to push him back down. "I insist, son. Least I can do. Take care of that girl of yours. And you—Piper, is it?—take care of that jackelope paw for me."

"I will!" she said. "And thank you."

"Thank you," said Alex. "Be safe."

"You all do the same." Gary dropped a fifty dollar bill on the counter and left.

"He was nice," said Piper, thumb running across the jack-elope paw.

"He was," said Alex softly. *I hope he makes it home.*

CHAPTER 6

The highway pass through the Cascades had been madness, and now a windstorm was picking up. Cameron gripped the wheel harder, knuckles jutting white against the backdrop of grey water pouring down the windshield. As anxious as Cameron was, Bettie was worse; knees pressed into the panel before her, she had one hand on the handle above her head and the other death-gripping the seat. Cameron's eyes kept drifting to the edge of the road just a frightening few feet away, past which was a hundred feet of empty space to the bottom of the canyon.

"Feel like music?" After the long silence they'd been driving in, Bettie actually jumped at the sound of Cameron's voice.

"No thanks," said Bettie. "Not just yet."

"We're almost off the freeway. The mountain road will be a lot better."

"It would have to be."

Cameron chuckled at that.

A few minutes later, Cameron breathed a sigh of relief as she spotted the turnoff ahead. The moment they were off the highway, the wind lessened. And now there was no precipitous fall just a few paces away, but land that rose away sharply to either side of them, like a funnel dragging them upward. Bettie relaxed at last, leaning back in her chair and closing her eyes.

"Good Lord, thank you."

"Wishing you stayed back home?"

"Not even a little bit. I'll take a windstorm over crazy white boys swinging their guns around any day."

Cameron clicked on the radio, this time without asking. With the tension leeching away, she felt the need for some background noise. But the speakers only blared static, no matter how many stations she flipped through.

"Probably no radio signal this far up in the mountains," said Bettie. "You got a CD?"

"Uh, sure," said Cameron, switching it to CD. She didn't voice the first thought in her mind: she'd driven this road a thousand times before, and radio reception was never a problem. This wasn't the mountains. It was the storm, or the solar flare, or some combination of the two.

The Dixie Chicks began fiddling away. Cameron turned it down to a comfortable ambiance. But now that the adrenaline was beginning to fade and she had nothing to focus on but the broken yellow line winding ahead, Cameron's thoughts drifted elsewhere. Where were Alex and Piper in all this? Safe, no doubt. Alex had already gotten them out of Manhattan. But safe for how long? The summer weather had turned crazy, and only looked to be getting worse.

"You're thinking about them, aren't you?"

Cameron shrugged. "Can't help it."

"I'm not blaming you. I'm thinking about my boy. He was supposed to come by the house today."

"I'm sure he stayed home. What with the weather."

"I'm sure he did," said Bettie. "Hope so, anyways."

They passed another bend in the road, and Cameron slammed on the brakes. There, just fifty feed ahead, a mammoth pine tree lay across the road, slanted, the bottom end closer to them.

"Damn it."

Bettie swallowed nervously. "What do we do?"

Cameron looked around. The ground on either side of the road stretched just a few yards before it sloped up sharply. There was just enough space between the top of the tree and the slope that she thought she could squeeze the Jeep around the left side, but it would be a tight fit.

"I think I can make it through that gap. But you should hop out and wait, just in case."

"Sure. Good thing we're driving this and not some little Toyota."

"Good thing for sure. Here, take my jacket."

She pulled her parka from the back seat and gave it to Bettie, who stepped out and began walking along the tree's length. The wind buffeted her hard, but she hunched down and pressed on through it.

Cameron edged the Jeep past her and beside the tree. The car soon filled with the crunching sound of tires on gravel. Slowly she edged up to the gap. She'd been wrong. There wasn't quite enough space.

"Run over the top of the tree, or edge up the slope?" she muttered to herself. If she drove with her left wheels on the incline, the Jeep could turn. But if she tried driving right over the tree, the tires might pop. They were strong, but not invulnerable. She had a spare, but she didn't relish the thought of unloading the supplies in the trunk to reach it.

Slope it is. She turned the steering wheel slightly right. The left tires began to lift. Soon she was almost 45 degrees, and crawling at a snail's pace. Heart in her throat, she passed the top of the tree and turned back down, and soon was on asphalt again, where she stopped. Bettie caught up soon and leapt in, blowing into her hands.

"Good Lord, I thought you were going over. Thank goodness I wasn't in the car. I probably would have had a heart attack."

"Over and done with," said Cameron, forcing a smile.

"Now we've had an adventure, and we can ride out the rest of this storm sitting around our cabin fire and drinking wine."

"Now you're talking. Any chance you got some within arm's reach?"

"Not open. We're driving."

"You really think anyone's gonna care all the way up here?"

The forced smile became real, became a laugh. "Just hang on, Hemingway. Twenty more minutes and I can get you nice and liquored up."

* * *

The sun had vanished behind the mountains by the time they reached the cabin community, but it was still mid-afternoon, and its light still filled the sky to show them the way. Cameron knew from long experience that real darkness wouldn't come for another couple of hours.

The iron gate stood closed. Cameron dug through the glove compartment for the clicker. But when she pressed the button, nothing happened. Frowning, she tried again, with the same result. She got out of the car and walked up to the gate. No one around. The little station at the front was empty.

"What the hell?" she muttered.

The passenger door slammed behind her. "What's wrong?" said Bettie.

"Door's not opening, and no one's posted. The caretaker must be slacking on the job. His name's Bill. Weird guy, though I guess he keeps to himself and lets others do the same."

"That him?"

Cameron stepped over to look past the guard house and follow Bettie's outstretched finger. There through the wind and the light drizzle that had begun to fall, she saw a figure approaching from the other side of the fence. As it got closer, she breathed a sigh of relief. It *was* Bill.

"Hey!" she called. "Hey, Bill! The gate opener's busted—or my clicker is, but I replaced the battery not too long ago."

"It ain't busted," said Bill, drawing to a stop just on the other side of the gate. He had a ridiculous brown hat on (*A Stetson, for chrissake,* thought Cameron) and it was pulled low over his brow. "I turned it off. Don't want just anybody trying to come in."

"How could just anybody come in?" said Cameron. "They'd need a clicker."

Bill leaned forward, looking at her through the gate's narrow bars. "Who's to say they owned the clicker? Might'a stole it offa somebody."

Cameron sighed and tried not to roll her eyes. "Okay, well, I didn't. You know me. Open the gate. Please."

His eyes drifted past her. "Who's your friend?"

"Happy to introduce you out of the weather. Open the gate, Bill."

"She got a name?"

"Bettie." Cameron's nostrils flared. "Open the damn gate."

"Hm. Awright. But maybe don't be bringing in a whole buncha other friends, you know?"

"I can bring who I want," said Cameron through gritted teeth. "It's my cabin."

"Sure, I guess that's right," said Bill. "Come on in."

He went to trip the switch. Cameron stalked back to the car, Bettie following a half pace behind. Once the Jeep's doors had closed, Cameron let out a frustrated growl and slammed her hand into the steering wheel.

"What an obnoxious prick. Every time I come up here I swear I'm gonna call the property manager and get Bill fired."

"Probably a little shorter with me here than he woulda been otherwise," said Bettie, her voice carefully nonchalant.

Cameron looked at her uneasily. "I . . . I don't think . . ."

"Honey, I've been seeing that look in people's eyes since before you were born. Trust me."

The gate was open. Cameron slowly pressed the gas and passed inside. "Promise—as soon as the storm's over with, I'll call and have his ass thrown out. Deal?"

"Sure," said Bettie, smiling a little. But she turned away to look out the window, and away from Bill.

* * *

Cameron's cabin was near the back of the property, so they passed a number of others on their way in. Some had cars in front, most didn't—but nearly all of them had big old campers or RVs. Common custom in the community was to bring the family up for a stay in the cabin, but to take the RV out and into the mountains for the "real" camping experience. Cameron didn't know that she considered an RV to be "real" camping, but these were mostly wealthy retirees, and she guessed they could do what they wanted with their money.

At last they reached the cabin. Higher than most of the others, on a little rise that looked over most of the surrounding land, it was a wonderful mix of cozy and spacious. Cameron and Alex had hunted for almost two years before they'd found their perfect spot. They'd nearly signed the deal on a few others, but once they walked in the doors of this one, it was game over.

"Well, this is lovely," said Bettie. "My goodness, why don't you just live up here all the time?"

Cameron smiled. "Not much work for nurses this deep in the woods. But trust me, Alex has tried to convince me to make this our home more than once."

"I don't blame him. Heck, hire me as your house sitter. I'll spend every day up here if you let me."

The garage door opened at her clicker. *Bill didn't turn that off, at least,* she thought. She backed the Jeep in and closed the door behind them. But rather than unload the supplies from the car right away, she went straight into the house. Nothing

60

would spoil, and she wanted to check the windows for wind damage. A quick tour of the house showed her everything was fine—there weren't any trees within fifty feet of the house—but she headed out to close the outdoor shutters anyway. When she got back, Bettie was wandering around the house admiring all the rooms.

"It's decorated to a tee," said Bettie. "This is a really nice place, honey."

"It's too hot in the summer," said Cameron, waving a hand dismissively. "Not that we've got that problem now."

Bettie rushed to the window and looked out back. "Is that a garden?"

"Yeah. Tried growing some flowers one year. They didn't take too well."

"Of course not. Those are rose bushes, and it looks like you tried to grow them in autumn."

Cameron looked over at her, taken aback. "How can you tell?"

"The way they grew—stunted like that, hardly any life in them. You can tell they started strong but it got too cold too quick."

"You know a lot about plants, huh?"

"Honey, I could grow a cornstalk in concrete."

Cameron chuckled. "Well, knock yourself out. We've got a ton of seed supplies downstairs."

"Downstairs?"

"Yeah, there's a basement. In fact, I was just going to check it."

She opened the door and descended the creaky wooden steps. She had to fumble for the light switch for a moment before she remembered where it was. Finally the single bare bulb in the ceiling came on, dousing the room in a dim orange glow.

There before them were stacks and stacks—pallets and pallets, in fact, since Alex wanted to keep them safe from potential flooding—of food. Boxed, canned, any form of packaging that enhanced the shelf life. Soup and powdered milk and hard, hard bread, the kind that was edible and nutritious long after it had gone hard and lost any semblance of flavor. Built into the back wall were metal doors to freezers full of meat ready for cooking.

Bettie gasped. "You could feed an army with all this."

"Or three people for about a year," said Cameron, smirking. "That's what Alex calculated, anyway. With a little room to spare."

Bettie looked at her askance. "Honey, there's preparing for the worst, and then there's crazy. Did your husband really think you'd ever need all this stuff?"

Cameron smiled ruefully and pointed back up the staircase. "Just look at what's happening to the world outside, Bettie. Maybe he right? You don't have to tell him I said that though."

CHAPTER 7

They drove in silence after they left the diner. A few times Alex caught himself looking over at Piper, feeling the urge to speak. But her gaze remained out the window and far away, and so he let the silence reign. The decision was even easier when he realized he didn't know what to say.

Near sundown, he flirted with the idea of driving through the night. But that didn't seem necessary, at least not yet. A voice in his head—hopeful, and therefore relegated to the very back where it couldn't make too much noise—said that he still might be blowing things out of proportion. But even if it was wrong, they might as well get sleep while they could. If things really did go to hell, as he thought they might, there were bound to be more than a few sleepless nights ahead of them.

A storm picked up and tipped the scales in favor of finding a place to stop, and he finally pulled off the freeway a few miles past the Indiana border. The downpour was getting torrential, and he jacked the wipers up to full as they crept along the side of the road. Finally he spotted a Best Western and pulled into the parking lot with a sigh of relief. Alex finally turned her eyes away from the window, and he winced internally at the anxiety he saw in her eyes.

"We've been in four states today."

She raised her eyebrows. "Cool?"

"Dang right it's cool. Hashtag on the road again."

He saw the way she tried to keep her brow furrowed, but

she couldn't stop a smile breaking through the dark mood. "Oh my god, shut up."

"Come on, let's get a room."

The hotel's front counter was manned by a young, lackadaisical girl who might have been a cousin to the girl who rented them their car that morning. She even gave Alex the same eye-roll when he tapped his fingers impatiently on the counter, spurred by the slow speed she took down his credit card number with pen and paper, since the computer wasn't working.

But eventually he got two keys, and they ran through the pouring rain to their hotel room. Again, Alex felt like maybe he and Piper should talk before they went to bed, but she just wrapped herself in her blankets and went out like a light—a light that wasn't working, because there still wasn't any electricity.

Maybe it's for the best, he thought. She'd seen a lot of stuff that day—more than he hoped she'd ever have to see in her life. Maybe a night's sleep was just what she needed. What they *both* needed.

But when he woke up just after dawn, sleep hadn't provided the answer to any of his problems. Outside, the rain was coming down twice as hard as the night before. There was frost on the ground, or perhaps small, icy bits of hail.

Hail. In March. He fought back a sudden shudder.

He turned from the window and started going through the room. There was no minibar, but he took nearly everything else that wasn't bolted down: the towels, the soap and the shampoo, the packets of coffee and sugar packets that sat near the TV. He was folding up his sheets and blankets, planning to take them, too, when Piper woke up. She peered at him from beneath the edge of her blanket, brow furrowed.

"Whayoudoing?" she mumbled.

"Grabbing these blankets. Might need them."

She blinked hard to banish the last of her sleep. "Dad, we can't just steal their blankets."

"They're cheap. They get a few people every once in a while who do this, and it's built into the cost. And yeah, normally I wouldn't be *that* guy, but this time I'm going to. Get up. We're grabbing yours, too."

For a moment he thought she'd keep protesting, but something came over her face. Maybe it was the memory of the plane crash the day before, or maybe their conversation with Gary at lunch. She rose silently and got dressed, and he folded her sheets and blanket into neat, tight little squares.

He'd only booked the one night, and there was no need to check out. He took the stolen hotel room items to the car quickly, hugging them tight to his chest against the rain, and soon they were back on the road. But he didn't make for the freeway. Instead he turned west, heading deeper into town.

"Where are we going?" said Piper.

"Walmart. There's one thing we need that we don't have. Coats. Didn't pack them, because I wasn't expecting . . . all of this." He waved his hand vaguely at the windshield, which was covered by a torrent of water the wipers couldn't begin to stave off, even though he had them full on.

Piper didn't argue. She was being very compliant, and it worried him. Not that he wanted her arguing with him at every turn, but he didn't want her to be miserable, either. Bad moods rarely helped anything, even in bad situations. And people who let sadness and grief bottle up often let them out at the worst possible time.

"How about some music?" he said, trying to sound cheerful. He clicked the radio on and pushed the scan button. Station after station was static. Finally he got a signal—but it was a news station, not music.

—the government now reporting that the effects of the solar flare are much worse than previously anticipated. All flights are grounded indefinitely. All citizens are urged to stay in their homes and conserve drinking water until the extent of the disaster has been—

His hand darted to the dial and twisted it all the way left.

Silence settled once more. "Maybe no radio just now," he muttered. Piper stared out the window again.

* * *

Walmart was berserk. The moment he pulled into the parking lot, Alex strongly considered turning around and heading right back to the freeway again. Every parking space was taken, so eventually he just took a handicapped spot. It gave him a momentary twinge of guilt, but no one was paying attention, and he knew exactly what he'd come here to get. They'd only be there a minute.

He realized his mistake once he got inside. If the parking lot was full, the store was stuffed to the gills. They actually had to fight their way through the crowd, and Alex wrapped a protective arm around Piper's shoulders as he shouldered his way through the other shoppers.

"Jesus," said Piper, keeping her voice muted. "This is insane."

Alex grunted. She was right. And the crowd itself wasn't even what worried him. He could *smell* the fear in these people. It had finally started to hit home to many of them that this wasn't just some storm, not just another power outage. He saw many eyes red and bloodshot, and many cheeks streaked with tears. Many here had lost someone—in plane crashes, in hospitals suddenly robbed of all power. Who knew how else. Hell, maybe the flare had even taken out electrical-only cars on the road.

These people were panicked, like a herd of cattle who smelled an approaching fire. And if this was how it was in a small town in Indiana, he could only imagine what the big cities looked like.

An earlier, half-formed decision solidified to unbreakable law in his mind: they wouldn't be going within fifty miles of any city if they had any other choice.

Once they got into the aisles, things eased up a bit. He hadn't bothered going for a shopping cart, and now he was glad. They wouldn't have been able to force their way through this press. Everyone else was going for perishables—food, mostly, plus kerosene for lamps and stoves. They were able to get two thick, waterproof parkas with little trouble, and Alex picked up two sleeping bags as an afterthought. Then he left Piper at the head of an aisle and dived into the commotion, going for a flat of water. He was elbowed twice trying to extract it—not from malice, but because no one was paying him any attention. Everyone had eyes only for what they needed.

The line at the front of the store took a full hour. Only a handful of the checkout registers were manned, and Alex cursed the store's management for not ordering in more cashiers. Then he realized—the manager probably *had* called in all the cashiers he had. But many of them wouldn't have come in. He thought back to Jersey, and how empty the bus had been, and the driver telling them about everyone staying home.

At last they emerged into the rain and ran for the car, feeling like they'd barely escaped with their lives.

* * *

After gassing up, they hit the freeway again. Piper was more quiet and withdrawn than she'd been before, if that was possible. With an inward sigh, Alex realized he was going to have to have a talk with her. Not to pull her out of this funk—he doubted he even could—but, probably, to make it even worse. He'd tried to sugarcoat things, at least a little. That was no longer an option.

"Piper," he began. "I need to tell you something."

She only glanced at him for a second before looking back out the window. He put a hand on her shoulder, and this time she kept her gaze on him.

"This is worse than I thought. I think it's worse than most people thought it was going to be. And so we need to treat it like what it is: an emergency. We can't just treat this like some fun road trip, as much as I'd like to."

"Okay," she said, a little uncertainly.

"I don't want to scare you. That's not what I'm trying to do here. But I do need you to understand. This trip is going to be . . . dangerous. A lot more dangerous than I thought it would be, anyway."

She glanced out the windshield. "I get it. This rain is absolutely insane."

"Not the weather, Piper. I mean, yes, that's something we have to think with, have to plan for. But we've got lots of gear. And I know how to deal with rain, with the wet and the cold, and even the snow, if it comes to that. Weather can change, but it can be predicted. And when it shows its face, you can plan for how to deal with it. Weather isn't what's going to be dangerous on this trip. It's people."

"Which people?"

His jaw clenched, hating what he knew he had to say, hating the effect he knew it would have on her. "All people. Everyone who's not you and me. We might meet a few more people like Gary on the road, or Elizabeth and Jackie from back in New York.

"But people are starting to realize that this isn't just some storm. This isn't winter just having some last hurrah before it gives way to spring. It looks like there's no power across the whole country, and I don't know when that will come back—or if they can even fix it. People are scared, and soon they're going to get more scared. When that happens, they'll stop being nice. They'll stop being helpful. They'll be more interested in protecting what they've got, their food and their homes."

"We're not going to steal their food and their homes," Piper said, frowning.

"Of course we're not. But we won't always get the chance to explain that to them. They'll be scared, and so they'll defend what they've got, because it's safer to overreact than to let someone take what you need to survive."

She shook her head. "So what, everyone's going to shoot first and ask questions later? That's stupid."

But it's what I would do, he thought to himself. Out loud, he only said, "Maybe yes. Maybe no. And not everyone will be that way. But we have to be cautious, too. If we want to stay safe, we have to act the same way as some of these people will. Assume that people might be dangerous, and be pleasantly surprised if they're not."

"Dad, I think you're over—"

"I'm not." He glanced away from the road for just a second, meeting her eyes so she could see the severity in his. "I'm not overreacting. I'm doing what I have to do to keep you safe. To keep *both* of us safe. And I need you to listen to me. You can never leave my eyesight. And you can never let any stranger get within arm's reach, not unless they've already proven that they're safe. You can't talk to anyone who's not me. It's the only way we can keep ourselves safe. And keeping you safe is my whole job right now. It's the only thing I'm thinking about."

He saw it then. Fear shone in her eyes, and her hands were trembling. His heart broke. The one thing he always wanted to do as a father was to make his daughter feel safe. From her childhood to an adolescence he wasn't quite ready for, it had been his number one priority. Every tragic news story had a soft, gentle explanation, a reason why that could never happen to *them.* Now the game had changed, and he'd been the one to change it. Now he was the one making her afraid.

But keeping her alive, he told himself.

Piper turned away, pulling her knees up to her chest and wrapping her arms around them.

Alex hated to press her, but he had to. "Do you understand, Piper?"

"Yes," she said, her voice impossibly small. He pressed the car on, through the rain and the small bits of hail that were once again falling out of the sky.

CHAPTER 8

O nce Cameron was satisfied that the house hadn't taken any damage, she unloaded the supplies from the back of the Jeep. When Bettie started to help, Cameron insisted she could handle it. But Bettie turned out to be even more stubborn, and by the time they were done, Cameron had to admit she was grateful for the extra hands. Everything was stowed neatly away in the kitchen cabinets and cupboard. To celebrate, she broke open a bottle of wine as promised— though not the most expensive. That was for when Alex and Piper arrived.

Cameron started a fire in the hearth. As they rested in the living room sipping at their glasses, her thoughts drifted to Alex and Piper again and again. Her phone had charged in the car, but she had no signal in the cabin. That, like the missing radio reception from before, was unusual. And it meant she couldn't even try to call him to see where he was. Were they still driving? Or had the airlines decided to resume flights? Maybe he'd caught a flight somewhere, Ohio, or Indiana, even, if they'd driven that far. Maybe he and Piper were on their way home, and they'd come driving up tomorrow.

Or maybe they were in the air when another burst of radiation hit, and took the planes down again.

She shuddered and took a gulp of wine. No. That was impossible. Alex would never risk getting in a plane, not after flights had been downed all across the country. He and Piper were still driving.

Unless something had happened on the road.

Her jaw was clenched tight, and she forced herself to relax. Worrying was useless—even if she was right, she couldn't do anything about it now.

Bettie must have caught her mood. The older woman looked at her with slightly narrowed eyes. "Listen, sweetie. I see you trying to fight back something on your mind. That ain't gonna work with just you sitting here doing nothing."

Cameron shrugged. "As opposed to what? Hitting the road and hoping I cross their path while I'm heading east?"

"No. But you gotta do something to keep your mind busy, or you'll eat yourself alive."

"All I've got is this fire and this wine. Thanks, Bettie, but I'll be fine."

"That's not all you got. But for now, you should get some rest. We both should. That drive got my nerves all shot to hell. Tomorrow, we'll see what else we can do to get your mind off it."

The sun had set long ago, so Cameron agreed easily enough. She feared she might have a restless night, plagued by thoughts and dreams of Alex and Piper. But the mountain road must have taken more of a toll than she thought, because she slept like a log and woke up long after the sun had already risen. The smell of coffee filled her nostrils as she sat up and stretched, and when she made her way to the kitchen, she saw that Bettie had put a pot on.

"Morning, sunshine. Get some of this in you."

Cameron took the cup gratefully, poured in some creamer and sipped. It wasn't until halfway through her first cup that she took stock of Bettie's clothes. The older woman had well-worn jeans and a flannel shirt on, and a pair of thick leather gloves tucked into her back pocket. Cameron raised an eyebrow.

72

"Planning on going somewhere?"

"Not very far. And you're underdressed. Today, you and I are going to go tackle that garden out back."

A wry smile crossed Cameron's lips. "That's your plan to get my mind off Alex and Piper? Gardening?"

"If it helps clear your head, so much the better. But the truth is, I can't stand to see a good garden go to waste, and I'll be damned if I'm going to bust my ass to fix your back yard and you're not even going to help me."

That forced a laugh, and once Cameron had had her coffee—two cups, the second with just a splash of Kahlúa—she got on more workmanlike clothing. Outside, the storm had finally abated, though the grey sky above threatened more rain, and the wind was still chilly. Cameron rubbed her arms vigorously as Bettie walked around, inspecting the earth.

"Shovels and stuff are over in the garage," said Cameron.

"I saw them. We aren't ready for them yet. Can't just start tearing up the ground without a plan. After all, that's what you did in the first place." A quick flash of white teeth showed Cameron the words weren't meant as harsh as they sounded.

Cameron shook her head with a chuckle. "Fine, fine. Just tell me what you need done."

Bettie did. She walked up and down the garden like a soldier on patrol, pointing out which plants should be torn out entirely and which might be saved. She shook her head and clucked her tongue at rows that had been planted too close to each other and would have to be torn up, and pointed at how they could have more plants around the edges of the garden, and not just in the middle, to use the space more efficiently.

"One problem," said Cameron, as Bettie pointed out a row of rosebushes that were going to get the chop. "We don't have more roses to replace these. All the seeds downstairs are vegetables."

"Oh, I know," said Bettie. "And so much the better. Roses look nice, but they've got no use. I always found I cared more about my plants, put more effort into taking care of them, when I knew I was gonna get a meal out of it at the end."

Cameron smiled. And she tried to banish the nagging thought at the back of her mind—the thought that sounded suspiciously like Alex, whispering that maybe they'd *need* to grow food if the storms from this flare kept up.

Once Bettie had finished surveying the ground, she and Cameron went into the garage to get the tools. And just as they reemerged into the back yard, the sun broke through the clouds at last, shining brightly down as they got to work. Soon Cameron had shed her flannel overshirt and was working in her black tank top. As she bent over to drag some particularly stubborn roots from the ground, Bettie happened to glance over.

"What's that?"

With raised eyebrows, Cameron looked down. The edge of her shirt had lifted up to reveal her tattoo, just above her belt line on the left side of her flat stomach. She traced it idly with her finger.

"It's called the Tree of Life," she said. "Though there's another name for it—*cann* something. I don't remember. It's Celtic."

"I can see that," said Bettie. "What's it mean?"

Cameron swallowed. But it was fine. Remembering what it meant didn't mean she had to think back to why she got it in the first place. She spoke by rote, like she was reciting a history lesson. "It's a symbol of balance. Harmony. The tree grows up, its branches reaching for the sky, but eventually they return to the earth, mingling with the roots, which spring up into the tree again. Death and rebirth. Growth and decay. Everything's a cycle. And, I guess, everything's connected."

"Well, that's nice. I'm glad you actually know what it means. Not like those idiot college kids who get Chinese letters tattooed on their backs, then find out it actually says 'dishwasher' or something."

To her surprise, Cameron barked a laugh, and her dark mood vanished. "No, I knew going in. Alex has one, too. It was his idea, actually."

"Same thing?"

"Yep. Same spot."

"Hey."

The new voice made them both jump, and they turned to the fence that rimmed the yard. There was Bill, leaning on the fence's top spar and chewing something. Cameron felt her hackles rise, and she tugged the hem of her shirt down until it covered her bare sliver of midriff.

"Bill. What do you want?"

"Gonna have a meeting down by the gatehouse. All the other cabin owners are coming."

Cameron barely kept herself from rolling her eyes. "*All* of them, huh? You're telling me every other cabin owner is here?"

He scowled a bit at that. "Course not. But them that is here, is coming. Why don't you come on down?"

"I think we'll skip it," said Cameron firmly. But Bettie put a hand on her arm.

"It's all right, Cameron. If there's other people around, I'd like to meet them."

She still felt uncomfortable under Bill's languid stare, but Cameron shrugged. "All right. If you want to go."

"I was only inviting the cabin owners . . ." Bill began.

That settled it. "Bettie's with me. She's coming. And we'll be *happy* to come. Let's go, Bettie."

She snatched up her flannel from where she'd hung it on a fencepost, and donned it quickly to cover up the skin of her arms and shoulders. Bill scowled again, but he turned and set off without a word. After dusting themselves off, Cameron and Bettie followed.

* * *

By the time they reached the gatehouse, most of the other cabin owners had already gathered. Bill stood at their head, just outside the door that lead to the gatehouse itself. Everyone else—Cameron counted seven—had their hands buried in their pockets, because despite the sunshine, it was still bitterly cold.

Too cold for March, Cameron thought. She pushed the thought away.

"All right, that's everyone," said Bill. "Now. We're gonna have to assign some jobs around here. Seeing as how I'm the one that knows what needs doing, makes the most sense for me to assign the jobs. You there. Russell, right? You got some muscle on you. Gonna need you to take guard duty. At least one shift."

No one answered him. Cameron looked around and saw the same look of wide-eyed confusion on all their faces that she felt herself.

"Bill, what the hell are you talking about?" she said. She was well tired of his crap already, and he'd called Bettie and Cameron away from the garden for *this?*

But Bill looked at her like she was the crazy one, and spat on the ground at his feet. "Jobs. For the cabin community. Everybody pitching in. What with the storms."

"What about the storms?" said Cameron, her anger rising.

He cocked an eyebrow. "Ain't you heard, sweetheart? World's going all to hell outside that gate. Power and everything else is down all across the country, and can't no one get it back up. Planes can't fly. Computers don't work. It's the end times."

She wasn't any less angry, but Cameron laughed anyway—loud and mocking, maybe even a little forced, because she could see the fear shining in the eyes of the others who were standing there listening. "End times? You sound like some homeless guy standing on the street corner with a cardboard sign and a megaphone."

Bill didn't rise to it. He only shook his head. "Don't much matter what you say, girl. The truth's the truth. Why'd so many of you show up here today, if you didn't know something was wrong? Any one of you want to turn around and drive back home?"

That was met with silence, and when Cameron looked around at the rest of them, they all seemed to be avoiding each other's eyes. Could they really all have been driven here by fear of this . . . this storm, the solar flares, whatever it was?

Isn't that why you came here? The question ran through her mind in a blink. And as she thought about it, she realized that Bill was right, at least for her part—given the chance, she wouldn't drive back home, either.

With no one to answer him, Bill smiled, growing bolder. "Now, that's what I thought. All right, so Russell—guard duty. I guess you and I can trade shifts. Anyone else want to volunteer? We should have at least three."

"I'll do it," said someone—an old guy, late sixties, maybe, wearing a Vietnam veteran's cap. Cameron thought his name was Scott.

"You all can't be serious," said Cameron. "Are you all taking this seriously? This is crazy. You live here—you *pay* Bill's paycheck."

"Paychecks are about to become a thing of the past," said Bill.

"Oh. My god," said Cameron, pinching the bridge of her nose. "Let me use the landline. I'm calling Fred, Bill. Your ass is going to be out of here by morning."

But Bill's smile was triumphant. "Can't call Fred even if I'd let you. Landlines are down. Have been all day. Told you, sweetheart—world outside's going all to hell."

A pencil-necked girl stepped forward, away from her equally pencil-necked husband, and looked back and forth with uneasy eyes. "He's right. We heard some news on our way up here. Storms are whipping out roads and some bridges all across the country. Most truckers won't even drive them. No one's run out of food yet, but some people think it's going to happen soon, and they're storming any store that still has supplies."

Cameron opened her mouth to speak. But suddenly she felt the smooth skin of Bettie's fingers clamp down on her arm. She glanced back as the older woman stepped in close.

"I'm not saying you're wrong, Cameron," she whispered. "But look around. This isn't the right time to argue the point."

And of course, she was right. Everyone there was scared. Bill's words had stoked the flames of those fears, and Miss Pencil-neck had sealed the deal.

Good lord, was she actually going to have to treat these people seriously, and not just laugh at them as they tried to create some new Mad Max-style government in this middle class cabin community?

"Aubrey's exactly right," Bill said. "Food's gonna run short real soon. Some people should go out to supermarkets and stores, anywhere within driving distance, and load up on supplies."

"Don't forget water," said the pencil-necked girl—Aubrey, he'd said her name was. She smiled slightly, as though she were very proud of herself for remembering this important detail. "It's one of the most important things you can stock up on in a disaster."

Cameron tried very hard not to roll her eyes, but did not succeed. "We are all on well water with solar power and generators back ups." Snapped Cameron. "And who's paying for these supplies, Bill? You?"

Bill's mouth set in a firm line—but he hedged at the last second, and for the first time he sounded doubtful. "Well, way I see it, they're gonna be taken by whoever wants them the most. Might as well be us."

She took one step forward. "I want to be very clear on this one. You're saying we should go out and *steal?*"

He didn't meet her eye. Everyone else shifted uncomfortably. "I didn't say that."

"Good. Because if you did, I'd throw you right over that gate on your ass, and good luck getting back in—I heard someone disabled all the clickers." That earned a light chuckle from the others, but Cameron pressed on, ignoring it. "We're not going to steal, and no one here is going to blow their savings accounts loading up on supplies that we don't even know we need yet. These storms could pass tomorrow, and then we'd be a thousand dollars poorer and look like a bunch of idiots."

"Or it could last for a month, a year, even, and then we'd all starve," said Bill, lifting his chin.

Cameron pointed to the first guy Bill had spoken to. "You. Russell, right? Do you have enough food to last the rest of the week?"

Russell shrugged. "More than that. Two weeks, maybe three if I stretch it out."

"Of course you do. We all do. Don't you?" She looked around, waiting for an answer. Slowly, they all nodded. She turned back to Bill. "Because we're not stupid, and none of us wants to drive half an hour to the nearest store every other day. So if we've all got enough food for almost another month, maybe chill out on panic button."

Relief washed through the rest of them—Cameron could feel it like a physical wave. But Bill didn't look relieved, he just looked angry.

"I think we're done here. Have fun on guard duty." She turned and walked away. Bettie hurried to follow, and after a moment she heard the shuffling of the rest of the group edging away.

"Well, you certainly didn't make friends with the man," said Bettie.

"He's a prick. I can't believe he called us down there for that joke of a meeting, or whatever it was supposed to be."

"Still, gotta admire someone who wants to be prepared.

We'll plant the fastest-growing veggies in the garden, just in case."

Cameron gaped at her. "You can't tell me you're taking him seriously."

Bettie shrugged. "We're gardening anyway. Why not grow something that'll be ready to eat quicker, on the off chance we're still here in a month and a half?"

No easy answer came. Cameron scowled and turned her eyes front again. "Fine."

"Good." Bettie looked over her shoulder to make sure no one was following too close, then continued in a low voice. "And by the way, I think that meeting was a lot more productive when you were talking than when Bill was. You ask me, you should be the one calling the shots."

Memories threatened to surface, memories linked to the tattoo on her stomach. "Not a chance," she said firmly. "Last thing I want to do is be responsible for a bunch of scared idiots who think the world is ending."

"Suit yourself," said Bettie. "I'm just letting you know *my* druthers."

Cameron didn't answer her, but only followed her back to the cabin and the garden, and began hoeing the dirt with much more fury than it probably deserved.

CHAPTER 9

Alex and Piper pulled up that evening in Normal, Illinois, after a terrible day on the road. They should have gotten at least twice as far as they had, but bad weather had held up traffic on the roads. Phones still couldn't pull up a GPS, so Alex had pored over maps trying to find an alternate route that avoided the freeways. It didn't work. Despite the fact that most people were staying home in this weather, the storms had caused enough accidents that the highways came to a standstill anyway.

"Wait, this place is *literally* called Normal?" said Piper.

"Yep. Named after a type of school, not because it's particularly average." Alex took a second glance at the buildings around them as they drove. "Though, of course, it is."

"How did you know that? Have you been here before?"

"No. There's probably hundreds of towns across the U.S. named Normal, and most of them for the same reason."

A large Best Western sign just off the freeway drew them in, but once they got close they saw the NO VACANCY sign glowing cheerily. Looking around the hotel's parking lot, Alex saw a bunch of people—some families, even—curled up in their seats, cars on and heaters blasting, ready to sleep through the night.

"Don't tell me we have to sleep in the car," Piper groaned.

"Waste too much gas," said Alex. "Might drain the battery, too. Come on. We'll look for another place."

They soon found what was almost a physical border—once they were out of sight of the freeway, things quickly took a turn for the boondocks. Houses became ramshackle, with spotted paint and rotting boards, and more than a few windows covered with bars. Alarm bells went off in Alex's mind, and he was just about to turn around when he spotted a sign up ahead that proclaimed, quite simply, "INN." He drove toward it, jaw clenched and hands ready to turn them around at a moment's notice.

The hotel was to the Best Western what the houses were to the homes closer to the freeway—ill-kept, dilapidated and looking like it might collapse under the fury of the storm. But a light burned in the front office, and the VACANCY sign shone bright. The parking lot was mostly full, but had plenty of spaces for them to pull in.

"Can I wait in the car?" said Piper.

Alex looked around at the place, and at the fading daylight in the sky overhead. "I'd rather you came in with me."

She gave him a nasty look, but obeyed without voicing any complaint. Inside they found caretakers whose appearance matched that of the hotel. The man had a few days' stubble and wore faded overalls atop a dirty flannel shirt, while the woman's gaudy flower-print dress barely contained her massive frame. She sat back on a stool, observing Alex and chewing something, while her husband stepped up to the counter. In his mind, Alex gave them the names of Doctor and Missus Hillbilly.

"Staying the night?" said Doctor.

"If you've got room."

"Got room," said Doctor. "Ain't take no credit cards, though."

"That's fine," said Alex, reaching for his wallet. "What's the charge?"

Doc folded his arms and leaned on the counter. "Well, normally it'd be fifty. But seein' as the Best Western's all full up, from what I hear, and what with them charging sixty-five, I think we gots to raise our prices to match. So it's sixty-five, and I hope you ain't hold that against me." Behind Doc, Missus leered.

Alex blinked. It was unusual to have someone scam you while being so . . . honest about it. But then he thought back to the New York hotel for $150 a night. "No problem at all. Business must be rough right now."

"It ain't business, it's the people," said Doc, shaking his head. "Acting like we never get storms around here. 'Course it's unseasonal, but ain't no call to go plumb crazy about it like y'all have been. Not meanin' you, o'course, but out of towners."

Piper had started to drift away, eyeing one of the chairs across the room. Alex reached out a hand and pulled her gently back. "Has it been bad here?"

Doc shrugged. "Ain't been good. Hear the cities got it worse. It'll all blow over, but 'till it does, everybody's lookin' out for them and theirs."

Alex handed him a hundred, and Doctor gave him a key along with the change. It was a metal key, old school, with a bit wooden tag hanging off the ring: 110.

"Checkout's at ten," said Doctor.

"We'll be leaving before then."

"One of us'll be around. Take care."

Alex led Piper outside, where they both threw up their hoods against the still-heavy rain. After the last town, Alex had thrown together two overnight bags for each of them, so they didn't need to unload anything else from the car. They settled into their beds, drawing the blinds against the darkness outside, and soon Piper fell asleep. Alex lay awake for quite a while before he could do the same, staring at the phone in his hand and waiting for signal bars that never came.

* * *

The sound of shattering glass woke him. He shot up in his bed, eyes wide as they roved the room. But Piper slept peacefully, and there was no one else there. His mind raced, processing the sounds that had woken him after the fact.

Outside.

He leapt up and ran to the window, pulling the curtains just apart to peer out through the blinds. Clouds still hid the moon in the sky, but the parking lot had one dismal yellow bulb to cast light. He squinted, trying to hasten his eyes as they adjusted.

There. Two figures. Standing by a car near the road, but moving down the line toward him.

They were robbing the cars. Two more, and they'd reach his.

He threw his boots on, fingers racing to tie them, then shrugged on his parka and zipped it up. The dark green would hide him fairly well in the darkness, but he didn't want to hide. He whispered a prayer that they didn't have any guns. He'd been half tempted to get his own firearm in the Walmart the day before, but hadn't wanted to do it with Piper right there. Now he cursed himself for being a fool.

He threw open the door and stepped out into the rain.

The thieves had reached the car next to his. Alex tried to make for the lamplight. If they did have guns, the last thing he wanted was to startle them. When he was a good few yards away and couldn't be any more brightly lit than he was, he raised his hands.

"Hey there," he said.

Both the thieves jumped and whirled to him. They wore black waterproof parkas over baseball caps, and with the parking lot light behind them, he couldn't make out their faces. But by the shapes of their bodies, he guessed two men, young, or at least skinny.

"Hey now," said Alex, spreading his hands to emphasize they were empty. "I don't want any trouble."

"Then get out of here," snarled one of the thieves—the closer one. He held a crowbar, but Alex didn't see another weapon. That was a good sign.

"Thing is, you're about to rob my car," said Alex. "And I can't let you do that. You've probably already got some good stuff from the other cars. Why don't you get on out of here, and we all get away happy?"

"Good stuff?" scoffed the thief. "One wallet with thirty bucks in it. What's the big deal with your car? Got something good in there?" He stepped forward, raising the crowbar so Alex couldn't miss it.

"Whoah, relax there, buddy," said Alex. "No need for a fight."

"Clock him, Mitch," said the other thief. He was at Alex's rear bumper now, holding a dull flashlight he was trying to shine in Alex's eyes. The heavy rain kept it from being blinding. "We'll see what he's got in a moment."

Mitch stepped forward, but his movement was slow, uncertain. Alex sprang. He grabbed the crowbar and twisted, his other hand punching Mitch in the throat. The kid fell back, coughing and wheezing, losing his grip on the crowbar. Alex turned to the other thief—but the kid had whipped out a knife. No little switchblade, either. It was at least six inches long and black, possibly military grade. Either the second thief was just big into the military, or he was a veteran; the calm look in his eye and the easy way his feet slid into a fighting stance told Alex it was the latter. His whole body tensed, ready for the thief to spring.

A gunshot ripped through the air, making them both jump. Without turning his back, Alex glanced over his shoulder. There was Doctor Hillbilly, a 12-gauge pointing at the sky.

"Get the fuck out of here, you goddamn degenerates," roared the good Doctor.

The second thief took off without a word. Mitch scrambled up from the asphalt and ran to follow him, crowbar forgotten.

Alex felt his adrenaline leave him in a rush, and his shoulders sagged. He turned to Doc, letting the crowbar slip from his limp fingers. "Thanks," he said.

"Told you. These lowlifes have decided it's every man for himself. You all right?"

"Fine. No chance to fight before you showed up." Alex gave the Doctor a weak smile. "Hey, I never caught your name."

"Heath. Wife's Marge. You?"

"Alex. My girl's Piper. The one I came in with."

"Sure, sure. Well, sorry this happened. Didn't get your car, did they?" Heath tucked the shotgun under his elbow and reached into his pocket for a cigarette, lighting it under the cover of his hand.

"Nope. Stopped them just in time. Hey, mind if I get one of those?"

Heath raised his eyes in surprise. "You're a smoker? Most you city folk quit when you have kids."

"I did, a long time ago. It's just, that's the closest I've gotten to a fight in more years than I can remember."

Heath chuckled, handed him the lit cigarette from his mouth—Alex chose to imagine the filter was wet from the rain—and lit another for himself. Together they moved under the awning that covered the walkway in front of all the hotel rooms, and smoked in silence. Alex's eyes roved across the hotel, the dim lights shining from a few windows, and the cars clustered together under the single dim bulb above. Then his gaze went to the roof, and he saw a wide metal antenna jutting up into the darkness.

"That's a radio antenna," he said, pointing.

Heath glanced up. "Sure is. Got us a setup in the offices. You a radio man?"

"I'm a forest ranger. And I've got my own setup at home.

Could I use your rig? I haven't been able to talk to my wife for a few days now."

"Hm." Heath took a long pull at his cigarette. "Don't usually let guests use it. You sure you know what you're doing?"

"I use one every day on my job. You've got nothing to worry about. I just want to call home."

Heath took another long drag, saying nothing. But then he tossed the cigarette into the gutter and turned, tossing his head for Alex to follow.

In the hotel's front office, Heath went to the desk to stow his shotgun behind it. Then he opened the back door, and Alex followed him through into a hallways that was claustrophobic in every direction but forward. They passed two rooms with entirely different, unpleasant smells—one chemical and antiseptic, the other musky and rotten—before they came to a padlocked door at the end of the hall. Heath was careful to cover the lock with his body as he spun the dial. After a moment it clicked, and the door swung open.

Stepping inside, Alex was pleased to find this room, at least, was fairly odorless, with only a faint whiff of electronic ozone. There was Heath's rig, and though dust had collected in the room's corners and rested on the shelves that lined the walls, the radio itself was polished and bright. It was an ancient-looking model, probably older than Alex was, though not as old as Heath.

"There she be," said Heath. "Have at it."

Alex sat down eagerly, and spun the dials to tune in to his home frequency. The radio in their cabin was always tuned the same, unless Cameron had changed the settings—which she wouldn't have. She'd have turned it on and left it going—probably with the volume turned near to full, so she could hear him from anywhere in the cabin if he happened to call.

"This is WA7OB looking for N7QJM."

The radio buzzed with static. Alex glanced over his shoulder. Heath was in the doorway, arms folded.

"WA7OB looking for N7QJM. Cameron, you there?"

Still silence. Of course, he couldn't have expected too much. She would certainly have reached the cabin by now, but he doubted she'd be sitting in the basement waiting for his voice to come in. She might be relaxing at the end of the day. Heck, she might be asleep. Heath gave up after about fifteen minutes and left him alone, then returned with a pair of beers and offered him one. Alex took it, but only sipped lightly as he kept trying to reach Cameron.

After twenty minutes he decided to change tack. He knew the emergency frequency of the stations in the area, so he tuned in to one. "WA7OB looking for W5YI. W5YI, come in."

For a moment, there was only buzzing static. Alex was about to call out again, but then a voice crackled out of the speakers. "WA7OB, this is W5YI. Alex, is that you?"

Alex felt weak and sagged in his seat. "Brent. Holy . . . it's good to hear you."

"Good to hear you, too, Alex. Everything okay in your neck of the woods?"

"I'm not in my neck of the woods, Brent. I'm with my daughter in Illinois. We're making our way back to the west coast, but we can't fly."

"No, you certainly can't. Well, what can I do for you?"

Alex leaned in. "There's a cabin community. It's about . . . I think it's about twenty miles southwest of you? I've got a place there, and my wife should be staying there. I haven't been able to reach her. Phones are down."

"You want a check-in?"

"If it's not too much trouble."

Brent's chuckle came out tinny and thin on the speakers. "Trouble? There's nothing to do up here. No one's hiking or camping. There's too much rain for fires, but not enough for floods. At least not yet. I'll be grateful for the diversion. I'll try to get down there tomorrow, all right?"

"Thanks, Brent. Her name's Cameron. The cabin community's called Widebrook."

"I know it. Anything you want me to tell her?"

"Tell her Piper and I are find, and we're on our way. Not sure how long it'll take us, but we'll see her soon."

"10-4. W5YI out."

Alex put the receiver down on the desk and swiped at his forehead—it was covered with a thin sheen of sweat. He hadn't realized—or hadn't *let* himself realize—just how worried he was about Cameron. Of course, he didn't know any more about her status than he had before, but now at least she'd know something about his.

"All done?" said Heath behind him. The man had clearly grown impatient while waiting for Alex to finish.

Alex gave him a weak smile. "Would it be too much trouble if I kept trying to reach my wife directly?" As Heath's eyes narrowed slightly, Alex hastily dug out his wallet. "Hey, listen, I appreciate you're doing me a favor. How about I give you an extra fifty bucks for the trouble?"

Heath took the fifty, but he still regarded Alex with suspicion. "It ain't about money. I can't stay here the whole night to watch you, and if you're the stealing type, there's a lotta stuff here worth more than just fifty bucks."

Paranoid much? thought Alex. But then he remembered Heath coming to his rescue with the shotgun. He reached into his wallet again. "Here you go. Driver's license, and both my credit cards. Hang on to them—plus the fifty. When I'm done, you check the place out. If even one cord's out of place, you keep the money."

Though he kept his frown, Heath eventually shrugged and shoved the cards and cash into his shirt breast pocket. Then he ambled out the door and down the hall toward the front desk, leaving Alex to tune the radio back to his home frequency.

He eyed his watch fitfully as he kept the broadcast up,

asking for Cameron again and again by callsign. The night wore on, two hours passing with no response. His eyelids were starting to drag, and he caught himself nodding more than once. Just as he was about to give up for the night, a voice crackled in the speakers, and he sat up straight.

"WA7OB, this is KK4SWV. Sorry I'm not who you're looking for, but I heard you while scanning."

Alex lowered his head to the desk, muttering out of the side of his mouth into the receiver. "Roger, KK4SWV. Sorry, but you got my hopes up."

There was a slight chuckle in the man's voice as he replied. "My apologies. Just hate to hear a man shouting into the void with no one there to hear him. Who you trying to reach?"

"My wife in Washington state. What are you doing up so late?"

"Early, actually. I'm in Ames, Iowa. I always get up early to watch the sunrise."

"You got a good view of the sunrise from your radio?"

That earned a sharp laugh. "All right, the sunrise ain't all it's cracked up to be. I like to check in on the radio before I start my day. Name's Pete."

Alex smiled. "I'm Alex. Ames, huh? I'm in Normal Illinois right now."

"Heading for Washington? Why, you're going to pass right through our area. If you want, you feel free to swing on by for a meal. It'll be better than trying to get a meal at some restaurant. The town's a little more dangerous than it has been."

An idea struck Alex, and he leaned in. "I'd be happy to take you up on that, Pete. And . . . if it's not too much to ask, could you do me one more favor? If you're around the radio at all, could you keep an ear on this frequency? My wife might try to reach me on it."

"Well, I'm not here all day," said Pete. "But sure. I'll keep the receiver open while I'm puttering around."

They exchanged information—Alex providing Cameron's

callsign, and Pete providing his home address. When they logged off at the end, Alex felt a wave of relief that easily over-rode his exhaustion after the long night. He rose and stumbled back to his room, falling into his bed and passing out immediately despite the sliver of grey dawn that tried to peek in through the curtains.

CHAPTER 10

The day after the "council" with Bill, Cameron's mood hadn't improved any. She and Bettie set out into the garden once more, and she attacked the soil with her hoe. Over and over she felt the urge to march down to the gatehouse and describe the multitudinous ways in which Bill was a stoat sphincter, but each time she repressed it. What with the weather, the lack of any outside communication, and the troubles that plagued the world outside, she figured interpersonal fighting was the last thing their cabin community needed just then.

She'd dealt with bigger assholes than Bill in the service. He wouldn't get to her now.

Bettie must have noticed Cameron's mood, but she was smart enough not to ask about it. Or maybe she already knew Cameron was still angry at Bill, and she just didn't care enough to get involved. It certainly didn't seem to bother her that Bill was a racist prick, though Cameron didn't know how that didn't rankle the old woman till she screamed.

They spoke rarely, and then only to ask each other to hand over this tool or that. They remarked on the sweat of their work or expressed thanks for the cool air that kept them from exhaustion. At noon they fixed lunch together, Bettie mixing a salad while Cameron threw together some sandwiches, and not a sentence was uttered more profound than "Can you hand me the pepper?"

Thus Cameron thought the whole day might pass without anything important happening.

And then they heard the screeching tires.

Screee. They were gone in an instant. Just one sharp blast. But their heads snapped up at the sound, and they stared in the direction of the cabin community's gate. Because there was no question: that was where the sound had come from.

They looked at each other, and then they made for the Jeep. Not running, exactly, but no leisurely walk either. It was that quiet hurry when you know something is wrong, but you don't want to admit it, because admitting it will make it real. So you walk, as quick as you can, but your heart is pulsing and you're wondering just how bad it's going to be.

Cameron hit the gas just a bit harder than she had to, and thundered down the road toward the front of the community with Bettie gripping the handle above her head. They saw the commotion long before they reached the gate: Bill standing just inside, next to the gatehouse. He was holding a shotgun, because of course he was, and he was shouting at someone through the gate. A few someones, in fact, because there was a gunmetal-gray pickup truck just outside. The driver had gotten out and had his hands up, and there were two other figures opposite him on the passenger side of the truck.

And then Cameron didn't see anything for a few moments. Because her eyes were fixed on the driver, and her mind was trying to process his face, and her mouth wouldn't move.

"Wade?" she finally managed to stammer.

"What?" said Bettie.

"Someone I know. From work."

Bettie leaned forward, the wrinkles around her eyes deepening as she peered through the windshield. "From Seattle?"

"Stay here."

Cameron pulled the car to a stop a few yards short of the gate and got out. Bill was in the middle of a heated tirade, but the moment he heard Cameron's car door slam shut, his lips stopped flapping and he looked back at her. His eyes squinted.

"Go on back to your cabin till I sort this out," he growled.

She ignored him, and only barely resisted giving him a dirty look. "Wade? What are you doing here?"

Relief crashed across his features like a wave on rocks. "Cameron. Thank god."

Bill squinted harder. "You two know each other?"

"You're quick, Bill. Wade, what's going on?"

"I found them on the road," said Wade, pointing to the family still in the truck. "And the daughter . . ."

That's when Cameron heard it. Whimpers of pain coming from the back seat of the pickup truck.

She ran forward, making for the gatehouse.

"Don't you open that gate!" roared Bill.

Cameron opened the gate.

* * *

The father had been riding shotgun, where he'd been glaring at Bill during the exchange. The mother was in the back seat, trying to make the daughter as comfortable as possible. Hasty introductions on the way inside told Cameron they were the Williams family, with Chad and Carla being the parents.

"And what's your name, sweetheart?" said Cameron. She'd jumped in the back seat of the pickup while Wade drove. She could always return for her Jeep later.

"Naomi." The girl's face was pale, her arm clutched to her chest.

"Naomi, I need to check your arm out. Can you hold it still for me, and tell me if I do something that hurts?"

She didn't need to ask. The moment she touched the spot where Naomi's arm seemed to bulge in an odd way, the girl cried out and recoiled from Cameron's hand. Carla's hands

94

jerked, a motherly instinct to protect her daughter, though quickly mastered.

"Okay. It looks like this is broken. Wade, make for that cabin there. That's mine."

They parked. Under Cameron's direction, Chad picked Naomi and carried her inside, being careful not to jostle the arm. Cameron had her sit in one of the dining room chairs, her arm laid out flat on the table. Though the girl whimpered every time Cameron touched it, and tears rolled down her face, she didn't move to get away.

Cameron gave her a smile. "You're being really brave, Naomi. Seriously. But I'm gonna need you to be even braver. I have to push your bone back into place."

Naomi blinked. "Will it hurt?"

A lot of people thought it was best to lie to kids. Cameron wasn't one of them. "Yes. It's going to hurt a lot. You can hold your dad's hand, and you can squeeze it as hard as you want. Although, try not to break it."

To her surprise, Naomi gasped out a quick laugh. That was good. The girl had some serious steel. Chad came up and took Naomi's hand. Carla paced behind them both, chewing on her fingernails as she watched.

"Are you ready?" said Cameron.

"Can you . . . count down or something?"

Cameron grimaced. "No."

She pushed the bone back into place. Naomi screamed, and Carla put her hands over her ears. Chad winced as Naomi crushed his fingers in her grip. But Cameron held it in place, and Naomi didn't try to drag her arm away, and in a second her screams died out.

"Good," Cameron murmured. "I'm sorry about that. You would have tensed up if I counted, and that would have made it harder. But the bone's set now. I'm going to give you a splint to hold it in place. Wade?"

She motioned to him as she rose and went to the back

of the house, where she had some backup medical supplies stashed. As she dug through them for a splint and some bandages, she started asking questions.

"What in the hell brought you here, Wade?"

He shrugged. "I remember you mentioning the name of the place. Managed to pull the name up on a GPS before the Internet went down."

"Went down where? And *why* would you come here?"

Wade didn't answer for a second. Cameron stopped her search and looked back at him. His look had gone dark, and in the set of his brow she saw a truth he didn't want to say.

"Wade? What is it?"

"I guess you didn't hear, then. I was in Leavenworth for the weekend. When the storms started, and the planes went down, I started heading back to Seattle. But then . . . Cameron, Seattle's mostly gone."

Again she froze in her search, but this time it was involuntary. She stared at her hands for a moment, trying to understand what the words meant. Then she stared at him.

"Gone?"

"Mostly. Storms kicked up some kind of killer tidal wave. It swept in and . . . well, a lot of people died, Cam. Then the few who were left went crazy—the ones who didn't leave, that is. Riots, civil unrest, the whole deal. It's a wasteland."

"Jesus," she whispered. "The hospital—"

He shook his head immediately. "Don't even think about it. I thought the same thing. It's gone, Cam. The building was hit hard. It's not even safe anymore. I doubt anyone's still there, and if they are, they're keeping their head down, same as everyone else. Same as we should be doing."

She wanted to disagree, wanted to jump in her Jeep and drive until she was back home, to help however she could. But she knew he was most likely right. And more importantly, Alex and Piper were on their way *here*, not Seattle. She'd never go there now, not if it meant Piper would try to follow her into what sounded like a war zone.

"I have to finish setting that arm," she muttered, and left Wade looking after her.

* * *

A while later, it was done. Naomi was resting, and Cameron had broken out another bottle of wine for the parents. Chad sat in an armchair staring at nothing, while Carla had her arms wrapped around her daughter like she'd never let go. It filled Cameron with a twinge of jealousy, if she were honest with herself.

She'd meant to let them rest as long as they needed. Maybe spend the night. But after a while, someone knocked at the door. Cameron sighed. It was probably Bill. He'd had sense enough to stay away till now, but apparently his smarts didn't last forever.

Sure enough, there he was when she opened the door. His bulbous, ruddy face was twisted in what was probably supposed to be a stern expression. Behind him were a few of the others from the cabin community; Cameron recognized Scott among them, as well as Russell and Debbie.

"You all done?"

"The bone's set," said Cameron, carefully blocking the doorway. "The girl's resting."

"Well, they gotta rest someplace else," said Bill. "Happy to help a little girl, of course, but we gotta look after ourselves now."

"What place else?" said Cameron. "What, are you kicking them out of the cabin community?"

"Damn right. They can't be here."

"I'm not kicking them out."

"We can't all be looking after them."

"You're on my doorstep, and if you think you're gonna tell me what to do with my own property, you can eat it."

She heard two sets of footsteps behind her and soon smelled a familiar cologne. "What's the problem?" said Wade, locking eyes with Bill. Bettie stepped up beside her other shoulder.

"We're not hanging on to those vagabonds, is the problem."

"They're in Cameron's house."

"Funny, I was just telling him that," said Cameron, giving Wade a dirty look.

"You ain't supposed to be here either," said Bill, sticking a fat finger in Wade's face. Cameron was half afraid Wade would break the man's hand, but then she was half hoping for it, too.

"I'm in Cameron's house, too."

"What's the problem letting them stay here?" said Bettie. "There's plenty of empty cabins, seems to me."

"They're not taking the cabins," said Bill.

"No one's in the cabins," said Cameron.

"They still belong to people. I'm the caretaker. This is exactly what I get paid to stop, and I ain't losing my job just because you've got a crisis of conscience."

Cameron pointed down the hall behind her. "There's a little girl back there in my living room. Can't be more than twelve. You try to kick her out of this cabin community, you and I are going to have problems. That's not a crisis of conscience, that's just a fact."

"You want to keep them in your house, that's your business, but—"

"They can stay in my RV," said Scott.

Bill stopped short and turned to look at him. Scott stepped forward, lips pursed beneath his thick bush of beard.

"That ain't . . ." Bill began. He turned back, squinting his ugliest squint at Cameron. "We're not taking in every poor sap who comes on that mountain road."

Cameron didn't bother shouting an answer as he turned

and stumped away, but she gave Scott a grateful nod once Bill was gone. Taking the Williams into her cabin would have made it a bit cramped, and throwing Wade into the mix would have made it unbearable.

They shut the door and went back to the living room. Chad and Carla were sitting up straight, worry plain in their eyes.

"Was that about us?" said Chad. "We don't want to be any trouble."

"No trouble," said Bettie. "Only some hopped-up yokel getting too big for his boots. You've got a place to stay, as long as you want to."

"And you'll stay," said Cameron, putting her hands to her hips. "I'll need to keep an eye on that arm."

They nodded in gratitude. Cameron beckoned Chad toward the door, so he could meet Scott and they could arrange to settle in. But as she left, she was aware of Wade watching her with an unreadable expression.

CHAPTER 11

Despite it being cramped, Cameron let the Williams family stay in her house that night, giving them her own bed while she slept on the couch. Scott gave Wade his RV for the night. They switched the next day, and Cameron busied herself helping the Williams move in. The RV had a bigger bed in the back where the parents could sleep, and a smaller pull-out sleeper for Naomi. They'd brought precious few possessions with them—just a few items for a camping trip. They had tents, as well, but Cameron quickly told them to keep that to themselves.

"If Bill finds out, he'll have you sleeping out in the rain," she said.

"Thanks," said Chad, lowering his gaze. "Sorry we're causing so much of a fuss."

"No fuss," said Cameron. "And if anyone complains, tell them to come and talk to me."

A bunch of the others from the cabin community came to help them settle in. Some offered food, others brought extra blankets, because the nights were getting colder—way past unseasonably cold for the time of year. Cameron told them where to put some items, or told them to take other supplies back to their homes if there wasn't room. They obeyed without question, most of them. She got the feeling they were just glad to have someone telling them what to do—and, too, they were probably happy it wasn't Bill.

Bill's behavior aside, the rest of the community was nothing but pleasant to the Williams. Chad was soon hanging out and sharing beers with some of the other guys, while Kira and Naomi were invited by the women to do a little miniature tour of all the occupied cabins. Bettie, in particular, hovered over Naomi like a grandma hen, which neither Naomi nor Kira seemed to mind at all. Even Wade began to get used to the new situation in his own way, though quite differently from the Williams. Cameron saw him wandering around the cabins and the woods with a camera, taking pictures of the homes and the forest beyond.

Once the Williams were more or less settled in, Cameron went back to the cabin and met up with Bettie. They got to work in the garden again. The soil had mostly been cleared of dead plants and was ready to be torn up for new ones. Bettie directed Cameron while she did the grunt work, then knelt down to get her own hands dirty by pulling up the few remaining weeds whose roots had refused to let go the soil.

"Where's that friend of yours?" she said after a while. "The one who came in with the Williams?"

Cameron paused, then looked up. "I'm not sure. He's been wandering around taking pictures. Could be anywhere."

"He works at the hospital, yeah?"

"Yeah," said Cameron. "Why?"

Bettie quickly shook her head. "No reason. Just didn't get to talk to him much. Seems like a capable young man. Strong."

"Strong enough," said Cameron, shrugging. "We spar sometimes. We're more work buddies than co-workers."

"Mm-hm."

Cameron got back to tearing up the ground with her hoe. Something about the set of Bettie's shoulders rubbed her the wrong way, but she couldn't put her finger on it.

* * *

The rest of the day passed with no sign of Wade, but he showed up early the next morning, just after Bettie and Cameron had had coffee and were getting to work on the garden again. He came up, leaning on the fence the way Bill had a few days ago—with the minor difference that Cameron didn't want to snap her hoe in half and drive one of the pointy ends through his face.

"Morning," he said. "Want to take a walk?"

Cameron blinked. "Sure, I guess. What's up?"

He frowned and shrugged. "Nothing serious. I just didn't make it over yesterday. We didn't really get to talk."

When Cameron looked over, Bettie waved her off. "I'm good here, for a little bit. Don't take too long, though—in a couple of hours we'll be ready to lay some seed."

So Cameron tossed off her gloves and hopped the fence. She and Wade set off along the hill, down a path that ran along the edge of the forest in a long, winding loop that eventually led to the front of the cabin community.

Despite asking her to talk, Wade was silent for a long while. In the end it was Cameron who had to break the silence.

"Saw you taking pictures yesterday. What was that all about?"

He looked at her askance. "What do you mean? I like taking pictures."

She stopped in her tracks and turned to him, folding her arms. "You. A photographer."

Something about his grin irked her. "What? Not what you expected?"

Cameron stared. Eventually his face faltered, and he shrugged.

"I got into it after I came back. You know that behavioral crap they make you do, if you're having trouble adjusting? Well, I tried a bunch of stuff, and photography was what eventually stuck. Saved up, got a decent camera—nothing crazy—and been taking pictures ever since."

Cameron considered that a moment. With that framing, it didn't seem quite so far-fetched. She knew people came back with all sorts of problems, and the government was less interested in solving them after the uniform came off. People did art, learned how to play an instrument. Photography seemed like another logical choice.

But even as her thoughts were growing to reconcile the idea with what she knew about Wade, his grin returned as he ruined it. "Plus, there's no faster way to get a girl's top off than to tell her you're a photographer."

"I knew it. I *knew* it." Cameron shook her head and turned to resume her stroll, while Wade hurried to fall into step. "I'd tell you to never change, but then again, you never have."

Wade barked a laugh, but then fell silent again for a long time. When he did speak, it was to change the subject. "I never got to thank you for helping us out at the gate."

"Please," said Cameron, shrugging. "Bill's just an asshole. But I didn't get to ask you—what happened to your car? That truck you came in wasn't yours, was it?"

"Nope, that was the Williams'. Mine is still down by the highway. Once I found them, I figured it was smarter to take one vehicle, and their truck was a lot steadier than my car would have been. Less cramped, too." He stopped for a moment and pointed. There, a little way off through the trees, Cameron could see the picket-and-wire fence that marked the edge of the community. "See that? Just a little bit farther, the fence is broken down, and something chewed a hole through the wire. It's old—nothing dangerous right now. But we should get out there and fix it when we can. I spent a lot of yesterday checking out the perimeter, seeing how secure everything was."

Cameron snorted and resumed her walk, forcing him to come along. "I haven't heard the words 'perimeter' or 'secure' in a long time, Wade. Don't tell me you're starting to have flashbacks."

He returned her grin, but there was something edgy in his—caution, or fear or something—Cameron couldn't quite place it, and wasn't sure she liked it. "I'm just thinking about keeping everything safe. Not even saying there's any danger now, or that there's going to be. But on the off chance there is, better safe than sorry, right?"

She frowned. "What's got you spooked, Wade? Is it what happened in Seattle?"

Wade balked, then shrugged. "Maybe a little bit. We saw some of it. TV was down, but there was a little bit of spotty cell phone reception, so I saw some videos posted online before everything went dark. It was a nuthouse, Cam. The power was out for so long, and the storms got so high . . . riots broke out in Belltown first. And right in the middle of that crazy, an earthquake hit, and maybe because of that, or maybe all on its own, waves came in and took half the city away. Some biblical shit."

A shudder ran up her spine. Cameron had known Wade for years. He didn't get spooked, not easily. He was the first one to make inappropriate jokes when some natural disaster happened out there across the world, like the Japan tsunami or the Kuala Lumpur earthquake. She tried to tell herself it was just because it was Seattle, because it was home, but she wasn't so sure.

"Anyway, the stores are empty and everyone's acting like paranoid freaks. No point going back to the city, not for a long time, anyway."

"I didn't have any plans to," said Cameron, sighing. "At first I wanted to. The hospital, you know. But Alex and Piper are coming here. Plus, I swear to god, if I leave Bill here running everything, everybody's going to be dead in a week."

Wade barked a laugh. "You don't honestly think Bill's running jack squat around here, do you?"

They were near the front of the community now, where the path crossed the main road, and Cameron stopped in the middle of it. She turned to Wade, hands on her hips. "What do you mean?"

He fixed her with that same sardonic smile, the one she'd always tried to discourage when they sparred back at the hospital. "Come on, Cameron. Don't play dumb."

She was about to press it, but then they both stopped. Out there beyond the gate, far off down the road, they heard the sound of a rumbling engine. After half a minute, a big brown Range Rover trundled into view, with Park Ranger logos emblazoned on all sides.

"Cam?"

"It's okay," she said. "It's a ranger. Nothing to worry about."

Then her stomach did a flip-flop, fear drawing whimpering caresses across her skin. Why would a ranger come here?

Alex.

She forced herself to take several calm, deep breaths. Alex wasn't in trouble. Or at least, she had no reason to think that, not yet. The ranger could be here for any number of reasons. Hell, she didn't even know if Alex was the only ranger who owned a place in the cabin community. Maybe someone else here was a retired ranger, or a parent of a ranger. There were any number of possible explanations.

The Range Rover stopped. Behind the wheel was a man of middle age, with a Magnum P.I. mustache. He opened the door and stepped from the vehicle.

"Hey there," he called out. "I'm looking for Cameron Robinson."

The sinking feeling redoubled. "That's me."

"Got a message from your husband, Alex."

"Is he—"

"He's all right," said the ranger, almost at the same instant she started to speak.

She burst out in a laugh, knowing and not caring that

it sounded hysterical. "Okay. All right. Hold on, I'll get the gate."

* * *

The Range Rover rolled through, and Cameron and Wade joined the ranger in the Rover. Cameron guided him up the road to her cabin with a strange sense of deja vu—this was the second time she'd taken the exact same trip in three days.

The ranger's name was Brent Williams, and he'd heard from Alex just a couple of days before. "Reached me on the HAM," he said. "Asked me to come down and check in on you, plus check your unit was working."

Cameron felt a hot flush creep into her cheeks. Jesus. How could she be so stupid? "I forgot about our radio," she said. She shook her head. "God damn it. I could have talked to them."

"Don't worry about it," said Wade. From the back seat he reached up, putting a hand on her shoulder.

"Anyway, he and your daughter—was it Piper?—they're all right. Still driving west. Storms are bad, but not so bad as all that, and Alex has stocked all up on supplies."

"Yeah, that's him," said Cameron.

"Right enough. I mean, we all take precautions at the station of course, but Alex was always next-level." Brent chuckled as he pulled the Rover to a stop right in front of Cameron's place.

She showed him inside and took him downstairs to the basement, where the HAM unit waited. Brent checked it out. Everything was in working order, so he fired it up and watched her send out her callsign. But no answer came.

"Probably driving," said Brent. "I'm afraid that while he's on the road, you're going to be on the receiving end most of the time. Just leave it on, and turned up loud enough that you can hear it upstairs if someone starts talking."

"I will," said Cameron. She put the handset back on its hook, trying not to let her disappointment show. Of course it was stupid to expect that Alex would still be there on the line when she showed up days later, but still. She'd have given a whole lot just to hear his voice. "Hey, you want something to eat? Drink? We've got food, coffee, wine."

"I should be driving back pronto, so no wine—but I'd kill for lunch and some coffee," said Brent.

"Sure. Come on up."

When they climbed the stairs, they found Bettie in the kitchen, washing her hands in the sink. After introductions, Bettie waved them all away. "I'll fix us all something. You sit and relax."

"You've been working in the garden," said Cameron. "Let me take care of it."

"Sit your butt down, Cameron, and relax," said Bettie, fixing her with a steely glare. "You're putting me up. It's the least I can do. Is he eating with us?"

Bettie pointed at Wade. Cameron blinked. "Of course. I mean, if you want to, Wade. No obligation."

Wade gave Bettie an odd look. "I'd love to. Thanks."

"Mm-hm." Bettie turned and began digging through cabinets for food and things to cook it with. Cameron took Brent and Wade into the living room, where they sank into the plush couches with a sigh.

"Things have gotten crazy in all the cities," said Brent. "But so far, our job's been easy enough out at the station. Definitely haven't had to worry about wildfires with all the rain, and we already got rid of the worst flood risks earlier in the year. Now we're mostly just worried about scared city folks running up into the mountains for safety."

Cameron frowned. That was a common theme these days, or so it seemed. She was glad to hear Alex and Piper were fine the last Brent had heard, but what about since then? How far did Alex realistically think he could get, if all the cities were madhouses the way she kept hearing?

Wade had been watching Cameron, but now he turned back to Brent. "Has that been happening?"

Brent frowned. "Not yet. But we're on the lookout. Seems like something that could happen easily, and all at once."

She opened her mouth to ask a follow up question. But at the edge of hearing, she heard something that stopped her cold.

sksssh "Hello? This is KK4SWV looking for N7QJM. Looking for N7QJM." *sksssh*

She was out of her couch in a flash and running down the stairs to the basement. The voice was unfamiliar, and she didn't recognize their callsign—but she knew hers. Cameron snatched up the handset.

"Hello? Hello, this is N7QJM. Who's this?"

"Howdy, N7QJM. This is Pete. Am I talking to Cameron?"

"Yes!" she said, louder than she meant to. "Yes. Hi, Pete. How did you get my callsign?" Though of course, she already knew the answer.

"Alex gave it to me."

"Did he have a message?"

"No." Her heart sank. "He just asked me to keep an eye out, keep trying to reach you if I could. He's on his way here now, though. Should be arriving any day. You'll get to talk to him yourself."

She frowned at the receiver. "He's headed to you? Where are you?"

"Ames," said Pete. "Iowa. A little off the route he was gonna take, but I offered a place to stay for the night. Some supplies, too, if they're still here when he arrives."

That sounded odd. "What do you mean? Why wouldn't they be?"

There was a moment's silence. "Sorry, didn't mean to give the wrong idea. Things are getting a little hairy here. But it's Ames, not a big city. Folks acting a little crazy doesn't mean

108

much. I'm on the outskirts of town, not in the middle of the crazy. It'll blow over."

The sinking feeling was back, and stronger than ever. But she forced herself to stay calm—or at least to *sound* calm. "Okay, Pete. You take care of yourself, okay? And tell Alex to make sure to radio me."

He chuckled. "Oh, don't worry. From how he sounded, there's nothing he wants to do more right now. I'm gonna sign off."

"Roger. And thank you. And please—tell him to call me as soon as he can, and that we're all fine here in the cabin community. Brent arrived. Tell him I'm sorry I didn't have the radio on before."

"My pleasure. KK4SWV out."

The radio clicked off, and the room filled with static. As she straightened and turned, Cameron realized Bettie, Brent and Wade were all standing behind her. She forced a smile.

"They're on the way," she said, feeling none of the confidence in her words.

CHAPTER 12

A lex knew something was wrong the second he pulled into Ames.

The streets were empty of people. Of course, they'd passed plenty of towns with empty streets on their way west. But most streets were empty of all signs of life. And, he supposed, that was true here, too. But here there were wrecked cars—some crashed, some flipped—and other signs of civil unrest. Alex saw more than one home where the front door had been smashed in and the windows shattered. He'd never visited Ames before, but from everything he knew, it wasn't a "loot and riot" sort of place.

This was something new. And it was definitely something dangerous.

Piper was staring out the window at everything as they passed. Suddenly she sat forward, pointing. "Look, Dad. There's some people."

Alex glanced over. He saw three tall, burly men sitting on the front porch of a house. The windows were broken in. One of them held an axe, and the other two crowbars.

"Don't look at them, honey." Alex stepped a little harder on the gas.

Fortunately they found no streets blocked by the wrecked cars or other signs of fighting, though once or twice they did have to drive slowly through thick clouds of black smoke. He had the route to Pete's address memorized, and crept slowly toward it, feeling every moment like he was going to have to stomp on the gas pedal and escape.

They finally reached Pete's house to find it broken into like all the rest.

Alex pulled the car into the driveway—but then he just sat there for a minute, thinking. He sure as hell wasn't going to leave Piper here in the car by herself. But neither did he want to bring her into that house. The black hole of the open door was like a gaping mouth waiting to suck them down into some evil unknown.

On the other hand, who knew if Pete was inside, bruised but alive, and waiting for them? Or maybe he was hurt, and needed help. In any case, there might still be food inside, or other supplies. And even if those had been stolen, thieves wouldn't have taken the HAM radio. Maybe a call to Cameron was just inside that black hole.

"We're going to go inside," he said. "But I need you to stay right next to me, and if I tell you to do something, you do it right away. No questions. Understand?"

"Okay," said Piper, her voice small and terrified.

He stepped out, then moved to her side of the car and opened her door for her. He led her up the stairs and toward the door, and there he stopped. For a moment he looked out, making sure there was no one else in sight. The last thing he wanted was someone following them in. He'd have enough to worry about keeping eyes front.

The door creaked slightly as he pushed it a little farther open. That's when the smell hit him—the smell of death. He knew it well—no ranger went more than a month without meeting some dead animal in the forest, and Alex had seen more than his fair share of human bodies, too. But it was worse in the house. Here the smell had collected, and gathered in the corners, and intensified.

Almost he turned around, got them back in the car, and took off. But there was still the HAM radio.

111

He gripped Piper's shoulder and took another step in. At least he didn't hear any sounds inside. If there were thieves—or worse—inside, they'd be moving, trying to take whatever they'd come for and get out as fast as they could. They wouldn't be lurking, waiting for him. Hell, they wouldn't have known Alex and Piper were coming.

They found Pete in the living room. Alex saw his foot first, poking out from behind the couch. But Piper was only half a second behind him. She cried out, covering her mouth with her hands. Too late, Alex took her shoulders and turned her away. He guided her around the corner, to where a wall blocked sight of the room.

"Stay here," he said. "Do not move." Then he went back into the living room.

It had been an axe, or so Alex guessed. Whatever had caused the wound, it was sizable, and had left a deep rent in Pete's chest. Pete himself looked a lot different than Alex had thought he would: bald, with a thick beard and a scrub of hair in a half ring from one ear to the other. His eyes were closed, so at least that was a mercy.

There was a throw blanket on one end of the couch. Alex threw it over the corpse, then returned to Piper.

"Come on," he said. "Don't go into the living room."

The HAM radio was in the back room. Alex looked it over. It was off now, but there was a notepad next to it. He glanced at it—then did a double take at the name *Cameron*.

Cameron to Alex: call as soon as you can. Brent arrived. Sorry she didn't have the radio on. Cabin community doing fine.

He gripped the paper tightly, feeling waves of relief wash through him. With scrabbling fingers he turned the HAM on and sent out his callsign. But he heard only static in response. After trying a little while, he turned away—but he left the radio on, static still blaring.

"Come on," he said to Piper. "Let's make sure the rest of the house is okay."

112

* * *

In the end, Alex decided to spend the night. Piper objected at first, and Alex didn't exactly relish the thought of sleeping in a house with a dead body. But he couldn't drive endlessly without stopping, and they had to take opportunities to rest while they could get them. Pete had a garage where the car might be safe, and the front door wasn't damaged, so Alex was able to lock it and block it easily.

That was a little curious—the door hadn't been broken open. The lock wasn't thrown, and the doorjamb didn't have so much as a scratch. Pete must have opened the door to a knock, and then had it kicked in on him. A hell of a way to go.

Opening the garage to secure the car revealed a new surprise: a dog. The dog's tag told them his name was Max, and he was clearly a mix—mostly German Shepherd, but with floppy ears and spots on the tongue that spoke to Alex of some Chow, plus who knew what else. The garage door had been shut, whether by accident or on purpose, and Max, though overjoyed when they let him out, also moved in a careful, slow way that spoke of hunger. Piper was happy to have something to do, so she kept feeding Max and giving him water until he ran in the back yard and threw up, and then came back in to keep eating. Alex wanted to tell her not to over-feed the poor guy, but it kept her busy, and he had his own work to do fortifying the house.

He padlocked the garage and placed what furniture he could in front of the door. The back door was a double sliding-glass deal, and impossible to totally block off, but he hoped that, with Max running free in the house, they'd have warning if anyone tried to come in that way.

"And he can watch out for us on the road, too," said Piper.

"Piper, we can't take his dog."

She glared at him. "Why not? Who's going to take care of

him if we don't? And if we have to sleep somewhere else, Max can watch out for us."

Alex wanted to argue, but that was a decent point. And besides, Piper still had a haunted look in her eye that he knew came from Pete's corpse. In the end, he couldn't say no.

Max had gone running over to the body the moment they let him in the house. He whined as he nudged Pete's shoes, and then lay down at the man's feet for a while. It broke Alex's heart, and Piper cried openly, though she still refused to go anywhere near the living room. After Max left, he avoided it just as hard, so that it became a place only Alex would go, and even then as little as possible.

He shuttered the windows that had shutters and locked the ones that didn't. The house only had one floor, and Pete's smell had permeated most of it, but the back bedroom was far away and mostly free of the smell. Alex cracked the window—it opened into the fenced-off back yard, not the street or anything—and made ready to sleep there for the night, sharing the bed with Piper. Just as they lay themselves down to rest, Max came barreling in and jumped up, burrowing into the blanket between them. Piper laughed, and Alex couldn't help but smile.

* * *

In the morning, Cameron answered the HAM on the third try.

"Cameron?" Alex sat straighter in his seat, gripping the handset tight.

"Mom?" Piper came running into the room, Max skipping at her heels.

"Alex? Piper?" Cameron laughed from the other end of the radio, her voice awash with relief. "Oh my god, it's so good to hear your voices."

"You too, honey," said Alex. "Are you all right?"

"I'm fine. We're all fine—everyone in the cabin community, I mean. Bettie says hi."

Alex blinked at the handset. "Bettie?"

"She came up with me from Seattle. She's staying at our place."

"Okay," said Alex, shrugging. "Tell her hi for us, I guess."

"I will. Piper, sweetheart, are you all right?"

Piper's face fell, and she looked over her shoulder. Alex knew she was thinking of Pete. With his finger off the handset, he whispered, "Remember she's far away and can't help us. Try not to make her worry more."

She nodded, then took the handset. "I'm fine, Mom."

"Are you eating enough? And how's your meds?"

"They're fine," she said, smiling. "Do you think Dad would really drive me across the country without having enough insulin?"

"I know, sweetie. I'm just worried. You're taking care of him, too, right?"

Piper rolled her eyes. "Of course, Mom."

"Good. Can I have him back?"

She relinquished the handset. Alex spoke low to her again. "Can you give me a minute, sweetheart?" Piper nodded and left the room, taking Max with her.

"You there?" he said.

"I'm not going anywhere. Not until you make me."

"I sent Piper out of the room. Is everything really all right at the cabins?"

"Yes, it's fine. Bill—you know, the caretaker—is being a total asshole. But everyone else is keeping to themselves. A family came here from the road. They got stranded. But we're taking care of them."

He breathed a sigh of relief. "Good. We're coming as fast as we can. But we have to take back roads, now more than ever. I thought Ames would be fine, but it's just as bad as I hear the cities have gotten."

"That's only going to get worse," she said, suddenly grave. "Brent didn't paint a pretty picture."

"There's no pretty picture to paint. Pete—the guy you talked to, whose house we're in—he's dead."

"What?" Cameron snapped. "What happened? Was Piper there?"

"No. We found him that way. She was a little shook up, but bounced back quickly. We, uh . . . we have a dog."

Silence for a moment. "A dog."

"Listen, it cheers her up."

"You always wanted a damn dog. Don't tell me this wasn't intentional."

Despite himself, and despite the seriousness of the situation, he smiled at the handset. "You think *I* set this up? What, did I cause the whole solar flares storms, too?"

"I wouldn't put it past you."

He laughed. But the laugh died away, and he spoke low, just in case Piper was trying to listen through the door. "We're going to be fine, Cam. I promise you I'll get Piper there. But things are getting really bad. I don't know what we might have to do, what detours we might have to take. So you keep yourself safe, and do your best not to worry. Focus on yourself. Keep the house ready for us when we arrive."

"I will," she said. "Promise."

"Okay. Love you."

"Christ, I love you. Take care of her."

"Always."

The radio clicked off, leaving only static.

CHAPTER 13

Before they left the house, Alex raided it for supplies. There wasn't all that much to take—Pete had a good supply of canned food, but Alex already had more than enough to eat on the trip, and they were well stocked on everything he thought they might need. But since Piper was set on taking Max, he loaded up a bag of dry dog food from the pantry, plus half a dozen cans of wet food. He wasn't going to give the dog any of their rations, which he'd already worked so hard to hoard. And Pete had two hand-chargers for electronics, so Alex grabbed them just in case.

"Dad? Why are you taking Pete's stuff?"

Alex froze in the doorway. Piper sat there at the kitchen table, looking up at him.

"Well . . ." Alex winced inwardly, but he kept his face calm for her as he sat down across from her at the table. "You know what happened to him."

Her eyes grew a little wider. "Yeah."

"So he doesn't need anything left here. But it might help us."

"So . . . that makes it okay?"

His lips twisted. "Not . . . not all the time. It's just that things are different right now. Dangerous, like I told you before. And we have to do some things that we wouldn't do normally. Just until all of this gets sorted out, and the world gets back to normal. After that, we go back to the old rules."

Piper looked around the house like she was expecting to find someone else inside it. "So then what are the new rules? The ones right now?"

Alex shrugged. "The most important rule is to keep ourselves safe, and we try not to hurt anyone else in the process. This might help keep us safe, and it's not going to hurt anybody."

She relaxed and nodded, like that was something comforting and not a pretty significant logical leap. "Okay. Do you need my help?"

A lurch hit his stomach. He might be able to tell her this was all right, that it was justified, but the thought of asking her to help him raid some dead guy's house . . . "No, sweetheart. I'll be done in a minute."

It wasn't a minute, but it wasn't much longer. The conversation had killed his interest in raiding for supplies, and soon they were in the car and heading away from Pete's house, Max crammed in the back seat, where he lay on top of the supplies. Not a moment too soon, it seemed—as they pulled out of the driveway, Alex saw a few guys standing across the street in the shadow of a home. They didn't look particularly threatening, but they were definitely watching Alex and Piper drive away. Behind the homes across the street, plumes of smoke were rising.

They'd almost reached the border of Ames when they heard several sharp, rapid pops. First there was a burst of them, and then a few more in scattered reply. Then silence. Piper frowned from the sound of the first one, leaning forward and looking out of her window.

"What was that?" she said.

"Not sure," said Alex. "Probably a car backfiring."

He'd stretched the truth with her a few times already on the trip. That was his first flat-out lie. He'd recognized the sounds at once. It was gun fire.

* * *

118

The car was quiet for so long that Alex began to wonder if Piper knew he'd lied to her. But he was distracted from such thoughts as he spotted the underbelly of a car off the side of the road. It had been flipped. He spotted it a long way off, and the freeway was empty, so it was easy to pull off to the shoulder. He got out of the car, then looked over to see Piper unbuckling her seatbelt.

"No," said Alex. "Stay here. Watch Max."

She looked up, and he was positive she'd ask why. But she didn't. She only nodded with wide eyes. Max gave a little whine.

Alex approached the car slowly. As soon as he was a dozen yards away, he spotted what he hadn't been able to see from the freeway: it was a cop car. The rooftop lights were smashed, but the top of the car hadn't crumpled when the car had flipped over.

That hadn't saved the cop, though. Alex found him dead in the driver's seat. Even upside down, one of his hands gripped the wheel, while the other hung down to the car's roof. Right side up, it would have looked like he was waving at someone.

Alex knew what he'd find, but he checked the guy's pulse anyway. Dead. He stood up and turned around, ready to leave.

He stopped.

Mind whirling, he turned and looked back at the dead cop.

Jesus, Alex, he thought to himself.

Keep her safe. That voice was Cameron's. She'd said it the night before. And he'd promised he would.

He kneeled down again, trying to hold his breath as he squeezed in through the shattered window and past the corpse. Thankfully the glass had broken clean, so he didn't have to worry about slicing himself open.

The cop's pistol was missing from his belt holster, but the belt still held all its other supplies—pepper spray, cuffs, everything but spare clips of ammo. Alex grabbed it all and shoved it into his pockets.

Whoever had raided the cruiser had left the shotgun. It was stuck in its mount beside the driver's seat. Alex gave it a tug. Wedged fast. Or at least, that's what some random scavenger would have thought. But rangers had pretty much the same vehicles, and they were often armed, too. Alex looked up at the butt of the shotgun and saw it: a thumbprint scanner.

Lips dragging back in a grimace, he took the cop's limp hand and extended the thumb, pressing it to the scanner. It gave a halfhearted *chirp,* and the shotgun came free. Alex tried to catch it, but the barrel came down hard on his finger. He jerked back, his head slamming into the steering wheel. Wincing, he sucked a deep breath in through his teeth. But after a moment, he loosed a soft chuckle.

"Almost got your ass kicked by a dead guy and a gun, Alex," he muttered to himself. "Maybe be a little more careful."

Slowly he slithered out of the window, shotgun in hand. Once more he turned to leave, but once more a hunch turned him around again. He reached in past the corpse again and pulled the trunk release. As the trunk popped open with a *thunk,* he heard the clatter of something heavy and metal.

Jackpot.

In the trunk he found a pistol and two mags of ammo, plus a box of shells for the shotgun. There were also some wool blankets and water. He had blankets. He had water. He took them anyway.

He must have looked ridiculous, coming back to the car carrying it all, his pockets bulging with the pepper spray and cuffs, because Piper gawked at him through the window with eyes as wide as dinner plates. At first he made some effort to hide the guns, but he soon gave it up. How could she miss them? So he stowed everything in the trunk, except the pistol, which he shoved in his waistband.

Piper stared at him as he slid back in behind the steering wheel.

"What happened to the car?"

Alex pursed his lips and shrugged. "Not sure. Whoever flipped it must have gotten away quick, but they left a bunch of stuff inside."

She opened her mouth to speak again, but his key turned in the ignition, and she was cut off by the engine revving to life. When the noise settled back down to a steady hum, she'd given up on whatever she was about to say.

* * *

After two corpses in twenty-four hours and a crap night of sleep, he shouldn't have blamed himself too badly for what happened next. He was nervous. On edge. He knew it by the way his hands were shaking on the steering wheel, and so he tried to ease himself. He stopped after a half hour and took Max out of the back to let him do his business by the side of the road. But when they got back on the road again, he didn't feel any better. His foot kept dropping harder on the accelerator, and he was always looking at the clock.

What time was it now?

How much farther had they driven?

How much farther did they have to go?

It was his mantra, and he repeated it every few seconds.

Piper's question shocked him from his thoughts, so abruptly that he found himself growing annoyed before he could help it. "You took stuff from that car. That was like Pete?"

"Yep," he said offhandedly.

"But Pete was dead."

His jaw worked as he tried to think of a smart answer. Goddammit. Why hadn't he thought his answer through? "Well, I don't know where the owner of that car was."

"But you took their stuff, like they were dead."

"I . . ." He trailed off. *Think, think.*

"Were they dead?"

Slowly he drummed his fingers on the steering wheel. "Yeah," he said finally. "He was dead. It was a cop car. That's why there were guns in it. The cop died in the crash."

Piper swallowed hard. "Okay."

"This is what I was talking about before, Piper. Things are dangerous now, and—"

"I get it," she said. "I got it the first time." Then she wrapped her arms around herself and turned away, looking out the window. Max pushed his head up and licked her cheek, but she pushed him away gently.

Alex's foot fell heavier on the accelerator. Then heavier. The freeways were empty, so he soon found himself at ninety before he realized it. But then, like driving through a curtain, they were in a rainstorm. Alex cursed under his breath as the rain forced him to slow the car.

"Don't swear," said Piper.

"Okay, *mom,*" said Alex. He glanced at her. She gave a little smile, and he returned it. Thank god she hadn't already forgotten how to smile.

Even with the rain, he kept going faster, before the steering wheel would jerk in his hands and he realized his speed had crept up too far. Then he'd slow down, only to realize he'd done it again a few miles later. The rain got worse, until it fell in grey sheets that kept them seeing farther than ten feet in any direction. Thunder and lightning began to rage around them, until Max was full-time whimpering in the back seat.

"Can you try to keep him calm, Piper?" said Alex. "I've got to focus on the road."

"He's afraid of the storm," she said, twisting in her seat to scratch behind the dog's ears. His whining only increased. "Maybe we should stop."

"Where?" said Alex, sharper than he'd meant to. He

waved a hand and went on more gently. "There's nothing around here, Piper. No farmhouses, definitely no hotels."

"We can sleep in the car," said Piper. "The rain is—" Her words were cut off as Max gave a loud bark. Alex jumped, and the steering wheel jerked in his hands.

"Jesus Christ," he growled. "Come on, Max. Piper, can you *please*—"

"It's not his fault," Piper said, getting angry now. "Look at the rain, dad."

Max barked again, and kept barking. And then lightning crashed into a tree right off the road, detonating it in a shower of sparks.

Alex slammed the brakes on instinct, even as his mind screamed, *Idiot!* The car spun out, skidding no matter how he tried to correct it with the steering wheel. Piper screamed, and Max howled as they careened off the road. There was a ditch, and as their wheels went over its edge, Alex thought, *We're going to flip over.* In his mind's eye he saw the cop car, and the dead cop inside it.

But the car didn't flip. It slid down the side of the ditch, slamming into the bottom with a jarring shake that wrenched the seat belt against Alex's neck. Piper's scream cut off abruptly, and for a heart-stopping moment Alex thought she'd slammed her head into the window. But then he saw she was just frozen in place. Her mouth was still open, though no sound came out, and she was shaking.

"Are you all right?" he croaked. His throat hurt like crazy.

She nodded.

"Okay. *Shit!*"

The driver's side rear window had shattered, and rain was pouring in. He dove back, looking for the bag with Piper's diabetic supplies in it.

"Your supplies are going to get all—"

"It's fine, dad. It's in ziplock bags, remember?"

Alex stopped his frantic digging. She was right, of course.

He'd have remembered that, if he had been thinking straight. What with all her swim meets, she'd dropped her supply bag in a pool once, and they'd had a waterproof one ever since, with everything in ziplock baggies, and had upgraded her pump to a water proof one as well, at no small cost.

"Right," he muttered. "Right. Okay. Let me try to get us out of here. Check on Max."

Piper did it, though Max was clearly all right, if shaken. Alex pressed the gas pedal. The car shuddered, but didn't move. He put it in reverse, but still got nothing. Groaning, he levered himself out of the driver's side door, though it was almost horizontal the way the car was leaning.

The rain beat on him like an angry drunk. And the moment he was out in it, he gave a frustrated sigh, because he knew the car wasn't going anywhere. Both left wheels were bent at crazy angles. The axles could be broken for all he knew—they were definitely bent far past any ability to drive.

"Well, you get your wish," he said after climbing back in the car and shutting the door against the storm. "We're not driving anywhere. We're going to wait in the car until this storm blows over."

"What?" said Piper. "The car's almost sideways. I don't want to wait here."

Alex arched an eyebrow. "You want to wait outside?"

She scowled and looked out. But then her brow furrowed deeper. "Dad, is that a train?"

He leaned over and peered out. It *was* a train. Maybe a quarter of a mile away, half-glimpsed through the rain. It wasn't moving. It looked old, maybe even rusted, likely a remnant on some abandoned track out here in the middle of nowhere.

"Yeah, I think so," he said.

"Why don't we wait in there?"

Instinct immediately told him *No*. But he gave it a second thought. He didn't want to stay, and likely sleep, in a tilted car any more than Piper did. And if the boxcars were unoccupied, they'd likely be safer than the car was with its broken window.

"All right," he said. "We'll check them out. If someone's already there, though, we're coming right back to the car."

"Of course. I don't want to sleep in a train car with some creepy old hobo."

From the back of the car, Alex pulled the shotgun and extra ammo, and then loaded up as much water and supplies as he could into two of the backpacks, giving the smaller one to Piper. They could always come back to the car after the storm let up, but someone else might come by before then, and he couldn't be sure their supplies would stay where they left them.

They both set off, half-jogging, neither one eager to remain in the storm a second longer than they had to. Alex kept scanning the area all around as they went, watchful for anyone approaching. He doubted anyone was out in this downpour, but if they were, he didn't want to be caught unaware.

No one showed their face by the time they reached the cars. Alex climbed the little half-ladder next to the big door and shoved it open. The car inside was empty—and dry. Piper gave an excited whoop and began to climb up into it.

"Hold on," said Alex. There were two other cars, one on either side of the first. He went to each of them and opened them as well. But they were empty as well, and he closed them against the rain before climbing into the middle car with Piper. Max leapt up into the car beside them, and Alex rolled the door shut.

It wasn't bright outside, but the darkness in the car was absolute. He pulled out his phone and used its flashlight, but only long enough to pull out two sleeping bags and lay them down next to each other. The moment they were laid out, Piper shucked off her raincoat and dove into one of them, hunching down in the warm fleece.

"Brrr. It's freezing out there."

"What are you talking about? It's summer." Alex kept a deadpan expression as she raised her eyebrows incredulously. Then he let his smile crack, and she laughed in response.

"You're so dumb."

"The dumbest." He clicked off the light and climbed into his own sleeping bag beside her. "Get some rest. I'm going to wake you up before sunrise, most likely, and I don't want to hear any complaining."

"Okay," she said, voice already sounding drowsy. It had been a long day.

"And Piper . . . if you get up in the middle of the night for anything, and I'm still asleep, don't touch the gun or go outside."

The train car sat in dark silence for a moment. "Okay," she whispered.

"You promise?"

"I promise."

"Thank you."

It was a while before he could drift off. He lay awake, wondering what kind of world this was that would make him draw such a promise from his daughter.

CHAPTER 14

The day after she spoke with Alex on the radio, another group of refugees came to the cabins.

Their arrival was heralded, as per usual, by shouting in the direction of the gate. Cameron and Bettie were out working in the garden—and whereas Cameron had leapt into action the last time they'd heard a fight breaking out, now she just sighed and straightened up, rolling her shoulders against the ache of stooping over the plants.

"Swear to God, if Bill is making trouble again, I'm going to deck him."

"He sure could use it," said Bettie, frowning. "Guess we'd better go and make sure no one kills each other."

She followed the words with a chuckle to soften them, but Cameron had to suppress a little shiver. Bill *was* a bit of a megalomaniac, and circumstances had become a bit extreme. Bettie's offhanded joke was an echo of a thought Cameron had been suppressing, pushing so far back she could pretend it wasn't there.

They hopped in the Jeep and headed for the front gate, though Cameron didn't lean on the gas too hard. When they got there, it was an all-too-familiar scene: Bill standing just inside the gate, hands on his hips, scowl on his face, and a truck outside the gate, the driver looking hesitant a couple of feet away from his door. Only this time the driver wasn't Wade or a park ranger, but some guy in a flannel shirt and jeans.

His arms muscular, if not bodybuilder-thick, and the set of his shoulders told Cameron he worked with his hands. There were a few other people in his car, but Cameron couldn't see them through the glare of the overcast sky on the windshield.

"What is it this time, Bill?" said Cameron.

"Damn it, you don't need to come down every time someone pulls up to the gate," said Bill, doubling down on his angry grimace.

"Past evidence indicates otherwise. You almost turned away a friend of mine, and then a park ranger who had news about my husband. I'll continue keeping an eye on things around *my* cabin community, if it's all the same to you." Then, while his face was slowly growing red and he was trying to come up with a scathing comeback, she brushed past him and went to the gate. "Hey there. How can we help you?"

"I . . . I'm hoping—that is, we were hoping we could take shelter here," said the man. "That is—"

"You can't," said Bill, seemingly determined to take the anger he was afraid to direct at Cameron and turn it on the man instead. "This isn't a hotel, and even if it was, we don't have any vacancies."

"Sure," said the man, mouth twitching. For such a solid-looking guy, he was surprisingly tongue-tied. "We thought the place would be abandoned."

Footsteps behind them made Cameron turn, and she saw Wade approaching at the head of some of the others in the community. Wade's dark eyes were narrowed, and he was looking at the man on the other side of the fence with a suspicion not unlike Bill's own, which only made Cameron even more nervous.

"The place ain't abandoned," said Bill, who hadn't seemed to notice the arrival of the others. "You can see that, so now you can turn around and go somewhere else."

"I—we don't know where," said the man, shrugging helplessly. "Listen, I—my name's Jeremy. That's my wife in the car.

Her name's Theresa. We're from Seattle. Or we were. But it's crazy there. We can't go home."

"Not our problem," said Bill.

"Oh, come on now," said Bettie. "What are you gonna do? Let them starve and freeze to death out there?"

Bill glared at her. "Lots of people gonna starve. Lots of people gonna freeze to death."

Cameron wished like hell that Bill wasn't such an asshole, because it made her want to disagree with him on principle—even when, like now, she knew he was basically right. If things really were going all to hell outside the borders of the cabin community, they didn't have the land or the resources to take in every single person affected by the disaster.

But they weren't talking about every single person. At least not yet. They were only talking about four people.

That brought to mind something else, however. "Who all's with you?" she said. "You've got more than just your wife."

As if those words were a signal, the back right door of the car burst open, and a girl got out—and that was how Cameron thought of her at once, *a girl*, because she had to be young, though she was old enough and endowed enough and carried herself like she knew exactly how much of a woman she was. Every movement swayed, and around her halter top and short denim shorts were a *lot* of tattoos, so that the eyes of every man present immediately snapped to her, and stayed.

"Jeremy, I'll take over," she said, voice lightly dusted with a Russian accent. She looked at Cameron and Bill and gave a little smile. "My parents have a cabin here. They're the Sokolovs. I don't know if you know them, but they do."

Bill shook off the look of her just enough to fold his arms over his chest. "Never seen you before. Anyone could say that."

"I'm Gina Sokolov. Are you the caretaker? You know my mom and dad, Simon and Yolanda. There should be pictures of me in the cabin."

That only deepened Bill's scowl, which was so full of leer

that Cameron wanted to deck him. But then the car's other back door opened, and the fourth passenger got out. Cameron's gut, which had already gone uneasy at the sight of Gina, began to roil in earnest.

The kid had to be even younger than Gina, though he sure tried to carry himself like he was older. His pants hung low, and his too-large sports jersey did nothing to cover the full tattoo sleeves that ran the whole length of his arms. Everything about him said he itched for a fight, like everyone present had insulted his mother and he'd come to settle the score. Cameron didn't like to make snap judgement, but she knew this was a kid from the streets. And that didn't bother her in and of itself—she met plenty of such kids in her line of work, and most of them were decent enough. But just as every man present had looked at Gina with immediate and barely-restrained lust, now they all focused on the new kid with ugly, angry appraisal. Whether he really was a troublemaker or not, they all thought he was, and that could easily become a self-fulfilling prophecy.

"Who the hell is this?" said Bill.

"He's with me," said Gina. But that wasn't really an explanation, and from the suddenly-nervous look on her face, it seemed that Gina knew it. "Can you open the gate now?"

"Not a chance," said Bill. "Even if you're who you say you are—"

"If her parents really do have a cabin here, we can prove that easily enough," said Bettie. "You can't just turn them away without even checking—"

"I can do whatever the hell I want."

They went on, voices steadily rising, but Cameron's attention went to Wade as he sidled up next to her.

"Bill's got one point—we can't take just anyone who comes by," said Wade, voice low so that only she could hear.

"Gina's family lives here," said Cameron.

Wade shook his head. "I get that. But look at her. If we do

have to look out for ourselves here, she doesn't look like she can help much."

Cameron arched an eyebrow. "Pretty quick to judge there."

He rolled his eyes. "Come on. Don't be like that. She clearly doesn't have a skill set to be useful. That Jeremy guy can probably be of use. But her . . ."

"So you'll take the construction worker who *doesn't* live here, instead of the manicured girl who actually does?"

Wade shrugged. "If things keep on the way they are, we're going to have to make some tough choices."

She didn't answer that. Instead, she set off for the gate house. Bill saw her almost too late, and ran over to get between her and the door.

"You're not doing that again," he said. "No one gets in or out without my say-so. Not again."

Cameron met his eyes, and fixed him with the stare she'd learned in the service. More than one guy who'd try to put a move on her saw that stare, right before they ended up in medical. "A man stood between me and a door the day before I came up here, Bill. I broke his arm. You want to see how?"

His flabby, stubbled throat twitched as he swallowed. Then he took a step to the side, and Cameron opened the gate.

* * *

They had the same argument as last time. Gina was allowed to move into her parents' cabin (after Bill made sure there really *were* pictures of her inside) but the other arrivals were consigned to RVs. Gina's cabin was one of the ones with an RV, and Hernando was stationed there at her insistence. Jeremy and Theresa, the couple, were relegated to an empty RV at one of the back cabins. Cameron was pretty certain she'd never seen anyone living in that cabin, but she didn't press the issue with Bill—she'd already pushed things far enough. *Pick your battles*, she reminded herself.

"He's a damn fool, and a cruel one besides," said Bettie. "Setting people up like second-class citizens. We've got space and enough food to spare, at least for a few people."

Once they'd gotten settled in to their new (temporary, or so Bill liked to keep reminding them) homes, Cameron invited all the new arrivals to her cabin to get acquainted. Some of the other compound residents—Christ, was she already thinking of it as a compound?—came by and introduced themselves. Bill showed up, too. Cameron thought about telling him to piss off, but thought better of it. She'd already won a battle against him today. But she locked the door to her basement. Bill didn't know about the food stores she had down there, and if she had her way, he'd stay ignorant.

In Cameron's living room, the young gangbanger-looking guy looked everywhere: the furniture, the pictures, the TV. It was like he was appraising the place. Cameron tried not to let it raise the hairs on the back of the neck. Hopefully he was just impressed—she doubted he came from a home that cared much about interior design. Gina seemed innocuous enough, though, and the couple, Jeremy and Theresa, were very polite, if a little out of their depth. Cameron kept catching them staring off vacantly into the distance, and wondered what they'd seen before they fled Seattle.

"Here, honey," said Bettie, coming to the gangbanger with a sandwich and a beer. "Eat up."

The kid blinked twice. His hands fidgeted for a moment before raising to take the food. "Thanks."

"No problem. What's your name, son?"

He took a bite and spoke with his mouth full. "Hernando."

"I'm Bettie. You need anything, you come and talk to me. All right?"

Hernando pursed his lips. "Yeah, all right."

"And you—it's Gina, right? You want a beer, too, sweetheart?"

Gina shook her head. "I don't drink beer. Do you have wine?" She blinked suddenly and looked to Cameron. "I mean, if it's no trouble."

"No trouble at all," said Cameron, loud enough to draw attention as she fixed Bill with a dark look. It took him a moment to notice. When he did, he jerked his gaze away from where it had been, trying to slide up Gina's short-shorts.

"Thank you," said Gina, blushing and crossing her legs.

"Mm-hm. I'll get you all some food, too." Bettie slid off towards the kitchen.

"So, what then?" said Bill, face flushed. "You're going to take care of them? Feed them?"

"I'm giving them a meal, Bill," said Cameron. "That a crime?"

"No, that's downright generous of you. But what about dinner tonight? What about tomorrow? You gonna just keep feeding them? It's only a matter of time before they're coming to the rest of us, asking for a meal. Food's gonna get scarce, and not just here."

"Well then we'll just have to find more food," said Bettie from the kitchen. "Or grow some."

That drew a snort from Bill. "Sure. Grow some. This isn't *Little House on the Prairie*. You got any idea how much work it is, farming to feed even this many people?"

Bettie gave him a cool look. Cameron was amazed the woman hadn't flown off the handle at him already. "I grew up on a farm. So the answer to that is yes, and that I'm guessing I know better than you do."

Bill's face grew a darker shade of red, and Cameron tensed. She hated to admit it, but she was almost hoping Bill would try something, just so she could have the pleasure of knocking him on his ass.

It seemed that Bill had just enough sense, though, to know that he couldn't backhand an old woman in the presence of so many others. "Even if you're right," he said slowly, grating the words out like they pained him, "that takes time. What do we do until then?"

Before Bettie could answer, Hernando spoke up, to the obvious surprise of everyone present. "There's food around we can grab," he said. "We saw a truck overturned on the highway coming up here. It looked like it held food, like a grocery store truck. Ralph's or something."

"It was Vons," said Gina.

Hernando frowned at her. "Okay, whatever. Point is, the back was still closed and locked. What with everything being so crazy, the driver probably left once they crashed it."

Cameron straightened in her seat. "You remember where that truck was?"

The boy shrugged. "Of course. It was right on the highway."

Wade looked to Cameron, and she nodded to him before turning to Bill. "All right, Bill. If you're really worried about feeding people, let's go get our hands on some grub."

Her stomach clenched as Bill sneered. "Sounds an awful lot like stealing. Would have thought you'd be too high and mighty for that kind of thing."

She knew she couldn't rise to his bait. He was looking for some little moral victory. If that's all he needed, she'd let him have it. Cameron rose from her chair, and Wade did the same. Hernando got to his feet more slowly. "Call it whatever you want. I'm not any more interested in starving than you are."

"I don't think everyone should go," interjected Wade. "Just people who can take care of themselves, and each other."

"Hernando, will you come with us?" said Cameron. "Just to show us where the truck is?"

"Sure. I can handle myself." Hernando rolled his shoulders and tilted his head to crack his neck. It was probably supposed to look badass, but Cameron had spent years bunking with Marines, and the gangbanger's slight frame was laughable if anything. Not that she felt the need to say so, of course.

"Good. Wade, you'll come too. Go and grab Russell—he's got a crew cab truck, we'll need it to bring back food, if there's any in the semi."

"What about . . ." Wade paused for a moment, frowning. "I mean, the roads are probably abandoned, but just in case there's others out there looking for stuff to steal—"

"I've got a pistol you can have, and a rifle for myself," said Cameron, taking his meaning at once. Hernando stood a little taller for a moment. Cameron's mouth twisted. "And no offense intended to anyone else, but I'm gonna keep guns in the hands of ex-military."

Hernando frowned, but he nodded without a word. On the other side of the room, Bill stood from his stool and hooked his thumbs in his belt. "Let's meet at the front gate in five minutes."

Cameron gave him a cool stare. "You're staying here, Bill. We've got two vehicles, and I want two people in each. We'll need the rest of the room to bring back the supplies." She turned and headed for the front door. "Besides, the community needs someone to watch the front gate, and that's the only thing I've seen you do. Now get out of my house."

CHAPTER 15

Alex awoke to the sound of knocking, and then the sound of Max's furious barking, which the boxcar walls amplified until it was louder than cannon fire.

In an instant he was wide awake, rolling over and feeling for Piper. She was on the floor right next to him. At first he thought she was asleep, but then he saw her eyes glinting in a thin shaft of light from a gap in the boxcar door. She remained utterly silent, frozen with fear.

"It's fine," he whispered—but his hand went to the shotgun on his other side, where she couldn't see. He raised his voice. "Quiet, Max. Quiet! Who's there?"

"You all right in there?" called a voice from outside. It sounded like a man, old, from the sound of it, and he had a thick accent—not southern, precisely, but definitely country. "Need anything?"

"We're fine," said Alex firmly. "We don't want any trouble, and we don't want any company, either." His hand tightened on the barrel of the shotgun.

"Oh, fair enough, fair enough, can't blame you, can't blame, you," said the man. Max started barking again, and the man fell silent until Alex got hold of the dog's collar and shut him up. "Just trying to help, that's all. The roads are a little more dangerous these days. People get along better if they help each other."

"Well, we're doing just fine," said Alex. "I'm gonna have to ask you to leave us alone."

There was a moment's silence—Alex could imagine the man looking offended—before the reply came. "All right, then. I won't knock again."

Alex didn't hear any receding footsteps, but then again he wasn't sure he'd be able to, what with the boxcar walls being decently thick. Max's ears were perked, but he didn't growl, and he didn't go running for the boxcar door when his collar was released. Still, Alex sat listening for a moment, trying to hear any indication that the man had retreated as asked—or that he had remained against their wishes.

"Who was that?" whispered Piper.

"No idea," whispered Alex. "But I think they're gone. You should go back to sleep."

She stared at him in the dim light, but when he only smiled, she rolled over. Max lay down beside her, and soon Alex heard her breathing deepen and slow down with sleep. But Alex was wide awake, and adrenaline didn't stop coursing through him for a long while. It was no longer raining outside, though if he had to guess, he would have said it was still cloudy and overcast, based on the color of the light he could see from outside. If the storm had passed, they should return to the car and get what supplies they could from it. The car itself was a lost cause—he'd seen the bent axle himself. But he didn't want to force Piper to rise if she could still sleep, and the encounter with the passerby outside had made him extra cautious. They could wait until Piper woke up on her own. A couple of hours wouldn't make much of a difference.

But then, less than half an hour after the man outside had spoken, Alex began to smell something. Something incredible. A smell known to any red-blooded American, and particularly beloved by Alex himself: the smell of bacon frying.

The man outside, he thought. He might have obeyed the letter of what Alex said, and left, but it seemed he hadn't gone very far. And despite all his best efforts, Alex's stomach was now growling—no, raging, at the smell wafting in from outside. He dug in his backpack for a protein bar and munched on it, but his appetite wasn't fooled. He could still smell the bacon, and the bar tasted like sawdust.

It wasn't long before the smell roused Piper from sleep. She sat up immediately, looking at the boxcar door with wide eyes. "Holy cow, what is that? It smells amazing."

"Keep your voice down," said Alex. She had forgotten to whisper.

"But I'm *hungry*," she said.

Alex sighed. There was no point in denying it—he was, too. And there was no way either of them was drifting off to sleep with that smell outside. Whoever the man outside had been, he was clearly cooking just outside to make a point, and to get them to come out. That in itself was a good sign—the boxcar didn't exactly have a lock on it, and if the man had evil intent, he could have just opened the door. Instead he was enticing them out with the smell of cooking food. *The best damn food I've smelled in days, too.*

"All right, we can go out and see," said Alex. "But stay behind me. And be careful."

"I will," promised Piper.

With another rueful shake of his head, Alex got to his feet and went to the door, making sure to bring the shotgun with him. Its rusted tracks screamed as he pulled it open. Outside, the world was a friendlier place than it had been when they went to sleep. He'd been right—the day was overcast and cloudy, but still pretty for all of that, and a green landscape stretched on ahead of them as far as the eye could see.

About ten yards away there was a small cooking fire, and by the fire sat an old hobo. His skin, hair, and nails were impossibly browned and wizened, but surprisingly clean—cleaner, certainly, than his clothes, though those were marked only by stains, and not by fresh sweat or grime. The hobo looked up at them as the door creaked open, and his wrinkled lips split in a smile to reveal fewer missing teeth than Alex would have expected.

"Why, good morning," said the man. "Name's Denny. I thought you wanted to be left alone, but if you insist on talking, you're welcome to come and have breakfast."

* * *

With the door already open, there didn't seem to be much use in shutting themselves inside any longer. Plus, Alex knew he could take Denny in a fight, if it came to that. The old man was wizened, but skinny as all get-out—the telltale, hunger-panged frame of a man who'd spent years without a proper home. Giving Piper a nod, Alex led the way over to the campfire, and they sat crosslegged beside it. Max ran nervously at Alex's heels, and lay on his stomach when they sat—between Alex and Denny.

A pan sat over the fire, the sort of pan that came in an outdoor camping kit. Wordlessly, Denny reached into the pan with a fork and pulled out a couple of strips of bacon, along with an egg he'd been frying, and slid them onto a metal plate, which he handed over. Alex inspected the plate for a second while trying not to look like he was inspecting the plate—but it was spic and span, with no trace of dirt.

"I'm not that dirty," said Denny, his grin growing wider.

There was no denying that the old man was charming. But Alex had spent this whole trip so far keying himself up to be distrustful of anyone they met on the road, and so he didn't smile. He looked Denny in the eye and gave him the blunt truth. "It's been a crazy road since New York, and I decided a ways back I couldn't leave anything to faith. Especially when it came to other people."

Denny only lifted his hands, spreading his fingers like a magician trying to show he wasn't hiding anything up his sleeves. "Like I already said—I can't blame you."

Max was licking his chops at the smell of the bacon. Alex lifted off a piece—the heat of it felt incredible after a cold night in the boxcar—and handed it to Piper. He picked up the other piece and bit off half of it, tossing the other half to Max, who caught it before it hit the ground.

"Good dog you got there," said Denny, nodding at Max. "He come with you from New York?"

Alex almost answered honestly, but then had a second thought. If Denny knew the dog hadn't always been theirs, he might get the idea that the dog wouldn't fight very hard to protect them. It was a paranoid thought, but Alex was okay with that. But he didn't know if he could rely on Piper to support a lie, so he changed the topic instead. "Where are you coming from? You're out in the middle of nowhere."

"Me? I come from everywhere." Denny waved his hand generally at the world all around them. "Ain't had a house of my own in . . . thirty years now? The ground's my bed, the sky's my roof, all that sh—stuff." He eyed Piper quickly as he barely avoided the curse word. She was staring at him with wide eyes, and when he gave her a little smile, it only made her shift nervously.

Licking his chops at the aftertaste of the bacon, Max got up and went over to Denny, sniffing at his knee. Denny tentatively reached out and scratched the dog behind his ears. Max pushed forward so that Denny was scratching his neck instead. That made Alex relax just a hair. Dogs could usually sense a threat better than humans could.

"Which way are you headed, then?" said Alex.

"Nowhere in particular," said Denny, giving a shrug. "I just walk until I find a place I want to set down for a while. Though with weather like it's been, south is sounding all right. How about yourselves?"

"Washington."

Denny flashed another broad grin. "I'm guessin' you mean the state, since you're heading the exact wrong way to reach D.C."

Alex allowed himself a smile. "Yeah. State."

The hobo leaned back, putting his hands on his knees and eyeing the both of them. "Well, I don't want to speak more than I'm welcome to. But from the sound of it, and from the look of you two, it's been a rough road west. And I'm guessing that car in the ditch over there belongs to the two of you." He tossed his head towards the road not far away. The car was just visible.

"Yep," said Alex. No point in denying it.

"Then, have you thought about passing through Cheyenne?"

He couldn't remember ever hearing of the place. "That a town? We're not from around here."

"Not the town. The people." Denny looked away to the northwest and pointed, as though there was something just there on the horizon for them to see. But Alex only saw grasslands. "The Cheyenne reservation. It's in Montana. A few days' walk from here."

Piper gave Alex a quizzical look, her eyes bright. No doubt the prospect of visiting a Native American reservation piqued her interest, but Alex had his doubts. "We were thinking we'd just stick to the roads."

"Suit yourself. But if you're worried they'll be unfriendly, don't be. I gotta say, every time I pass through, they're a lot more helpful than . . . well, put it bluntly, a lot more helpful than white folks."

"You've done it before?"

Denny nodded emphatically. "Oh, sure. I stay off roads and out of towns for the most part, unless I need to pick something up from a store or such like. And a lot of places, walking open country means walking reservations."

Alex shook his head slowly. He was surprised to find himself even considering the idea. But with their car wrecked . . . "You really don't think they'd object?"

"They aren't gonna run you off their land on horseback, if that's what you mean." Denny gave him a cool, appraising look, and Alex almost thought the hobo might regret having made the offer in the first place.

"I only mean—look, it's just the two of us. Three, I guess, if we all go together. I could understand people not wanting to help a couple of stragglers who don't have anything to offer in return."

The hobo's wizened old face softened. "I gotcha. But not everyone's looking for something to gain when they help other people out."

Alex raised his eyebrows. "Are you talking about the Cheyenne, or yourself?"

Denny grinned. "Either or, I guess."

* * *

Once they finished eating, Alex took Piper to the car to get what supplies they could out of it. Max accompanied them, while Denny stayed behind near the cooking fire. There wasn't much more they could fit into the backpacks—he'd packed in a hurry when they were trying to escape the storm, but he'd still taken nearly all of the essentials. All he managed to do was cram a little more food in, until the backpacks were so stuffed that he could barely zip them shut. At first he put all the insulin and pump supplies into his pack, but then he thought better of it and put half of them in Piper's. No point in putting all their eggs in one basket.

"Dad, are we really going with him?" said Piper.

Alex gave her a glance. "I'm planning on it."

She looked down at her feet. "I thought we weren't supposed to trust anyone."

He looked over the top of her head, back to where Denny sat by the fire. The hobo wasn't looking at them. "Trust is a strong word. I'm not going to let him steal anything from us, or hurt us."

Piper looked over her shoulder. "But he's . . . he's homeless."

Alex sighed and shook his head. "That doesn't mean he's a bad person, sweetheart." She shrugged and looked away. He could tell she wasn't convinced. He turned around and planted his butt on the car's rear bumper, looking her in the eye. "Listen. Hey, come on. Listen to me. I told you we had to be careful because I don't want you to get hurt. I don't want you to let somebody take advantage of you, or us. But I also don't want you to be terrified of everyone and afraid to let people help. We've got to be careful, yes. If we're not careful, bad people could try to hurt us. But going through life being afraid of everything, turning down people who actually want to help—well, that could do more harm than good. Do you understand?"

"I guess," she mumbled.

He frowned. Then he saw Max, who was sitting on his haunches and grinning up at them. "Hey, come on. Max seems to like Denny. How bad could he be?"

Piper snorted. "Max is a dummy." But the tension in her face fled like a passing cloud.

"He sure is," said Alex. "But he's a dummy who seems to like us. I think we'll be all right. Max won't let anything happen to us either."

She nodded. Alex stood and put a hand on her shoulder. "Okay. Let's start walking. It's a long way to Montana."

CHAPTER 16

Hernando was right. The truck was impossible to miss, overturned and blocking almost all of the mountain highway. It ran all the way to the mountainside on the one side, and protruded into the opposite lane, so that there was barely enough room there to drive a car through without pitching off the side and into the canyon far below. From the driver's seat of her Jeep, Cameron studied it for a second.

"You guys drove through this?"

"Yeah," said Hernando. She'd chosen to bring him with her, and put Wade in Russell's truck. "It was a tight squeeze, and Gina drove it way too fast. The whole time, I was afraid we were gonna go over the side."

"Can't blame you," said Cameron. She killed the engine and got out. Hernando was quick to follow a second later, and Wade and Russell emerged from the truck. It turned out Russell had a shotgun in his truck, and Cameron had let him keep it, going against her earlier decision. For one thing, Russell had an air of confidence and competence with the weapon that let her know he wouldn't accidentally blow of his own foot. For another, he'd carefully kept the shotgun secret until Bill wasn't around to hear it. It was a smart decision, and gave Cameron even more confidence in him.

They were about a hundred yards from the accident. Over the top of the truck, Cameron could see another pair of cars.

It looked like they were right up against the semi's undercarriage, looking like they'd crashed there.

"Those cars," said Cameron. "Were they there when you passed by?"

Hernando shook his head. "They must have crashed after."

"Could be people inside," said Wade. His hand was already on the pistol in its holster, and Cameron saw his grip tighten.

"They could be hurt," she said, staring at him until he met her gaze. He nodded slowly. "We should go check them first—to make sure we're safe, and to help them if they need it."

"No way someone would just sit here if they crashed," said Hernando. "If there's anyone if those cars, they're dead. I don't fuck with dead people."

Cameron had to stop herself from rolling her eyes. "You came to the cabins and asked us to help you. Now we're going to make sure no one else here needs our help. You can always sit here and wait if you're too scared to come check with us."

That had the desired effect. Hernando puffed up his chest and glared at her. "I'm not afraid. I just don't fuck with dead people. Whatever, the cars are probably empty anyway. Let's go."

He took a step toward the truck, but Cameron stopped him with a hand on his shoulder. His glare deepened. "Not so fast. Come with me around that side. Wade and Russell will take the other."

Hernando gave a sarcastic little bow and waved her on. "Whatever you say, boss lady."

Come on, kid, she thought. *I'm trying to give you the best chance I can. Don't give me another Bill to deal with.* But she walked forward without answering, and Hernando was right behind her. Once they reached the truck, both parties split around either side. On Cameron's side was a crashed Toyota truck, old and spotted with rust. She couldn't see Wade and Russell on the other side of the semi.

"Okay, I'm keeping an eye out," said Cameron, speaking in a low voice. "Go around the other side of the Toyota and make sure there's no one there, or inside it."

"You go," said Hernando, balking. "You've got the gun."

"It's a rifle, not a handgun," she said. "I can protect you with it fine from right here."

He scowled. "Then give me the gun and you go up to the truck."

She barely restrained a curse. "God almighty, Hernando, just go. The damn thing's probably empty."

Hernando's jaw worked and he shook his head like he was going to refuse. But in a moment he started walking for the Toyota. He approached it cautiously, almost walking on tiptoes, and peered in the passenger side window. After looking back to her and shaking his head, he went around the other side. Cameron felt her body tense, just in case. Then Hernando vanished behind the cab, and Cameron muttered in disgust.

"Stay where I can see you, you dumb—"

A gunshot rang out.

In an instant Cameron was on her feet and sprinting for the Toyota. She rounded the back of it just as Russell and Wade came into view from the other side, guns raised.

There was Hernando—but he wasn't injured. In fact, he was the one holding the gun. A little smoke still wafted from the barrel of a 9mm clutched in his shaking hand. At his feet lay the bloodied, lifeless body of his target—a raccoon.

Cameron gave a sigh, but relief quickly turned to anger as she stalked up to him. She snatched the pistol from his hand and ejected the clip, as well as the chambered round. "You idiot. Why didn't you tell me you had a gun?"

"I—I thought you were gonna take it," he stammered.

"I might not have, but I sure as hell am now," she said, stuffing the pistol into her waistband and pocketing the clip. "This is why I didn't want anyone carrying a piece besides me and Wade—do you get it now?"

From behind her, Wade had burst into laughter and was now leaning over, hands on his waist. "Holy crap," he said, still chuckling. "That poor raccoon. Did it jump out at you, kid? Was it frothing at the mouth? *Rragh, arrrrgh!*" he cried, making feral snarling noises that sounded somewhere in between a raccoon and a zombie from *The Walking Dead*.

"Hey, shut up, man!" said Hernando angrily. "It popped out of the bottom of the truck. I thought it was someone trying to grab me!"

"With its tiny little raccoon hands?" said Wade. He pinched at the air with his thumbs and forefingers. "*Rragh!*"

"Enough, Wade," said Cameron. Hernando was already ticked enough—and he was the kind of kid to carry a gun without telling anyone about it. Not that there was anything wrong with that necessarily, and he didn't seem the violent type, necessarily, but it meant he wasn't an entirely known factor.

Hernando turned away from the other men, still scowling. "Anyways, I just—I got freaked out. There's someone in the truck."

Cameron's heart skipped. "Someone . . . ?"

"Dead," muttered Hernando.

She paused for a second at that before going to the driver's side window. Inside, she saw the shape of the body laid out across the front bench seat. The head was bent at a terrible angle, but the window was dirty and hard to see through. The door wasn't locked, and she pulled it open.

"Jesus," said Hernando, stepping away and covering his mouth and nose with his hands. He took several quick, deep breaths.

"He's definitely dead," said Cameron, looking the man over. He was middle-aged and portly, with grey hair and a thick mustache. His whole face was a mess. She would have guessed his head slammed into the steering wheel when he crashed. He'd probably died instantly, though she couldn't find much comfort in that fact.

"Truck looks fine," said Wade lightly. He was at the front of the truck, inspecting it where it was wedged up against the bottom of the semi trailer. "A little bumper damage, of course, but I'd bet it still drives."

Cameron gingerly leaned into the cab to see the key. It was in the On position. "Out of gas," she said. "It probably kept running after the accident, until eventually it stopped."

"Well, let's siphon some gas and get it going," said Wade. "It'd be useful to have another truck."

"Jesus Christ, man," said Hernando. "There's a dead body right there." Russell, too, looked grim, and maybe a shade paler than normal.

Wade rolled his eyes. "Yeah, and that means he's not gonna give a shit if we use his truck. Grow a pair, kid."

Hernando bit the inside of his cheek and cocked his head. Every time Wade called him "kid," Cameron saw him grow a little more agitated. She'd have to have a word with Wade about it. But now wasn't the time.

"How about the other car?" she said, pointing toward the other vehicle that Russell and Wade had already checked out.

"Empty," said Russell.

"All right," said Cameron. "Then let's get what we came here for."

* * *

The semi was sealed with a padlock, but Russell had bolt cutters in his truck. She saw Wade give Russell an odd look, but she didn't question the presence of the cutters—for one thing, they were useful, and for another, there were a lot of legitimate reasons for a logger to carry them, and she preferred to think that those reasons were the correct ones. The padlock went clattering to the asphalt, and one of the doors fell open to the ground—the other hung there, swinging slightly off the back of the overturned trailer.

With her Maglite, Cameron inspected the contents. It wasn't a refrigerated truck, so everything was dry, thankfully, and it appeared nothing needed to be kept refrigerated. She saw multiple pallets of canned food—they'd gone crashing into the wall when the truck overturned, of course, but it looked like a whole lot of them would still be intact. But her eyes caught immediately on a pallet right at the back that had two pieces of equipment strapped on to it, surrounded only by a few thin layers of plastic wrap to help secure them and keep them clean—power generators.

"Gold mine," she muttered. Then, louder, she called out to the others, "There's generators in here and a whole lot of food. Way more than we can carry in one trip. We're gonna have to go back and forth to the cabins a few times."

"We'll bring more people next time," said Wade. "Many hands, light work, and all that."

"I've got a trailer we can use, too," said Russell. "Shoulda brought it this time, I just wanted to know what we were getting into."

"Yeah, that's all fine," said Cameron. She stood on tiptoes, trying to see over the piles of fallen food stocks, but didn't see anything else interesting. "All right. Let's get the truck running and load up as much as we can."

It ended up taking them a couple of hours. First Wade dragged the corpse out of the cab and tossed it by the side of the road—literally tossed it, in such a cavalier way that Cameron almost chastised him for it. Then he made a token effort to scrub the blood off the seat of the truck's cab, though there were still stains when he was done. They siphoned the gas easily enough, and then backed all three of the vehicles up to the rear of the semi trailer. The pallets couldn't be moved of course, and Cameron didn't want to take whole flats of the canned food—individual cans could easily have been punctured by the impact, and even a small hole could lead to botulism if they weren't careful. So she took the cans one by one and checked them, and then handed them off to Russell, Hernando, and Wade, each one of whom took charge of filling up one of the vehicles. It was slow, grueling work, and by the end of it Cameron felt practically cross-eyed from inspecting all the cans. About halfway through the process, the generators were uncovered enough to be moved, and they brought them out and put them to the side. The generators came aboard last, wedged in between the piles of canned food and the backs of the two pickup trucks.

"All righty," said Wade, slamming the tailgate shut. He'd drive the newly-appropriated truck back to the cabin community. "We ready to go?"

"Yep," said Cameron. "Take it slow going back—you've got a heavy load now, and the roads are slick."

"Yes, *mom.*" Wade grinned and hopped in the cab. Cameron tried not to imagine the blood of the driver staining his jeans.

The truck started up and trundled off. Russell soon followed in his own pickup, while Cameron and Hernando hopped into her Jeep. But before she started the engine, Cameron gave him a hard look.

"You get why I was pissed off about your gun?" she said.

He propped one elbow up on the window and leaned his head into his hand. "Yeah, sure, whatever. It's just, look—I was right, wasn't I? You just took it as soon as you found out."

Cameron shook her head. Then she reached into her waistband and pulled out the pistol, holding it out to him. Hernando took it slowly. She pulled out the magazine and passed him that, too.

"I'm already dealing with enough shit at the cabins," she said. "I don't want us to be up in each other's faces. Okay?"

"Yeah," he said quietly. He popped the clip into the pistol—and put the safety on, she was relieved to see. "Sure. That Bill guy is an asshole."

"He is. 100% Grade A asshole," said Cameron. That got

a little chuckle out of Hernando. "I don't think you're an asshole. Prove me right. Don't do anything stupid with that gun like you did today. And in fact, don't even tell anyone you have it. Especially not Bill. Okay? I'm okay if you want to keep yourself safe, just don't brandish it around like a goddamn cowboy."

He looked her in the eye for a long moment. "Yeah, sure," he said finally, solemnly. "Okay. And, uh . . . thanks."

"Just, please don't make me regret it." She fired up the Jeep and turned it around, heading up the road where Wade and Russell had already vanished.

CHAPTER 17

The trailer was empty after only two runs—much faster than Cameron had thought. It turned out that a lot more of the cans had been damaged than it looked like from the rear, and most of the damaged ones were towards the front. Once they'd sorted through about half of the cans, she wasn't finding any more than were intact, and gave the rest of the trailer up as a bad job.

Everyone in the community helped unload the food into the community clubhouse near the front of the compound. When it was all done, they all stood back in a little group to look it over. There were literally thousands of cans—everything from soup, to fruit, to pickled vegetables—as well as boxed rice and more macaroni and cheese than Cameron thought she could eat in a lifetime. Though she suspected that, if things stayed the way they were, that limit might be tested.

"So what do we do with it now?" said Russell. "Should we divvy it all up among the cabins?"

Cameron thought about it, and then thought about the food she already had stashed in her basement. It wouldn't be fair to take an equal portion to everyone else when she already had that—and if the others found out about her stash later, which they would at some point, it could easily spark tempers. "No," she said. "Let's leave it here. If it comes to the point where we need it, we'll set someone up in charge of cooking and maintaining the supplies, and they'll distribute it meal by meal."

"I'll take care of that, of course," said Bill. "It's in the clubhouse, after all."

She met his look with an equally determined one of her own. "It's in the clubhouse, Bill, not your cabin. This place belongs to all of us, so there's no 'of course' about it. Besides, are you gonna be all of our personal chef? Slaving away in the kitchen to make sure we all have our bellies full?"

That made him scowl, which was nice, but Cameron immediately wondered if she'd made a mistake. Framing it that way didn't make it any more appealing to anyone else there than it did to Bill. Bettie, of course, would know why Cameron had put it that way, and she'd probably be more than willing to cook for the community, but they'd need Bettie to manage the foraging and gardening, if indeed they were going to stay in this place for the long haul.

The long haul, she thought. She was already thinking of it. Turning this little cabin community into a permanent little settlement. The idea seemed ridiculous on the face of it. But the first stake had been planted the second she heard what happened to Seattle, and every scrap of news they received from the outside world only drove the point deeper. She knew there was no way she would try to take Alex and Piper back to the city when they arrived, not for several weeks at least. For now, at least, they were going to have to turn this place into a home. And in the meantime, she knew from her time in the service that it was what they all needed, anyway.

Everyone in the clubhouse had gone quiet, and she realized she'd drifted away while the conversation continued. She squared her shoulders in the silence and gave everyone a long look. "All right. We've danced around this topic before, but it's time we get explicit. We're going to assign jobs to everyone here. The number one priority is food—gathering, hunting, everything. But we're going to need other things as well—little repairs and upgrades to cabins and whatnot. We're not all going to go on some crazy work schedule yet; a few hours a day should be fine, for now."

Gina looked around, frowning. "We're being put to work? But we live here."

Bill gave her a lascivious sneer, and the rest of them shifted uncomfortably. But Cameron spoke before anyone else could. "You're right. And you don't have to do anything if you don't want to. But we're all going to share our resources to get through this—and we're all going to work together, too. If you're well stocked in your cabin already, then have a great time sitting around and playing crossword puzzles, since that's about the only thing there is to do now that TV isn't an option. But as for the rest of us—you work to help the community, and you get food from the community. That's the deal. Everyone agreed?"

No one moved or said anything for a second. Then Wade muttered, "You got it, boss." Slowly, one by one, everyone in the room nodded.

"All right," said Cameron, releasing a breath she hadn't known she was holding. "Let's figure out what we're all going to be doing."

* * *

The first job assignment was easy: Bettie was put in charge of gardening and growing "crops," such as they were. Cameron was tempted to join her, but she knew her talents would be of better use elsewhere, and so she put up a call for volunteers.

"I'll help her with that," said Hernando immediately.

"Really?" said Cameron, raising an eyebrow. "Gardening."

Hernando's nostrils flared, and he rolled his shoulders. "Yeah. Sure. Why not?"

Bettie stepped over to him and patted his arm. "I can't wait. We're gonna have such fun." Hernando ducked his head.

Debbie, Russell's wife, joined the gardening team as well. Next Cameron asked who had experience with firearms. A surprising number of people raised their hands—her and Wade, of course, as well as Scott, Russell, Bill, and Chad, the father who'd arrived with the first group of stragglers. A woman named Aubrey, who Cameron barely knew, also raised her hand, though her husband Ken didn't.

"My dad used to take me shooting," she said, lowering her eyes as if embarrassed. "I'm . . . I'm not a crack shot, or anything, but I can fire a handgun, shotgun, rifle, whatever."

"All right," said Cameron, nodding and pursing her lips. "Then Wade, Russell, Chad, Aubrey and are going to hunt—wait, Aubrey, do you know how to clean an animal?"

The girl went a shade paler. "No, I–I don't. And, sorry, but I don't want to learn."

"No problem. You can still help us bring them down, and we'll take care of the rest." Cameron gave a reassuring smile and then turned to Scott. "Scott, I know you can shoot, but you're also sort of a handyman, right?"

"Uh-huh," said Scott, nodding. "Mostly electrician, but I can do other little stuff—patch holes, hang things, whatnot."

"I'd rather put you on that, if it's all right," said Cameron. "What with the weather, if any cabin's got leaks in the roof, we're going to find out about it real quick, if we haven't already. Windows might need fixing, and a lot of electrical systems have been fried, especially if they were connected to a computer. I don't think anyone else here has the skill set to deal with that."

"Happy to," said Scott, nodding. He probably knew what she wasn't saying—that he was a little old to be traipsing through the woods shooting at deer and rabbits—but she got the feeling that he appreciated the way she framed it.

"I'd, uh—ahem." Aubrey's husband, Ken, raised his hand suddenly, clearing his throat as though he was surprised to have heard himself speak. "I'd be willing to help Scott. If that's all right. I've never really be the handyman type, but I've always wanted to learn, and I'm happy to carry and hold things to help him."

"Sure thing," said Cameron. "If it's all right with you, Scott?"

"Better you lugging supplies around than me," said Scott. He stuck out a hand for Ken's and shook it vigorously. Ken smiled weakly. Cameron was pretty sure the guy was a lawyer or paralegal or something like that, and hoped he wasn't going to treat this as some sort of field trip.

"What about me?" said Bill. "Why aren't I going to go hunting?"

Because I don't want you wandering around the woods with a gun, and we all know it, and you just called attention to it, you absolute moron, thought Cameron. But she only said, "Because I was going to put you in charge of security. I mean, that seems to be what you're most concerned about, anyway."

An ugly gleam showed in Bill's eye, and Cameron hoped she wasn't making a terrible mistake. "That makes sense. Maybe the new girl can work with me."

He gave Gina a wink, and she carefully avoided his gaze. "I'll work with Bettie and Hernando, if that's all right."

Before Bill could snap back at her, Cameron interjected. "Jeremy, can you help Bill out?"

Jeremy, who had come in the same car as Gina and Hernando, gave Bill a little side-eye. But he nodded after only a moment's hesitation. "Sure."

"Good. And everyone who doesn't have a job yet, you're going to work with Bill, too, at least temporarily. The first thing we've got to do is check the fencing all around the cabins and make sure it's secure, and it'll be useful to have more than two people working on that until it's done. Once the fence is secure, we'll figure out more permanent jobs for you."

"Even me?" Naomi, the girl who had come with the first stragglers, piped up from near the back of the room. Cameron had barely noticed her. Her injured arm was still in its splint and sling.

"I don't think you can help much on fence repairs, Naomi," said Cameron. "But can you help Bettie with the gardening? I'm sure she'd love to teach you how to grow plants and things."

"I'd love to," said Bettie, smiling at the girl.

"Sure," said Naomi, giving a nervous little smile.

"In that case, I'd like to work with them as well, and not on the fence," said Kira, the girl's mother.

"Absolutely," said Cameron. "Okay. Everyone knows what they're doing? Good. It's too late to begin today, but we'll start tomorrow. And, really quick—thank you all. I appreciate everyone being understanding and willing to help. I think we're going to have a pretty good time."

There was a chorus of assenting murmurs, and they all began to drift out of the clubhouse. Once most of the eyes were off her, Cameron left, too, slipping out the clubhouse door with Bettie close behind. Bettie waited until they were a little ways off from the clubhouse and no one else was within earshot, and then she stepped closer to speak quietly to Cameron.

"So you're setting us up for the long haul, huh? You think it's really that bad?"

Cameron glanced over her shoulder to double check no one was close enough to hear. "Honestly? I doubt it. I think things'll go back to normal soon. But it's what could happen in the meantime that worries me. Even if we're only here for a month, or a couple of weeks—you pen twenty people up in an enclosed space for fourteen days, and you don't give them anything to do? You're gonna have problems. At that point, hurricanes and blizzards aren't close to as dangerous as people."

Bettie nodded slowly. "So you keep everyone busy and you keep them out of trouble. That it?"

Bill came to mind, and Gina, and Hernando. Cameron gave a little grimace. "That's the idea, anyway. Let's hope it works."

CHAPTER 18

The wide open plains of South Dakota made their road west an easy one. They walked on open land for the most part. Alex noted that Denny always kept a road in sight, but never too close. It was the same thing Alex would have done. With the road in sight, they could take advantage if they saw an abandoned car, or maybe a truck carrying useful supplies. Meanwhile, by keeping it a safe distance away, they could get out of Dodge if anyone spotted them and headed out to investigate.

But they didn't see any abandoned vehicles, and no one spotted them or came out towards them. In fact, they didn't see anybody at all. The roads were eerily abandoned, both the freeway and the smaller country roads they passed. They walked wide around the farmhouses and microtowns in their path, but Alex began to feel like they didn't need to worry about it. No one seemed to be home to see them pass.

After lightening the morning they met Denny, the rain grew stronger again as the day wore on. Alex broke out the rainproof jackets he'd purchased for himself and Piper. He'd brought a spare, and after only a moment's hesitation he gave it to Denny. It seemed like the least he could do after Denny was willing to guide them, and even if Denny snuck off with the jacket, it was only a spare.

As their journey went on, however, passing into a second and then a third day, Alex grew less and less convinced that

Denny was the type to sneak off and leave them high and dry—or high and soaked, with the weather being what it was. Whenever they stopped to eat, Denny provided his own food, and shared some with Alex and Piper as well. He had tastier provisions than the almost military rations Alex had stocked up on, and the bacon in particular was a welcome addition to their diet. As they walked together, Denny would tell them stories about the lands they were passing through, about his personal experiences there or the bits of history he'd picked up from his time on the road. Pretty soon Alex became convinced that Denny was just glad for the company, and wasn't going to do anything to jeopardize the presence of the first people he'd traveled with in a long time.

It wasn't long before even Piper began to warm up to the old hobo. Alex was glad to see it, though he knew he was the reason she'd started off somewhat paranoid in the first place. By the middle of the second day she was laughing at Denny's lame jokes, and she'd engage him in small snatches of conversation as they walked, or when they ate. And Max had warmed to the old man almost from the moment they'd met him, so that the whole group's journey together became a pleasant one, despite the darkness of the circumstances that had driven them together.

"How long have you been homeless?" asked Piper, on the morning on the third day. They'd just emerged from their tents and were eating a quick meal, heated on a fire Alex had built under a little rain screen.

"Piper," said Alex.

"Nah, it's all right," said Denny, waving off Alex's concern. "I've been wandering since I was younger than your dad is now. I didn't exactly pick it—always thought my life would be a lot different than this—but once I got used to it, I found out it actually wasn't so bad."

Piper's brow furrowed. "But you don't have a house. Don't you want a house?"

"Not so much," said Denny. He gave Alex a quick glance. "Don't get me wrong—I'm sure your mom and dad are happy to have a house. They want to take care of you. And you probably like it, too. That's fine. But me? I can go anywhere I want." He waved an arm at the land around them, gray and rain-soaked though it was. "Living in a house, I can't just pick up and go anywhere I want any time I want. Right now, I can. And that's the kind of life I want. A lot of the time, I think it's what I'm meant for. Maybe that's why . . . well, maybe that's why I ended up where I am."

He cut himself off abruptly and stared down at his food. It drew Alex's attention, and he studied the hobo with renewed interest. His gaze drifted to Denny's ring finger. There was no band there, but something told Alex there might have been, once upon a time.

Denny shook himself, as though he were shrugging an old blanket off his shoulders. "Anyway. Most people wouldn't do well at this. You're lucky to have two parents who keep a roof over your head and food in your belly. Don't forget that, okay? You're lucky."

Piper glanced at Alex, and quickly turned away when she saw he was already looking at her. "Okay," she murmured.

* * *

The weather only got worse the farther they traveled. Soon, in order to keep the road in sight, they had to walk less than half a mile away from it. Their jackets kept the rain off them, but didn't do much to stop the cold, which whipped at them on winds that were almost strong enough to knock Piper over. She took to holding Alex's hand as they walked, leaning forward into the wind. Max no longer ranged ahead and around them, instead plodding along miserably at Alex's heels. Denny and Alex both tried to keep away from trees, knowing that in

161

the wind, a branch could easily snap and strike any one of them.

They weren't careful enough—or maybe the wind was stronger than they'd thought. One moment they were struggling down a long slope covered in mud and slippery, and the next Alex heard a *whoosh* as a branch flew from nowhere and struck Denny in the chest. Denny gave a shout as he lost his footing. His rear struck the ground hard, and he started to slide. Alex tried to grab for him, but missed, and had to fall to his knees to keep from falling over himself. He planted hands and feet wide, crouching like a crab. He could only watch helplessly as Denny tumbled down the hill, striking a sizable rock halfway down. When he reached the bottom, he lay still.

"Denny!" cried Alex, shouting to be heard over the storm. But if Denny heard him, he gave no answer. Max went running down the slope, which was no trouble on four legs, apparently. Alex looked to Piper. "Come on. Carefully."

Step by hesitant, shaky step, they made their way to the bottom of the little dell. Just as they finished the awkward climb, Alex felt a rush of relief—Denny's hand rose to pet Max, who was sniffing at the hobo's face. Just as they reached him, Denny slowly pushed himself up to sitting with a groan.

"Holy fuck," he said, grimacing. His eyes darted to Piper. "Sorry."

"Forget it. Are you hurt?" said Alex.

Denny arched his back, then lifted his knees. "Doesn't seem like anything's broken. Hurts like all get-out, though." He tried to stand, winced hard, and put a hand to his side. "Hitting that rock didn't help. But I think my ribs are all right."

"Sometimes they can break, and it's hard to—"

The hobo cut him off with a look. "I've broken a rib before, son. Trust me—I think I'm fine."

Alex loosed a sigh and offered a hand. Denny took it gratefully, and allowed himself to be pulled up. "All right," said Alex. "We can rest a second. I—"

Piper fell down hard on her butt, drawing his attention. She lifted her knees and put her head between them, breathing heavily.

"Piper?" said Alex. He knelt beside her, putting a hand on her shoulder. "Sweetie, what's wrong?"

"Just . . . my head," she said. She blinked hard. "Sorry, I just . . ."

Her words trailed off. Alex cursed inwardly. The shock of Denny's fall must have spiked her adrenalin, and she was hyperglycemic.

He looked around. They were surrounded by hills, but the slopes were too gentle and the rises were too low to offer much protection against the storms. They needed to rest, but they needed to rest somewhere the entire sky wasn't trying to beat the crap out of them. There was a river just over the next line of hills, and from far away Alex had seen a group of trees and boulders that might make for a nice shelter, if a temporary one.

"We have to go on a little bit farther, then we can rest for a while," said Alex. "Just a little bit farther, okay?"

"Okay," said Piper, nodding. She pulled on his shoulder to stand, but he barely felt the tug. "Help me stand up."

He bit his tongue against another curse. If she couldn't stand, there was no way she was going to make the walk. He looked at Denny. "Can you carry her pack?"

"Sure," said Denny. He, too, struggled as he tried to rise, but Alex could see him restraining any complaints. Likely he saw Alex's worry and didn't want to add to it, which Alex appreciated.

Denny reached out a hand, and Alex took Piper's pack from her back to hand to him. Then he picked Piper up, holding her arms like a child.

"I can walk," she said. But her face was ghost-white, and

he could tell that her face was soaked with sweat as well as rainwater.

"It's not far," said Alex. "I've got you."

They pressed on towards the river. Though Piper wrapped her arms around his neck, she was almost a dead weight in his arms, and Alex was struggling by the time they neared the water. The river had risen far above normal levels, and was all rushing whitewater besides, but there was a cluster of trees and boulders that were still well above the waterline. Alex made for them. The tree branches would still pose a threat, but he hoped that by being right underneath them, the risk would be low.

He put Piper down a little harder than he'd meant to and helped Denny settle down, back against one of the boulders. From his pack he took a tarp, which he attached to two trees and a chink in the rock with bungee cords. A palpable wave of relief went through all three of them as the rain finally stopped beating on their heads.

"Sorry, dad," said Piper.

"Nothing to be sorry for," said Alex. "Catch a breather. Maybe we take the rest of the day off, and start fresh tomorrow."

"You know, there's a town just north of here," said Denny. "We might shoot for it instead."

Alex frowned. "I don't think towns are a great idea right now."

"No, it's a small place," said Denny. "And they're all good people. Place called Broadus. I've been there before, and most people there know me. I've done work for a lot of 'em, and they're good folk. Plus, the two of you could maybe get a hotel room for cheap—or they might just give it to you. Like I said, good people."

He tilted his head towards Piper almost imperceptibly. Alex gave her another look. Some color was coming back into her cheeks, but she was still too pale for his liking, and she was sweating profusely despite the cold. She needed rest for sure, but right now they weren't in a very restful place. She'd do better under a roof, and with maybe one night in a bed—and with some food in her belly. Plus, the town would probably have a pharmacy or corner drug store, and they could restock on insulin. That thought sealed it.

Alex ducked out from under the tarp for a moment, looking north. But the weather was too heavy for him to see very far, and the town was nowhere in sight. Frowning, he returned to the tent.

"How far?" he asked Denny.

* * *

It ended up being farther than he might have hoped, but not as far as he had feared. The rain lightened a little as they began their walk north, and almost immediately the town came into view. Just south of it there was a small bridge with country roads on either side, which they used to cross the flooded river. Alex carried Piper across it, eyeing the water uneasily—it was less than a yard beneath the edge of the bridge.

When they finally reached the town, they found the streets completely empty. Just as Alex had guessed, there was a corner store, but all the lights were off inside. Alex peered in through the glass, but there was no sign of activity inside.

"Let's head for the diner," said Denny. "Maybe someone there knows the shop owner—and if not, we can rest, anyway."

"Good idea," said Alex.

"You can put me down, Dad," said Piper. "I'm feeling all right." He did, carefully, and she kept her feet easily. But she kept a hand on his arm as they walked.

The diner was at the other end of the block. They didn't run into anyone on their way there, but Alex saw a few cars in the parking lot. It seemed the whole town wasn't abandoned after all—a fact that was confirmed the moment they stepped in the front door. Not only were a hostess and two waiters on duty, but over half the tables in the place were full. Alex got the feeling this was an unusually large crowd, even if they'd arrived during lunch hour, which they hadn't. Denny drew more than a few looks with his ratty clothes and dirty, sun-browned skin, but the hostess didn't say anything about him. Alex figured that with weather the way it was, the diner wasn't exactly going to throw anyone out.

"Hi there," said the hostess. "Can I get you a table?"

"That'd be great," said Alex. "But we were also hoping to shop at the corner store down the street. Do you know when it opens?"

The hostess clicked her tongue. "Midge's dad runs it. He's . . ." She stopped and scanned the room behind her. "Nope, he's not here right now. But I'll put you in her section, and you can ask her."

"Thank you so much," said Alex. The hostess smiled in reply and led them to a booth in the corner. With the crowd, it was a short while before their waitress arrived, but when she did, Alex saw *Midge* on her name tag.

"Hey y'all," she said. "Sorry about the wait. Can I start you off with some coffee, or do you already know what you want?"

"I think we'll all take burgers, and coffee would be great," said Alex. "But we were hoping you could help us with something else. The hostess said your father runs the corner store down the street?"

"Oh, sure," said Midge. She smiled, but it was halfheart-ed. "He just closed it up, what with the weather. Most places in town are closed up except this one. I'll give him a call after I put your order in."

Their food came quicker than the service had, and they ate quickly. Piper wolfed down her food, and Alex could al-most see the strength flood back into her. It made him breathe easier, and he was able to enjoy his own food with gusto. It wasn't like they were starving on the road, but their rations sure got old.

As they ate, Alex noted how many Native Americans were in the restaurant. They must be drawing near to the reservation Denny had mentioned. He'd been so caught up with pushing on through the rain and keeping Piper safe that it had been a long while since he'd asked Denny how much farther they had to go. The locals, Native American and not, gave Alex's table a few curious looks, but mostly they kept their eyes on their food.

When they finished, Denny tried to pay for his own meal, but Alex waved him off and dropped a hundred on the check. Midge scooped it up a moment later.

"I'll get you some change, honey."

"No need," said Alex.

She paused, taken aback, and then smiled. "Why . . . why thank you, sweetheart. You all have a great day, then. And my dad said he was heading over to the store, so you should find it open for you now."

"Thanks," said Alex. "We appreciate it."

Midge gave them a final smile and hurried off to the next table. Alex led Piper and Denny out of the restaurant, all of them bundling up in their jackets against the rain.

The storm had grown worse, and more than once they stumbled against its fury. It almost threw Piper into the buildings they were walking by, and Alex had to take her arm a couple of times. But her blood sugar levels seemed to have stabilized. She looked miles better than she had when they reached the town. Still, Alex was leery of pushing too hard.

"We'll stock up on your insulin, and then we'll head for the town's motel. Okay?"

Piper frowned. "We can keep going. I'm fine."

"I'm sure you are, but I don't think we're going to find too many more towns like this one where it's safe to stop. Might as well rest while we can."

Her frown deepened, but she nodded, and he thought she looked a little relieved. She was putting on a brave face, but Alex doubted she wanted to press on through the storm any more than he did.

Denny was looking up at the sky. One hand absentmindedly rubbed his chest where the branch had struck him earlier, and he wore a troubled expression. Alex didn't like it, but he thought better than to ask what was wrong. If the hobo knew something was wrong, it was likely to freak Piper out even more. That could wait until they were safe from the storm.

They found the corner store open, and a wizened, bent old man was at the counter. As soon as they walked in the door he hailed them with a friendly wave.

"Howdy. Midge told me y'all needed some things. Name's Fred. Sorry we were closed up."

"Can't blame you. I'm Alex. We need insulin, for my daughter, if you have some."

"Sure do, lots" said Fred. "Right over here."

He led Alex towards the back left corner. Alex asked for every vial of insulin out of the cooler, prompting Fred to raise his eyebrows. "I should be getting more in soon, and you usually need a prescription for it, but with the weather I say no need, how far are ya'll going? Fred asked.

"Still got a long way to go," said Alex.

"West coast?"

"Almost Seattle."

"Well. Good luck." Fred's tone wasn't as encouraging as his words.

As Fred rang them up, Alex noticed that Denny had remained near the front of the store. His face was almost pressed against the glass, and he was still staring at the sky. It got Alex's nerves up, and he scooped up the insulin almost before Fred had handed back his change, hurrying towards Denny with Piper in tow.

"What is it?" said Alex.

"Bad sky," said Denny. "The storm's bad enough here, but it's worse close by, and—"

A sudden roar cut him off. The ground shuddered beneath their feet, and Alex tightened his grip on Piper's arm. Looking back, he saw Fred's knuckles white on the countertop, a look of confusion on the old man's face. Whatever this was, it wasn't normal for Broadus.

"What the hell was—"

"Flood," said Denny, almost whispering. Then he turned and shouted so Fred could hear him. "Flash flood! Get out!"

Fred vanished into the back of the shop. Alex, Piper and Denny ran out the front. "Come on!" shouted Alex, as they pounded down the street towards the center of town. "The hotel! If we can reach it, we can—"

He skidded to a halt, Piper and Denny doing the same beside him.

They were too late.

Broadus' main street stretched on ahead of them. It gave them a clear view straight through the other side of the town. There they saw a solid wall of water rushing towards them. It was almost twenty feet high, and it was rushing faster than a train. The motel was near the town's north end, and the floodwaters were closer to it than Alex was.

"Dad," cried Piper.

"I—we have to—" Alex shook himself. "Back inside the pharmacy. Quick, before—"

"Glass storefront," said Denny. "It's a deathtrap."

Alex almost snapped at him, asking for a better idea. But just then, tires screeched nearby, and he clutched Piper to him. A beat-up old truck skidded around one of the town's street corners. For a moment it seemed it would speed right past them, but then it screamed to a halt. One massive door flew open, and Alex barely registered the sight of a Native American couple in the cab.

"Get in!" cried the man behind the wheel.

Without hesitation, Alex practically threw Piper into the cab's back seat and scrambled in after her. Denny followed half a second later, and the man punched the gas almost before the hobo's feet had left asphalt. The woman in shotgun struggled to pull the door closed behind them, and the truck sped away.

Alex turned to look out the back window, just as the wall of water struck the first buildings in Broadus. The smaller houses erupted into fountains of timber and kindling. He saw at least two cars picked up in the flood and thrown through the walls of the larger buildings. He turned away, his heart sick, and whispered a prayer for the safety of Midge and the rest of the people of Broadus, as he and his friends sped away from the town's death.

CHAPTER 19

The cabin community took to their new jobs with gusto. Despite the heavy rain, Bettie's new helpers spent almost all day long in Cameron's back yard, and when their work was done each day, Bettie directed the laying of new gardens in other locations. Cameron barely managed to keep the smirk from her face when she saw Hernando grubbing in the dirt and digging holes for tomato seeds, all the while trying to keep the tough guy look on his face and in his posture.

Where the gardening team turned the soil and planted their seeds, Scott would follow behind and throw up crude wire fences to keep animals away, helped in large part by Ken. The two of them were the perfect Odd Couple, with Scott grousing and grumping as he directed Ken, who was almost too eager to help. Often Ken would set to work with drill and saw before Scott had half finished giving directions, and have to undo some part of what he'd done in order to make the fence more secure. Cameron didn't mind. Half of the point of it all was to keep everyone busy, after all, and Ken was definitely busy.

The only problem, to no one's surprise, was Bill. It took less than a day for him and his team to check the fence surrounding the cabin community, and then everyone but Jeremy was assigned to one of the other teams. After that, Bill's idea of "security" appeared to be nosing into everyone else's business, and he would putter from team to team—the gardeners, the hunters, Scott and Ken—and just observe, giving the occasional snide remark. Without any direction, Jeremy soon stopped accompanying Bill on his trips, since it seemed obvious he hated them almost as much as the people Bill stood and leered over.

Cameron wondered often if she should do anything about it, but she decided against it for the time being. If Bill posed a real problem to the community, she could deal with him then. Until that time, she didn't want to be his excuse to be even more of an asshole.

But a few days after the work assignments, Cameron was returning from a hunting trip when she heard shouts at the community. She'd gone out with Aubrey, and they'd managed to shoot a couple of rabbits. When they heard the raised voices ahead of them, they shared a quick glance before breaking out into a sprint to burst out of the woods.

She saw the problem at once. Russell was standing just outside the clubhouse near the front gate, out in the middle of the street and waving his arms in fury. The target of his anger was lolling on its side in the clubhouse door: a black bear, sitting in a mess of torn food packets. The bear didn't seem particularly impressed by Russell's attempts to ward it off.

"Shit!" said Aubrey. She raised her handgun, but Cameron grabbed her arm and pushed it down.

"No way," she said. "You'll just piss it off." She unslung her rifle from her back. Her pulse was pounding in her ears as she slowly approached the clubhouse.

Russell spotted her as she drew within ten yards. He stopped screaming and waving his arms. "Careful," he called out. "If you don't hit it dead in the—"

"I know," said Cameron. She hoisted the rifle to her shoulder. The bear hardly seemed to notice her, giving her only a passing glance before it ducked its head down to a bag of apples it had already torn open. She took a deep breath. If she didn't kill it, it would get up and charge. She couldn't guarantee a second hit if it was moving around. Her hands were steady, though she felt like they should be shaking.

"I can take the shot if you want," said Russell.

"I got it."

She looked down the sights. Exhaled. Pulled the trigger.

The slug went straight through the left eye. The bear jerked once, then slumped to the floor.

Cameron loosed a sharp breath, almost a grunt. Her hands fell to point the rifle at the ground, and now they started shaking as she let the adrenalin have its way with her. Russell sighed with relief and bent over, hands on his knees. Aubrey giggled, a nervous sound, not a happy one.

"How did it get in?" said Cameron.

"No idea," said Russell. "I was coming down here to grab a snack, and I found it sitting there."

Cameron looked to the north. The gunshot had drawn attention, and now a bunch of the community were running towards them. In the middle of the pack was Bill. Cameron slung her rifle over her shoulder again and made for him.

"Bill!" she said, louder than she'd really meant to. "What the hell?"

He stopped short, as did the rest of the group. All eyes turned to Bill, as he folded his arms and scowled at her.

"What the hell, what?" he said.

Cameron pointed at the bear. "What the hell that. How did a bear get in here? You're security, remember?"

His mouth fell open, but nothing came out. His arms unfolded, and he looked left and right, like he was expecting to find the answer just over either shoulder. "I . . . I don't know! I didn't let it in!"

"Jesus Christ," said Cameron, pinching the bridge of her nose. "Bill and Jeremy, check the damn fence. Find out how it got in. Russell, Aubrey, can you go with them?"

Both of them murmured in assent. Bill, for once, didn't argue at being ordered around, and set off with the group in tow to find the hole. Bettie came up, with Hernando and the rest of her gardening team lurking just a few yards behind, looking uncertain. Bettie appraised the dead bear with raised eyebrows.

"Well, that's a little meat, at least."

"If you want to look on the bright side," muttered Cameron.

"Always seemed to me to be the best way to go through life," said Bettie. "But you gotta plan for the bad days, too."

Cameron looked again at the bear. "You're right. We'll have a meeting once they get back from checking the fence."

* * *

They gathered in the clubhouse an hour later, which Bettie and her helpers had cleaned up. Bill and the others came in out of the cold, shaking rainwater from their coats and rubbing their arms to warm them. Cameron sat in a chair at the front of the room near the stockpiled supplies. The bear hadn't gotten into as much food as they'd all feared, and they still had plenty to go around. By that time Wade had arrived—he'd been sleeping earlier, and had missed all the hubbub about the bear—and he sat silently by Cameron's left side.

"There was a loose post about a quarter mile away," said Bill. "Looks like the bear pushed the fence over there. No way to know it woulda done that."

"Sure," said Cameron, nodding. Of course Bill could have checked the fence posts, but it wasn't worth arguing about now. "We'll go and check the rest of it for any other loose posts along the line."

"Fair enough," said Bill.

"We're also going to need to post guards," said Cameron. "Two, always, on rotations."

Everyone went quiet, looking around at each other. Aubrey was the first one to speak. "But everyone already has jobs."

"They'll be in addition to normal jobs," said Cameron. "I'll stand watch, same as Wade. Russell, Hernando, I'd appreciate it if you stepped up."

"Sure," said Russell. Behind him, Hernando nodded.

"Two during the day, two at night," said Cameron. "The night watch gets to sleep the day after their rotation on guard duty."

"And I'm in charge of the rotations?" said Bill.

Cameron winced inwardly. "You're the head of security."

Bill's mouth twisted. He'd noticed she hadn't said *Of course*, or even *Yes*. But he didn't press it. "Fine. I'll work out a schedule."

"Always two. We've got three rifles. At night each guard can have one. But during the day the hunters will need two, so the other guard will take Scott's shotgun, and everyone carries handguns, all the time."

"I thought handguns didn't work against bears," said Aubrey.

"There's other animals out there besides bears," said Wade. "Wolves, cougars. Other people."

That sent a chill rippling through the room. "We're not going to shoot people," said Aubrey.

"Of course not, if they're peaceful," said Wade. "But they might not be. And everyone's a little bit more friendly when you're showing a piece."

That drew a bark of laughter from Bill. "Dang, you thought I was a jerk for saying things like that. I guess your boyfriend has special privileges."

Wade shot out of his chair and took two steps towards Bill. Cameron got up and snatched the back of his shirt, dragging him around. "Knock it off, Wade." She stepped past him right in front of Bill—who, to his credit, didn't back away, though it seemed clear he wanted to. "Bill, you're in charge of everyone's safety. Maybe don't make things more dangerous by being a complete asshole. Everyone else, we're not turning into

175

an army. We're not putting guns in the hands of trigger-happy idiots. But today a bear broke into the cabins. Thank god it came for the clubhouse and our food. What if it had gone for one of the cabins? Someone could have died. All we're doing is making sure that doesn't happen next time—if there even is a next time. Got it?"

A slow, quiet murmur of assent rippled through the room.

"Good. No one leaves the fence line alone, and with a firearm more powerful than a handgun. That's all we got. Everyone get back to it—or take today off, if you want. It's been stressful, and we deserve it."

Everyone drifted away. Cameron brushed past Bettie and walked out into the rain, alone.

* * *

She didn't head back for her cabin, but instead headed for the tree line and took a little walk through the woods, enjoying the relative shelter the branches gave from the rain. If she were honest with herself, it wasn't the woods she wanted— she'd already spent hours beneath the trees earlier when she was hunting with Aubrey. But if she went back to the cabin, Bettie would want to talk to her, and right now she wanted to be alone.

"Cam!"

Her jaw clenched. *So much for that.*

Wade approached, jogging to catch up to her. "Where you going?"

"For a walk."

"You've been out all day."

Cameron shrugged and turned to walk on. Wade fell into stride next to her.

"It's smart," he said. "Posting guards. I know it feels like Bill's fear-mongering horse shit, but it's smart."

"I know," said Cameron.

"It's not going to be long before people start getting desperate. Everything on the radio makes it sound like it's getting worse and worse out there."

"I *know*," said Cameron, a bit too much venom in her voice. They'd all heard the scattered radio reports. They didn't come often, and only lasted a few minutes at a time, but word spread quickly whenever voices came through the static. No one had figured out how to restore the national power grids, and things were starting to get desperate in a lot of the cities.

Wade studied her from the corner of his eye. He probably thought she didn't notice, but she did. Cameron knew she often gave the appearance of being lost in thought, and when she did, people didn't think she was paying attention to her surroundings. It had been that way a long time, and people always used to comment on it in the service. What they didn't realize was that she was always paying attention to what was going on around her, trying to use it to pull her *away* from her thoughts. When a lot was on her mind, she was at her most observant.

"I can't imagine what it must be like out there for someone right now," said Wade in a low voice.

Cameron barely kept herself from shaking her head. He was subtly hinting at Alex and Piper, but Wade had about as much subtlety as a brick. If he wanted to talk around it, though, she wouldn't stop him. "I'm sure it's pretty hard. At least we're safe here."

"Yeah. But even this isn't exactly peachy. The bear, the weather. Guard duty, for chrissake. Everyone can see you're taking a lot on your shoulders." She gave him a look, and he shrugged. "I'm just saying, I'm here. You know? We were both in the service. We both know what it's like to have a lot riding on you, and to be worried about other people."

All right, enough subtlety, thought Cameron. She looked him dead in the eye. "Alex is going to bring Piper home," she said. "I know it. I'm not worried about it. I'm only worried about keeping the cabins here until he does."

Wade pursed his lips, and then raised his hands as if he was surrendering. "All right," he said. "No problem. Just offering."

He turned and walked away, heading back for the cabins. Cameron watched him go for a moment before she turned and walked back off into the trees. She wondered briefly if he knew she was lying.

CHAPTER 20

The truck was dead silent as they drove away from the wreckage of Broadus. The road turned west just south of the town, and the flash flood passed harmlessly by them. Alex tried not to look back at it, tried not to see the cars and bits of houses floating on the tide, and wonder how many people were caught in the waters.

The shock began to fade, and he blinked hard as he realized not a word had been spoken since the town. He looked at the couple in the truck's front seat. Both of them had their gaze fixed on the horizon ahead, as though they weren't even aware of his existence.

"Thank you," said Alex quietly. "We would have . . . thank you."

"Of course," said the man driving. His black hair hung down to his shoulders, resting on a faded red and white flannel shirt. His knuckles on the wheel looked soft and free from calluses.

The woman riding shotgun loosed a half-sob, covering her mouth with one hand. The driver reached over and took her left hand in his right, squeezing her fingers in his own.

"I . . . did you know anyone?" said Alex.

"No family, but a lot of friends," said the driver. He glanced over his shoulder at Alex, but not for long. The rain had intensified, and the road wasn't well-maintained. "I'm Graham, by the way. This is my wife, Willow."

"I'm Alex. This is Piper, and Denny."

"Where'd you come from?"

"New York. But our home's in Washington. That's where we were headed."

"On foot?" Graham shook his head. "You're brave or crazy."

"We had a car, but it got wrecked. The rain."

"Well, we'll take you to the reservation," said Graham. "We were headed that way ourselves, though we weren't planning on getting on the road till tonight. I can't go farther than that."

"I understand, of course," said Alex. "We're incredibly grateful."

"No problem," said Graham. He shook his head, looking at the storm outside. "All this rain, and almost summer. I never thought I'd live to see anything like that flare. I mean, it was only a matter of time, but the odds . . ."

Alex and Denny looked at each other, frowning. Denny shrugged. Piper barely seemed aware that a conversation was taking place. "What do you know about the solar flare?"

"Not enough, but a bit more than most," said Graham. "I'm a meteorologist. Actually I was a weather guy on a local station, which broadcast out of Broadus. We got a warning almost as soon as the flare went off. A lot of the bigger orgs tried to warn people—NASA got on the horn about it, everyone was trying to say this was going to be big. But I don't think they knew just how big it was going to be, and D.C. didn't take it seriously. I guess they thought some crazy scientists were trying to live out their *Armageddon* fantasies."

"Armageddon," said Alex. He snorted. "Sounds about right. So what *is* this? I thought solar flares were common. Is this one just bigger than normal?"

"Bigger than normal, but not even close to the biggest," said Graham. "There's bigger ones all the time, but you gotta realize, the odds of one doing this are practically non-existent.

The sun is huge, in case you hadn't noticed. If it were a basketball, Earth wouldn't be a ping pong ball, or even a marble. It would be smaller than a pea."

"Small target," said Denny.

"Exactly. Flares send out pulses of electromagnetic radiation all the time, but they're like needles firing out in a straight line, and Earth is a long, long way away. It's like spinning in a circle in the middle of a football field, blindfolded, shooting a sniper rifle every few seconds. Even if someone's standing on the edge of the field, the odds you'll actually hit them are tiny. But eventually, even a blind man gets lucky. Heck, two years ago there was a flare twice as big as this one—but it was on the other side of the sun."

Alex shuddered. "You mean this could have been twice as bad?"

"No, man. Twice as strong is a million times as bad. This flare just sent a glancing blow off the edge of our atmosphere. You know Earth's got a magnetic field, right? Well, that's what keeps us from being nuked by the sun's radiation. But that glancing blow disrupted the field, and that's why the flare had the EMP effect. Took out all the electronics. And meanwhile, it sort of . . . cooked the atmosphere a little bit. Messed everything up, like climate change kicked into fast forward. If the solar flare had been even ten percent stronger, it could have wiped us out. Still might, the way things are looking."

Piper's attention was finally drawn to the conversation. "How do you know all this? It hasn't happened before, has it? I think I would have learned about that in school."

"Huh. You'd think," said Graham. "But there's been five mass extinction events in Earth's history, and we're not a hundred percent sure what a couple of them were. Schools don't think it's very helpful to tell kids, 'Hey, all life on the planet could be wiped out in an instant, and there's no way to tell when it's gonna happen.'"

"Graham," said Willow reproachfully. She wiped a couple of tears from the edge of her eyes. "You'll scare the girl."

"It's fine," mumbled Piper. But her eyes were wide with fear.

"So if you know what's happened, do you know what's still in store?" said Alex. "Is there an end to all this?"

"That's . . . a little harder to know," said Graham. "People have been running simulation models on this sort of thing for decades. But there's not a lot of sample data."

Alex's jaw clenched as he saw Piper go a shade paler. He tried again. "Is there a best-case scenario?"

"Best-case? After some heavy weather, the climate—and the magnetic field—resets itself with a series of massive storms."

"Wait, what?" said Piper. "These *are* massive storms."

"Oh, no, girl," said Graham. "Sorry. But even in the best case, the worst isn't on the horizon yet."

* * *

The truck was quiet again after that.

Alex put his arm around Piper, trying to give her some comfort, though he knew it was probably an exercise in futility. He could hardly blame Graham for telling the truth, but he wished the guy had tried to soften the blow at least a little. Alex doubted Graham and Willow had kids. There were some things you just didn't tell children, your own or other people's. Some things were unimaginable.

After a while, though, Piper started to squirm. She looked uncomfortably around, frowning.

"What's wrong?" said Alex.

"I . . . I, uh . . ." Piper's frown deepened. She leaned closer to whisper. "I have to go to the bathroom. I don't feel good."

Alex looked ahead through the windshield. There were no buildings in sight anywhere. "Can you wait? Just till we find a gas station or something."

Her cheeks flushed, and she shook her head. "I told you I don't feel good. I don't think I can wait."

It probably wasn't wise to try and push her now. "Graham, I'm sorry, but can we make a pit stop? Piper needs a second."

"Pit stop? Can it wait until we get to a gas station? There's a one just about ten miles away."

Alex gave Piper a quick look. Ten miles would take a half hour in this weather. "I don't think so."

"Suit yourself," said Graham.

He pulled the truck over to the side of the road, leaving the engine running. Alex slid out so Piper could exit the cab, both of them throwing up their hoods against the rain, as Max jumped from the bed of the truck to join them, Denny stayed in the truck, uncharacteristically silent.

There were a bunch of bushes and shrubs near the freeway, and Alex walked Piper towards them. When they reached one tall enough to hide her from the truck, he waited discreetly while she went around the other side. He looked back towards the truck, where Graham, Willow and Denny waited with a light on inside.

All the world around them was gray, from the clouded sky to the road to the land around them. When it rained in the Pacific Northwest, everything sprang out in brilliant green, so bright and colorful it looked Photoshopped, even when you viewed it with the naked eye. But whether it was this part of the country, or the sheer fury of the rainstorm, the ground was just a slimy gray mud that clung to the boots and got in everything. When they eventually made it to the cabins in Washington, Alex fully planned to spend an entire week inside, away from the rain, in his pajamas, and sit near the fire as often as he possibly could, just enjoying the lack of weather constantly assaulting him.

Piper had been out of sight a moment too long for his liking. "Piper?" he called out. "You okay?"

"I'm fine," she said, a little too quickly.

Alex frowned. "What is it?"

"I . . . I think I . . ." He heard her squelching footsteps, and she emerged from around the bush. Her skin was ghostly pale.

"Are you okay?" said Alex, truly concerned now. "Did you throw up?"

Piper shook her head, biting on her lower lip. She turned around, and Alex saw a red spot on the rear of her jeans.

He stood frozen, staring at it, his throat suddenly dry.

"Okay," he said quickly. "Okay, this is fine. That's—ah, that's fine. Okay, fine. Um. Let's get back to . . . to the truck. This is fine."

"I *know* it's fine," said Piper. "Jesus, Dad."

"Nope, this is okay. Really. Don't worry about it," said Alex, aware of how nonsensical he sounded. Inside he was screaming, *Seriously? Seriously, right now?*

They made their way back to the truck, Piper looking more and more miserable with every step. When they were a few yards away, Alex stopped her and ran up to the cab, tapping on Willow's window. She frowned at him through the glass as she rolled it down.

"Ah," said Alex. "So . . . do you, um. Do you have any . . . I mean, Piper just—" He cut himself off and closed his eyes. *Jesus Christ, Alex, you're not a teenage boy.* He took a deep breath and tried again. "Piper just got her period. It's . . . her first one. Do you have any . . ."

Graham's eyes went wide, and Willow rolled her eyes. "Oh, lord. Poor girl. I wish I had some pads or tampons with me, but I don't. Here."

She opened the door and pushed past Alex, shaking her head with a little smile. She went to Piper and took her arm, leading her toward the truck with an arm over the girl's shoulders. Piper just stared at her feet, her cheeks now beet-red. *Better than pale and bloodless, I guess,* thought Alex. Then he mentally kicked himself for using the word *bloodless* at a time like this.

From the back of the truck, Willow pulled Graham's tool box from the bed, and encouraged Max to get back in. "We don't need you in the way right now, boy." She said with a smile. Inside the tool box was a pile of rags, clean, thankfully. Willow took a couple of them and folded them over.

"Here," she said, handing them to Piper. "You can use these as temporary pads until we get you the real thing, which we'll do soon. Okay? It's going to be uncomfortable. I'm sorry."

"No, it's fine," mumbled Piper. "Thank you."

"You should head back out to put those in. You know what to do?"

"I think so," said Piper, and then repeated, "Thank you." She wandered around the back of the truck where no one could see.

Willow cocked her head as she looked at Alex. "You're not catching any breaks on this trip."

"We sure aren't," said Alex. "I appreciate your help. I'm not . . . exactly the best person to help her with this."

"Don't tell me you're one of those husbands who acts like his wife's a leper when she's on her period." Willow folded their arms and looked at him appraisingly.

"No, not at all," said Alex. He shrugged helplessly. "It's just . . . my area of expertise is limited to running to the store and getting her some Maxi-Pads. I don't know a lot about the . . . particulars."

Willow rolled her eyes. "Men. Well, we need to get her some real pads. Those rags are hardly very sanitary, and they won't soak up much, anyway."

Piper emerged from around the rear of the truck. She still kept her eyes on her feet, and her cheeks hadn't lost a speck of their color. "Okay," she mumbled. "I'm, uh, done."

"Good job, sweetheart," said Willow, patting her shoulder. "And I've got some Advil in the glove box. If you don't need it already, you will soon."

Alex led the way back to the cab where Graham and Denny were waiting. Both men studiously avoided looking at Piper as she climbed back into the cab. Alex wished they wouldn't make things even more awkward. But Willow turned to Graham as soon as the doors were shut against the rain.

"Stop at the next town," she said. "We need to make another pit stop—a real one this time."

* * *

The next town was called Muddy, and just now, it deserved the name. Little more than a collection of gas stations and shops, it sat squalid and filthy in the rain. But about a mile off the road Alex saw an All-N-All, one of the warehouse store chains that had sprung up in the Midwest in recent years. Graham exited the freeway and made for the store, creeping along the town's streets slowly.

Almost immediately Alex felt that something was wrong. The lights were off at the gas station, and none of the other stores or little houses were lit. He might have expected the places of business to be abandoned, but the homes gave the town an ominous feel. His nerves were raw by the time they pulled into the store's sizable parking lot. Graham stopped just off the street, putting the truck in park and leaving the engine to idle.

The front doors of the All-N-All were open, but in front of them had been laid a barricade of shopping carts, tables and other furniture. Alex couldn't see anybody manning the barricade, but it seemed clear it had been erected to keep people out, not in. That meant there were people inside the store, and if they'd built a barrier, he doubted they were friendly.

"I'm gonna let you take care of this one," said Graham. "We'll wait here."

Piper seized Alex's arm. "Dad, don't," she said. "I'll be fine, I promise. We can wait until we—"

"It's fine, Piper," said Alex. "Don't worry. I'll be fine."

He didn't feel nearly as confident as he managed to sound, climbing out of the truck cab into the pouring rain. He approached the All-N-All slowly, resisting the urge to put his hands in the air. If there was anyone inside, they'd have set a watch. They'd see him coming. He only hoped that the fact he was alone, and hadn't brought his gun, would keep them from killing him on sight.

A gunshot rang out.

Alex jumped. But the bullet ricocheted from the parking lot's asphalt, at least five yards away. Either the people inside were terrible shots, or that was a warning shot. Alex desperately hoped it was the latter, a hope that seemed bolstered the longer he stood there without a second shot following the first. He hadn't seen the shooter, only their muzzle flash from the blackness of the doorway.

"Whoever you are, fuck off!" came a voice—a man. "Everything in here is ours!"

"I'm not here to hurt you or steal anything," called Alex, and now he did raise his hands. "I'm here to—"

"We don't care! I said fuck off!"

Another gunshot. This one hit the parking lot as well, but closer.

"I don't want food!" said Alex. "Please! I just need some pads!"

Dead silence from the store. Alex waited for a reply, but none came.

"Pads, or tampons," he called out. "We—listen, my daughter and I are traveling west, and . . . and she just—well, she just started her period. And it's her first one, and we . . . listen, please. Please help us out here."

Whatever expected, it wasn't what he got: a woman's wild, almost hysterical guffaw burst out from the darkness of the store. It sounded like she was on the verge of having a conniption fit, but with who knew how many guns trained on him,

Alex couldn't share in the mirth. Still there was no actual reply, but only a prolonged silence.

Then, out of the darkness of the store, a huge bulk-pack of Maxi Pads came flying out. It was followed half a second later by another. They landed on the asphalt only a few yards away from the store, a good distance away from Alex.

"Thank you!" he called out. "Thank you, thank you so much!" He almost ran for the package, but thought better of it and approached slowly instead. He reached the two huge bulk packs and stooped to retrieve them, then turned back towards the truck.

"Wait!" Alex stopped short and turned. It was the woman's voice. He still couldn't see her. But after another moment's silence, two more packages came flying out of the All-N-All. He didn't recognize them at first, until they landed and skidded to his feet. One was a bulk-pack of Midol. The other was a huge twelve-pack of Nutella.

"God bless you!" called Alex. He wasn't much for religion, but it was the Midwest—they probably were. "I hope like hell you make it through this!"

He scooped up his prizes and ran for the truck like all get-out.

CHAPTER 21

Though the camp was on edge after the bear attack, things soon settled out back to normal. But Cameron gradually became aware of another problem. The first sign was when Bettie asked for help finding gardening tools for her team—there was only one shovel, and she didn't have enough work to keep more than one person busy without more. But none of the other cabins had another shovel, or trowels, or tools for weeding.

Then Scott went a whole day without working because he was trying to find shingles and tools to install them, but there weren't any spares around. Cameron thought privately to herself that that was the sort of thing she would have expected Bill to have on hand.

When next the community all got together, Cameron addressed them as a group to discuss the problem.

"We're pretty good on food, at least for a while," she said. "But that's not all we're going to need. We're short on a lot of tools we need to build and repair things, not to mention the gardening. Plus, I've got next to nothing when it comes to medical supplies and medicine. I want to send out a few parties to collect what we can from locations we can reach easily and safely."

"What places?" said Gina. "There aren't any towns on the way up here."

Wade chimed in. "Not the way you drove up, but further in the mountains there's a couple of small towns. Barely anything more than a collection of fast food joints and gas stations, really. People don't live there, they just work there."

"Which means those stores are probably abandoned," said Cameron.

"So you're talking about looting," said Bill.

"If anyone's still manning the stores, we'll pay for what we need," said Cameron. "If not, we'll take it. If it'll help you sleep at night, Bill, I can promise I'll make good on whatever we take after everything calms down. If it does."

"I'm not the one whose conscience needs stroking, honey." For the thousandth time, she wanted to deck him. She turned away instead, addressing the rest of the group.

"I'm going out, and I'm taking Bill, Russell and Chad with me. Bettie, Scott and I have made a list of what we need. We'll pick up those items first, and then fill the rest of any vehicle space with non-perishable food. Can't have too much of that."

"We should gas up while we're at it," said Russell. The big man was frowning in his beard. Cameron guessed he didn't like the idea of raiding stores for goods. Truth be told, she wasn't overjoyed at it, either, but she was grateful he didn't argue.

"Good call," said Cameron. "Everyone else, do what you can with what you have until we get back."

"I should come," said Wade.

Cameron had expected that. "No. Two to each vehicle."

"Then let me swap out," said Wade. "No offense to Chad and Russell. But you and I are vets. It only makes sense." Cameron smiled inwardly as she noted he'd left Bill out of the *no offense* comment.

"We're not going into a war zone," said Cameron. "We'll be armed, but we're not going to start any trouble, and I'm not expecting to find any. But I do need someone here to watch out for everyone while we're gone. We're taking all but one gun."

Wade's jaw worked. But in the end he nodded, settling back down in his chair.

"All right," said Cameron. "We'll load up and drive out in fifteen minutes. Use the bathroom if you need to, or so help me, I'll turn the car around and drive straight back."

That drew a chuckle from everyone, even Bill, and the group broke up to get to work.

* * *

By unspoken agreement, Russell took Bill in his truck, while Cameron drove with Chad. Cameron was grateful—she knew she'd do something stupid if she had to be in the truck with Bill for half an hour, but the little weasel was always a lot more polite around Russell and his massive logger's arms. Chad was mostly silent as Cameron drove the Jeep carefully through the rain, winding along the road deeper into the Cascades. He drummed the first two knuckles of his right hand on the window every so often, but not enough to be annoying. After a long silence, he turned abruptly to Cameron.

"So were you, like, an officer?"

Cameron blew a sigh through her nose. "Technically, yes. I was a medic, and that means I was an officer almost from day one. But I didn't have a command. It's more of an honorary thing."

"Oh." Chad looked back out the window. "You just . . . you take charge. It seems like you're used to it."

Cameron smirked. "In my experience, doctors are more likely to tell people what to do—and better at it—than officers."

Chad snorted. "Fair enough. It must have been wild. I mean, I'm a trucker. It's rare enough seeing women in my line of work, and they don't always have the easiest time of it when you do. Not that I mind," he said quickly, raising his hands. "It's just not every guy with an eighteen-wheeler thinks the same way I do. I can only imagine what it was like in the military."

"Not great, honestly," said Cameron. "I mean, listen. Everyone tries not to bring it up, to act like it's normal. But it's something you can feel. Little looks, little comments. Not from everyone, but from enough."

"Did you serve active duty? Combat?"

Her jaw clenched. "Some."

Thankfully Chad took the terse answer as a hint, and he didn't press. He stayed quiet the rest of the drive.

Soon afterward, they pulled into Merritt, a tiny little cluster of buildings nestled in a dell that looked like something straight out of a fantasy movie—if it weren't for the garish Shell station sign poking over the trees that was visible for miles. Two gas stations, a McDonalds, a Burger King, a diner for fancy eating, and an All-N-All. That's what passed for a town this deep in the mountains.

Cameron pulled into the Shell station, and Russell pulled his truck in just behind her. The raised roof protected them from the rain while Russell broke open the pump and fiddled with the insides to make it produce gas. Cameron would happily have paid for it, but there was no attendant, and the card readers at the pumps were offline, just like most computers had been ever since the flare. Bill and Chad stayed in the Jeep and the truck while Cameron stood guard, rifle slung over her shoulder.

Soon both vehicles and all the extra gas can were full. They loaded up once more and drove the short distance to the All-N-All. The huge warehouse store had its lights off and the front sliding door closed. There was an overhang protecting the door from rain. They backed the vehicles up right underneath it, backs to the door.

"Okay," said Cameron. "We know what's on the list. Get our stuff, load up, and let's get back as quick as we can."

Everyone grabbed shopping carts and headed in. The All-N-All was considerably smaller than the one she was used to shopping in just outside of Seattle, but it had the same high roof and high stacks of bulk goods. Such supplies were even more in demand here, not because of penny-pinching suburban moms, but because here the customers were often stocking cabins for months at a time. Cameron headed over to the pharmacy, where she went down her shopping list of medicines, bandages and other supplies.

She saw a case of insulin in a refrigerator and picked it up. Staring at it in her hands, her thoughts drifted east, and she wondered what Piper was doing now. Probably complaining at something Alex was making her do in order to stay safe. A smirk tugged at Cameron's lips, but her eyes began to sting. She blinked hard, lifting her chin and taking a deep breath. The insulin case *clinked* as she dropped it in the cart.

Shouting erupted from the back of the All-N-All.

Cameron abandoned her cart and pounded for the rear of the store, slinging the rifle off her back. She skidded around the last corner and into the back aisle, raising the gun.

There stood Bill, brandishing his pistol. Russell and Chad were nowhere in sight. Ten feet away from Bill was a tall black man, hands raised in front of himself. He wore a backpack that bulged.

"Get the fuck down on the ground!" screamed Bill. "Lay down!"

"Don't shoot! I just came for food!" the man screamed back.

"Put your hands up and lay down!"

"Bill!" shouted Cameron. "Bill, stop!"

She sprinted for him, turning the rifle in her hands and raising the butt of it. But her movement made the man think Bill was distracted. He turned to flee for the back door of the All-N-All.

Bill's finger squeezed on the trigger three times. The stranger fell to the floor.

Too late, Cameron brought the butt of the rifle crashing into the back of Bill's head. He fell to the floor with a cry, the handgun falling from his grip and skidding across the floor. Chad and Russell finally appeared from the other side of the store.

Bill rolled over and glared up at her. "What the fuck?"

"Excuse me?" Cameron grabbed his shirt and dragged him to his feet, then threw him into a shelf of cereal. But then she thought of the man on the ground, and she ran past Bill to go to him.

Russell knelt by the man's side, three fingers to the neck. He looked up at her solemnly and shook his head.

"God damn it!" cried Cameron. She turned away and put her hands on her hips, raising her face and closing her eyes. *Calm. Breathe. Or you'll do something you shouldn't.*

She heard footsteps from Bill's direction and turned. She saw him walking towards his handgun, stooping to pick it up. His movements were slow, unhurried. He picked it up and shoved it in the back of his waistband.

Cameron approached him. He tensed, raising his hands to ward off a punch—but she took one hand and twisted it around behind his back until he squealed. With her other hand she took the pistol from his belt, and then she shoved him away.

"Give that back," said Bill, rounding on her.

"Like hell. You've lost firearm privileges."

"Give it back! It's *my* gun!"

Russell pushed past Cameron and seized the front of Bill's shirt, shoving him against the refrigerators that lined the back of the store. The glass cracked. "Shut up, asshole. You just killed a guy. You're lucky we don't just leave you here." He glanced over his shoulder at Cameron. "We're not just gonna leave him here, are we?"

Cameron had been thinking the same thing. That or giving Bill the same treatment he'd given the stranger. But she shook her head.

"No," she said, growling. "But he loses firearm privileges and he's off security. Get your ass out of here Bill. We'll get the supplies and load them up."

Russell shoved Bill toward the front of the store, and Bill slunk off, glancing back darkly over his shoulder every few steps. Cameron watched until he was out of sight. Then she glanced at Russell.

"You've got the key to your truck, right?" she said.

"Yeah. I can't believe that guy."

Cameron stalked off toward her shopping cart.

* * *

As they drove back into the cabin community, Cameron felt that something was wrong. That was confirmed as Scott came running towards her Jeep from the clubhouse, waving his arms in the air. Cameron pulled to a stop and rolled down the window.

"What is it?"

"Bettie's hurt," said Scott. "She's in your cabin, some guys attacked them and they—"

Cameron punched the accelerator, cutting off the last of his words. She sped the short distance to the cabin and screeched into the driveway, diving out of the driver's seat and running in through the front door.

Bettie lay on the couch in the living room. Her dark skin was a couple of shades paler. A white cloth was wrapped around her arm, and it was stained with blood. Hernando and Gina were with her.

"What happened?" said Cameron. She kept the panic out of her voice, but her hands were shaking as she began to unwrap the bandage.

"I'm fine," said Bettie, trying to push her away. But her touch was feather light. Chad came in the front door, looking at them all with wide eyes.

"What happened?" said Cameron, looking up at Hernando.

"We went out fishing," said Hernando. "I wasn't there, but some guys showed up. They tried to rob her and Scott, and—"

"Go get Scott," said Cameron.

"I'm here," said Scott, pounding in through the front door.

Cameron didn't look up at him, keeping her eyes on Bettie's arm. The bandage came off, revealing a deep cut across her bicep. Fresh blood seeped out as the cloth came off.

"How many were there?' said Cameron.

"Four. They found Bettie and Megan alone. I showed up a second—"

"Megan?"

"She's fine. When I showed up, a guy with a hatchet went for Bettie. I shot him, and the rest scattered."

Cameron motioned Hernando to her and put the bandage back on the arm. "Hold this on. Pressure. Hard."

Hernando pushed, and Bettie winced. "Sorry," he said.

"It's fine," said Bettie.

Cameron went and got her medical bag, digging through it to pull out a needle and thread, alcohol and swabs. She returned and pushed Hernando gently aside. Removing the bandage once more, she cleaned the wound and began to stitch it shut.

"Sorry I don't have anesthetic."

"I'm all right," said Bettie. "I've had kids. You know this ain't nothing compared to that."

Cameron allowed herself a smirk. Everyone waited in tense silence while she finished. When it was done, she wrapped the gauze right around the wound and taped it shut. She stood and went to the sink, washing the blood from her hands. She gave Scott a look.

"Bettie and Megan shouldn't have been alone," she said.

"I know," said Scott. He ducked his gaze, looking down at his feet with his hands on his feet. "I'm sorry."

"That can't happen again."

"It won't."

She sighed. "All right. It's hardly the worst thing to happen today."

Hernando frowned. "What happened? Someone get hurt while you all were out?"

Cameron's jaw clenched. "We'll talk about it later. Right now we need to figure out some things on security. Bill's not in charge anymore."

"Is he . . . ?" said Bettie.

"A goddamn idiot? Yes," said Cameron. "I said we'll discuss it. You need to rest. Hernando, help me get her to bed."

"I don't need to go to bed," said Bettie. "We're planting peas and I—"

"Doctor's orders," said Cameron. "Hernando."

They got her to bed despite her protests, and Cameron assigned Gina to watch her. Gina did it willingly, sitting by Bettie and striking up a conversation at once. That eased Cameron's mind a bit, made it easier for her to leave and not hover.

Back out in the living room, a few of the others had gathered. Russell and Ken had arrived, Bill in tow. He wasn't tied up or anything, but he definitely had an air of a defiant prisoner, and Russell beside him looked like a guard ready to restrain him at a moment's notice.

"Bill, you're off all work duties. You'll stay in your cabin and do whatever the hell you want, but you're off the teams. Food will be brought to you."

His eyes flashed. For a second she wondered if he was going to mouth off, and for another second she hoped he would. She wasn't too proud to admit to herself she'd enjoy kicking his ass. But instead he only scowled down at his boots.

"Russell, take him," said Cameron. "And when you get there, search his cabin. Make sure he doesn't have any more guns hidden away. If he does, take them. You're the new head of security. We'll figure out what to do with Bill later."

He blinked. "All right. But what about hunting?"

"We'll figure it out," said Cameron. "Take him, please."

Russell got Bill out. Cameron sighed and pinched the bridge of her nose. She gave herself a moment to breathe, and then she turned to address the rest of the group.

"We ran into someone else foraging for supplies. Bill shot him."

There was a collective intake of breath, and then the room went silent. After a moment, Ken spoke up. "Did the guy, like, attack you? Or—"

"He was running away," said Cameron. "He didn't do anything. Bill just shot him. Today some of us were attacked by other people desperate for food and supplies. They were the bad guys, and we kept ourselves safe. But we were the bad guys in someone else's story, and they weren't as lucky as Bettie was."

No one answered that. The rain intensified, slamming down on the roof like a swarm of locusts.

"The world's gone to hell, and I doubt this is the last time something like this is going to happen," said Cameron. "But we need to make sure we stay the good guys. As good as we can be. If we can help someone, we will. But mostly, we look out for each other. As of now, every one of you has a job: keep the community safe, and keep everyone in it alive. We all keep doing our jobs. But that's the reason behind everything we do. Got it?"

There were nods, murmurs of assent. She hadn't seen a group look so frightened since Iraq.

"We're going to be fine. As long as we look out for each

other, we're going to be fine. And I am going make sure of it. I promise."

She said the words without thinking, and her gut did a turn. There it was—a promise of safety, the thing she'd been avoiding ever since her first inkling that this crazy storm wasn't some temporary thing. But now it was said, and she couldn't take it back. They all looked at her, and she saw the relief spread across their faces, almost palpable.

"Let's get back to work," she said. "Come on, chop chop."

They stepped to it. She waited until everyone was gone. Then she sat in the living room's plush armchair, burying her face in her hands.

CHAPTER 22

A scream woke Cameron in the middle of the night.

She was awake like a shot, from a light sleep to standing in the middle of her bedroom in less than a second. Her brain took a second to process what had woken her, and then she ran to Bettie's room. But the old woman was sitting up in her bed, alive and unhurt, her eyes wide.

"Outside."

Cameron ran almost before Bettie said the word. She was in pajamas and didn't bother with anything heavier, just threw on a raincoat and boots with no socks. The screams had resumed, and they were clearly a man's—and far off. Almost without thinking about it, she scooped up her rifle as she ran out into the night. The rain had let up, thank god, and so she listened again.

Another scream, near the front gate. It was muffled. Inside a cabin. She ran for it.

Others appeared out of the darkness. She saw Scott, Wade, both of them running the same direction as her. Then Hernando, who carried a shotgun—he was on guard duty, Cameron remembered. He must have been on the other side of the cabin community when the noise started.

The screams were coming from Bill's cabin. The front door was slightly ajar. Even as she kicked it in, thoughts raced through her mind: *bear, wolf, looter?* She'd never been in the place before, and it stank. One more scream sounded, from the back on the first floor. The bedroom. She ran to it and kicked open the door.

There was Bill, lying on the bed. He was soaked in his own blood, clutching at his stomach.

Over him stood Gina, holding a carving knife. She, too, was blood-soaked, and Cameron knew at once that none of it was hers.

Cameron leapt at Bill and rolled him over, trying to get at the wound in his stomach. But Gina screamed and went at her, grabbing her shoulder with a free hand and trying to pull her off.

"Don't! Let him die! Let him die!"

Wade was there in an instant, pulling Gina away. In one smooth motion he snatched the knife from her hand and threw it at the wall. It embedded itself in the wood, quivering. Cameron tried to lift Bill's shirt off the hole in his stomach, but he was screaming and writhing too hard for her to see the wound.

"Hold still. Still!" said Cameron.

Bill ignored her. He looked past her to where Gina stood, now with Wade holding both her arms behind her back. He grimaced, blood bubbling up from between his teeth.

"Fucking bitch," he hissed. "Asssked for it."

He gurgled and went still. Cameron threw him on his back and made ready to give him CPR. Then she saw his stomach. And she saw, lower, more blood pouring from between his legs. Gina had cut something off down there.

She stood up and backed away. CPR wouldn't help this. The thing in the bed was a corpse now.

* * *

"Let go of her," Cameron told Wade.

"Cameron, she—"

"Now, Wade."

201

He released Gina's arms, and Cameron took the girl's hand. She led her out of the room and out of the house, away from the smell of Bill's mess, as well as his body. She didn't look behind to see if any of the men were following her—she hoped Hernando and Scott would take care of the mess, but right now there were living people who needed her more.

Time in the service had taught her a few things, and one of them was how to judge a scene with little more than a single glance. First impressions told her a lot now, and more details were becoming clear the more she took in. She'd seen the wild rage in Gina's eye when she stepped in the room, but also the fear. She'd seen Gina wince when Wade seized her. She saw the way Gina walked gingerly now, almost painfully, and felt how the girl's fingers trembled in her own.

Gina's cabin was open, but Cameron locked it once she'd brought the girl inside. She led Gina to the living room and sat her down.

"I need you to take off anything that's got blood on it," she said.

Gina looked up at her, eyes fearful and brimming with tears.

"Do you want me to leave the room?" said Cameron softly.

"I . . . no, it's okay," said Gina.

Slowly she got her clothes off, and Cameron inspected her. Bruises on her wrists and on one cheek. Minor scrapes here and there. Cameron took a deep breath.

"I need to check you out," she said.

Gina swallowed hard and shook her head.

"Gina, there could be lasting injuries. Tears, abrasions that could get infected. If that happens, I don't have the ability to treat it outside of a hospital. I have to prevent it now instead."

"I can't," whispered Gina.

Cameron knelt in front of her. She thought about putting

her hands on Gina's arms, but thought better of it. "I know," she said. "I know what it's like, but you have to take care of—"

"Has it ever happened to you?" snapped Gina. Cameron looked at her a long moment in silence. "Then how the hell do you know what it's like?" Her voice finally broke, and she started to cry.

"I was a medic in the Army," said Cameron. "It didn't happen to me, but it happened enough."

Gina didn't answer for a long moment, but only looked into Cameron's eyes. After what seemed like forever, she gave a loud sniff and nodded. Then she stood, peeling off her underwear.

"Lay down. I'll be as fast as I possibly can."

Gina complied, turning her head away to stare into the back of the couch. It didn't take Cameron as long as she feared, and there was no sign of anything that wouldn't heal easily with time. The second she was sure, she moved away quickly and took Gina's hand.

"Okay. You're fine. You're absolutely fine." She helped Gina sit up and grabbed a throw blanket to cover her with. Then she sat by the girl, let her bury her head in Cameron's shoulder, and cry.

When the heavy, wracking sobs had subsided, Cameron leaned away to look at Gina. The girl looked back above tear-streaked cheeks, on the verge of breaking down again any minute.

"I need to know what happened," said Cameron. "It's not fair to make you tell me, not right now. But the group is going to need answers. We need to handle this quickly, or it's going to be an even bigger problem."

"How? How could it be bigger?" said Gina. But she sniffed and swiped at her nose with the back of her hand. "I was on guard duty. Hernando and I were walking around the cabins, going in opposite directions. I was to the north when Bill stumbled at me out of the darkness. I almost shot him until

I realized it was him. Now I wish I had. I could smell he was drunk. I asked him what he was doing, but almost before I could say anything he hit the gun out of my hand and knocked me down. Then he . . ." There was a moment of silence before she continued. "I blacked out, or something. When I came to, I went straight to his house. You know the rest."

Cameron took a deep breath, releasing it slowly through her nose. "Okay. Okay."

"I'm not sorry," said Gina, her eyes flashing. "I'd do it again if I could, right now."

"I know," said Cameron. "But I need you not to say that. I need you not to say anything to anyone. Okay?"

"Why?" said Gina. "I don't care."

"Because they're going to want to punish you."

Gina shot up off the couch. "Punish *me?* What the hell do you mean—"

Cameron stood to face her, looking her right in the eye. "Gina. Stop it. What do you do for a living?"

For a moment Gina didn't answer. She crossed her arms. "I'm a dancer."

"Right. And not ballet. So you know how people are—men and women. You know this is never fair. We never get an even break at this stuff. Okay? If the whole world was normal, maybe we could try to do something about that. Right now, it's not, and we can't."

Shaking her head, Gina looked up toward the ceiling. "This is . . . that's bullshit."

"But you know it's true. So are you going to help me help you?"

The girl's shoulders sagged. She looked down at her feet, and suddenly her confidence, her anger seemed to flow out of her. "Yeah. Yeah, okay."

* * *

After swaddling her in a thick waterproof jacket, Cameron led her out of the house. Hernando was waiting outside, sitting on the front porch smoking a cigarette. As soon as they came into view, he stood and tossed it into the dirt.

"Gina. You okay? I mean . . . you know."

Gina nodded. Cameron drew Hernando's attention back to her. "Where is everyone?"

"The clubhouse. I was there for a second, but I felt ready to knock somebody the fu—I mean, I thought I should probably go."

"Smart," said Cameron wryly. "But let's head over there. And whatever you do, don't mouth off. Or hit anyone. Actually, stand behind me and don't say anything. Okay?"

Hernando fell into step behind her with an unintelligible mutter. It didn't exactly sound like agreement, but he wasn't arguing, either. Cameron noticed how he walked by Gina, but didn't try to touch her, even to put an arm around her shoulders. The kid was a lot smarter than he looked, and smarter than most people here wanted to give him credit for.

At the clubhouse she found about half the community gathered around. Wade stood at the head of the room, though he stepped aside the second he saw Cameron, making room for her to take her spot. Scott and Russell were there, as were Debbie, Aubrey, Jeremy, and Theresa.

"Hey Cam," said Wade.

"Let's get this over with," said Cameron. "We all know why we're here."

"Damn straight," said Jeremy. He pointed at Gina. "She just killed somebody."

Cameron met his eye for a moment, and then she looked around at everyone. "Does anyone here really think that's all? Or do you all know what actually happened tonight?"

No one answered for a second. Eventually it was Theresa's husband Jeremy who spoke up. "Yeah, but she still killed someone."

Theresa rounded on him. "Seriously? He raped her."

Cameron tensed, her gaze darting to Gina. The girl flinched and wrapped her arms around herself.

Jeremy had the decency to hang his head, but he still looked troubled. "Yeah, I know, but . . . you can't just kill people!"

Theresa snorted. "Really? I would."

There were a few murmurs throughout the room—some angry, but some of agreement. Cameron could feel the tension like a hand around her throat. She stepped forward, drawing everyone's attention back to her.

"Stop. We're not having a hypothetical argument here. We're dealing with what's actually happened. And what actually happened isn't just some random murder."

"We know, Cam," said Wade. "But at the same time . . . we can't *not* have rules, we can't just let people—"

"My name is Cameron," she said, fixing him with a look. "And I didn't say anything about rules, or *letting* people do anything."

His nostrils flared, but he only shook his head in silence. Jeremy spoke up again. "We could—we should exile her. You can't kill someone in the community and get away with it."

"We're not exiling her," said Cameron.

"But she *killed* someone," said Jeremy.

"Not 'someone,'" said Russell. "A goddamn rapist!"

His wife, Debbie, shook her head slowly. "I . . . that's awful, but she still murdered someone. Sending her away seems right. It's not like we're killing her."

"Except we would be killing her," said Bettie. She turned to Jeremy with her hands on her hips. "We kick her out, she's dead. So, an eye for an eye. Except it's not. We all know what happened tonight—*everything* that happened. And you all know that Bill shot someone, a total stranger, just today. So let's not pretend this is some random killing, like she's some sicko or even just someone on a power trip. That was Bill, not Gina. We gave him every chance, and maybe we gave him more chances than we should have. But Jeremy, you look me in the eye right now and tell me he didn't deserve to die."

The room went dead silent. Cameron winced internally. Bettie had said it. They all knew that they'd all been thinking it, but still, she'd said it. And Cameron felt it descending upon her like the weight of a truck: the world really *was* different now. This was a world where you talked about who did and didn't deserve life itself, where there were no cops or courts to take care of the messy, violent side of life that always lived at the edges of civilization. She wanted to run out of the clubhouse and jump in her Jeep, and then just drive east until she found Alex and Piper. Instead she stood stock still, matching Jeremy's gaze until at last he looked away.

"So what about the next person who deserves to die?" said Jeremy. "Anybody else on that list? You gonna send Gina after them?"

Cameron ignored that—it was the argument of a child losing an argument, and everyone there knew it. She looked at Wade instead. "I say Gina gets manual labor. Hard stuff, digging new fence posts, reinforcing the fences, digging any holes that need doing. Twelve-hour shifts under supervision, and reduced rations."

Wade snorted. "Getting real military around here."

"I'll do it," said Gina.

"We're not asking you," said Cameron immediately. She looked into Gina's eyes, trying to plead with her. *Please shut up. I'm doing everything I can.* Gina understood, or else she was hurt, because she looked back down at her boots. Either way, she wasn't talking any more, and Cameron was grateful.

"It's gotta be for a long time, though," said Jeremy. "At least . . . at least a month."

"I was thinking six weeks," said Cameron. "It would be a lot longer than that in a court, since it wasn't self-defense. But the courts also aren't good at recognizing mitigating circumstances. And we can be better than that. I mean, tell me, Jeremy—if it had been Theresa, wouldn't you have been the one holding the knife?"

He wouldn't meet her gaze. "Okay. Six weeks." He said it guiltily, as though he'd pushed for the extra time instead of Cameron. That was good. If he had thought Gina was getting off easy, he might have been vindictive in the future. Guilt had a way of making men much more forgiving.

"All right," said Cameron. "Then everyone get back to sleep. Wade, take Gina's spot on guard duty tonight."

"Yes, boss," said Wade. Cameron didn't correct him as she led Gina out of the clubhouse.

CHAPTER 23

Alex recognized Flathead territory almost the second they entered it. In an instant the land went from green and lush to brown, almost-desert, with only thin scrubs and trees clinging bitterly to the landscape. He shifted in his seat, suddenly a little uncomfortable.

"Welcome to the reservation," said Graham. "It doesn't normally look this bad. Just in summer."

"I think it's nice," said Piper. Alex could hear the lie in her voice, and he suspected everyone else in the truck could, too.

The truck was moving at barely a crawl, trundling along in four-wheel drive as it pushed its way through what seemed to be a solid wall of rain. Alex could have walked faster than the truck was moving—or at least, he could have in clear weather, if he didn't think the wind might pick him up and carry him off.

"Should we keep pushing on through this?" said Alex. "The wind's getting pretty bad."

"I'd rather not stop here if we can help it," said Graham. "We're almost to the reservation, and it's got much better protection against the weather. We'll be a lot safer there if anything really serious hits."

"Really serious?" said Piper. "Like what?"

"Like that," said Denny from beside her.

"Graham." Willow clutched at his sleeve.

Alex leaned over Piper, looking out the left-side window.

There, just a few miles away, the weather had begun to clear. But the rain hadn't ceased to fall—instead, it was being drawn into the whirling, sucking vortex of a tornado.

It touched down, and Alex saw a great plume of dirt and rock erupt into the air. It rose, and then touched down again. It was moving west, following their course—but it was also coming closer.

"We can't be here," said Graham. "Gotta get off the road. We're dead in this truck."

"We're dead outside of it, too," said Alex. "It's all open space. How close is the reservation?"

"Not close enough," said Graham.

"The bridge." Willow pointed through the windshield, and Alex saw it ahead through the rain. It was thick, four lanes wide, and looked decently new. Below it and off to the side was a narrow railroad trestle, running just a few yards above a rushing river below.

"Okay, hang on," said Graham. He stepped a little harder on the gas. The truck began to slip and slide, and he had to wrestle the steering wheel to keep them on course. But their speed increased, and soon they'd pulled up just in front of the bridge.

"Hurry," said Alex, throwing open his door. The twister was less than a mile away. "Come on, Piper. Max Come boy!"

He took her arm and hustled her towards the bridge. The slope leading down was muddy and slippery, and he barely tried to stay upright, half-sliding down it. Beneath the bridge were huge concrete walls that extended out along its length, forming a sort of man-made cave protected on all sides but the front. From the second he stepped inside it, the wind lessened, and the air was almost calm.

Graham and Willow huddled together, sitting against the wall, and Alex pressed close to them with Piper in between. Denny sat, too, a few feet to Alex's left.

"No use getting shy now," said Alex. He grabbed the hobo's sleeve and dragged him closer. "Come on."

Denny gave a brief chuckle as he pressed in closer. They waited like that in silence, watching the sky's fury rush by in the air just outside their little shelter. The hail was like a sheet of tiny bullets constantly firing, almost horizontal with the strength of the wind.

Then the wind increased even more, screaming like a demon from hell. The tornado was close. Maybe right above them. Alex clutched Piper closer, and held tightly to Max's collar. He could feel the wind tugging at him, at all of them, almost strong enough to pick up one of the adults. He shuddered and tried to banish an image from his mind: Piper, out in the gale, swept away by the fury of the storm.

A blast of sound struck them, and they all jumped. There came a great rending scream of steel, and then another crash. Alex recognized it the second time: it was the truck. The twister had picked it up and flipped it over—twice, from the sound of it. Another great screaming, scraping shriek, and then silence.

THOOM

Across the river, the truck came careening down out of the sky. It struck the bridge's very edge and spun, tumbling far, far down into the river below. It only barely missed the railroad trestle, which extended out almost from the mouth of their little cave.

"I'm sorry," said Alex.

"Don't be," said Graham. "It was a piece of junk. And if we manage to survive all this, the insurance payout's gonna be great."

Alex knew it was funny, but he couldn't bring himself to laugh.

* * *

The tornado passed, and the wind began to lessen slightly. But when Piper asked Alex if they should move on, he shook his head.

"Now that we're here, and since the truck is gone, we should stay. There might be another break in the rain, and when there is, it'll be safer to keep going."

Willow nodded. "If the rain lightens up, we can reach the town in just a few hours. But with the weather like this, it could take a few days."

"And what if it doesn't stop raining?" said Piper.

Alex shrugged. "Then I'd rather try to make that journey after a good night's sleep."

Of course, a *good* night's sleep wasn't going to happen. But as the day waned, and the sun's pale glow through the clouds began to vanish, Alex readied himself to build the two tents. He realized he wouldn't be able to stake them down, here in this concrete cave, and he briefly considered pitching them out in the open instead. But then he realized that the wind would be worse out there, canceling the benefits of the stakes. They'd have to rely on their body weight to hold them in place.

Just as he'd slung the backpack off his back and started to dig through it, he looked up and noticed Denny. The hobo was sitting up straight, his brow furrowed, head cocked like he was listening.

"Denny?" said Alex. "What is it?"

"Sky," said Denny. "Sky, and the . . . do you hear something?"

Alex froze. He listened, but he couldn't hear it. Yet now that Denny had spoken, he could almost *sense* something—a rumble underfoot. His mind flashed back to Broadus.

"Flood," he said.

Piper clutched his arm.

"We have to cross the bridge," said Graham.

"We should climb up," said Willow. "Let's go back where it's—"

"The bridge could get wiped out," said Denny. "Then we're stranded. Come on. The railroad trestle."

Alex's eyes went to it. It was just a few yards away. He saw Denny's point immediately: climbing up the hill to run across the bridge would take minutes they didn't have. But they could book it across the trestle in no time. He snatched Piper's hand and pulled her forward.

"Dad, wait!"

He stopped, and she reached for her backpack. She'd taken it off and put it on the ground. He shuddered, realizing he'd almost left half her meds behind.

"Come on!" he said, pulling her on again. Max running ahead and running back to them.

They all ran like hell, their feet slipping in the mud. Somehow Alex remained upright until he reached the trestle, and then there was a low railing he could clutch. A wild, insane part of his mind said they shouldn't be walking on railroad tracks. But the trains were dead now, and maybe would be forever.

Movement caught his eye, and he looked towards it. The river ran straight for a mile or more to the north, where it bent away west.

Around the bend, a solid wall of water came rushing. In front of it came a storm of debris, torn trees and rocks and dirt. Alex saw a car in the mix.

"Move!"

They redoubled their pace, uncaring that it made them slip and slide as long as they kept moving forward. Alex was in the lead with Piper, with Graham and Willow just behind. Denny brought up the rear.

He tried not to look at the river. So he didn't see the tree until the instant it came crashing into the trestle.

BOOM

The whole trestle swayed, and Alex fell to hands and knees. The tracks bent till they were nearly vertical, throwing him into the railing, which had turned into a floor.

Piper's hand slipped from his. She screamed as she fell.

"No!" he screamed, reaching.

If she'd hit the water, she'd have been swept away in an instant. Instead, by some miracle, she landed on the edge of the riverbank. Her backpack wasn't so lucky—it fell from her grip and vanished into the water.

Alex's outstretched hand was at least six feet above hers. He withdrew his hand and prepared to dive over the railing for her. It was a madman's plan, but he had to try something.

But Denny hadn't fallen, and he moved before Alex could. The hobo dove over the railing to land on the riverbank beside Piper. Max at the top of the bank barking frantically.

Just as she fought to her feet, he seized her under the armpits. Then, with a strength it didn't seem like he should possess, Denny threw her straight up. She screamed and flailed—and Alex snatched her whipping hand. He heaved, and she landed on the trestle.

And in the exact same instant, a rock came flying from the water and struck Denny in the chest. It was moving as fast as a cannonball—Alex could almost hear the ribs shatter.

Denny fell beneath the surface. The river swept him away in an instant.

Piper screamed. But Alex picked her up and dragged her on. The end of the trestle was only a few paces away. They reached it and fell onto the land on the other side, Graham and Willow only a second behind.

The river struck the trestle. Its anchors were torn from the earth. Alex hid his face and put an arm over Piper as they went slicing through the air, but they were far out of reach. The metal structure vanished into the water and went rushing away south, following Denny's corpse.

CHAPTER 24

Piper wanted to go find him. Even if it was just to find his body, she said. They should bury him, at least. But Alex put his foot down, even though he almost had to drag her away at the end. They'd never find Denny, and they couldn't afford the time they'd waste trying. Alex knew it, and he pulled Piper away from the river knowing it—but he couldn't help the pain he felt deep in his chest, or the lead weight of his limbs that seemed harder to move the farther they went.

Less than a week, he thought. *Less than a week we knew the guy.* But Denny's loss had hit him harder than most of the family he'd lost in his life, other than his parents.

Graham and Willow led them down the road. The couple hadn't been very talkative before, but after losing Denny they went dead quiet. Graham just walked on, head down and hands shoved in his jacket pockets, while Willow followed behind. Piper fell into step with Alex at last, though she kept crying long after the river was lost from sight behind them.

Alex felt a little guilty about how quickly his thoughts turned to the road ahead, but he was filled with a sudden sense of urgency and dread at the loss of Piper's backpack. He hadn't put all his eggs in one basket—not all of her meds were in her pack, and he had some in his own. But he needed to count it up and see how long it would last. If he remembered correctly, he'd put enough in his pack to make it to the cabins—if all went well. But he'd long ago given up on the notion that nothing else would go wrong on their journey. That was a lie, and the evidence lay behind them, was maybe even now washing up on the banks of the river.

At some point, Graham called them all to a stop. They stood outside a little home, and with some shock Alex realized it was Graham's and Willow's. Half-glimpsed through the storm, Alex saw the shapes of other homes close by, the scattered dwellings of some small town. He hadn't even realized they were on the reservation. There had been no clear demarcation point, no line or border that marked this part of the land as being any different. Or maybe there had been, and Alex had just missed it. He'd barely looked up as they trudged along, and when he had, it was hard to see very far in any direction through the pouring rain and the mist.

The house was simple inside, and it felt warm, though that was only because the wind stopped blasting them the second they stepped inside. Graham went to turn on the heater while Willow went to the kitchen to make everyone food. Soon their bellies were full of sandwiches and coffee, and then they simply waited for the water to dry out of their clothing and hair.

Before long there came a knock at the front door. Alex jerked up, instinct making him nervous. But when Graham answered, it was only another native couple on the other side of the door. They were surprised to see Alex and Piper inside, and they stayed on the doorstep. But Graham spoke soft words Alex couldn't hear, and the uneasy looks of the other couple softened. After a few seconds of whispered conversation, they clapped Graham on the shoulder, waved to Willow, and left.

The house was silent again. This time, it stayed that way for every longer.

It was Piper who broke the quiet next. She shifted on the couch, frowning and blushing all at once. "Um, where's your restroom?" she said softly. "I need to . . ."

Willow jumped up at once. "I'll show you. I have more pads." Piper's had been in the bag that went into the river.

"Thank you," muttered Piper, refusing to meet anyone else's gaze as she followed the woman into the back of the house.

When the girls were gone, Graham fixed Alex with a look. "You two can stay here if you want. As long as you need to."

"Thank you," said Alex. "But I don't think we'll stay long. My wife's still waiting. All of . . . this—" he waved his hand generally at the world outside the shuttered windows "—is only going to keep getting worse. I want to keep Piper safe, but I'm afraid for Cameron too, and I can keep them both safer if we're all together."

"Of course," said Graham, giving a slow nod. "You'll need a car, though. I'll hop on the HAM—phones are still down—and see if we can find anyone who's got a spare they can lend you."

Alex shot up in his seat. "You have a radio?"

* * *

"Alex, is that—?"

He'd been trying for fifteen minutes, and now he clutched the receiver like a lifeline. Piper had been sitting beside him, and she shot bolt upright in her chair. "Hello? Who's that?" said Alex.

"Alex, can you hear—?" The voice on the other end was shouting now—and suddenly Alex recognized it. He almost burst out laughing.

"Bettie, is that you?"

"You can hear me? I don't know how this thing—"

"Yes! Yes, I can hear you. You just—hold the button down until you're completely finished talking."

"Like—"

"A little longer."

"How about now?"

"Yes, you've got it."

Piper took the receiver from his hand and pressed the button. "Hi Bettie!"

"Lord above, is that Piper?"

"Yes!" Piper giggled. "It's me. How are you?"

"I'm fine, honey, just fine."

"Piper." Alex took the receiver back from her. "Bettie, is Cameron there?"

"Not right now, but I can get her. She's out with some of the others. I forget if she's hunting or building a fence. I've mostly been keeping to the garden. It's dang hard to grow anything in all this rain, and if I turn my back on those plants for a second they start trying to die on me. But heck, you don't want to hear about me right now. I'll be right back with Cameron."

The line went silent. Piper almost bounced in her seat. But the silence stretched long, until she was slumped in her seat and Alex's feet were tapping with impatience.

Almost an hour later, the radio crackled to life again. "Alex?"

His eyes stung, and he tried not to let Piper see it. "Cam?"

"Oh my god. Are you all right?"

Piper snatched the receiver again. "Mommy?"

* * *

"Piper."

Cameron's voice went thick, her throat constricting around the words, and tears sprang to life in her eyes. It wasn't weeping, not quite, but it was close enough. Bettie had been standing in the doorway behind her. Cameron heard the slow creak of hinges, followed by the *click* of the door closing.

"Mom, oh my god, Mom, I miss you." Even through the static of the radio, Cameron heard tears in her daughter's voice.

"Jesus, I miss you too, sweetie," said Cameron. "Are you safe? Are you okay?"

"We're—we're safe, Mom. I'm okay, but—"

The line went silent.

* * *

"Don't talk about Denny," said Alex. "I'll tell her, but right now she needs to know that you're alive, and that neither one of us has been hurt. Let me tell her about . . . about *that*, in a minute, okay?"

Cameron's voice crackled from the speaker again. "Piper? Alex? Are you there?"

Piper swallowed hard and nodded at Alex, swiping at her eyes. "I'm here. Sorry. We're fine. Are you okay?"

"Don't worry about me, sweetie."

That sent alarm bells ringing in the back of Alex's mind, and his hackles rose. Why hadn't Cameron just said *Yes, I'm okay?*

But Piper didn't notice, and her smile broadened. "I can't wait to see you. I think we're getting close." She looked quizzically at Alex, and he nodded. "Yeah, Dad says we are."

"I'm so glad, honey," said Cameron. "Are you taking your meds?"

Piper rolled her eyes. "I'm with Dad. Do you think he'd let me forget?"

There was a moment of silence, and Alex guessed that Cameron was laughing. It was confirmed when she spoke again, and Alex could hear the smile in her voice. "I guess he wouldn't."

Alex put a hand on Piper's shoulder. "Okay, sweetie. I need you to wrap up so Mom and I can talk alone."

She nodded. "I'm gonna let you and Dad talk, Mom. We'll see you soon. Okay?"

"Okay," said Cameron. "I love you. So much."

219

"I love you, too." Piper handed the receiver to Alex and left the room.

Alex rose to close the door behind her before sitting down and picking up the receiver again.

"Cameron, what's wrong?"

* * *

Cameron's heart skipped a beat. She kept her tone carefully neutral as she pressed the button to talk. "What do you mean?"

The line was silent for a while. When Alex spoke again, it wasn't with an answer. "Come on. What's happening?"

She sighed. "What did I say?"

"It was when Piper asked if you were okay. Did something happen?"

Cameron pinched the bridge of her nose. "Nothing serious. I mean—no, it *was* serious. But it's okay. I've got it under control."

"Well *that's* reassuring."

"Do you remember Bill? The groundskeeper who worked here?"

"Holy—why past tense? What happened?"

She had to fight with two warring emotions—anxiousness at confessing that something bad had happened, and anger at Bill's memory. "Short version? He died."

"The storm? Wild animal?"

Gina flashed through Cameron's mind. How the heck could she explain *that* over such a long distance?

"Not exactly."

"Someone in the cabin community?" Alex's voice had risen half an octave.

"Look—I know how it sounds. But it's complicated. It wasn't self-defense, but it was close."

"Cameron—"

"Please. Don't . . . can you just trust me? It's under control. Everyone here is safe, now. I'm more worried about you two."

The line was silent for a long, long time. Long enough that Cameron wondered if they'd somehow lost the connection. But eventually Alex spoke—and to her relief, it seemed he'd chosen to let the matter rest. At least for now.

"The road's been rough."

"Are either of you hurt?"

"Not us." He sighed. "We met someone on the road. A— well, a hobo, honestly. But he was decent, and he traveled with us for a while. Name of Denny."

Cameron stared incredulously at the receiver in her hand, as though it were her husband's face. If she'd been asked to write a list of activities that were distinctly un-Alex, traveling cross-country with a homeless man would have been pretty close to the top of that list. But the way Alex was so reluctant to talk about the man . . . "What did he do?"

Static. Then, "He died. Today. Or, yesterday? I can barely even tell when the days pass any more."

The tone of his voice was a curious thing: it threw Cameron right back into her days in the service. It was the low, hollow, shell-shocked sound of someone who'd watched a war buddy turned to red paste by an IED. One minute there, the next—not even a body to bury. She had no idea what had happened between Alex and Piper, and this Denny. But she could hear the weight of it in Alex's words.

"I'm sorry, baby."

"It's okay." His voice gave lie to the words, even more emotional than it had been when they first got on the line together. "I don't—we barely even knew him, you know? And then, bam."

"How's Piper taking it?"

"Harder than I am."

That wasn't good. "Make sure you spend time with her.

She might want to talk about it, or she might not. Give her the option."

"I know." Static for a moment, or it might have been a sigh. "We're close, but I'm worried. It seems like every mile is harder than the last."

"Maybe you two should stay there. Wait for this to blow over."

"Cameron. Come on. I haven't seen anything that indicates any of this is going to blow over. Have you?"

She stared at the receiver, trying to think of an answer. Nothing came.

"Are you there?"

"I'm here. I just . . . okay. Where are you, anyway? How close?"

"A Flathead reservation in Montana. If things were normal, we wouldn't even be talking because I'd already be driving. It's only seven hours away from you on a clear day with no traffic. But right now . . ."

She sighed. "So, what? Two days? Three?"

"Should be."

Cameron frowned before realizing he couldn't see it. "Don't *should* me. You two need to get here."

"Yes ma'am."

She fought the smile. "I'm serious. Get here."

"Yes *ma'am*. I will. I promise."

"Okay." She leaned back in the chair, swiping the back of a hand across her forehead. "Okay. I can't wait."

"Me either. And now I should go. We've got to get some rest so we can figure out how we're getting the rest of the way here. I'm going to have to figure out a way to buy a car with no money."

"Give them an I.O.U. Tell them you'll give them three times what the car's worth when you can come back after the storm."

"Yeah . . . I'm not going to look a Native American in the

face, on their own land, and promise them, "No, seriously, I'm *definitely* going to pay you later for something you give me today.' I have a feeling we used up all our chances at that some couple of hundred years ago."

Cameron snorted. "Maybe steal a horse?"

"That is the opposite of a better solution."

Finally she laughed, and heard him on the other end doing the same thing. "I love you."

"I love you, too."

The radio clicked off. But she listened to the static for a long time. She was supposed to be doing something, patrol, or hunting, she'd forgotten. But she didn't make one move away from the radio.

CHAPTER 25

Cameron woke the next morning feeling better than she had since the first call she'd received from Alex, back when he was in New York. She was still in the cabin community. The sky still threatened a constant storm, still broke into rain every few hours, when it let up at all. But now she went about her day with an ear cocked, expecting at any minute to hear the thunder of a car's engine approaching the cabin community gate—a car that would carry Alex and Piper, and bring an end to the waking nightmare she'd been living for weeks. It had begun to wear on her, a constant presence at the back of her mind even when she wasn't thinking directly about it. It was only now that the ever-present fear had vanished that she knew it had been there at all, and what a weight it had been.

The mood lasted for a good couple of hours, until Wade approached her with a dark look on his face.

"Got a minute?" he said.

She'd been heading for the clubhouse. Scott was on watch there, and she was his morning relief. Raising an eyebrow, she motioned for Wade to follow.

"With an expression like that, I guess I have to. What's up?"

He surveyed the cabins for a moment before he answered. It took a moment for Cameron to realize he was looking to make sure they wouldn't be overheard. "Someone stole my camera."

A tremor passed through Cameron's stomach—a feeling not of an immediate danger, but one approaching quick, and difficult to see. The same way she'd felt when she heard Bill's screams, and *knew* this wasn't just another false scare.

"What makes you think it was stolen? Maybe you misplaced—"

He shot her a look, and she fell silent. She respected him enough, at least, to not treat him like that much of an idiot.

"Okay. So, what?"

"What do you mean, what?"

Cameron spread her hands. "What do you want to do? People are already worked up after what happened with Bill and Gina. I don't want to go on a witch hunt for your camera."

"So, what? We just let whoever stole it, keep it?" He slammed his right fist into his other hand. "Not a goddamn chance."

Cameron looked away, her mind racing. She didn't like the idea of a thief running loose any more than Wade did, but she didn't know how to go about finding one. But Wade's next words threw all such thoughts from her mind.

"Besides, it's not like we don't know who took it."

She heard the words, and thought about them, and then she thought about them again. Each time, she tried not to hear the meaning she knew was behind them, but each time, she couldn't hear anything else. So she met Wade's gaze and narrowed her eyes.

"Oh? Care to explain that?"

If she was expecting him to back down, she was disappointed. He only folded his arms and scowled harder. "I don't need to. You know who I'm talking about. There's a suspect list of one."

"Spell it out for me."

"You want that? Fine. Hernando."

"The Mexican."

"The Mexican *teenager* who showed up looking like a gangster and talks like—"

"Yeah, I'm gonna cut the racism off right about there. If that's all you've got, this conversation is over."

"Tell me I'm wrong. Who else would do it?"

Cameron rolled her eyes and turned away. But even as she did, and no matter how much she hated herself for thinking it, she found herself agreeing with him. Who else *would* have done it? Putting race aside, everyone else in the cabin community was upper-middle class, with no possible reason to steal a camera. Anyone who had a property here dropped enough in monthly bills to pay for five cameras like Wade's. Everyone but Bettie, but that thought almost made Cameron laugh out loud.

Except . . . She turned on the spot. "It easily could have been Bill. He was way more of a—"

"I've used it since Bill died," said Wade.

"Shit." She put her hands on her hips and turned away again. "Shit."

"See? Who else, Cam? There's a reason neither one of us can put even one person on the list."

"Let's entertain the notion for one second. Just one," said Cameron. "You think he wouldn't guess that we'd find out about it? The cabin community is tiny. There's only so many people it could be. He'd know we'd suspect him."

"So what? Thieves always steal in their own communities, even when they've got a record. Even when they know the cops are gonna come ask them first."

"We're not cops."

"And maybe that's the problem. Maybe he thinks we wouldn't go looking if something went missing." Wade cracked his knuckles and looked towards Cameron's house—where Bettie and Hernando, along with some others, were working even now. "Punk's got another think coming."

Cameron wanted to send him away, to tell him she'd handle it on her own. But she couldn't think of a good excuse to do so, and she knew that in his current mood, Wade wouldn't agree no matter what. So she thrust a finger under his nose to draw his attention back to her.

"We confront him, and we search his stuff for the camera. If we don't find it immediately, we search everyone else's stuff just the same. We don't look for more secret hiding places. Everyone gets the same treatment."

"And if he has it, we—"

"If he has it, you don't touch him," said Cameron. "Is that explicitly clear?"

"I'm not gonna let him—"

"You're not letting anyone do anything. I get your word, right now, that you don't touch him, or I don't take one step towards the kid, and I'll stop you if you try."

Wade's nostrils flared. A deep red began creeping up his neck. "You want him to get—"

"No. Nope. Stop. This is non-negotiable. If your answer is no, I make a public announcement to the whole community. I tell them the camera's gone, and whoever stole it can leave it anonymously on my back porch, with no consequences. That's your only other option."

He fumed, shoulders hunching forward, the color in his cheeks darkening further. She met his look with one of steel. For half a heartbeat, she thought it wouldn't be enough. That it would come to a fight, turning all their months of sparring into mere rehearsal for the real deal.

Wade slammed his fist into his hand again. Then he let loose a heavy *whoosh* of breath, all the contents of his lungs dumped at once.

"Fine," he growled. "I don't touch him. But he doesn't get off free, either."

Cameron nodded slowly. "Good enough. Let's go."

* * *

227

They entered the back yard together, Wade just half a step behind Cameron. Hernando was helping Bettie rig up a tarp roof over the garden. The rains were too heavy, and threatened to flood all the plants they were growing, so the roof was meant to help keep them at least somewhat dry.

As soon as Hernando saw Cameron and Wade together, he stopped moving. Slowly his hands lowered from where they were holding up the tarp, and an expression of quiet resolution slid over his features.

Shit, thought Cameron.

But she kept the thought well contained as they crossed the garden. Bettie saw them halfway across, and she must have seen something in Cameron's face—or maybe Wade's—because she stopped moving, too. Naomi and Kira were there, too, and they picked up on the mood, so that by the time Cameron and Wade stood in front of Hernando, the whole back yard had gone graveyard-still.

"Hernando," said Cameron.

"What's up?" Hernando didn't look afraid, or angry. Just calm. Way too calm.

"That's our question," said Cameron. "Anything you want to tell us? If so, I'd much rather you volunteer it."

"Before we have to beat it out of you," snarled Wade.

"Wade."

"Whoa, *what* is going on?" said Bettie. She stepped in front of Hernando, putting her hands on her hips to match Cameron's.

"He stole my camera." Wade thrust forth a finger, pointing right under Hernando's nose. The kid didn't even flinch.

Cameron seized the hand and pushed it down. "Hernando, I'm asking you. Anything you want to say?"

"Do I gotta say anything?"

Wade took half a step forward. "No one's reading you any Miranda rights."

"Did you take Wade's camera?" said Cameron.

Bettie looked at her, horrorstruck. "You can't be serious. You believe this?"

Cameron shook her head. "I'm asking."

"Oh yeah?" said Hernando. "Why you asking me? Why not her?" He pointed over Cameron's shoulder, where Naomi and Kira were standing mute and frozen.

"Get real," snarled Wade.

"What, I look like someone who'd steal a camera? Is that it?"

"If you'd show us your stuff," said Cameron. "Your backpack, whatever."

Wade looked past Hernando, and his eyes narrowed. "Hey, there's your backpack right now. Maybe it's in there. Why don't we—"

He tried to step past the group, but Bettie scooted over and put herself in front of him, both hands up in front of his chest.

"You hold up!" she shouted. "Nobody's searching anybody's things. You ain't the cops."

"There are no cops," said Wade. "Just us. And this punk—"

"I think a lot higher of this punk than I think of you right now."

Cameron wanted to agree with Bettie. Wade wasn't helping anything, the way he was acting. But she couldn't shake one persistent thought that nagged at the back of her mind: every time Hernando had lied since he arrived, it was easy to tell. The kid was a terrible bluff. And he still hadn't denied stealing the camera.

She caught his look and forced him to look her in the eye. "Hernando. If you didn't take the camera, just say so."

His nostrils flared in anger. But before he could speak, Wade interjected. "Who cares what he says? Let's just look in his backpack. It's *right there.*"

Cameron shook her head. "Hernando—"

"Dammit, Cam!" said Wade, rounding on her. "Even if

he says no, what then? We're gonna search everyone's stuff, right? *Right?*"

"We'll find your camera," said Cameron.

"Then look!"

Cameron met Bettie's eyes. The old woman looked doubtful now. Unsure. She glanced briefly at Hernando, and the corners of her mouth turned down.

"Hernando," said Cameron. "Open your backpack. Please."

Hernando's mouth twitched. Then he looked skyward and shook his head slightly. Turning, he went to the backpack and unzipped it. Then he reached inside and pulled out Wade's camera.

"Motherf—" Wade lunged for him.

"Wade!"

Cameron caught the back of his shirt and dragged him around. But he slapped away her hand, forcing her to catch his wrist to restrain him. He flipped his arm around hers, and her grip loosened. But she'd managed to place herself in between him and Hernando. He stopped dead, shoulders heaving, chest rising and falling with furious pants.

"You don't touch him," said Cameron. "That was the deal."

"He stole—"

"I was right here. Doesn't matter. You don't touch him."

It was more than a desire for some kind of civil justice that drove Cameron to make her stand. She'd fought with Wade—just sparring, but plenty of it. He had a streak of something, something she recognized from the service. It wasn't a mean streak, exactly, but something less emotional. She knew if he got his hands on Hernando, he'd take the kid apart.

Bettie moved, and for a second Cameron thought she was going for Wade. But she strode right up to Hernando and slapped him right across the face.

"You damn fool!" she shouted. "What in the sam hell were you thinking?"

Hernando blinked at her, rubbing his cheek. He opened his mouth, and for one second, Cameron thought he was actually going to answer. But then his gaze slid past her, locking on Cameron and Wade. His face hardened.

"Like I'm gonna say crap to these two. They already made up their minds about me."

"You'll explain whatever we want you to, punk!" said Wade.

"Wade, enough." Cameron sighed and pinched the bridge of her nose. "Hernando, you're on half rations. And you're on the same work schedule as Gina for a week."

"Yo, what?" said Hernando. "She *killed* someone. I get the same treatment?"

"For a week," said Cameron. "Gina's on until we decide otherwise. You want to complain? Don't take people's shit."

She went to him and took the camera, then turned to put it in Wade's hands. She searched his face until he finally met her gaze.

"We're done here," she told him.

He snorted. For one second his eyes flitted to Hernando before darting away. Then he turned on his heel and marched off. Cameron watched him go, hoping that was the end of it, knowing somehow that it wasn't.

CHAPTER 26

It turned out that Alex didn't need to do any bargaining at all. Graham went and spoke to the other family, the ones who'd come briefly to visit when Alex and Piper first arrived. When Graham returned, he had the keys to a car. It was a beat-up old '93 Toyota Camry, its heater didn't work, and one of its rear doors wouldn't unlock. But Alex didn't care about any of that, since it had four wheels and would roll on them. The gift left him with a hefty load of guilt, and he swore up and down he'd return to the reservation and repay them as soon as he could. Graham nodded and accepted the promise, but he regarded Alex with a cool expression. Alex wondered if the man really believed him.

He spent some time studying a Thomas Guide before they set out on the road, and planned a winding route that would take them about a hundred miles north of Spokane. Alex still wasn't willing to get within sight of a city. He shuddered to think what they must be like by now—all the same situations he'd seen out in the open country, but playing out on narrow streets chock full of humanity. No. No, they'd give Spokane a wide berth.

Just as they were loading up the car and getting ready to go, Willow appeared from the garage lugging something big. As soon as he saw it, Alex ran to help—but as soon as it was in his hands, he paused and studied it. It was some kind of hand pump, with about a dozen feet of hose and a main unit that was bigger than his head.

"For gas," said Willow. "You should need about four tanks to get where you're going, but you've been on the road—gas stations are going to be abandoned. You can use this to take it from their ground wells. I hope you know how to work it?"

"I can figure it out," said Alex. "And thank you."

Her gaze drifted over his shoulder to where Piper was waiting in the car, sheltering from the rain. "Just make sure you get home safely."

They set off with Alex feeling better than when they'd arrived, but with a new worry: with half of Piper's meds lost in the flash flood, he was concerned they might not have enough to finish the trip. But he was out of any ideas about how to get more. Any big stores were likely to be taken over like the All-N-All they'd visited earlier. Small towns seemed a risky proposition—they might be like Broadus, or they might be full of paranoid country folk who were dang proud of their impressive gun collections, and Denny wasn't there to give his recommendation or advice. Alex resolved to keep an eye out for any place that might have more meds, and in the meantime to press on as quickly as he could, in hopes of reaching the cabins before they ran out.

Unfortunately, they weren't able to move nearly as fast as he wanted. The storms weren't quite as bad as they'd been under the bridge a few days ago, but they were close. He didn't feel comfortable at anything above half highway speed, for fear that any slight tap on the brakes would send them careening off the road again. And slow going meant less fuel efficiency, so their gas problem would be even worse than he'd planned.

On the first day, he called it quits at the apex of their northward journey, just across a lake the map said was called Pend Oreille and within sight of a town called Sandpoint. He didn't risk driving into the town, and made sure they parked overnight on a very, very high piece of land—he wasn't taking any chances of another flood making things any worse than they already were.

They slept an uncomfortable night in the car—or at least Alex did. Piper climbed in the back seat and curled up with her head on Max's belly. The dog's presence eased Alex's mind a bit. No one was going to sneak up on the car while Max was in it. But no matter how far he leaned back his seat, no matter how he twisted and turned, he couldn't force his body to drift off until well into the night, and he woke early in the morning feeling supremely unrested.

The first thing he did was drive along Sandpoint's outskirts looking for a gas station. He found one at last, a non-chain joint that was probably locally owned. No one challenged them when he parked next to the ground tanks. A socket wrench and crowbar got the manhole-like cover off, and he found the insert point for the pump easily enough. The hand crank clearly wasn't well-used, and his arms had begun to burn by the time he finally saw the liquid passing through the pipe. But the well was close to full, and soon the car's tank was full. He had an extra little five-gallon canister, and he filled that too before tossing it in the trunk. Then they hit the road again.

It was half an hour later before Alex realized that Piper hadn't asked him about stealing the gas. The thought was a little disquieting, and he did his best to push it away.

Piper asked for a bathroom break just before they stopped. She'd been taking them every few hours to change her pads, always an awkward and uncomfortable affair, seeing as how Alex still wasn't willing to let her wander too far out of his sight, and the sudden dearth of publicly available restrooms. Now, though, they were in luck—as the sun set, they found another abandoned gas station, and this one had a toilet that didn't make Piper want to puke when she saw it. As she ducked into the restroom, Alex repeated his performance with the station's underground tank.

But when he tried to pump it, nothing happened. Piper finished and returned to him, and still Alex hadn't pumped so much as a drop into the car. Quickly he went to the other underground tanks and tried them, but they were all empty as well.

He sat back on his heels, draping his arms over his knees, and gave a little snort of laughter. "Guess someone got paranoid and stocked up on fuel."

Piper shoved her hands in her pockets. She glanced at Max, who was poking his nose around the station's dumpster not far away. "What are we going to do?"

"We'll sleep now and find another place in the morning, like we did today. It makes sense that someone would steal from the stations, but most of them won't have been touched."

The next morning, however, he found that the opposite was true. It seemed the station he'd found in Sandpoint was an exception. He managed to trundle the car to five gas stations, but all of them had been drained dry. Finally, on the sixth, he found a ground tank that hadn't been touched. He filled the car and the extra canister, a flood of relief washing through him.

"See?" he told Piper. "No sweat."

She didn't look very reassured, and neither was Alex.

As the day neared its end, Alex started pulling off the road every few miles to check the gas stations. But every one he checked was empty, except for a few that were jealously guarded by hard-eyed men with shotguns. Alex took one look and drove right by those, figuring it wasn't worth the risk of trying to barter. Not that they had any supplies they could afford to trade, anyway.

He went to sleep that night reassuring himself that he'd find another full station the next day. Morning proved him a liar. After trying every station within a reasonable distance, he set out on the 2 freeway heading west, his knuckles white on the wheel and a grim set to his jaw. Piper had to know what was wrong, but she remained mercifully silent.

The car finally guttered and died just before noon, right

after they'd passed a town called Reardan. They were in Washington. They'd crossed almost the entire country. But they still had a whole state to cross.

Max paced around the car while Alex loaded up their supplies into two backpacks again. After all the times he'd had to do it on the trip, the routine came quickly, and it afforded him some extra attention to spend counting Piper's meds. They were low. She'd be fine for now, but he'd have to find more long before they reached the cabins. If he didn't, she'd never make it.

Enough of that. He wouldn't let himself go down that road. They'd handled everything they'd come across so far. He could get some stupid insulin. He *would*, because the alternative was unthinkable.

Piper stood beside the trunk of the car, her hood up, her eyes lowered to the road. Alex caught her eye and gave her a smile.

"You okay walking, princess?"

She didn't even roll her eyes. "Sure."

He went over to her and wrapped an arm around her shoulders. "Just for a little while. We'll find something else, just like we have before—a car, a truck. Heck, maybe I'll steal a bus. We'll cruise up to the cabins in a tour bus. How about that?"

It worked, but barely. Her lips summoned a quivering smile, but her eyes couldn't quite join in. "Okay."

"All right. Feed Max before we go, huh? We can't bring all his food with us, so we might as well let him fill up before we start off."

Piper nodded and went to do as he asked. When her back was turned and she was near the front of the car, he loaded up the pistol he'd taken from the cop car days ago, and shoved it in the back of his waistband.

* * *

236

Walking again brought back painful memories of Denny, but that was tempered by the fact that the storms were much lighter than usual. The road's high elevation, combined with its well-built shoulders, meant they didn't have to deal with mud or rough terrain as they walked. In fact they were practically on the road itself, which Alex would once have avoided, but now a total lack of people eased his mind.

That changed when they saw a prison in the distance. It was far from the road but not quite far enough for Alex's liking. At first he didn't pay it too much mind; it wasn't as though prisons were a rare sight in the countryside. But then he got to thinking, and he wondered what prisons must be like in the middle of this planetary reboot. The prisoners couldn't possibly have been released. But what, then? Did the guards keep reporting for duty every day? He knew he wouldn't be clocking in if he were them, with the whole social structure crumbling. Had the prisoners starved to death, with no one to let them out of their cells? Or, left to their own devices, had some of them managed to get out? Had they, perhaps, released the others?

All these thoughts and more swirled around his mind, until he stopped even pretending to keep his gaze from the prison. Then, when the freeway turned and brought them around the other side of it, he saw something that chilled his heart: on the prison's western side, the fence had been torn down. By what exactly, he didn't know, but a big vehicle, certainly—a truck, maybe, or at least a prison van. The door leading into the prison itself was shut, but he doubted very much that it was locked.

Piper didn't seem to have noticed, and he'd be damned if he was going to bring it up only to freak her out. So he kept his mouth shut, and they pressed on until they saw another small town up ahead. Then Alex took them off the freeway and onto some smaller side country roads to wind their way around it. If he remembered correctly, the town was called

Davenport. Whoever had broken out of the prison, he didn't doubt they would have gone straight for the town. Maybe they'd snatched up some supplies and run along, but maybe not. Best to play it safe.

When they made it back to the 2 without seeing another soul, Alex began to breathe easier. As the sun began to set, he led Piper and Max off the freeway. A small road led up a rise and into a thicket of oaks. Once under their boughs, he built their tent out of sight of the road. Piper dropped off almost immediately, but Alex lay awake a little while, listening to her breathing and the occasional rustling of Max outside. He felt a little bad leaving the dog in the rain, but the tent wasn't big enough for all three of them, and he didn't want to wake up to a load of crap dropped on the tent's floor because he'd left the door closed all night.

Sleep found him at last, and he woke to a grey dawn that promised the rain was coming back strong. Alex watched the sky distrustfully as they ate a meager breakfast and pressed on. As the heaviness of the rain began to steadily increase, he began to search for something, anything, to speed up the rest of the trip—or at least to ease it. Another vehicle would be ideal, but at this point he'd even have taken a pair of umbrellas—until he thought of fighting their wind resistance day and night, and tossed that away as a bad idea.

The only pleasant part about any of it was the way Washington looked in the midst of all the rain. It was the beginning of summer, and already the state's most beautiful time of year. Rain didn't exactly make the day cheery, but weeks of it had caused an explosion of greenery that sometimes made him stop and stare in wonder. Wildflowers had sprung to life in such numbers that they covered some entire fields, and had even come burrowing up through cracks in the road—and without cars passing by to batter them back down into submission, the freeway itself had become a sparse garden tended by Nature's hand. The lack of any passers by, whether on foot

238

or in a vehicle, had been eerie and tiring. Now it made the whole experience surreal, and somehow more beautiful. It was as if he and Piper were being given a gift, a special glimpse at Earth after humanity had passed from it.

The world didn't need them, he suddenly realized. Or rather, he'd known that all his life—he was a park ranger, after all. He was no stranger to the ways of the wild. But now that simple fact, the adage of pioneers and outdoorsmen for all the centuries of America's existence, was made clear and given tangible proof. His quest to return home to his wife had a new and invalidating perspective. Who cared if their family reunited? Who cared if humanity survived the flare at all? If it wasn't the flare, it would be an asteroid, or humanity's own industrial poisons, or their insane obsession with nuclear weapons.

Someday they'd all be gone. Earth would still be here. It wouldn't even notice.

CHAPTER 27

The rain grew steadily worse as the day wore on, and toward evening Alex began looking for a place to hole up for the night. At first he was only looking for a hill or a copse, but he found something much better: a barn in the middle of an open field. Its red walls sagged a bit, but they looked sturdy enough. A new-looking lock on the property's gate told him it might be inhabited. But with luck, the ranchers would be holed up in their own home, or living on some other property, and wouldn't notice a pair of weary refugees huddling in their barn for one night against the rain.

They hopped the fence and made their way across the field towards the barn. Now they walked on mud, and it sucked at their feet like it was trying to make up for the days of clear road they'd had. But as they drew near the barn's huge front door, Alex was drawn up short by a sudden sound from inside: the whinny of horses.

On instinct, Alex's hand darted in front of Piper to shield her, moments before his mind even registered what the sound had been. When he recognized it, he relaxed—and then he smiled.

"Dad?" said Piper. "What is it?"

"Horses in the barn," said Alex. "I know it's been a few years, but you remember how to ride one, right?"

Piper frowned. "Sure, but . . ."

She stopped and ducked her gaze. Maybe she'd been about

to point out that the horses no doubt belonged to someone, and a horse could easily cost as much as a cheap used car. But Alex was grateful she didn't finish the statement, because nothing was going to change his mind. Horses weren't as fast as a car, but they were a heck of a lot faster than walking, and best of all he wouldn't have to worry about fuel. The horses probably couldn't go on grass forever, but they'd last the couple of days it would take to reach the cabins.

The barn's front door wasn't locked—a chain hung in two loops, but it hung loose, with nothing securing it. Even a few days ago, that might have triggered alarm bells in Alex's mind, but just now he was tired and could only think of Piper's dwindling meds. He seized the handles of the door and wrenched it sideways.

He didn't see the shotgun butt until after it struck him in the forehead.

Alex went crashing to the ground, stars dancing in his eyes. Piper screamed and threw herself over his body, protecting him with her arms. Max went berserk, standing in front of both of them and barking like hell. Alex blinked hard, trying to clear the spots in his vision.

When they cleared, he saw his assailant. A black man, big, maybe six inches taller than Alex and well-muscled. He'd flipped the shotgun around to point it at them. And Alex's stomach clenched as he saw the man's orange jumpsuit, and handcuffs with a severed chain dangling from each wrist. A convict from the prison.

The shotgun barrel pointing at Piper gave Alex a fresh surge of strength. He pushed up, seizing Piper and throwing her behind him. In the same motion he drew the pistol from his waistband and pointed it, flipping the safety off. The convict tensed, but didn't move.

For a long moment they had a Mexican standoff, gazing into each other's eyes. Max had subsided to angry growls, low in the back of his throat.

"Your safety's on," said Alex.

The convict didn't blink. "Shotguns don't have a safety."

Damn. It would have been a moment's distraction, at least. "Listen. We needed shelter from the rain. We don't want any trouble."

"Then put the gun down."

"And you'll put down the shotgun?"

"I might take a slug and live. You ain't taking a shell."

"That's not reassuring."

"I'm not your therapist."

Alex's jaw worked. Instinct told him the convict would just blow him away if he backed down. But instinct had a tendency to escalate situations. He didn't see murder in the man's eyes. And it might have been anything, but Max had mostly subsided. Either the man wasn't as aggressive as he looked, and Max could smell it, or they were simply facing a cold-blooded killer. In which case, Alex doubted they were getting out of this anyway.

Slowly, Alex lowered the pistol.

Five heartbeats thundered in his ears. Then, the shotgun lowered.

"Thank you."

The convict didn't smile. "You can come in after I've left."

"Just let us get out of the rain."

"Sure. After I get my horse and go."

Alex sighed inwardly. He supposed prison tended to cultivate men who weren't willing to give an inch, on anything. It was probably a miracle the guy had lowered his weapon at all.

Then Alex took another look at the cuffs on the guy's wrists. The only other thing he knew about prison, really, was that it was a culture of favors. Help someone else out with something, they'd tend to do you a solid back. Granting and owing favors was as much a part of survival as being known as the biggest badass on the block.

"You want those cuffs off?" said Alex. "There's gotta be a hacksaw in this barn."

The convict blinked. His eyes flicked to his wrists. Alex could see the skin had been rubbed raw in a few places. He met Alex's gaze a moment longer.

"The girl and the dog can sit by the front." Then he tossed his head, indicating for Alex to follow him, before turning and entering the barn.

"Dad, I'm scared," muttered Piper.

"It's going to be okay," said Alex. "Get inside and keep Max with you. If anything goes wrong, run. But nothing will. Okay?"

She didn't answer, but she did as he asked. Alex followed the convict deeper into the barn, where there was a shed built into the wall. Tools filled it, and the man was digging through them. He turned just as Alex approached, holding a hacksaw.

"You try to cut me, I can kill you easily."

"I believe you," said Alex. He held out his hand. The convict handed him the hacksaw, then turned and put his arm out on the table next to them.

Alex set to work. He had to hold the guy's wrist to keep the cut steady, which was an awkward moment of skin contact. He ran the blade sideways across the guy's arm, like cutting fruit or veggies in a kitchen and keeping his fingers parallel with the blade so it didn't have the opportunity to cut. Soon he fell into a rhythm, but he was still dealing with high-grade steel, and progress was slow. Soon he was sweating and puffing, and he felt the urge to take a break to go soak in some cold rain.

His hand cramped up, and he muttered a curse as he dropped the hacksaw. The convict tensed, but when he saw Alex shaking his hand with pain, he eased up. He regarded Alex coolly for a moment, not moving his arm from the table.

"Where you headed?" said Alex, flexing his fingers.

"Seattle."

"Seattle's been wiped out, I heard."

"I heard it, too. But I got family there, so I'm going anyway."

Alex nodded. "We're from there, but my wife is in the mountains outside the cabin. That's where we're headed."

The man didn't answer.

Alex tried to smile, but it felt fake, so he dropped it. He picked up the hacksaw. "Let's give this another shot."

The barn filled with the rasping, repetitive sound of sawing. After what felt like an eternity, the cuff split, the pieces falling to the floor. Alex gave a huge sigh of relief. The convict stood and stretched, flexing his wrist.

"One more," said Alex.

"Thanks."

"You're welcome. I'm Alex, by the way."

The guy's mouth twitched. "Lamont."

"Good to meet you, Lamont. Come on." Alex waved for his other wrist, and Lamont laid it out for him. Alex decided to risk another conversation while he was working. "Is it rude to ask what you were in for?"

"Most people would call that rude as hell, yeah."

"Well, the world's going to hell, so what the hey. What were you in for?"

To his immense shock, that drew a laugh from Lamont. "I'm black. What do you think?"

Black, and with a chip on his shoulder. "Drugs?"

Lamont inclined his head. "Not even anything hard. Just weed. A lot of it, but hell."

"Sorry to hear that," said Alex, and he meant it. "Maybe stay in Washington next time. It's legal there, if you hadn't heard."

"If legal even matters anymore."

That was a sobering thought, and it left them both in silence the rest of the time Alex was working. Finally the second handcuff fell to the straw of the barn floor. Alex had cast off his rainproof jacket by then, and he wiped a sweaty arm across his brow.

"Thanks again," said Lamont.

"My pleasure. Thanks for not shooting us."

"I never killed nobody."

"Me neither. High five."

The look in Lamont's eyes told him that wasn't happening. The convict went to the stalls across the barn. Four of them were occupied. He went to the biggest horse, a big bay, and reached out a tentative hand. The horse sniffed his hand and didn't try to bite. That seemed good enough for Lamont, who turned to find himself a saddle.

He froze when he saw Alex, and it made Alex tense up immediately. He didn't know what was wrong, until he looked down at his feet. Leaning on the wall within easy reach, and at least four yards from Lamont, was the shotgun. Alex looked up and met the man's gaze for a moment. Then he took a slow, deliberate step away from the weapon.

"We're good," he said.

Lamont let out a breath. He hesitated for a moment. But then he went and picked up the shot gun anyway. When he looked at Alex, he seemed almost chagrined.

"I just—"

"It's fine," said Alex. "I get it."

Lamont got his saddle and brought it to the horse. He put it on the right way around, but once he started fiddling with the saddle straps, it became clear he had no idea what he was doing. After watching for a moment in slight amusement, Alex approached.

"You need a blanket first," he said. "Otherwise the saddle's going to rub him raw. Here."

He lifted off the saddle and tossed on the blanket before replacing it, and then cinched up the straps. He put on the horse's bridle, snug but not too tight, and then he turned to Lamont.

"You don't have to take the saddle off during the journey, but if you keep him once you reach Seattle, you can't just leave it on."

"Okay," said Lamont.

"You know, we're on the same road for a long, long time. We could—"

"No."

Alex's mouth twisted. "Sure. Right. Okay. You're all set."

Lamont stepped past him, shotgun in hand. He held it in one hand while he led the horse out with the other. Once they were outside, he threw up the hood of his jacket—which looked like it had been stolen from a prison guard—and mounted up. It was less awkward than Alex had been expecting. Once he was mounted up, he looked down at Alex.

"Sorry about your head." His eyes went to Piper. "Take care of yourself. Good luck."

"You too," said Alex. "I hope your family's okay."

Lamont nodded. Then he tugged on the horse's reins. He seemed a little surprised as it wheeled around, but soon he was leading it off west across the plain, and before long he was out of sight.

CHAPTER 28

Cameron woke to a morning without any noise except the rain falling on the roof. A gentle gray light through the window. For a second she just lay there under the covers, taking long blinks and longer breaths. Maybe she could stay in bed today. Maybe she could stay in bed until Alex and Piper finally got home.

Yeah, right.

She'd just managed to sit upright and swing her legs over the edge of her bed when she heard a pounding at her front door. She sighed and tilted her head back. What was it now?

The front door burst open. Cameron shot to her feet.

"Cameron!"

It was Scott, and she could tell in his voice something was wrong. Not run-of-the-mill wrong.

"Hang on," she called out, throwing on her jeans and a tank top as fast as she could.

"Hurry! It's Hernando. And—and Wade."

God damn it, Wade. She threw on her boots and ran out of the room without bothering to lace them. But Scott caught her arm as she tried to rush past him in the living room.

"You don't need to run. It's over."

"Who started it? Was it Wade? Where's Hernando?" If Wade had decided to take out his frustration on the kid, she'd probably need to clean some wounds, maybe stitch something up—before she beat the crap out of Wade herself, of course.

Scott shook his head slowly. "He's down by the clubhouse. But he's—Hernando's dead."

Cameron stared at him. The living room was dead silent for a full minute.

"What do you mean, dead?"

The voice came from behind her. Cameron turned to find Bettie in the doorway of the guest room. She had on a thick robe, and her fingers were white as they gripped the lapels of it.

Cameron turned and ran out the front door.

* * *

A half dozen people were gathered around Hernando's body, looking down at it in morose silence. Cameron didn't take the time to inventory them. She fell to her knees by Hernando's side, feeling for a pulse. His eyes were closed, and his chest wasn't moving.

Nothing. And from the temperature of his skin, it had been some time since he died. She could feel something wrong beneath the skin, something poking, and she knew his neck had been broken.

Rage started to rise up inside her. It was a feeling she was familiar with from her time in the service. She had long practice in suppressing emotion; it didn't help on the job, and it wasn't pleasant to go through in any case. When you were a doctor or a nurse, you couldn't afford to get too attached, because there were always some who weren't going to make it. But one thing always made her blood boil regardless: the senseless deaths, the needless ones that came from sheer stupidity instead of the enemy. The sentry who shot a friendly patrol because they got spooked; the driver who broke their neck because they were too goddamn stupid to wear a seatbelt; the new recruit who got too drunk on leave and took a knife in a bar fight.

248

Now Hernando was dead, but Cameron knew the stupidity was hers. She should have known Wade would do this, should have known he—

Then she saw Wade.

He was just a few yards away, sitting on the ground with his back to the clubhouse. And he was covered in blood. She could tell at a glance that most, if not all of it, was his. A knife had slashed him in several places, mostly on his arms, and it looked like he might have been stabbed in the side. She couldn't see his face, because it was buried in his hands, and his shoulders were shaking.

Cameron's eyes narrowed. If she was honest with herself, she maybe didn't know Wade *that* well. But she'd never have pegged him for a crier.

She got to her feet and went to him. She saw Russell out of the corner of her eye. He took a step toward her, like he was going to stop her. But she shot him a look that rooted him, and stood over Wade with her arms folded.

"What happened?"

Wade looked up. His cheeks were wet with tears, soon joined by the rainwater that pelted down. He sniffed and swiped at his nose with the back of his forearm.

"We were on guard duty. I was all pissed at him, so I kept him out of sight. But then he came at me, out of the darkness. He had a knife, and he . . . we fought, and before I knew what happened, he was—"

He buried his face in his hands again. Cameron was about to order him to get up—or maybe just to kick the crap out of him sitting down, she wasn't sure—when she heard a scream behind her. She whirled.

Gina came running. She looked like she'd started running while still half-dressed and hadn't completely finished the job on the way. She grabbed Hernando's shoulders—which now Cameron could see had one or two cuts as well, though not nearly as bad as the ones on Wade—and began to shake him, screaming for him to get up, to wake up. The way Hernando's head lolled back and forth made Cameron feel sick.

She went to the girl and took her by the arm, lifting her firmly up. Gina fought, but Cameron turned her gently away. People always wanted to look at the body, like if they only stared enough, they could bring the person back to life. They never could, of course, and Cameron had learned that it only made the pain worse.

"Come on," she said, ushering Gina away despite the girl's protests. "He's gone. He's gone."

Then Bettie was there, appearing out of the rain like a ghost. She took Gina and wrapped her arms around her, giving the embrace and comfort that Cameron had almost forgotten after so many years. But over Gina's shoulder, Bettie couldn't remove her eyes from Hernando's body.

"Shush, baby," she murmured. "Quiet now."

Cameron heard footsteps behind her, and she turned to find Wade had risen. He stepped forward, as if he was actually about to approach Bettie and Gina. Cameron planted herself between him and the girls. He ignored her, looking over her shoulder.

"I'm so sorry," he said. "I'm sorry, I wish—"

"You shut your mouth!" Bettie's scream was so sudden, so unexpected, that even Cameron jumped. "You goddamn bastard!"

"It wasn't my fault!" said Wade, fresh tears welling.

"Wade, shut up," said Cameron. "And get out of here. I'll deal with you later."

"Cam, you have to—"

"*Out!*" she roared.

Wade recoiled like a slapped puppy and slunk off.

"Don't you dare let him get away with this," said Bettie. "Don't you dare let that monster—"

Cameron cut her off with a raised hand. "Bettie, stop. Hernando sliced him up. He's covered with cuts and blood."

"You really believe that?"

Did she? Admittedly, it was hard to imagine Wade slicing himself up after murdering Hernando. That was something a crazy person would do. Or a really, really angry one. And she couldn't forget the look on Wade's face the day before when they'd found his camera in Hernando's bag.

But why would he kill Hernando like this after? The camera had been returned, and Hernando never would have been stupid enough to try taking it again.

Why had he been stupid enough to take it in the first place?

Even if Wade *had* been that angry, why do it like this? He was crafty. He could have made it look like an accident. So maybe Hernando *had* attacked him.

Except that didn't make any sense either.

God damn it. She had a thousand questions and exactly zero answers. But if she didn't make a decision, *any* decision, this would tear the cabin community apart. That was another thing she knew well from the service.

"Both of them are hurt badly," said Cameron. "The cuts could point in either direction. And Hernando got caught stealing Wade's stuff."

Bettie scowled. "If you even believe that. He could have put the camera in Hernando's backpack himself."

Cameron remembered the look of resignation in Hernando's face as he pulled the camera out. "I don't think that's true. But we can't know. All we know is that Hernando's dead, and he sliced Wade up good before he died."

That only made the lines on Bettie's face deepen. She turned away, her disappointment in Cameron practically radiating off her.

"Get Gina out of here and look after her," said Cameron. She turned to the onlookers and pointed to Scott and Russell. "Help me bury the body."

The body. That's all he was now.

* * *

Once Hernando was shrouded and in the wet ground, they had a little gathering around the grave. Bettie and Gina wept openly. Everyone else just sort of stared at the loose earth and shuffled their feet uncomfortably. No one said a word.

The Williams were the first to leave. After that, everyone wandered off one by one until it was only Cameron, Bettie, and Gina. Then Bettie patted Gina's shoulder and urged her away.

"Go home and rest, sweetheart. I'll come see you in a minute."

Cameron sighed. Bettie wanted to speak, no doubt. She'd expected it, but she still wasn't looking forward to it.

Once Gina was out of earshot, Bettie folded her arms and fixed Cameron with a look. "Hernando and *that man* never should have been out last night at the same time."

"I couldn't agree more. I didn't double-check the watch schedule after what happened yesterday. That's on me."

"I don't believe what Wade said for one second."

Cameron looked down at her hand. Mud from the grave had spattered the back of it. She wiped it against the front of her shirt. "There's no evidence to say anything other than what he told us."

"Ain't that convenient. We're standing on the grave of the only other person who was there. What if it's someone else tomorrow? What if he cuts himself up again? Would you believe him then, too?"

"That would be different, and you know it."

Bettie scoffed. "Because Hernando was just some Mexican kid you didn't like the look of. Save it."

She headed off towards Cameron's house, old legs swinging in a march filled with purpose. Cameron watched her go. A feeling nagged her. A feeling she'd felt just the day before, when she saw Wade walk off just the same way.

This still wasn't over.

CHAPTER 29

Another day brought them to Banks Lake. Thicker at its north end than the south, it was shaped like a T-bone steak someone had stretched out on some medieval torture device. Unlike most of Washington's gentle lakes, Banks was bordered mostly by cliffs, with an island in the middle that rose straight up and had sides as flat cake icing. It was one of those places that made you wonder if ancient explorers named things just to mess with those who came after; Banks hardly had any banks at all.

Once, before Piper had been born, Alex and Cameron had come and vacationed here. Then, they'd stayed near the lake's northern end, where it fed into the Columbia River just before that waterway hooked and ran south to form the border with Oregon. But now his road with Piper brought him to Banks' southern end and a little town called, creatively enough, Banks Lake South. Well outside the town, they found a tiny motel and a truck stop. Both were abandoned. There was a semi trailer there, too, half full of fresh-cut hay. There was also a fenced area at the rear of the hotel where they could put the horses overnight.

"We'll stop here," said Alex. "I don't think we'll find a better spot than this." He didn't voice the rest of his thought: that he'd hoped to find another vehicle for them to take as well. A pen and food for the horses seemed too lucky a find to start complaining about their fortune.

Piper helped him coop up the horses and get them some hay. Alex poked his head into the greenhouse, but if there had been any vegetables in there, they were long gone now. He led Piper back to the hotel. The place was ancient, so the doors didn't have modern hotel locks, which were almost impossible to break. Alex was able to kick one open easily. Max padded in and started sniffing around in the room's corners. Alex was able to push the door handle mostly back into the door, and when he pushed it closed again, it seemed fairly secure. The place was still cold, but that would change soon with three bodies inside. The temperature had been dropping steadily, and Alex thought it couldn't be very far above freezing. Another product of the solar burst he supposed—summer shouldn't have been anything close to this cold. He dreaded the thought that it might snow soon. As if the going wasn't tough enough already.

He shook away his worries, along with the rainwater all over his jacket. "This'll do," said Alex. "Take a load off."

She complied immediately, throwing off her backpack and flinging herself down on one of the beds with a sigh. "Oh my god. This feels so much better than the ground. Or even a car seat."

Alex smiled. "You're getting spoiled. You know it's only been a few days since we were at Graham's place."

"Yeah, well, I slept on a couch there, so this is still better."

He snorted. But mention of Graham almost reminded him of Denny, and his mind shied away at that. He sat on the other bed, and he couldn't help a sigh of his own. A real mattress had become an almost unimaginable luxury, even if this one was low quality and likely flea-ridden. He thought he might actually melt when they finally made it to the cabin, and he could finally relax in his own bed.

Mine and Cameron's, that is.

Holy cow, were they going to have some catching up to do.

That was another thing he didn't want to think about just

now, though. So he pulled off his boots and peeled off his soaking wet socks. His boots were solid enough, but there was just no keeping out the constant rain. They took all their wet clothes and hung them around the room on chairs and doors, for the best possible chance to dry out while they slept. As she flexed her bare feet, Piper looked up at him with a frown.

"I don't want to sound like a little kid, but—how much longer?"

"Till the cabins?" Alex pursed his lips and thought about it. "I remember the maps, but I was planning on us still being in a car. That would only take us a few hours. On foot, it would be more like a week. So, somewhere in between, I guess. Four days, maybe three if we push the horses hard. But I'm mostly guessing."

"I can't wait," said Piper quietly. "I love you, Dad, but this has not been a fun vacation."

She smiled weakly as she said it, and Alex laughed. "I don't blame you, kiddo. This wasn't exactly how I planned our trip, either. But it's almost over."

Piper scowled with mock ferocity. "Don't you dare jinx it."

Alex raised his hands as if surrendering. "Whatever you say. Check your blood sugar. Tomorrow we should get halfway to the mountains."

Alex went to the window, where the drapes were almost completely drawn. Outside it was all grey skies and falling rain. He could only barely see the truck stop just a few dozen yards away, and the town farther off was completely obscured. That, as much as anything else, should keep them safe here for the night. But just to be safe, he pulled the curtains all the way closed before he went to his pack and started unpacking a cold, cheerless dinner.

* * *

In the middle of the night, Max shot up to all four legs and began growling.

Alex started awake from a light sleep. He shook his head, trying to clear his vision, before he realized the room was completely dark. He slithered out of bed and crawled to the window—and when he pulled aside the curtain, he was shocked to see silvery light outside.

Stars and the moon. The sky was clear. How in all hell was the sky clear?

Then another light appeared, shining right in his eye and almost blinding him. Headlights. He dropped to the floor until they passed over the window, then got back up on one knee again. Cracking the curtain, he peered out into the night.

Not a car. A van. A black van with an insignia on the side. It read *Geiger Corrections Center.*

Alex held his breath as a door opened. The man who got out wasn't wearing the uniform of a guard, but a thick green coat tossed over an orange jumpsuit.

Shit.

Why were they stopping?

They must have seen the horses. He'd left the saddles on—a clear sign someone was in the hotel.

Max growled again. "Shush," said Alex, putting a hand on the dog's head.

Still crouching, he crept across the room to where Piper was still asleep. He shook her until her eyes shot wide and covered her mouth.

"Quiet," he said. "We need to go, now. Get dressed and get your bag."

Neither of them had taken off more than their jackets and boots, so they were ready to go in less than a minute. The convicts outside hadn't seemed to notice the hotel room door that was slightly ajar, for which he was thankful.

They took their packs and slipped out the hotel room's back door into the communal area with the pool. As they hit the below-freezing air, Alex slipped his pistol from his waistband, but he held it low, trying to keep it out of Piper's sight.

A back gate let them out into the grassland behind the hotel, which would allow them to sneak around to where the horses were. Alex tried to think a few steps ahead. If the convicts weren't near the horses, he and Piper would hop on their saddles and ride out into the wilderness, away from the road. Even if they were followed, the van's tires would likely pop at some point.

If the horses *were* guarded, they'd strike out into the wilderness on foot. Their chances of being spotted at night were slim to none. They couldn't make the rest of the journey on foot, but right now they had to survive. He could figure out the next step later.

And what if they do spot you? he thought. *What then?*

He was trying to come up with an answer when a figure in an orange jumpsuit leapt from the shadows and punched him in the jaw.

Stars danced in his vision for the second time in as many days. The blow didn't land where Lamont had hit him with the shotgun, but his head was still sore from that hit. Somehow he managed to keep his feet, managed to keep from dropping the gun. He shoved Piper away, no time to be gentle, and raised the pistol.

A muzzle flash lit the night, the sound like a thunderclap. The convict dropped.

They had to run now. No time to go for the horses.

"Piper—"

He'd thought the man was alone. He was wrong. Two more came into view around the hotel's corner. Alex got off one shot that missed by a mile before they tackled him, and the Glock went spinning away across the concrete.

Alex landed badly, and something in his pack jabbed hard into his back. But he managed to twist out of the men's grip anyway. He was free just long enough to deck one of them, but the convict didn't go down. Then they had him by the arms again, and one of them drove a meaty fist into his gut.

"Get his shit!"

"Take him down!"

They knocked him down, trying to pull the pack from his shoulders. But all of Piper's remaining meds were in there. Alex fought like hell, thrashing and trying to free himself again.

Hands seized him by the shoulders and lifted before slamming his head into the ground. The world went red and blurry.

"Let him go!" Piper's panicked voice made Alex's head jerk up.

God, no. Piper stood there with the Glock in her hand, swinging it back and forth between the two convicts.

One of them laughed and took a step forward. Piper panicked, or maybe she meant to—but she pulled the trigger. The convict spun, screaming, and fell to the ground clutching his side. Piper's face went ghost white.

A savage, vicious snarling came from Alex's right. Max came flying from the dark, his jaws locking on the other man's arm. The convict shouted, and his grip on Alex loosened. Alex fought to his knees. But when he tried to rise higher, the world swam and he almost fell again.

More shouts. More footsteps. More convicts came running from around the hotel.

"Piper," croaked Alex. "Run."

She didn't hear him, or maybe she ignored him. But she stood there frozen, the gun not even fully raised. There were at least six of them, and her hesitation was going to rob her of the time to stop even one.

BOOM

A gunshot—far louder than the Glock. A crater opened in one of the men's stomachs. He probed it with shaking hands before sinking to his knees, then falling flat on his face. The rest skidded to a halt.

BOOM

258

Another convict lost his leg at the knee. He fell with a high-pitched shriek.

A huge figure stepped forward into the light of the motel's single, crappy lamp. Lamont, shotgun raised.

The rest of the convicts turned and ran.

To Alex's right, Max yelped. The convict had kicked him and finally shaken him loose.

The man ran off into the dark—but not before scooping up Alex's pack, which he'd finally managed to get off Alex's back.

"No," moaned Alex, reaching out a hand.

He finally found his feet, but it was no use. Each step nearly sent him back to the ground again, and his vision was still blurred. The convict vanished.

Alex came to a stop, hand still outstretched. Slowly, he lowered it to his side.

He heard light, quick breaths behind him and turned. Piper. She was shaking now, the gun dangling from fingers that were almost completely limp. Alex went to her as quickly as he could, and pried the Glock from her grip.

"It's okay," he whispered. "You're okay. You did good."

She didn't answer. It didn't even seem like she'd heard him, as she stared through his chest and off into the distance. If Alex knew anything, she was seeing the man she'd shot—the man who was probably even now bleeding out on the pavement just a few feet away.

"Come on," he said. "Let's get away from this place."

He tried to lead her off, but he almost fell again. That got her out of her fugue, and she took his arm to put across her shoulders.

"H-here," she stammered, shivering from fear or from the cold. "Let me help."

They ambled slowly away from the courtyard and towards the field where they'd find the horses. From the other side of the hotel, Alex heard the sound of tires screeching as the van made a getaway. Lamont still stood where he'd stepped out of the shadows, and Alex stopped for a second to look up at him.

"Thank you," he said. His voice cracked. "We'd be—"

"'S'all good," said Lamont. "I knew some of these guys. Good riddance."

Alex nodded. "How'd you find us?"

"Was in the truck stop," said Lamont, tilting his head towards where it sat in the near distance. "I guess you were in the hotel. I thought about that, but I thought it might attract more attention. But when I heard the pistol shots, I came over."

"We're glad you did," said Alex. He tried to take another step, but his legs almost gave out, and Piper had to steady him. Lamont put out a hand on his shoulder, too.

"Take it easy. Sorry about your head—but I guess they hit you a little harder than I did."

Alex chuckled. "Just a little. I'm fine, though. Fine." He stood straighter and took his arm from Piper. His head was starting to clear. "Just shows you, though, that we really are heading the same way. You sure you don't want to—"

"Still no," said Lamont. "You did me a solid, I'm glad to do one back. But this was a one-time thing. I'm not in the business of babysitting."

"Fair enough," said Alex. "Then thank you. And good luck."

"You too."

Lamont turned to go. But Piper burst away from Alex and ran to him. The convict tensed as she threw her arms around his waist in a hug. She could barely reach all the way around him.

"Thank you," she whispered.

His brow furrowing, Lamont looked over at Alex with something like terror. Alex could only give him a weak smile. Soon Piper disengaged herself and pulled away, returning to Alex's side.

"Uh, yeah," said Lamont. "Sure thing. Y'all stay safe—safer, this time, I guess."

He walked away, still looking somewhat awkward, and soon he was lost in the night.

CHAPTER 30

It began to snow.

The flakes were huge, the biggest Cameron had ever seen. Some were almost as wide as her palm. And they fell thick, buffeted by a strong wind that seemed to be trying to make up for the one clear night they'd had two days ago.

It was four days since Hernando had been killed, and seven since she'd last spoke with Alex.

Four days, he'd said. She'd made him promise. Now a week had passed, and no sign.

They were all right. She knew they were, because any other possibility was simply unacceptable.

That was what she told herself, at least, in the long hours she spent cooped up, a prisoner in her own home, pacing back and forth and all around. She'd stood guard the night before, and had no work shifts during the day. She was supposed to be sleeping, what with having been up most of the previous night, but thoughts of Alex and Cameron made that impossible. So she stirred restlessly about, and watched the snow slowly stack up outside, and checked on her supplies over and over again, and generally made herself and Bettie miserable.

Bettie was stuck inside too, of course. She wasn't fit for guard duty, and there was nothing to do in the garden other than check for weeds—something she did in the morning, effectively clearing her schedule for the rest of the day. She had nothing more to fill her time with than Cameron, and after making coffee, then breakfast, she slowly migrated from chair to couch and back again as she waited for the miserable snow day to pass.

If it will even pass at all. Who knew but that tomorrow would be the same as today, or even worse?

If it had been two weeks earlier, Cameron would happily have spent her time curled up under a blanket in the living room, chatting with Bettie and trading stories, and maybe enjoying herself even more than it was a work day. But Hernando's death had thrown Bettie into a foul mood she seemed unwilling to pull herself out of.

Not that Cameron could blame her. Of *course* it was horrible. Of *course* it didn't make sense, and Bettie had every excuse to harbor a grudge against Wade for what had gone down. But Cameron knew, or at least had a strong feeling, that Bettie wanted something from her—something she wasn't sure she could, or wanted to, provide.

The quiet expectation hung between them all morning and promised to make the rest of the day just as bad. But fortunately for them both, Bettie seemed to have more courage than Cameron did, because just as Cameron was starting to think about having lunch and then finding some excuse to leave the house for the rest of the day, the old woman sighed and threw her hands in the air.

"Lord almighty, girl, we gotta talk, because if this goes on much longer I'm going to march out into the cold and keep walking until I keel over."

Cameron had been on her way to the kitchen, and the first sound of Bettie's voice made her freeze in her tracks. But she'd been expecting the start of a fight, and so Bettie's words struck her as even funnier than they would have in normal circumstances, and she barked a loud laugh before she could help herself. Strain bled from the room like blood from a sliced vein, and Cameron settled herself on one of the stools by the kitchen bar.

"You'd better not," said Cameron. "But I guess you're right that it's been pretty miserable."

"You think? You stalking all around here like a cat about to pop out kittens, and I'd be the same except the cold's got my damn knee keeping me from walking."

Again Cameron laughed, this time warm, genuine, pure enjoyment and not the release of tension. "I'll get us some wine."

Bettie raised an eyebrow. "It's eleven."

"I think society's standards of acceptable behavior went out the window a long time ago. Don't think I haven't seen you sneaking Kahlúa into your coffee on occasion."

"Touché, and fill me up good, honey."

Cameron did, fetching two glasses of merlot that she filled very near to the brim. Once she'd handed one to Bettie, she started a fire in the fireplace, and then finally settled down on the chair beside the couch. For a moment they let the quiet stretch, both of them appreciating that it was no longer an angry silence.

But, too, they both knew it couldn't last forever, and Bettie was the one who finally broke it with a sigh. "So, can we talk about this without going back to hissy fits? For both of us, I mean."

"I can do my best."

"Appreciate it. I can't imagine how worried you must be with Alex and Piper out there."

Cameron stared down at her glass and said nothing.

"Sorry," said Bettie. "Probably shouldn't have led with that."

"It's fine. It doesn't get better just because we avoid talking about it. And it's half the reason today's so frustrating."

"And the other half?"

Cameron took a deep sip of wine. "The other half is the thing you really want to talk to me about. So, let's give it a whirl."

"It's Wade. He's bad news."

"He got angry."

"He murdered—"

"We don't know that."

"Come on."

Cameron took another sip and used her free hand to rub at her temples. "I . . . listen, I realize the only people who know, were there, and one of them is dead. But I don't know how to deal with that, Bettie. There have to be rules. People have rules. And we can't—"

"Ain't you just tell me something about society's standards and windows?"

"Makes a lot of sense for drinking before noon. I'm less comfortable when it comes to criminal justice."

"And what about Hernando's justice?"

Cameron slowly shook her head. "I hear what you're saying. But . . . okay, can I explain something and you promise not to get mad until I'm finished?"

Bettie leaned back into the couch at that, her brows drawing close. "I can promise to try. And I can promise not to say anything, at least."

"Let's say the worst is true. Let's say Wade hated Hernando, and he planned to kill him, and he set it up to do it in the middle of the night, when no one was around to witness it, and he stabbed himself and cut himself to make it look like self-defense. Let's say all that is true. I have no idea how to prove it, and then to deal with it, in a way that doesn't open up even more problems and turn the cabin community into a lawless hellhole where anyone's word is enough to get someone killed."

That sent Bettie into long silence. Cameron studied her, watching the gears whirr. Both took plentiful sips of their wine. Then Bettie's eyes flashed, and she met Cameron's gaze.

"What if this was the service? What woulda happened then?"

It took Cameron aback. She hadn't thought of it like that. She tried to picture it—out on the forefront, very little logistical support from command, and a soldier found killed by another soldier. Even claims of self-defense wouldn't stop an investigation. But . . .

"There'd be inquiries, investigations. But according to procedure. The MPs would—" Bettie's brow furrowed "—Military Police. Cops for soldiers. And they have rules and procedures that help them find the truth, hopefully. And I wasn't an MP. No idea how to even start going about it."

"You could question people."

"You mean Wade. He's already given his story, and I doubt it's going to change."

Bettie studied her a moment. When she spoke, it was tentative. Almost nervous. "Can I ask something, and you promise not to get mad until I'm finished?"

Cameron steeled herself. "I can promise to try."

"I think you might be better about thinking up a way to get to the truth, if it wasn't Wade we were dealing with."

"Thought that might be where you were going."

Bettie sighed. It sounded like relief. "So you can admit there might be reason to think so. That's more than I was expecting."

"I wouldn't go that far."

"He sucks up to you."

"He backs my calls. It's a military thing."

"Is it a military thing when he smiles at you, and says things a man says when he's trying to get a girl on her back?"

A jolt of anger shot through her, burning in her chest. But Cameron was self-reflective enough to recognize it for what it was: a recognition of the truth. "I know Wade flirts. Always has. Doesn't mean I return it."

"Never said it did. If I thought you were that type, I wouldn't like you as much as I do."

Cameron rolled her eyes. "Flattery? Really?"

"Ain't a flatterer. But I also ain't so crusty that I don't remember what it was like when I was a younger woman. You don't have to bat your eyes back at him to be influenced by the way he acts. It feels good when a man thinks we're beautiful—especially a strong man, who knows his business and ain't bad to look at himself."

"You've gotta be kidding me. I'm not a teenager."

Bettie pointed to the wrinkles on her face. "Compared to me, you're damn right you are. And it ain't just how Wade acts towards you—when you look away, he doesn't. He's always got his eye on you. Has since day one. I never brought it up because I know you're smart. But the longer Alex takes to get here, the more Wade's pressing things. And now Hernando . . . it's like he's testing his limits. Seeing what he can do to get you on his side, even against every one else's best interests."

Cameron's hand tightened on her wine glass, and she forced it to loosen. "If you think I'd chase a pair of biceps at the expense of the community, you don't know a goddamn thing about me."

"I don't think that. But maybe Wade does."

She took a deep breath. Closed her eyes. Forced herself to consider it. It was dumb. It was playing one person against the next, sucking up to someone with some modicum of power. It sounded like stupid, petty, high school politics bullshit.

Her eyes popped open, and she felt sick with dread. It was the perfect description of life in the military. At least for some.

Bettie must have seen the look on Cameron's face, must have sensed she was making progress. "There's another thing. Hernando had a phone, but it wasn't on him when he died."

Back to this. "Bettie—"

"No, hang on. I helped clean out his stuff. It wasn't there, either. So I've been thinking about it, right? Two possibilities. Hernando had the phone on him when he died, and Wade took it. Or, Hernando hid the phone somewhere, and Wade wanted it. He tried to get Hernando to give it to him, and when Hernando wouldn't give it up, Wade killed him."

"Or, possibility three: Hernando was pissed at Wade for siccing us on him just because he was Mexican, and he attacked Wade, just like Wade said."

Bettie tilted her head up just a bit. "First of all, Hernando was Guatemalan, not Mexican. Second of all, you just admitted there's three possibilities. Not just one."

Cameron realized her glass was empty. She went and fetched the bottle to refill it, and then filled Bettie's proffered glass. It gave her time she desperately needed to think of a retort. "What would even be on the phone? What, you think Hernando managed to get some kind of incriminating documents on Wade?"

"I don't know."

"Hernando had a laptop, didn't he? Even if there was something on his phone, wouldn't it also be on his laptop?"

"Unless he was afraid of his laptop being searched."

"Why the hell would he—"

Cameron stopped short. Yeah, why *would* Hernando be afraid of his laptop being searched? Why *would* he be so paranoid as to copy the files onto his phone instead, and hide the phone so no one could reach it? What could possibly make him think he'd be under suspicion?

"Fuck."

"Language. But you got it. You and Wade came after him for the camera. As far as Hernando knew, you were on Wade's side. He wasn't exactly the kind of kid who could trust authority figures after they ganged up on him. *Both* of us have some experience with that."

Cameron scrubbed at her forehead with the heel of her hand. She couldn't believe she'd been led down this train of thought. Analytically, it still seemed crazy. But now she couldn't stop seeing the connections between seemingly disparate facts.

"Okay. What—I have to think about this. About the next step."

"Can't we search Wade's stuff for the phone? Or does that rule only apply to Mexicans, even if they ain't really Mexican?"

"Useless. If—and it is *still* an if—if Wade did get the phone from Hernando, he'd have destroyed it by now. Or hidden it somewhere we'll never find it. We've got to look for the phone ourselves, on the chance Hernando hid it before he died. And in the meantime, I'll keep an eye on Wade. See if I can catch any glimpse of something off, that Hernando might have stumbled on."

Bettie heaved a huge sigh and leaned back on the couch. "Thank you. Was that so hard?"

"Hey, don't jump to conclusions. I'm still betting this is all a load of bull. And if it is, if we don't find anything, I'm dropping it. You understand?"

"Perfectly." Bettie smiled a huge gap-toothed grin and spread her hands. "Now, why don't we get some knitting done? Everybody's gonna need some sweaters with all this weather."

Cameron stared at her. The silence stretched for what felt like forever.

"Knitting."

Bettie's smile didn't falter, even as she gestured out the window to the hand-sized snowflakes drifting down. "You got something better to do?"

Cameron raised a finger. Her mouth opened. It closed again. She lowered the finger. She sighed.

"I'm getting another drink."

CHAPTER 31

Alex lost count of the number of times he whispered a quiet prayer of thanks for finding the horses. The snow piled up each night and melted away the next day, but always leaving a little bit more than there had been before. If they'd had to trudge through it, he doubted they would have made it even a few days. As it was, they let the horses take it at their own pace, only giving them occasional nudges to keep them headed the right direction.

The endless flat plains of eastern Washington had been brown and dead with the earliest summer heat, and now the snow mixed with the dirt and clay to turn the whole landscape into a thick sludge that sucked at their mounts' hooves. Alex kept them on the road as much as he could, only heading away from it when there were wrecks to avoid, or towns loomed up out of the ghostly white air.

Eventually flatlands began to rise. First the land sprang up around them in abrupt hillocks and miniature plateaus, thrusting straight into the air like impacts from the fists of impossibly large subterranean monsters. Then, abruptly, the road began to rise, and the land with it. Now they were almost always headed up, except when the road had to navigate around obstacles, weaving its way through a countryside that seemed to be trying its best to put walls in the path.

Some days after they had fought the convicts at the hotel, they reached the east bank of the Columbia River. They were at the very feet of Washington's Cascades. Just across the water, which slushed against its banks at the edge of freezing, was a long line of high hills, not quite the foothills but close enough. It was like one final great wall trying to block their path.

On the other side of those hills was the road that led to Cameron. But before that they had to ride south, along the river to the town of Wenatchee, the closest bridge that would take them over the river.

But they had another problem.

On the morning of the day that would take them to Wenatchee, Piper shook her last bottle of Insulin, the last one she'd had in her pocket when the convicts stole the rest in Alex's pack. Now she was empty—not even enough moisture on the inside of the bottle to form a single drop.

"I'm out," she said.

"I know, sweetheart," said Alex. He was checking his horse's saddle before mounting up. "We're almost there."

"No, Dad. I'm totally empty."

Alex yanked on the saddle strap. The horse shifted, and he splayed his hand across its coat, trying to calm himself. "I know," he said quietly.

Piper didn't produce insulin on her own. Zero, zilch. Before the end of the day she'd start having headaches. Next—maybe tomorrow—would come abdominal pains, nausea, vomiting. Probably some blurry vision before a coma, and then total brain death.

They were four good, fast days away from the cabins. Piper didn't have half that long. And she knew it as well as he did—maybe better. Doctors always read kids the riot act on what would happen if they missed their doses, or else you had them doing stupid stuff like skipping out to try and feel "normal."

"We'll look for something in Wenatchee," he said. She gulped, and he caught her gaze so that she was looking into his eyes. "Hey. We'll find some. I promise."

Piper stared at him a moment before nodding. "Okay," she whispered.

Wenatchee didn't have much of a northern border. They kept following the road, and then, rounding one snow-covered hillock, there were abruptly houses all around them. The horses picked their careful way down the street, with Max snuffling along at their heels.

No houses had their lights on. No one was out to observe them pass. The town was deserted, or everyone was staying away from the strangers riding through. Either way, Alex was relieved not to have to worry about threats.

Until he noticed the prison van.

It was off to the side of the road, halfway hidden behind two trees on the edge of someone's yard. The only good news was that it was covered by about as much snow as all the other vehicles around. The convicts must have reached this place the day after their fight with Alex and Piper, and abandoned the van then. Maybe they'd moved on by now.

Then again, maybe not.

He pointed the vehicle out to Piper. "We can't stop here."

Her eyes widened as she whirled to him. "Dad—"

"There's a smaller town just past Wenatchee. Cashmere. We'll look there."

"Smaller? But what if they don't have any insulin?"

Alex's jaw worked, chewing the inside of his cheek. Wenatchee was far more likely to have some available. But Cashmere wasn't some Podunk four-home town. They'd have more than one pharmacy, some drug stores. And Wenatchee seemed more than large enough for the convicts to want to stay here—tons of abandoned homes to choose from for shelter, and doubtless lots of food in the supermarkets and restaurants, for hard men who didn't mind getting their hands dirty.

"Not in Wenatchee. It's not safe. Cashmere will have insulin."

"What if they don't?"

272

"They will."

For just a second he thought she'd argue further. But she shut her mouth with a *click* and looked away.

"They will," he said again.

He hoped to god he was right.

* * *

It took them less than two hours to pass through the town, but it might have been the most frightening part of the whole journey. Everything was dead quiet—made more so by the snow as it fell and piled on the ground, killing hoof-beats and the soft pad of Max's feet on the ground. No lights shone from the homes. No vehicles moved, no people around to move them. If anyone was there, they were hiding, watching Alex and Piper pass and hoping not to be noticed.

But that line of thinking led Alex to suspect eyes in every corner, every shadow of the homes they passed. They were small houses, the kind you found in any small town in America, but fear turned them into cavernous, gaping faces that watched the travelers with malice.

Halfway through the town, they reached the east end of the bridge. Alex stopped, and Piper did the same a moment later. The sound of the river was a gentle, lapping monotone, a gentle splashing against the mud of the bank. There were no vehicles on the bridge—a narrow strip of white across the black water, that was all. Still no one in sight.

Alex nudged his horse forward.

If anyone was watching, they'd surely see the two of them now. The bridge was in the middle of the town, and their dark shapes would stand out against the snow and the stormy sky. But there were no challenges, no shouts, and no gunshots—something Alex half expected—and soon they'd reached the other side. He loosed a long sigh of relief as his horse's hooves touched the opposite bank. Just a mile more, and they'd be in open country again, and then soon to Cashmere.

Footsteps crunched on the snow.

Alex reined in the second he heard them. Piper was a little slower to react, and by the time her horse stopped, the sound was gone. Max drew closer, his head lifted, ears perked.

"Dad?" she said. "What is it?"

He stared north, where he'd heard the sound. Buildings pressed close to the road here, a little strip mall with a diner and another building with a sign declaring *Doghouse Motorsports*. He thought the sounds had come from the diner, but he couldn't be sure.

"Nothing," he said. "Let's keep going."

He heard the sounds twice more before they reached the town's border, but nothing more. He never took his hand from the grip of the pistol in his belt.

* * *

Open country eased Alex's nerves, but not by much. Now there were high hills on both sides, and little ridges running beside the road. If someone was following them, they had plenty of places to hide while keeping the trail. The only advantage now was that Alex had about twenty yards to see them coming, instead of only five.

The town of Cashmere came upon them gradually, more and more buildings appearing at a time until suddenly they were in the middle of a town without realizing they'd passed its borders. The snow wasn't piled up quite so high on these streets as it had been in Wenatchee. Someone had clearly come out to plow it in the not-too-distant past.

Alex felt a little jolt of hope. If there was any semblance of infrastructure here, maybe there wouldn't have been the same looting and chaos they'd seen for the last few weeks. He even half let himself imagine that they could still find an open store, or any place they wouldn't have to break into to find the insulin they needed so badly.

That hope died once they found the town's pharmacy. A squat, square building, little more than a cube, he could see a pale seventies pink stucco under the snow that covered it. All the front windows were smashed, and through their gaping holes he could see most of the merchandise had been taken from the shelves. What was left lay on the floor, scattered all around in great garbage piles.

He looked over his shoulder. They had to at least check inside, to see if there was any insulin at all. It might be the last chance they had. But he was still keenly aware that they might have some unwanted guests. He hadn't heard any footsteps since they left Wenatchee, but that didn't mean they weren't there.

"We're going inside," he said. "Stick close to me."

Piper nodded silently and helped him tie up the horses. The front doors were busted in like the windows, but they had crossbars and were chained shut. Alex helped her step in through the windows, careful to avoid the sharp glass. Max poked his nose in after them, but seemed reluctant to come in.

"Stay," said Alex, holding up a hand in front of the dog's nose. "We'll be right back."

Max whined, but he stopped trying to follow.

Inside was just what he'd expected—or feared. What scant few products remained inside were all over the floor. The shelves were absolutely empty. He checked all of them, even after he went to the section where the insulin should have been, even after he saw the shelves were empty and boxes were scattered all over the floor.

There was nothing.

"It's empty," said Piper.

"I know," said Alex. "We'll find someplace else."

"Where else? This is the only place."

"There's going to be another one."

"How do you know? We should have looked in the last town."

Her face was ghost-white. She shoved her shaking hands into her armpits, wrapping her arms around herself. Alex stepped forward in concern.

"Are you all right? How's your head?" He put a hand to her forehead.

Piper slapped it away. "I'm fine. I don't have a fever, or a headache—yet. I'm *freaked out*, Dad."

"It's okay. It's going to be okay. We'll find something."

He hated the words, because he had no way of knowing how he was going to back them up. But what the hell else could he say to her? As if she sensed his doubt, she turned away from him, breathing heavy, the fog of it drifting out the window.

Alex stared over her shoulder, at the buildings across the street, and the land farther south, where it rose up and into the foothills of mountains. Maybe someone up there could help. If it were him living in this town, he'd have a house up in those hills. The perfect place to retreat for the end of the world. Just you and the other richer inhabitants of the town, perched up above it all with lots of space in between each home. Nothing up there to attract crowds, or any people at all, except—

His eyes fell on a low, red brick building.

"The school."

Piper turned to him. "What?"

Alex pointed to it where it looked over the town from atop the hill. "That school. The nurse's office. They'll have insulin. More than enough to get us home."

Piper stared at it for a moment, then spun to look at him. In her eyes he saw something priceless: she believed him.

"Well then let's go!" she cried. "Come on!"

They practically leapt out through the broken front windows, and once they were mounted Alex spurred the horses to a trot. Max sped along behind them, as though he'd picked up their mood, and together they made their way up the hill to where the school was waiting.

CHAPTER 32

The school's front door was locked, but didn't hold up long once Alex threw his shoulder into it. On the third try it flew open, slamming into the wall behind and sending a deep reverberating blast echoing through the linoleum halls.

Alex stepped in, closely followed by Piper and Max. Max stepped just ahead of him and raised his nose, sniffing. Alex looked down the hall stretching ahead, as well as the ones that ran left and right. Empty. Not that he'd expected to find anyone inside—the locked front door was a pretty clear indicator no one had come here since the weather began. Still, it made him breathe easier.

They couldn't see the nurse's office from where they'd forced their way in, so Alex led the way down the hall. If he had to guess, the school would place the nurse somewhere near the middle of the campus, so medical help was as close as possible no matter where kids got injured.

Every footstep sent long echoes bouncing all around. Alex could only remember two times he'd been in an empty school, both during high school, and he doubted Piper ever had. It was unnerving. The halls were so obviously built for crowds and sound, the thrum of young humanity on its way to adulthood, that when that life was stripped away, they seemed far more empty and cadaverous than open country. It was even worse than passing through Wenatchee and then Cashmere, no matter that they'd been reduced to Cashmere.

But thoughts of the town reminded him of the prison van, and the lingering footsteps behind. He glanced over his shoulder before he could stop himself. The school's front door was now out of sight. But with the dead quiet in the school, he hoped they'd hear it if anyone came in after them.

"Faster, sweetheart," he said. "Let's find what we need and get out of here."

The hallway ended in a t-split, and Alex only hesitated a moment before turning right. In fact he had no idea which direction the nurse's office might be, but one was as good as another.

They didn't find the nurse's office right away, but they came across something else that made Piper stop and stare in awe, her eyes wide and her jaw hanging open.

"Dad," she gasped, and stepped forward. She spread her hands across the glass front of a vending machine absolutely packed with sweet, sugary goodness.

Alex couldn't help but smile at the look on her face, though his mood dampened again quickly. "All right, step back," he said. "Get Max back, too."

Across the hall was the cafeteria. He picked up one of the chairs—a heavy, metal job—and chucked it into the vending machine. But the glass didn't break. It was some kind of plexiglass.

"Step into the cafeteria and around the corner," he said. Piper did so quickly.

He pointed the Glock at the top corner of the plexiglass and pulled the trigger. The gunshot blasted through the halls, deafening them. A neat hole appeared, along with a spiderweb of cracks across the whole thing. When he threw the chair again, the glass shattered to fall and spread across the hallway floor.

"Oh my god," said Piper.

She went straight for the Kettle chips, ripping open a bag

and shoving a handful of them into her mouth. Her eyes rolled back in her head as she moaned.

"Sooo good. Do you want some?"

She thrust the bag towards him, flecks of potato flying from her lips. Alex's stomach growled at the sight and smell of it. They'd spent weeks now eating nothing but bare-bones rations, and something with salt and lots of trans fat sounded like heaven. But he was so nervous at the idea of being followed, he didn't think he'd be able to keep down even such a small bite of food.

"I'm fine, sweetheart. Go nuts, but hurry up. We didn't come for snacks."

She downed the rest of the bag and shoved several more into her pockets, along with some candy bars. Alex hurried her on before she was fully done. They needed to find the insulin, and then they needed to get moving. Maybe he was just being paranoid, but the sooner they were out of Cashmere, the safer he'd feel.

Fate didn't seem interested in kowtowing to his anxiety, however. It was another fifteen minutes before they finally found the nurse's office. The door was thick wood and locked, but there was a glass window in the middle of it. It was real glass, and broke easily under the butt of his pistol, and then they were in.

In the back room was a medical table, the uncomfortable kind that seemed designed to make every kid's visit to the school nurse as unpleasant as possible. But in the back of the room was a tall locked cabinet. Like everything else, it was built to stop a curious child from breaking in and stealing something to get high, but wasn't sturdy enough to stop a determined attempt to break in. Soon Alex had the door hanging from its hinges.

On the top shelf in a small refrigerator was a whole box of insulin bottles. He almost wept with relief.

Piper did, at least a little.

"Here," he said, pulling the box down with shaking fingers, and peering inside at the four vials of precious liquid. He got one bottle out, opened his back pack, grabbed the pump supplies and filled the reservoir for the pump while Piper removed her old cannula and inserted a new one. Piper then sat down for a dose right there, while Max curled up by her thigh, resting his head in her lap. "Glad we kept a few supplies in each pack . . . see, your dad isn't as crazy as you thought he was," Alex said with a tired smile. "And we're not taking any risks with these, for sure."

Of the four, he put one in his jacket, and one in Piper's, and then tucked one into his sock, and another in hers.

"Backups of our backups."

"For once, I don't think you're a paranoid freak," said Piper, smiling a little.

"See?" said Alex. "That's why I've been crazy all your life. For just such a situation."

She arched an eyebrow. "Sure. For some kind of solar flare that destroyed the whole world. Totally makes sense."

He was about to answer, maybe give her a hard time, but a sharp sound cut him off. It was the sound of a metal door slamming open, striking the wall behind it.

The front door of the school.

They both froze, staring at each other in horror, while Max lifted his head from Piper's head and began to growl. There came a long, screaming squeak of hinges, before the front door slammed shut again.

Then, far off, they heard footsteps. More than one pair, moving into the school's halls.

Max sprang to the door of the nurse's office and poked his head at the door, bristling. A low growl issued from his throat.

Alex looked to Piper. Her eyes were wide as radar dishes, and her face was paler than it had been before the insulin.

"We have to get out," he whispered. "Follow me. And be as quiet as you possibly can."

Terrified, she nodded. They packed up her insulin pump. Alex slid out the door and down the hall, one hand trailing behind him to remain on Piper's arm. The other hand led, holding the Glock.

Max followed on their heels. Alex wondered briefly if it wouldn't be better to leave the dog behind somehow. Dogs didn't exactly understand the concept of stealth. But Max wasn't making any noise now that they were on the move. And if Alex and Piper were found, he wouldn't mind having the dog's fangs on his side.

"You there, asshole?"

The shout was so sudden and loud, Alex almost popped off a shot. He and Piper both froze in the hallway. His mind raced, trying to figure out where the voice had come from. Not very close, but not far enough away.

"We saw you come in, man. You and your little girl. Where are you?"

Behind them. That was good. Alex nudged Piper forward. If he remembered, the next left took them toward the front door.

"You killed my cousin, man, and two of my friends. That's fucked up. We weren't even gonna kill you, and you blew them away. Now? Now we're gonna kill you."

Piper squeaked with fright. Alex stopped and turned to her, putting a finger against his lips. The convicts were trying to frighten them. They wanted Alex and Piper to be afraid, to make a mistake, make a noise, so they could be found.

The Glock was covered in sweat. He prayed it wouldn't slip if he had to use it. Where was the goddamn front door? They should have reached the turn already. He was lost.

Footsteps. Just around the corner. Max lunged forward, snarling.

Alex dove into a classroom, pulling Piper after him.

"What the fuck?"

Max's mad, furious barking tore the air. After the quiet

stalking through the hallways, it sounded like the apocalypse. Footsteps scuffed a hasty retreat.

"You got 'em? Where are you?"

"Nah, man! It's their fucking dog!"

"Kill it!"

"I'm not getting near that fucking thing!"

God bless you, Max, thought Alex.

He'd been an idiot. He'd been listening to the voice, the one convict who was shouting after them. But there was more than one, and the other—or were there more than two?—had been sneaking along silently, trying to catch Alex and Piper as they were driven out into the open.

The classroom door's hinges squeaked slightly. Alex tensed. But then the pitter-pat of dog feet announced Max's approach just before the dog came into view, whining and licking Alex's hand.

"Good boy," whispered Alex.

"Dad, there's another door," said Piper.

He followed her pointing finger. The classroom had a back door. He was pretty sure it went the wrong way, but right now he'd do anything to get out of the school. They could figure out how to recover the horses, or get the other transport. But right now they had to survive.

They made a beeline for the door. A short hallway led to the school's back exit. Through the windows he could see a courtyard with tables for students to sit and eat—all abandoned, all covered with snow.

Almost home free.

No stealth now. Just running. He sprinted for the door, dragging Piper after him.

A man the size of a linebacker leapt from nowhere. He tackled Alex into the window. Glass shattered as both of them flew out to land in the snow.

Pain lanced the shoulder of the arm holding the Glock. He thought it was from the landing, but it was the wrong side.

He and the convict rolled away from each other. When he tried to raise the gun, pain flared again. Grimacing, he felt the shoulder. His hand came away with blood.

Glass. Laceration. No way to tell how bad it—

The convict's fist slammed into his face, too fast for him to raise the gun.

Alex dropped. The man loomed over him—face thick and wide, and a deep cut in one cheek. The glass had been indiscriminate.

"My fucking cousin, asshole!"

He kicked. Hard. Alex tried to roll with the blow, but barely softened it. He groaned, hoping he hadn't just felt a rib break.

Shink.

Looking up, Alex saw a knife in the man's hand. Barely a knife—a prison shiv.

There was a bestial snarl half a second before a flash of brown and black fur took the convict down. Max was on top of him, snarling and tearing at his arms.

"Fuck!"

The shiv slashed. But the man couldn't get it up for a stab, and it just cut a gash in Max's flank. The dog yelped and darted away.

Alex was halfway to his feet. He heard crushed glass and looked to the window. Another convict was climbing out.

Where's Piper?

Out of sight. He hoped to high heaven she was doing the smart thing and hiding.

The new arrival raised his fists and charged.

Alex lifted the Glock and put two rounds in his belly. The convict's eyes widened as he stumbled back. Blood spattered the white snow. He looked down at his own ruined torso as he fell, and didn't move again.

Movement to Alex's left.

Then a blinding flash of pain as the shiv sank into Alex's guts.

He gasped. His left hand came up to grip the convict's bicep, like he was holding him for comfort. The man's face was an inch away, rank breath washing up Alex's nostrils.

"Motherfucker," the man growled.

Alex's hand tightened on his shirt. Then the Glock came up under the man's chin, and Alex popped off two shots.

Blood spattered his face as the convict's eyes went vacant, and he fell to the ground.

Alex sank to his knees. He stared at the shiv in his belly.

Some organs have to be shredded. Internal bleeding for sure. Do I pull it out? Could bleed more. On the other hand, can't move with this thing stuck in me.

His thoughts were way too clinical. It had to be shock. That was bad.

The nurse's office.

But first . . .

One fist closed over the shiv's handle. He took two deep, wheezing breaths.

He yanked it out.

If there's anything that will sharpen your wits, it's the unbelievable pain of pulling a blade out of your own innards. Alex screamed, screamed till he thought his throat would break. His fingers almost wouldn't uncurl from around the shiv, but at least he forced them to, and it plummeted from his shaking grasp.

He looked up, his eyes darting all over the place. Snow was still falling. It was starting to pile up on his shoulders. Was that because it was falling so heavy, or because he'd been there longer than he realized?

Damn it. Shock might be settling in again. He couldn't let his thoughts wander.

Max appeared at his side. The dog was whining. He sniffed at Alex's hand tentatively. Alex's fingers sank into his fur, stroking him, drinking in the dog's warmth. It helped him focus.

"Good boy," whispered Alex. "Good."

He got a hand on the dog's haunch and managed to lever himself to standing. Slowly, a step at a time, he hobbled for the school's back door. No way he was trying to climb in through the window in this condition. Both hands were pressed tight over the wound in his gut. It wasn't bleeding as much as he'd been afraid it would.

"Dad?"

Piper was at the shattered window. Her pale face reflected the grey sunlight from the clouds, and the white of the snow beneath. It made her look ghostly, or elfin, like something from a fairy tale. Unless that was in Alex's head, too.

"Pipes," he said. "Can you make sure the back door isn't locked?"

"I . . ." She glanced down at his stomach, and her eyes widened still more. "Oh my god."

"I'm fine. Really. Just . . . just please open the door."

She did, and then she helped him hobble to the nurse's office. Over and over again he mumbled how he was fine, just fine, he'd be okay. She wasn't even asking.

She probably knew he was lying.

The nurse's office had gauze, and bandages. But he needed fluids. He couldn't very well set up an IV—they had to get moving—but if he didn't get something in his body to help produce more blood, he was dead.

"Piper," he gasped. "Water. Please, as much of it as you can get."

"I—where?" she said.

"There was a drink machine next to the vending machine. Get another chair."

She nodded and rose to go.

"Pipes!"

Instantly she stopped. "What?"

He lifted the Glock. "Just in case."

She shivered, but she took it with her.

Moments later, Alex heard glass shattering. Soon Piper returned with half a dozen one-liter water bottles in her arms. Alex had managed to patch himself up. The hole wasn't as bad as he feared, but he didn't like to imagine what was going on inside his belly. Every movement hurt.

He downed two water bottles and shoved the rest in his pack. Then he got to his feet. Pain wouldn't let him stay silent, and he cried out as he felt something shift inside him.

"Dad, you should sit back down . . . you should rest, you're hurt . . ."

"Can't rest," he said. He lifted one hand to grip her shoulder and gave her a smile, though he knew it looked weak. "I'll have to heal up on the road. I'll be fine till we get to the cabins, at least. Then mom can have a look at me. Okay?"

She didn't answer for a moment. Her bottom lip was quivering.

He gave her a gentle little shake. "Hey. I'm gonna be okay. Trust me. Come on."

"Yeah," she whispered. Her eyes brimmed with tears. "Yeah, okay. Come on. I'll help you get back to the horses."

"That's the spirit," he said, grinning. He put an arm over her shoulders and leaned on her as they stumbled out of the office and through the halls of the school.

It was a lie. Every word of it. Alex knew it, and from the look in her eyes, Piper knew it, too.

But they kept walking.

CHAPTER 33

It was two days after Cameron and Bettie had talked, and Cameron was leading a hunting party out in the woods. She liked hunting. It was clean. Uncomplicated. Just her and her gun and some others from the community, and whatever they were looking to kill. All her worries about the cabin community faded away as she tried to get some food for them to eat.

Even when one of the sources of her worry was in the woods with her.

Wade was with her, along with Chad and Russell. They'd split up less than an hour's walk from the community. Now Russell and Cameron were in the woods to the south, while Wade and Chad had taken the river to the east.

Cameron's rifle was ice cold, and she kept running her hands over it to keep it from picking up frost. The snow had stopped falling, but it was still thick on the ground and heavy in the trees. The sky was the same grey overcast it had been since the solar reboot had started—that was what the girl Naomi had called it a few days ago, and the name had stuck—but the winds and storms had abated, at least for a little bit. The world was quiet except for their footsteps, free from birdsong or the calls of animals. Sound couldn't travel far with so much snow around to muffle it. Despite herself, despite her focus, Cameron kept coming to a stop as she walked. Everything was so pretty it didn't look real, like a picture on a holiday greeting card that had clearly gone through too many passes in Photoshop. After a moment she'd come to her senses, or Russell would clear his throat, and they'd press on.

At first they'd feared game might be hard to find, what with this strange winter in the middle of summer. It turned out to be the opposite. Animals were everywhere, running about freely as if it was summer, but standing out in stark contrast against the snow. They'd managed a couple of rabbits in just an hour. Then, shortly after noon, Russell stopped Cameron with a hand on her arm and pointed. Not too far away was a young white-tailed doe. She stood nuzzling the snow on the ground, probably looking for green shoots beneath it. She was upwind, and hadn't noticed them yet.

Cameron gave a quick glance around for a fawn—it was the right season for them, though the snow didn't make it look that way. But she realized, with no small amount of guilt, that she'd bring the doe down regardless. They weren't desperate for food yet, but that would only remain the case if they took what they could get when they could get it.

She lifted the rifle to her shoulder. *Sorry*, she thought, imagining she was speaking to the deer. *My family needs me more than yours needs you. I'm sure you'd disagree, but I'm the one with the gun.*

CRACK

A nearby branch snapped. The trees were overloaded with snow. Branches were dropping like crazy. It was a miracle no one had been hurt yet.

The sound startled the deer. But she didn't run. She lifted her head and looked right into Cameron's eyes.

Cameron's heart skipped a beat. She pulled the trigger.

The doe fell to the ground, a bullet through its brain.

Russell whistled. "Damn good shot."

"Not really. I was aiming for the lungs."

He balked and looked at her. She stared at him deadpan for a moment before cracking a wry smile. Russell chuckled and shook his head. Together they set off across the meadow towards the deer's body.

"You learn to shoot like that in the force?"

"Yeah. Not that I was in combat, but nobody gets away without learning how a gun works."

"True enough, but not everybody comes out shooting like that. You're a natural."

Cameron frowned, somewhat uncomfortable. "I'm more proud of knowing how to save lives than take them."

Russell shrugged. "Sure, sure. Just saying. You're good at it. No point in denying it."

"Come on."

They lifted the doe up together, and Russell slung it over his shoulders. They followed their own footsteps back towards the cabin, a measured trail of indents marching away from a small pool of blood.

They hadn't been walking for ten minutes before they heard a distant shout. Cameron froze in her tracks, Russell stopping a moment later.

The forest went dead silent.

The shout came again. *Cameron!*

Russell looked at her. "Is that Chad?"

She didn't bother to nod before setting off at a run. Russell, still carrying the doe, trotted behind.

Her mind was already racing. Shouting would disturb any game. Chad would know that, so if he was shouting it meant he wasn't hunting, and didn't care if he scared off whatever Cameron was hunting. That meant something was wrong.

Wade.

Chad appeared a moment later, stepping out from behind a tree so suddenly that Cameron almost decked him. She skidded to a halt in the snow.

"What is it? What's wrong?"

"Wade," he said. "I lost him."

"Lost him where? Never mind. Take me to where you saw him last."

He set off at a jog, and Cameron kept pace easily. He huffed out a hurried explanation. "It was like it vanished. One second we were together, within sight of each other, and then I was alone. I looked for a while before I came for you."

Cameron didn't answer, just kept running east. They were in a narrow valley that ran straight north, with the cabin community resting at its mouth. The valley ended at two good-sized lakes at the foot of a mountain, a good source of clean water and the reason for all the wildlife nearby. The lake ran off into a river on the valley's east end, where it spun wide around the cabins and fell into the pass where the freeway had been built. Visions rushed through her mind of Wade falling into the river and being swept away, vanishing over the falls miles away. Her stomach clenched.

Then again, maybe he murdered Hernando. In which case, good riddance.

She banished the thought as soon as it came. Wade had the benefit of the doubt for now. He was part of the community. That meant his safety was her job.

And then she reached the river, and there was Wade.

He was kneeling at the bank, washing his hands in the water. His head snapped up the second Cameron and Chad came into view, drawn by the sound of their running footsteps. When he recognized them, he raised his brows.

"What's the rush?"

"Wade, man! Where'd you go?" said Chad.

Wade made a show of looking back and forth before spreading his hands. "Right here? Where did *you* go?"

"I . . . I lost you, and when I couldn't find you I went looking for Cameron." Chad scratched at the back of his neck, frowning like he was doubting his own story.

"Well, when we were out here, I thought I saw a rabbit, so I whispered for you to follow me and went after it. Didn't realize you hadn't followed me until later. But I got the rabbit." He lifted it from the ground, swinging it back and forth slightly. "You had the gun, so I had to use my knife."

He put the rabbit back down and lowered his hands to the water again, scrubbing away the last of its blood.

Something had Cameron's nerves on edge. It was hard to put a finger on it. Nothing seemed all that strange about the story. Wade *did* have the rabbit. Chad could easily have lost track of him for a second.

But she found it harder to believe that Wade would lose Chad. Something about his story seemed too polished. Almost rehearsed. And combined with the misgivings she already held, what she'd talked about with Bettie . . .

Wade looked up from the river at her. His lips spread in that easy grin of his. "How about you and Russ? Get anything?"

Cameron heard footsteps from behind. She waved a hand behind her without looking. "More than a rabbit."

Russell trudged into view, huffing a cloud of steam with each breath. The doe's head lolled against his arm. "Hey. Everyone all right?"

"Everything's fine," said Wade. He picked up his rabbit again and stood. "Guess we should head back out again."

"Why don't we head back," said Cameron. "A deer's a good enough haul for one day."

"Might find another one."

Cameron met his gaze. "Let's head back."

Wade tilted his head and shrugged. "You got it, boss."

* * *

Ken was on gate duty when they returned, nose buried in some fantasy novel. He didn't notice the approaching party until they were almost on top of him, but once he did he hurried to open the gate.

"Bettie wanted to see you," he told Cameron.

Cameron frowned. "Why?"

"Didn't say. But she seemed pretty upset. She wanted to go out looking for you right away, but of course I told her told to wait 'til you came back."

Cameron glanced back at the rest of the party. Wade waved her off.

"Go. We can skin and clean them."

She set off for her cabin at a brisk walk. But she could tell it was empty almost from the moment she opened the door. A quick search confirmed it, and she headed back out to search the rest of the community.

Bettie was nowhere to be found. Most people had seen her running around. She'd spoken to a few of them, and everyone confirmed what Ken had said: she'd seemed pretty upset.

She stopped short after checking on the last cabin. Still no Bettie. Where the hell would she have gone? There was nothing else within the fence line except some trees.

The fence line.

She went to the area where Gina was working, moving at a jog now. Her nerves were already on high alert from Wade's mysterious disappearance, and none of this was helping.

Please let her be there. Please let her be talking with Gina, and all right.

Gina was there. Bettie wasn't. Gina had a small section of the fence down and two holes dug, putting new, fresh-cut posts in to replace two that were nearly rotten away. She looked up at Cameron's approach and must have seen some of the worry in her expression.

"What is it?" she said. "Is everything all right?"

"Have you seen Bettie?" said Cameron.

Gina frowned. "Sure. She was here not too long ago."

"Where did she go?"

A moment's silence stretched as Gina cocked her head. "I . . . I'm not really sure," she said. "She came over to talk and see how I was doing, bring me some water. But then she told me to go take a bathroom break and she'd watch the gap in the fence. But, um. When I came back, she was gone. I guess she got tired of waiting, but I swear I wasn't gone that long."

Panic clutched Cameron's throat. She turned and sprinted all the way back to the front gate. Wade, Russell, and Chad were nearby, doing their grisly work with the day's haul.

"Bettie's in the woods. Outside the cabins. We need to go find her."

Russell and Chad froze, but Wade shot to his feet. "You sure she's out there?"

"I'm sure. Get everyone who can take care of themselves. We're leaving five minutes ago."

* * *

Eight of them set out from the cabins, and Cameron split them up into two parties of four, with instructions for each party to split up again once they'd spread out a little ways. Part of her wanted to put Wade in charge of the other team, but another part of her—the part she ended up listening to—wanted to keep him where she could see him. They headed east while the other party headed west, covering much of the same ground they'd seen while they were out hunting. If Cameron guessed right, Bettie had passed them while they were heading back to camp, and would have stayed out searching east to west for Cameron rather than pushing farther north.

But why was she out here in the first place?

That question could wait till they'd found her.

When they reached the mountain's wide southeastern ridge, Cameron ordered the party to split up again. She sent Jeremy and Ken east, following the ridge down until it hit the river, while she and Wade went west, following the land up.

Wade spoke almost as soon as the other two men were out of sight. "She'll be fine, Cam. We'll find her."

"I know we will," she said. "Keep quiet so we can hear if she calls out."

He fell silent.

The first hour revealed nothing. After another, they met Chad and Russell coming from the west. They split up again, with Chad and Russell heading southwest while Cameron and Wade struck southeast, forming a sort of web pattern.

The third hour passed. Still nothing. Each team had a gun, and there was one back at the cabins as well. Anyone who found something was supposed to let off a shot to let the others know. But the silence of the mountains kept pressing down on them. Cameron could almost feel its weight on her shoulders.

Someone will find her. They have to.

They reached the outskirts of the camp. Wade halted.

"Maybe she went farther north," he muttered.

"Maybe," said Cameron. "Let's go."

They turned and headed back towards the mountain. They spread out now, walking just within sight of each other to cover as much ground as possible. The slope increased. They were both fit, but it wasn't long before their breath came heavy and hot, shooting into the air in clouds.

"We might have gone far—" Wade began.

CRACK

A rifle shot.

They stopped dead and turned, looking down behind them. There, just visible in the far distance, was the cabin community.

A moment's silence stretched.

Nothing else. Not a gunfight. A report.

They broke into a run.

Scott flagged them down before they reached the cabins and directed them east towards the river. He didn't say much, but his face was grim. Cameron recognized it and felt herself start to shut down inside. It was the calm face she put on in the ER when she knew she was about to watch someone die. When a heart rate monitor let out a long, steady beep that would never end. When she knew she was about to bring two parents the worst news they'd ever hear.

They'd found Bettie in the river. By the time Cameron reached the spot, they'd already pulled her out and laid her on the bank. Cameron knelt beside her. Eyes closed, skin cold and clammy.

She flipped over the corpse—that's what it was now, after all.

Blunt force trauma to the back of the head. Heavy. One clean blow. It had been quick, at least. Could easily have happened from a falling branch. The trees were overloaded with snow.

But she didn't say that. She waited for Wade to say it.

"Must have been a tree branch," said Wade. "They've been falling like crazy."

"Christ," muttered Russell. "What was she even doing out here?"

Me. She was looking for me.

Cameron turned Bettie back over, laying her down gently. She stood and turned to the men.

"Make a litter," she said. "Bring her back to the cabins."

Wade met her gaze. His brow was furrowed, worry clear in his eyes. "You okay?"

Cameron stared at him. He didn't blink. She turned on her heel and headed towards the cabins.

CHAPTER 34

The burial was short and sweet. They put her in Cameron's back yard, right next to the garden. In lieu of a coffin, Cameron wrapped her in clean white sheets. Once they'd buried her, they built a small mound of stones at the head of the grave. Cameron vowed to herself that if the world ever got back to normal, she'd get a gravestone—a proper one—and put it there.

If the world ever got back to normal. Christ. Bettie had family. A son she hadn't been able to contact when everything went to hell. Cameron would have to find him. She'd have to tell him about all this.

A few people spoke at the grave. Afterwards, Cameron didn't remember who. She didn't remember the words they said. She watched Wade the whole time. He stared respect-fully at the grave. He paid dutiful attention to each speaker in turn. And he glanced Cameron's way occasionally. When their eyes met, he'd give her a sad little smile before turning away again—not too quickly, not with any visible guilt. He was the perfect picture of a sorrowful mourner, and a concerned friend.

The sun had gone down by the time people started to drift away from the grave. Naomi, the kid, was first. She'd cried through most of it, and eventually her mother led her away with soothing murmurs. One by one they all left.

Cameron didn't wait until it was just her and him. She

turned and headed for the cabin when there were only a few of them left. She'd almost reached the back door when she heard his voice.

"Cam."

She didn't turn around. "What."

"You want to talk?"

"No."

"Can I come inside? We can have a drink. You shouldn't be alone right now."

I sure as hell don't want to be alone with you. "I'll be all right."

"Come on. Don't put on your work voice. It's me, and we're not at the hospital."

She rounded on him. He was closer than she'd thought he was. Almost inappropriately close. His feet were slightly spread, powerful arms by his sides. Cameron couldn't believe she'd ever looked at those arms, at all of him, with anything but contempt. That she'd ever checked him out, even secretly.

"I'm going into my home now. I want to be alone."

His jaw twitched. Just the tiniest hint of anger, but she could see it. "Come on, Cam. Don't be stupid. You know better than most people—"

"You're not coming in. End of discussion."

She didn't wait for his answer before she turned and went inside, slamming the door. But even before he spoke, she'd seen the shock on his face—and the fury that had just begun to flare before he was out of her sight.

* * *

She sat on the couch and downed half a bottle of wine in about five minutes, fully intending to keep that pace until she passed out.

The cabin felt empty. She and Bettie hadn't even spent that much time together here, but the older woman's presence had been a tangible thing even when she wasn't in the room. Now that presence was gone, and Cameron felt aimless.

Her eyes went to the door of Bettie's room. There was a bag in there, and it was full of Bettie's things. There was a bathroom on the other side, and it had Bettie's toothbrush. All these . . . *things* now, and no owner to claim them. And now Cameron would have to clean them all out.

What should she do with Bettie's things? If the world ever returned to normal, she felt some obligation to collect everything up and return it to her family, wherever they might be. But what, then? She didn't want them around the house, she knew that much. She didn't want them sitting here when Alex and Piper reached the cabins, if they ever did. That was a conversation she didn't even want to have once, though she knew she'd have to tell Alex about it.

Her thoughts drifted to Wade. She forced him from her mind.

Bettie's knitting bag sat by the old leather armchair, the one by the back door where she'd liked to sit. That was one bag. It would be easy to tackle. One thing at a time.

Cameron went to the bag. She picked it up and folded the bag's handles around the rest of it. She'd put it in a box. Everything of Bettie's could go in a box. Then the box could sit in the basement, hidden away behind Alex's endless piles of supplies, and she could deal with it whenever she felt like it.

Her hands tightened on the bag.

No. No, she'd keep the bag. Yes, everything else could go in the box. But the knitting bag she'd keep. It would be something to do on her downtime. And it would be a memory of Bettie. Maybe she was being foolish, but she thought she'd like to have something around as a reminder.

She pulled the bag open. There were the needles, the yarn. Some half-finished project Bettie was in the middle of— which she'd never complete now. Maybe Cameron could. Not now, of course. She barely knew what she was doing. But once she got a little better at it, she could finish whatever it was that Bettie had started.

Deep in the bag, something glinted.

Cameron frowned and reached for it. Out came a phone. She stared at it for a moment, not understanding. Then she recognized it.

It was Hernando's phone.

He'd always been on the damn thing when he first arrived. Cameron remembered thinking it was odd, because there was no cell reception and he couldn't be texting anyone. Then she realized he must be playing some stupid game to pass the time. And then, before she had died, Bettie had made a big stink about the phone.

And now it was in Cameron's hand.

How did Bettie find it? Why was it in her knitting bag?

She hit the home button. The phone opened right up. No password. That seemed odd. Hernando had stolen Wade's camera. Thieves were usually pretty paranoid about protecting their own stuff.

Cameron stared at it, puzzled. The thing was packed with apps, some she recognized and some that were completely unfamiliar. She scrolled through some of the recently opened ones.

The camera was the last app used. Had Bettie been looking through Hernando's photos?

She opened the camera. A photo roll came up, and she started to scroll through.

Two pictures in, she stopped.

It was a picture of her. Cameron stared at herself on the phone screen.

She was standing on the back patio of the cabin, looking off to the right, not at the camera. Cameron scrolled left. Another picture of her on the patio. Then one of her by the front gate.

Then one of her in her bedroom.

Her shirt was off, but not her bra. It looked like she was getting ready for bed. Another photo—this one entirely nude. She was in the bathroom, just getting out of the shower.

Cameron's blood boiled. *Goddamn pervert,* she thought. Hernando must have been sneaking around her cabin, sticking his phone up to the windows to catch shots of her. He probably took them back to his bed and . . . well. Cameron had never experienced anything like this. Her pulse thundered in her ears. She wished Hernando was still alive so she could beat the snot out of him.

She scrolled to another photo. But this one was just a shot of the forest, and the mountains looming above them. It was peaceful. Beautiful.

Too beautiful.

Cameron blinked, trying to understand. Why did this photo look out of place? Finally she got it. It was too high quality. She couldn't believe it had been taken on a phone. After a moment's thought, she scrolled back. To the pictures from the bedroom, the bathroom.

Yes. It was the same. The focus was too sharp, the lighting too good. There was no grain in the photos at all. And . . . and she couldn't be sure, but it was like the pictures had been taken on a really long lens. Way longer than a phone. Even the most modern smartphones didn't take pictures this good.

Cameron's head came up, and she stared at nothing. The phone almost fell from her hand, forgotten.

Phones didn't take pictures this good. But cameras did.

Cameras like Wade's.

Her hands clenched to fists.

Wade had been taking pictures of her like a dirty peeping Tom. Hernando must have seen him doing it, or become suspicious for some reason. He didn't steal Wade's camera because he actually *wanted* the camera. He was trying to get evidence of what Wade had been doing.

Then Cameron had come after him. And when he saw

how quick she was to judge him, Hernando shut down. How could she have been so stupid? He'd been trying to help, and she'd rushed to judgement. Just the way Hernando said she had.

What then? Wade must have known Hernando stole the photos. And he killed him. It wasn't self-defense after all.

And Bettie? She'd had the phone. It wasn't locked. She'd found the photos—only earlier that day—and she'd immediately rushed out to find Cameron.

But she'd died.

Or been killed.

The time when Wade was lost for a moment. Bettie found him, or he found her. Knowing Bettie, she'd probably confronted him with what she'd learned. And Wade had made sure she'd never reveal it.

Cameron threw the phone into the cushions of her couch and rushed for the front door. But she paused before going outside. She ran into the basement and grabbed one more thing, shoving it into the back of her waistband. Then she threw on a jacket and ran out into the night, making for Wade's cabin.

* * *

She found him just as he was throwing his bags into the car.

The lights were on inside Wade's truck, but he hadn't started the engine yet. No doubt he didn't want anyone else to hear it, didn't want them to have any warning before he tried to flee the cabin community forever. Had he guessed that Cameron would figure out what was going on? Or was the weight of two corpses just too much for him? Either way, Cameron had no intention of letting him get away with what he'd done.

"Wade."

He froze, leaning halfway through the back passenger

door. Slowly he withdrew and straightened up. He turned to her—and he winked. He *winked.*

Motherfucker.

"Cam," he said. "What's up?"

"Cut the crap. I found Hernando's phone."

Wade frowned. "Okay."

"He had the photos."

The frown vanished. Wade's face went deadpan. Emotionless.

"Yeah. That makes sense."

"You bastard. It was . . . they were *pictures.* Yeah, it's fucked up and you're a goddamn creep. But were they really worth killing people over?"

Wade rolled his eyes and shook his head. "Get real, Cameron. Who *cares?* You're smarter than this. The world's changed, and it's never going back. I wanted something, and when I tried to get it, people got in my way. So I took care of them."

"You *wanted* something? What about what Bettie wanted? What Hernando wanted?"

He shrugged. "The new world isn't a democracy. Your big problem is that you keep trying to pretend that's not true."

With a little toss of his fingers, he closed the car door and made for the driver's seat. But Cameron darted forward, placing herself in front of him.

"You're not going anywhere."

Wade sighed. "Come on, Cameron. Best thing now is to just let me go. I'm not stupid. I know I can't stay here. But you don't want to kill me, and you can't keep me around. What, you're going to . . . what? Imprison me? Put me on work detail? Sorry. Not interested. I'm out. Finding somewhere else that's a little more friendly."

He took a step forward. Cameron didn't budge.

"You say you're not interested? I don't care. I'm not interested in you murdering my friend and just walking away."

His eyes hardened. "Come on, Cam. We've sparred enough times." He started to count off on his fingers. "I'm bigger, I'm stronger. You're faster, but that only goes so far. I win every time I don't decide to let *you* win."

"Oh yeah?" said Cameron. "You're talking a lot of crap for a scared little boy who just got caught trying to run away."

Wade put his hands on his hips. A long sigh blew out through his nose as he shook his head. He looked for all the world like he was disappointed in her.

Then, without warning, he attacked.

His hand flew from nowhere, and Cameron barely blocked it. He tried another punch, and when that missed, a kick. It caught Cameron in the knee, and she almost buckled.

But she screamed with rage and launched herself at him instead, clawing for his eyes. That wasn't a feature in their sparring matches, and it took him by surprise. Her nails raked long gashes down his cheek, and he cried out.

"Bitch!" he said, taking a step back and placing a hand on his face.

She didn't respond. She just went for him again. But this time he blocked her swipe, and then his fist hit her in the gut. He didn't pull the punch either. Cameron fell to one knee, gasping, but she still had enough presence of mind to block the knee he sent flying toward her face. It put her at the perfect position to punch him in the balls, and she did. He saw it at the last second and jumped back to soften the blow, but it connected. He took two stumbling steps back, wheezing.

"Okay, fuck this," he snarled. His hand went to the back of his belt and came back with a knife. There was a *snikt* as he flipped it open.

Cameron smiled. "You were wrong, Wade. I *do* want to kill you. So thank you."

Her hand went to the back of her belt just like his had. But hers came back with a gun. She flipped off the safety and squeezed the trigger twice.

Wade fell to the ground, gasping and clutching at the holes in his chest. Cameron did her best not to enjoy the sound as his last breath wheezed out of him. And then it was over.

CHAPTER 35

Alex couldn't tell if it was the day after the school, or the day after that. His thoughts swam. His vision had gone blurry. He was slumping in his saddle. He thought he'd stopped bleeding from the wound in his stomach, but he couldn't be sure. It seemed like a terrible idea to pull off his bandages and check. If he wasn't going to die already, that would surely seal the deal.

Storms had struck again as they left Wenatchee. Snow had come thick and hard, the same dinner-plate-sized snowflakes slamming into each other on wind currents. Max struggled through drifts that were almost above his head. The weather had battered Alex and Piper and the horses, but Alex had refused to stop. Stopping would lead to rest, which would lead to sleep, which might lead to never waking up again. And they weren't home yet.

Not that he really expected to get home. Not anymore.

Even without opening the bandages to check his wound, he could feel his life slipping away. It flowed from him with the blood. How many guys took a knife in the gut and lived through it, even before the world had gone all to hell? Not many. Stomach wounds were the worst type to get. It was amazing he'd lasted as long as he had. That told him the real vitals hadn't been hit—gall bladder, spleen, kidneys. But something was deeply wrong inside him. He didn't need to have Cameron's medical training to know that.

The horses had stopped. When had they stopped?

Alex lifted his head. They were in the mountains. Not far in, with the land still rising up and up before them. They'd just passed Leavenworth. Alex hadn't even tried to take them on a side road around the town. If someone saw them and wanted to kill them, they would. But Alex had faced up to one fact: he wasn't going to make it to the cabins. The only thing he could—the *last* thing he could do—was get as far as possible, and hope that Piper could carry on the rest of the way by herself.

"Dad?"

Piper's voice brought him back to the moment. His thoughts kept wandering. Was that shock? Shock did that, but he'd always thought shock was a more sudden thing. Damn it, he *knew* what shock was. Part of park ranger training. But it was drifting away along with the rest of the thoughts in his head.

Thoughts drifting. He turned to Piper. "What, honey?"

Her eyes were wide, her face pale. Was she pale because of how little sun they'd been getting recently? Or was it fear.

Definitely fear. He could see it in her expression. She might not have known how close he was to collapsing, but she knew he wasn't all right.

Thoughts drifting.

"I . . . I thought you stopped." Alex shook his head. "Sorry. We should keep going."

Piper looked back down the road. They weren't half a mile out from the town, and the last few western houses were in view—though they were partially buried in snow. "Maybe we should stop. Someone in the town can help. They can . . . they can help you with the—"

"No. Gotta keep going. We should reach the cabins tonight." A lie, but he hoped she wouldn't guess that. "Mom can help me."

"Dad, it *is* night. Or, it almost is."

He looked up again. Behind all the clouds, the sky *was* darker than normal. If he'd been able to rise up into the sky, up above the clouds, he'd likely see the sun sliding behind the edge of the world. What a sight that would be. It was one of his favorite things on plane trips. Like the trip he'd taken with Piper, going to New York. Just a few days ago, really! Or, weeks. But weeks were just multiples of days.

God damn it, he had to get a grip on his thoughts. He tried, focusing hard, closing his eyes and pinching the bridge of his nose.

Suddenly he was on the ground.

"Dad!"

The impact of his fall jarred the wound in his stomach, and he gasped as he looked up at the horse. It bounced on its hooves, backing away from him nervously. He hadn't meant to get off the saddle. *Get off, hell,* he thought. He'd just slid off. Like . . . like his legs weren't working any more.

He tried to move one. A toe wiggled in his boot. Phew. That was a relief.

Piper was on the ground, kneeling by his head. She lifted him up, and he felt a wetness in his hair. Blood? Had he struck his head when he landed?

"No, you idiot," he mumbled. "It's snow." Then he realized he hadn't meant to speak out loud.

It didn't seem to matter to Piper, who ignored his words. "Dad. Dad! Can you get up? You need to get back on the horse."

"Can't," he muttered. It was true. He couldn't even move his arms. "Can't get up. Definitely can't climb up on a horse."

"You have to!" she cried. Tears sprang to her eyes, sliding down her cheeks.

"No, you have to . . . you have to keep riding."

She ignored that, too, and pulled on his shoulders. "Come on. Just get up. I'll help you get back up. We'll go back to Leavenworth."

A surge of adrenaline shot through him, but even that was only enough to raise an arm. He gripped the sleeve of her jacket, holding her gaze with his.

"We can't," he said. "I can't. You've got to keep going. Keep riding . . . this road. It goes all the way up. Up to the cabins. It turns off. You'll remember where. Been there before." Each word felt like it took everything he had. Stars were swimming at the edge of his vision, and they were beginning to crowd around Piper's face. There was a high whine at the edge of his hearing.

"I'm not going on without you. I'm not."

Alex gasped with pain, and clenched his teeth to keep it from turning into a scream. "You are. Everything . . . everything this whole way, was to get you home. Me, Denny. Even Max. Just to get you there. If you stop now, it all failed."

"You have to get home, too," said Piper. Tears still poured from her eyes, but she was hardly crying. She was angry. She wanted to fight.

So much like her mother, thought Alex. And with that came a crashing wave of grief, rocking him where he lay on the ground. He wouldn't see her again. Wouldn't see Cameron.

It was getting harder to see. Sun going down? Or the very last bit of his life leaching away?

"Go," he whispered. "Please. Or it was all for nothing."

The world went black.

* * *

In the middle of the night, a thundering crash shook Cameron's cabin.

She was out of her bed like a shot. She jerked on her clothes, but before she was even done she heard shouting outside. Others in the cabin community, all of them running. Tugging on her boots, she snatched up her rifle from beside the bed. Even after Wade, she slept with the weapon close.

This was it. Cameron didn't know what "it" was, but it had come. Bandits attacking the cabins? A final storm to end them all? She didn't know, but it was the culmination. She could feel it in her skin, could hear it in the panicked voices outside.

She threw the front door open and pounded out into the snow. There was Scott, and Russell, and even Debbie, and they were all running. Not from a threat, but towards the sound of the crash, the explosion, whatever it had been. Something had come, and they were going to face it together. Even if it was the end, the last, final gasp.

It was the middle of the night, but there were lights on in the club house near the front of the community. By those dim lights, Cameron could see the front gate through the swirling snow storm. But the gate wasn't standing there anymore. It had been thrown to the ground beneath the tires of a huge truck. A tow truck?

God. Bandits, then. Someone coming to attack this little pocket of community and steal whatever resources they could. Cameron lifted the rifle, holding it ready to fire at the first sign of life.

But no one emerged from the tow truck. Whoever was inside, they were waiting for a target.

Chad reached the truck first. He pressed his pistol up against the driver's side window. "Hands up!" he screamed. "Hands up, god damn it! Put your hands where—"

He froze, his words falling to silence. Cameron was still struggling through the snow, and she couldn't see his face. What was it? Did they have a gun trained on him? What were they waiting for?

Chad turned away from the truck, looking towards the others who were running towards him at full tilt.

"Help!" he cried.

Cameron almost stopped in her tracks, but she kept her feet moving. But she lowered her rifle. No longer looking to shoot, but only to understand.

A white face appeared in the windshield. Small, and so low it was almost covered by the steering wheel. Wide, terrified eyes, looking out into the light of Russell's flashlight, which he'd just trained on the tow truck.

This time, Cameron *did* stop in her tracks.

"Piper?" she whispered.

Then Piper recognized her.

"*Mom!*"

"*Piper!*"

Cameron threw the rifle aside and ran for the tow truck. She shoved Chad aside and yanked open the driver's side door. Then Piper fell out of the cab and into her arms, and Cameron dropped to her knees, holding her daughter close, burying her face in the girl's hair.

"Piper, Jesus, Piper, baby, I'm here, it's okay, you're—"

"Mom, stop, Mom," said Piper, trying to push her away. "Mom, listen—"

"Piper, for God's sakes, I thought I'd lost you!" said Cameron, not easing up on her grip in the slightest. "Just let me have—"

"No, *Mom!*" cried Piper, finally pushing her away. "It's Dad."

Cameron's heart nearly stopped. In the shock at seeing Piper, all thought of Alex had fled. "Piper, where is he?"

"The back seat," said Piper, tears spilling from her eyes. "He's—it's bad."

Cameron leaped to her feet and threw open the back door. There was Alex, wrapped in blankets. Blood had soaked the ones laid over his midsection.

"Alex!" cried Cameron. No response. She threw herself into the cab and felt for his pulse. She froze, her fingers on his neck. She felt nothing. God, no. Please, not this. Not like—

There. There it was. Faint. God, so faint.

She turned. "Scott. Russell. Get a table from the clubhouse and break off the legs, then bring it out here. We're taking him to my place."

311

They didn't answer, didn't even nod, but just ran off to do as she said. Cameron climbed back out of the truck, and Piper grabbed her arm.

"Can you . . . is he going to . . . ?"

Cameron had heard the question a thousand times from a thousand mouths. Hospital policy—and human decency—always dictated that she not answer. You could never guarantee someone would pull through. Hope was a wonderful thing—but take that away, and the world became a little darker, and it stayed that way forever. Better to tell them the truth, that all things were uncertain, that you could only do your best.

She looked down into her daughter's eyes. Her mouth set in a firm line.

"He's going to live," she said. "I promise."

CHAPTER 36

Blinding white light pierced his eyelids.

For a long while, the pain of it was all he could focus on. Then the pain of the rest of his body came flooding in, and the pain in his eyes became a mere pinprick. Alex groaned—or he tried to. He managed only a thin whimper, dribbling out between cracked lips.

Holy cow, I'm alive, was his first thought. He had a momentary thought that he didn't *know* he was alive. But the pain seemed a pretty good hint. He'd never had any strong opinion about what happened after death, but he was decently sure that pain wasn't part of it.

He opened his eyes.

Wood panel ceiling. Familiar grain. Where had he seen that before?

The realization crashed in on him like a thunderstorm. The cabin. *His* cabin. His and Cameron's.

He tried to sit up, and his whole body made him immediately regret it. He fell back on the pillow, gritting his teeth with a hiss. It took a moment for the pain to subside, a longer moment than he thought it should. Without moving too much, he turned his head.

Cameron.

Just seeing her was like Christmas and a birthday all in one. She was in an armchair by the bed. The armchair didn't belong here, in their bedroom. She must have brought it in, to be with him while he rested. While he rested from . . .

The knife wound. He remembered now. Remembered Piper, too, kneeling over him and crying in the snow. Through the bedroom window, the outside world was a wall of white. Gingerly, he moved a hand and probed at his stomach. Bandages, again. They were new, though. Applied by Cameron, no doubt, after she'd done whatever she'd done to him. Fixed him, it seemed like.

It seemed unbelievable, but he'd actually made it. He was home. Or the closest thing to home that still existed any more.

"Cameron," he croaked.

Her head jerked, and she shot straight up in the armchair. "Alex!"

Alex gave her his best smile. "Hey, babe."

She sat on the bed beside him, then leaned over to give him a kiss. Not too deep, and it didn't last too long. She must know how ginger he was, because she barely touched him with her hands. But he could feel the passion in it, a driving urgency that spoke to all the long days and weeks they'd been apart.

When it was over, she sat up straight, and suddenly she was all business. She pulled back the blanket, looking down at the bandages that wrapped his middle. Alex tried to lift his head to see. He couldn't get a very good look, but it didn't look like there was any visible blood. That was a good thing, he hoped.

"What's the prognosis, doc?" he said.

"Now? A lot better than when you got here," said Cameron. "That punk could hardly have picked a worse place to stab you."

That brought back memories of the attack, and then Piper again. "Oh my god—where's Piper? Is she—"

"She's fine," said Cameron. "In fact, I'll bet she's up. Hold on."

She leaned over and kissed him again, on the forehead this time, and then left the room. But Alex had barely settled further into his pillows before the door opened again, and Piper came bouncing in followed by Max.

"Dad!" she said. She froze by the bed, her fingers twisting around each other, clearly holding herself back.

"Hey, sweetie," said Alex. "What's wrong?"

"Nothing," said Cameron, stepping into the room behind Piper. "But I gave her very, *very* strict orders not to jump on you when she came in. She actually listened. I'm shocked."

Piper shot her a glare, but it was half-hearted. "Are you feeling okay? Do you need anything? I just made some soup, I could make another can."

"No solid food," said Cameron. "But here."

Beside the bed was a cup of water with a straw. She handed it to Piper, and Piper put the straw in Alex's mouth. He gulped deeply at it. Part of him was a little embarrassed to be served like this by his own daughter, but most of him just thought the water was the best thing he'd ever tasted.

He nodded when he was done, and Piper returned the cup to the side table. He looked up at her with a smile for a moment, but then his mood dampened. "Cam, how'd you find me? I never thought you'd come that far east of the cabins, even if you were scouting out food sources or something."

Cameron arched an eyebrow. "We didn't find you. Piper found us."

Alex frowned and looked at her. Piper blushed and looked down at her hands, which had begun to fidget again. "When you fainted, I didn't keep on the road like you told me to. I went back to Leavenworth with Max. I couldn't find anybody there—either they'd all gone, or they kept their doors closed and ignored me. So I started checking cars. Most of them were locked shut. Finally I found a tow truck, and there were keys in the visor above the steering wheel. So I . . . I drove back to you. You got up and got into the car. Don't you remember?"

Alex frowned. "I . . . don't. I must have been out of it."

Piper ducked her head. "Well, anyway. You fell into the back seat. And then I drove you here."

"You *what?*" said Alex. "Piper, you can't drive!"

"Damn right she can't," said Cameron, barely hiding a smile. "You should see the tow truck. It's totaled—and that's before she crashed it through the cabin community's front gate."

"But the mountain road . . . the snow . . ." said Alex.

"I just went slow," said Piper. "I . . . I stopped all the time, any time I felt like I was slipping. It was hard, and for a while I thought I'd missed the cabins. But then I saw the turnoff. And then when I saw the gate, I . . . I got excited, and I stepped on the gas, and then I forgot where the brake was, and . . ." Her words gradually trailed off. "I'm sorry."

"Sorry?" Alex shook his head, though even that little movement brought pain. "Piper, that's . . . that's amazing. I'm sure I would have told you to stop if I was awake to see it, just like I told you to leave me. But that was wrong. You were right. You were brilliant."

He smiled at her again, but she didn't return it. Instead she burst into tears and fell forward, forgetting Cameron's orders and hugging him tight.

"I was scared," she said. "I . . . I thought you died in the car while I was driving. Don't ever do that again. When you told me to leave, I thought—"

"I know," said Alex quietly. "I did, too. But it's okay. I'm here. We're all here." Fingers gripped his own, and he looked up to see Cameron looking down at them. Tears shone in her eyes, though she kept them from falling.

"We're all here," he repeated. "We're all okay."

Piper sniffed and lifted her head. "Well, sort of. There's, like, twenty people here, and all but one of them is a grown-up. You've only been out for a few days, but I'm getting *bored*."

Alex snorted, and Cameron rolled her eyes. It was such

a perfect—such a *normal* moment, that Alex could almost feel the last four weeks of tension and fear melting away, to be replaced by an immense sense of gratitude that he was alive to enjoy it.

"Come on, kiddo," said Cameron. "Get out of here so your dad can get some rest."

"I *hate* when you call me kiddo," said Piper. But after giving Alex's hand one final squeeze, she rose and left the room, following Cameron. Alex smiled after them—and then his eyelids began to droop. Before Cameron came back to check on him, he'd drifted off again.

* * *

It was more than a week before Cameron finally let him get out of bed, and even then, he had to hold on to her to move around. During that time, he met everyone else in the cabin community. Some of them he'd seen before, while others were refugees, and brand new. They all seemed inordinately happy to see him—he guessed they'd heard about him and Piper. No doubt most of them had thought they'd never actually make it to the cabins. The fact that they had seemed like a small victory, even when weighed against the chaos of everything else.

Sometimes as they talked to him, or when Cameron told him some stories of how the community had fared, he caught a dark look in their eyes. Occasionally someone would stop speaking, giving Cameron a furtive look before changing the subject. Cameron, too, was clearly hiding something, though she was better at it than most of them. Alex let it ride for two days before late one night, he finally had her sit down and tell him everything. She told him everything from the very beginning—about Bill, and then Hernando, Bettie, and finally Wade.

The whole story came out in a dead monotone—even the ending. In her eyes was the same look she'd worn when she came back from deployment, the look that it had taken him so long to coax her out of in the first place. When the story was done, she looked down at him, her face an impassive mask.

He reached up and took her hand. "I'm sorry, sweetheart," he whispered. "I should have been here for you. But I'm here now."

The look in her eyes passed like a storm. She leaned down and kissed his forehead.

"Damn right," Cameron whispered.

Now, some days later, he was finally out of bed. One arm over Cameron's shoulders and one over Piper's, he hobbled out to the living room and sat on the couch there. The pain in his stomach was now a dull, lingering ache, greatly eased by wine or Scotch—both of which they had in plentiful supply. He sat looking out the wide rear windows, into a world that was all white and silent as death. For a moment that's all he did—sit there staring.

"The windows lose a lot of heat," he finally said. "We should try to insulate them somehow."

"None of that," said Cameron. "You're still recovering. You can worry about solving the world's problems when you're finally back to normal."

Alex chuckled.

A knock came at the front door. Cameron's head snapped up at once. "Come in," she called.

The door opened just enough for Russell to poke his head in. "Gina's finished the western fence, boss," he said. "I've got her on the front gate already, but I thought you'd want to come check the work."

"Thanks," said Cameron. "I'll be out soon."

Russell nodded and vanished, closing the door behind him.

Alex looked up at Cameron and arched an eyebrow. "Boss?"

Cameron's mouth twisted. "That's another story."

"I bet. But it makes sense. Suits you."

"Is it always going to be like this?" said Piper. "Is the world ever going to go back to normal?"

Cameron turned to look at Alex, and he pulled his gaze away from the window to look at her. In unison, they sighed and turned to Piper.

"I don't know, sweetheart," said Alex. "It might not. But then again, it might. All we can do is whatever we can: taking care of each other, and of everyone else in the cabins. If the weather goes back to normal, we'll be ready. If it doesn't . . . well, we'll figure it out."

Piper shivered. "It's all different. Everything seems . . . dangerous."

"It is," said Cameron, matter-of-factly. "But we'll take care of you."

"We will," promised Alex. "And so will others. There *are* dangers out there—the weather, and the people, too. But you and I saw the same things, Pipes. There's always people who are willing to help. And if you think about it, there were more of them than people who wanted to hurt us."

She looked thoughtful for a moment. Alex wondered if her thoughts, like his, had turned to the many people they'd met on the road. Pete, who'd inadvertently given them Max, and Denny, and Graham and Willow. Even the nameless woman, who'd thrown out a package of pads from the darkness of a supermarket; and Lamont, the convict who wouldn't travel by their side, but also wouldn't let a pack of criminals kill them and steal everything they owned.

"I guess you're right," said Piper slowly.

"Of course I am," said Alex. "And no matter what, you've got me and Mom. I got you all the way across the country all by myself. Now there's two of us. We'll be fine."

Max came padding into the living room and lay down at Alex's feet. Cameron rolled her eyes at the dog, but sat by

Alex's side and took his hand. Piper, rather than answering, just nuzzled deeper into his shoulder.

Alex squeezed Cameron's hand and met her gaze. "We'll be fine," he said again, quietly.

To his own great surprise, he believed it.

ACKNOWLEDGEMENTS

First and foremost I'd like to thank (because it's good for my health) my wife for putting up with me. . . Oh and for being supportive while I was writing this book.

I'd also like to thank Garrett Robinson for editing, being a friend, being supportive, and just being Garrett. And a special thank you to his wife Meghan, for riding herd on both of us and making sure that we didn't get distracted by every shiny thing that crossed our path, instead of working. And in conclusion I'd like to thank all of my friends and family who have been so supportive while I've been writing this book – you know who you are.

ABOUT THE AUTHOR

Matthew lives in the Pacific Northwest with his wife and three children, two cats, and a fish. He recently made a life change and started working in film as an actor/producer/writer, which set him on the path to this book. His youngest child is a ninja princess, his middle child is an aspiring time machine creator (or endocrinologist, he hasn't quite decided yet) and also a type 1 diabetic, and his oldest child is a tween girl, so this book could have easily turned into a horror or situational comedy. The two cats and the fish don't seem to care that there even is a book. When Matthew isn't working, he enjoys playing with his children and their RC cars, and whatever other goofy game they come up with and volunteering at their school. Matthew's other passions include: Coffee.